Adoring Amy

Adoring Amy

A multicultural, best friends to lovers, office romance book.

Heart's Destiny Book 4

Leah Mae Wright

Copyright

Contents

Dedication

I originally planned to dedicate this book to all the science teachers who had to deal with having me in class over the years. I thought it would be a nice way to show them that I understood their lessons, even though I haven't retained as much of them as I probably should have since I was in school.

But as I've gone through the writing process, my characters have taken over as usual. Justin and Amy didn't want their story to be as focused on their time in the lab as I originally planned. Instead, they took me on an emotional journey to deal with my feelings after my own Ancestry experience.

This book has helped me deal with my disappointment at not being able to solve some family mysteries by giving the Burlesons a happy ending with their long-lost loved ones. In exchange for giving me a small sense of closure over the family members I may never find, I shared a small segment of my real life through Amy.

The emotions she feels surrounding finding her biological father were all written straight from my heart, though I gave her dad to her twenty years earlier in life than when I found mine. The texts when she first reaches out to him are almost word for word the same as when I first contacted my Dad three years ago, with the names and relationships changed to protect our family privacy. Though everything else about their interactions in the book were solely made up to fit the story, the thoughts Amy had before contacting him were all based on the things I've struggled with personally.

I started this series with two characters whose appearances I based on my mom and adoptive father as a way to deal with the grief of losing both of them way too early in life. This book has truly helped me to deal with my feelings of guilt for finding my biological father after their passing. Therefore, I feel it's only right to dedicate it to all three of my parents.

To Mom and Daddy for understanding that my reaching out to Dad isn't because I'm trying to replace you now that you're gone. Even if we could change the past so the two of you were both still here with me, I'd still need to love him as much as I love you.

To Dad for welcoming me with open arms when you found out I'm yours. If distance and medical limitations ever let us finally meet in the same place, you can expect the tear-filled bear hug I wrote for Amy and her dad in this book. I love you.

Introduction

Justin Burleson lived a charmed, happy life on his family ranch in Heart's Destiny, Texas. He worked in his dream job in the family business as the head of the research and development department in the Burleson Energy division of Burleson Incorporated. While he technically had a vice president title, he had the freedom to spend his time in the lab more than in the executive offices with the rest of his family. He appreciated being able to spend his time working on finding alternative fuels to help Burleson Energy be a more environmentally-friendly company than the oil conglomerate his ancestors had started without realizing how damaging to the land and surrounding ecosystems their endeavors would be a hundred years later.

Unfortunately, spending all his time with his family, either at work or on the ranch, meant he didn't have as much time for dating. So, settling down, as his mother and aunt seemed to want for all their children, wasn't his top priority. It wasn't that he was reluctant to romance, more that he wasn't interested in romancing the women his mother kept setting him up with at every event in town. He wasn't looking for just any woman to marry and carry on the family name. He was seeking his soulmate.

Amy Lawton wasn't sure she was really interested in dating anyone seriously after growing up watching her mother's string of relationship failures. Dealing with her own abandonment issues after losing her grandparents was only made harder by feeling abandoned by her father and several pseudo stepfathers over the years. Not wanting to feel the pain of heartbreak when a man inevitably left the relationship, Amy

Leah Mae Wright

put up walls and wouldn't let herself fall in love, like her mother and sister seemed to do each week with someone new.

When Amy came to Heart's Destiny, Texas, for her best friend's sister's wedding, Justin thought he'd finally met his soulmate. Their common interest in chemical engineering was far more important to him than their racial or socioeconomic differences. He didn't just see a woman of color; he saw a woman of character, a woman he wanted to get to know better.

Amy felt an instant attraction to Justin when she met him, but she was reluctant to pursue a romance with the man who was so obviously different from her and anyone she'd ever dated. Even though they seemed to have a lot of common interests when they talked about their professional lives, she doubted a Black woman white man romance would ever develop between them. Though she'd seen such a pairing work for her grandparents, her mother's string of failed relationships with mostly white men had made it clear to her that a multicultural romance would never last, so she vowed to save herself the heartbreak by keeping him in the friend zone.

When the Burlesons offered her more than double her current salary to move to Texas and work in their research and development department, Amy couldn't turn down the opportunity for career advancement. Justin wanted to use their daily interaction at work to move them from friends to lovers, but Amy kept fighting her instalove with her possessive boss.

Could Justin show Amy that he's the man of her dreams and she's the woman of his? Or would Amy be too afraid to take their chemistry outside the lab?

DISCLAIMER: This multicultural, best friends to lovers, office romance book contains profanity, graphic sex scenes, shocking DNA test results, and emotional moments of meeting long-lost family. It is intended for adult readers (18+) who are not easily offended.

x

Prologue

Justin Burleson struggled all afternoon to tear his gaze away from the bronze beauty that caught his eye the instant she arrived on the family ranch for the cookout his family was hosting for all the out-of-town guests coming to his cousin's wedding. He'd barely been introduced to Amy Lawton before she was whisked away with the wedding party to go into town. But once she'd gotten back to the ranch and changed out of her dress into jeans and boots to join in on the horseback riding, he couldn't stop himself from watching her every move.

Coming from a family of firm believers in love at first sight, he'd heard for years that meeting *The One* felt a lot like being struck by lightning. One look into Amy's eyes, which were so dark brown they were almost black, reminding him of the volcanic glass he saw at Obsidian Cliff in Yellowstone National Park when he went on a trip to Wyoming with his brother a couple years back, was all it took to convince him that his family had been right all along. Love at first sight was a real thing, and she was it for him.

He only hoped the African American goddess wasn't turned off by a pale white boy with more brains than brawn. With so many of his cousin's coworkers in attendance for the wedding, she certainly had her choice of more muscular wrestlers to be attracted to, regardless of her skin tone preference. Seeing as how he wasn't nearly as extroverted as the brawny bunch of sports entertainers, Justin wasn't sure he even had a sliver of a chance of Amy remembering his name at the end of the week, much less being willing to go on a date with him.

Not that Justin really lacked self-confidence. When it came to his position in the family business, he was more than confident in his ability to head up the research and development department of

Burleson Energy, which was what they were rebranding the former oil division of Burleson Incorporated into, in order to show the world that the current generation of Burlesons wanted the company to be a more environmentally-friendly entity. His time in the lab was when he felt like he was truly able to be his best self, especially when he was successful in developing new alternatives for biofuel.

He normally didn't lack self-confidence when talking to women either, knowing he was considered one of the most eligible bachelors in Texas. But he also knew that status was based on his family wealth, and generally attracted women of a similar socioeconomic status, or women who wanted him for his. Those women were easy to talk to because he knew what they wanted. He could be cordial and friendly whenever he was approached at various social events, without leading them on that it would ever be more. He'd even managed to scratch an itch a few times over the years without anyone getting hurt because everyone knew the score before their clothes came off.

Amy was different, though, and he didn't mean because they weren't the same race. From getting to know his soon-to-be cousin-in-law, he'd gleaned a little information about the friends she'd invited down for the wedding. Kay hadn't even mentioned race or ethnicity when telling his family about Amy or Deanna, her other friend who was actually participating in the wedding. Justin had been happy to see that his cousin's future wife seemed to be as racially inclusive as the rest of the Burleson family.

When Kay told his family about Amy, she spoke of her sister's best friend as if she considered her to be another sister of the heart, though there were no legal or blood ties between them. Kay described Amy as shy and sweet, telling them how she'd used her brain to earn the scholarships that paid for her college education in chemical engineering.

Justin's interest had initially been piqued when he heard they shared the same major, but he'd tried not to let that show, so his mother and aunt wouldn't get any matchmaking ideas with him as the target. He didn't think they'd noticed how avidly he was listening to Kay, when she'd told them all how Amy and her sister had been raised by a single mother, using his focus on the food he was consuming at Sunday supper as his way of covering his longing to know more. He only hoped he was as successful covering his interest in Amy while his whole family was watching earlier in the day, as he felt he was the month before when Kay was telling them about her.

Now that they were out at the joint bachelor and bachelorette party for Anthony and Kay, and out from under the watchful eyes of his matchmaking momma, he found it was getting harder for him to keep his eyes off the raven-haired beauty. They'd started the evening off with the men in the back room of Tully's Roadhouse playing pool and the women in the main bar area at the front playing their party games.

Justin had enjoyed a beer, toasting to his cousin Anthony and his impending nuptials, before switching to water and playing a few games with his family and friends. But as soon as the ladies had started filtering into the back room, and a few of the other guys had gone to the front to dance with their girlfriends, or the women they were trying to pick up for the night, Justin had been drawn back into his intense need to watch Amy Lawton like it was his job.

Amy had initially followed Randi Lee back to the pool table where James Hunter was playing a game with one of the other GWA wrestlers, who were in town for the wedding. But when James and Randi went back up front to dance, Amy had stayed in the back, watching the other games going on around the room.

Justin wanted to go over and ask her if she wanted to play a game. But when he saw her mutely turn down the wrestler, who James had just been shooting pool with, by briskly shaking her head in the negative, Justin didn't think she'd be any more receptive to talking to him than the muscular African American man she'd just rebuffed.

"You should go ask her to dance." Justin's cousin, Josh, nodded his head in Amy's direction.

"Yeah, with the way she just turned down James's friend," Justin disagreed, shaking his head. "I doubt she'd dance with me."

"Maybe you're more her type than Dion." Josh covered his grin by taking a sip of his bottled water.

"Whatever," Justin replied with a self-deprecating chuckle. "We both know that women prefer buff guys like you and all these wrestlers to scrawny nerds like me."

"Naw," Josh disagreed as his twin, Jake, walked up. "If that were the case, Jake wouldn't get laid nearly as often as he does."

"What the fuck are you talkin' about, Bro?" Jake looked back and forth between Josh and Justin.

"Justin doesn't think he has a chance with Amy," Josh explained, not laying out his reason why.

"And what does that hafta do with how often I get laid?" Jake tilted his head and looked up at his slightly taller, more muscular twin.

Justin realized at that moment that he was the shortest of all the Burleson men, having maxed out at six-foot-two. The rest of the men in the family were at least six-foot-three, like Justin's cousin, Jake, Justin's older brother, JJ, and their father, Jon. His Uncle Bob and cousin Josh were both six-foot-four, while his cousin Bobby was six-foot-five, and his cousin Anthony was six-foot-six. Since he didn't even break the two-hundred pound mark, Justin assumed they all outweighed him as well.

"He thinks women prefer muscle over math skills." Josh smirked. "I told him that if that were the case, you wouldn't get laid as much as you do."

"Whatever," Jake chuckled, shaking his head at his brother.

"I told him he needs to go ask her to dance since she's lookin' at him almost as often as he's lookin' at her." Josh tipped his head toward Amy, who dropped her gaze to the floor a moment after Justin looked her way.

He'd only barely caught her eyes on him, but that fleeting second when their eyes met from across the room made Justin tingle in a way he'd never admit to his cousins, knowing they'd pick on him for being smitten.

"Damn, I hate to say it, but Josh is right. You should go ask her to dance."

Justin's head snapped around to look at his cousin Jake, surprised at his statement.

"What?" Jake half-shrugged at Justin's incredulous look. "Bobby's already trying to make sure enough of us are still sober to drive everyone home. And I know you've already switched to water for that exact purpose. So, go dance with the girl. Then you'll more likely be the one she leans on to drive her back to the ranch tonight."

"Dude, I'm not gonna take advantage of her being drunk to…"

"No, I know you won't." Jake interrupted Justin, holding his hands up in a sign of surrender. "I just thought you'd prefer to be the one to drive her back to Mom and Dad's tonight instead of one of us."

"Or one of the wrestlers," Josh interjected.

"Yeah, okay." Justin nodded at his cousins, then swallowed down the last of his bottled water.

I can do this. What's the worst that can happen? She says, "no." It's just a dance. And maybe a ride back to the ranch. It's not like I'm asking her to marry me.

If she declines a dance, maybe we can at least strike up a conversation about our jobs, something we have in common. If we can find common ground to start a friendship, maybe she won't turn me down for more in the future.

Putting on an air of confidence he wasn't really feeling, Justin walked over to where Amy was standing on the other side of the room.

"Hey, having a good time?" Justin smiled when he stopped a few feet away from the raven-haired woman of his dreams.

Amy's obsidian eyes widened when she realized he was talking to her. "Ya-yes," she stuttered. "Just taking a breather back here, where it's a little quieter, before the girls drag me back out on the dance floor, or hand me another shot that's way stronger than I'm used to drinking. This isn't my normal scene, but everyone's been so friendly and welcoming. So, I'm having a really good time, but it's a little outside my comfort zone, if ya know what I mean."

Her tawny brown cheeks took on a more terra-cotta tone the longer she spoke, making Justin wonder why she was blushing. She hadn't said anything to be embarrassed about, so Justin had to wonder if it was merely his presence that was affecting her.

"Sorry, I don't normally ramble like that." Amy slightly shook her head as she looked down at the floor, no longer meeting Justin's gaze. "That's probably a sign I should cut off the alcohol for the night."

"Don't apologize." Justin leaned against the pool table closest to them, tilting his head as he bent down to get within her sightline once more. He smiled when her dark-brown, almost black eyes met his baby blues, eliciting a slight upturn of her lips in response. "You have a nice voice, so I don't mind listening to you ramble."

Her shy smile spread a little wider, causing Justin to notice how much fuller her bottom lip was than the top. *Fuck, I wanna suck that pouty lip into my mouth. Too bad I can't even kiss her tonight because of how much she's apparently had to drink.*

Justin shifted back, standing back up to his full height, so he didn't seem like a creep leaning in too close to her. And to keep himself from pushing in a little closer to steal the kiss he so desperately wanted. He hated that when he pulled back, he was no longer close enough to get a whiff of her beachy scent.

"So, if you're cutting off the alcohol and need a breather before going back to dance, wanna play a game of pool?"

"No." Amy shook her head with a self-deprecating chuckle. "I've already embarrassed myself enough for tonight. I don't need to make it worse by letting anyone see how bad I am at shooting pool."

He wasn't a fan of her lack of self-confidence, but he was glad she was looking up at him and laughing, instead of shying away in embarrassment. *I wish I could help her see herself as I see her — capable of anything she wants to achieve.*

"Please, you're a scientist. I highly doubt you're as bad as you think, since pool is just a mix of physics and geometry."

"Yeah, I don't really use much physics or geometry when I'm mixing chemicals in the lab." Amy's light chuckle turned into a full-on laugh.

Justin's cock responded to the melodic sound, starting to press against the back of his zipper in a rather uncomfortable way. Hoping to stop his half-chub from turning into a full-blown hard-on, Justin decided to change the subject to work, thinking that wouldn't be as arousing as making her laugh.

"Kay said you're also a chemical engineer. What're you working on now?"

"Environmentally-friendly cleaning agents," Amy replied, shrugging. "I don't know if any of them will ever be good enough to mass-produce to replace the harsher chemicals on the market, but my lab smells amazing with all the essential oils I've been playing with recently."

"Probably a lot better than mine," Justin grimaced. "Maybe I should get you to bring some of those essential oils in to help me make our new biofuels smell more appealing to the public."

"You're working on a new biofuel?"

Justin nodded in the affirmative, though his current project wasn't truly a new biofuel, more a new process to manufacture it.

"I didn't think biofuel smelled as bad as regular gasoline. Being plant-based, I'd think it'd smell more like the corn or whatever it was made from."

"Yeah, and I'm kinda wishing I was making biodiesel outta used coffee grounds, like those students at Lancaster University I read about last year."

"I saw that article!" Amy's face lit up with excitement. "It made me wish my car could run on biodiesel, so instead of smog, I could smell my morning coffee on the way to work."

"Yeah, that would definitely be a benefit." Justin chuckled along with Amy.

"So, what does your biofuel smell like?"

Justin rubbed a hand over the back of his neck, hating that he was probably going to kill any positive vibes he had going with Amy by admitting what he was working with instead. "I'm actually working on converting methane from cow manure into methanol to be used as racing fuel and as an additive to our current gasoline production. And while methanol actually has a faintly sweet smell, several people in the lab swear they still smell the manure."

"Oh, that's just a psychological thing because they know where it came from, right?" Amy tilted her head, thoughtfully looking up at Justin and causing his pants to tighten once more.

"Yeah, but it doesn't stop me from feeling like I need to stop by the house to take a shower before heading into the lab, when I've had to spend a morning on the west side of the ranch, where we have the collection and conversion facilities set up across the road from the refinery." Justin shifted his stance, hoping to hide the way his body was reacting to hers like a teenager unable to control when he got an erection. *Fuck, I haven't had this much trouble controlling my cock in over a decade.*

"So, your lab isn't at the same location?"

"We have a lab at the refinery in Heart's Destiny, but it's more for quality testing of everything that goes through the refinery. And we'll put another quality control lab in the new methane production facility when we get it up and running. But the R and D lab, where I spend most of my time, is in our main office in San Antonio."

They ended up moving over to a table to sit down and chat because Amy was starting to feel the effects of all the shots the ladies had consumed, and she was less than steady on her feet. They spent the next hour talking about all the other projects Justin had going on in the lab, while sipping on a couple fresh bottles of water. At the mention of the other ways Justin was trying to make his family business into a more environmentally-friendly company, Amy told him about the things she'd discovered in her job that seemed to overlap with his ideas.

By the time Leo Walker gave the last call for alcohol, Amy seemed to have sobered up some, but Justin still offered her a ride back to the ranch. She looked around the room, clearly unsure if she was willing to accept a ride from him, or if she needed to find the women she'd rode to the bar with instead.

"How 'bout we go check in with my cousin Bobby?" Justin held out his hand to help her stand. When Amy just looked at his outstretched arm and didn't make a move to accept his assistance, he elaborated. "He's the police chief, and the one makin' sure everyone has a sober ride home or to wherever they're stayin' while they're in town. I bet your girlfriends are already being paired up with rides, so we can make sure ya'll get back to the ranch safely."

"Oh, okay," Amy agreed, tentatively reaching her hand out to clasp his, so he could assist her in standing without stumbling.

The tingles Justin felt when he held her hand only multiplied when she tripped over her own feet and came crashing into him. His free arm went around her, holding her body against his, chest-to-chest. He couldn't resist inhaling deeply to fill his soul with her beachy scent.

"Whoa! I got ya."

"Sorry, too many shots," Amy mumbled, pressing her forehead into his shoulder. "Shots and heels don't mix. Bad chemical composition. Won't try that experiment again."

Justin just chuckled at her drunken silliness. "It's alright, Sweetheart. Just lean on me."

Sweetheart? What the fuck? Just because I think she's **The One***, doesn't mean I should be starting in with the terms of endearment when she's too drunk to even remember it.*

Justin looped one of Amy's arms over his shoulders, holding her hand to keep it there while he wrapped his other arm around her torso to walk her slowly toward the front of the bar.

Bobby was checking everyone at the door, making sure that anyone who was driving had stopped with only one drink at the beginning of the night before letting them leave the bar. It seemed that Amy wasn't the only woman there who'd overindulged. Justin's sisters, Jen and

Julie, ended up getting a ride home with their brother, JJ. His cousins, Charlotte and Becky, were carried out by their brothers, Josh and Jake. Anthony was taking his fiancée, Kay, home, but he stopped Justin on the way to the door to make sure the other bridesmaid, Deanna, also had a ride.

"Since you've got Amy, maybe you can also get Deanna?" Anthony looked hopefully at Justin. "They're both staying at Mom and Dad's."

"Yeah, but I'll need help getting her to my truck," Justin replied, wishing he could be alone with Amy.

"I guess I'll help you with her," Dean Hunter sighed, motioning over to the woman hugging Kay as if it was the last time she'd see her. "Your ma will probably be thrilled to see me carrying her in for the night."

"Cool, Amy's in Charlotte's old room and Deanna's in Becky's, if ya'll end up having to carry them in." Anthony smirked at Dean.

"You could probably go swap riders with JJ," Justin teased as he watched Dean head toward the bawling bridesmaid with a grimace. Dean looked over to where JJ was struggling to get both Jen and Julie out the door and shook his head.

Justin knew his older brother had a thing for the other bridesmaid, and thought the way his Aunt Hazel was pushing Dean toward Deanna at the cookout earlier was a ploy to make JJ jealous enough to act on his feelings. But apparently, Dean didn't know he wasn't really being fixed up with the second bridesmaid, like his brother James was being fixed up with Kay's sister Randi.

Speaking of the other members of the bridal party, Justin stopped on their walk to his truck to say goodnight to the couple, who didn't appear to be upset about being set up. Once all the pleasantries were handled, he helped Amy up into his truck, where she promptly passed out.

He made sure she was buckled in before heading for home, wishing he could carry her into his house on the ranch instead of into his aunt and uncle's house, where she was staying for the duration of the time she would be in town for the wedding. It took all his willpower to carry her up the stairs and lay her gently on the bed without crawling in beside her.

Leah Mae Wright

He removed her shoes, but he left her in the dress she'd changed back into before going to the bachelor and bachelorette party. He covered her with the quilt from the foot of the bed and placed a bottle of water and some over-the-counter painkillers on the bedside table.

"Goodnight, Sweetheart." Justin brushed his lips over her forehead, unable to stop himself from showing her affection, even though he knew she would never remember it. "Dream of me, like I'll be dreaming of you."

He paused when he got to the door, taking one last, longing look at the woman he had no idea how to pursue. He had to figure out how to win her over in the week she'd be in town. Or else he thought he might have to move to Tulsa, Oklahoma.

~~~

Sunday, November 18, 2018

Amy Lawton was really enjoying the vacation she was taking with her best friend and roommate, Randi Lee, to go to Randi's sister's wedding, even if she did have a little bit of a hangover after the bachelorette party the night before.

She'd been skeptical of really being welcomed in the small Texas town when Kay had first issued the invitation for her to come to the wedding, but Randi had convinced her that Kay would never marry into a racist family. So, Amy had relented and decided to go along, if only to see how the uber-rich lived.

She might currently be earning a middle-class income, but having grown up as the mixed-race daughter of a single mom, she'd certainly seen enough of low-income living in the course of her life. So, she wanted to at least have a glimpse of the good life.

After the group chat, where she learned the Burlesons had oil money, she expected the wedding and all the events leading up to it to be high society affairs. That's why she'd packed every nice dress she owned and didn't listen to Randi when she told her to bring jeans and boots. She still felt a little bad about having to tag along to go pick up the bridesmaids' dresses, so Kay could take her and Deanna to buy
~~~

ranch wear because they hadn't realized just how normal and down-to-earth the Burlesons actually were.

Yeah, their houses were large and lavish, and they all had brand-new vehicles, but they weren't flaunting their wealth in any way. Their vehicles weren't high-end luxury cars or chauffeur-driven limos, either. Even a new pickup truck was still more of a work truck than a luxury vehicle. And even though they were dressed up for church and the wedding shower on Sunday, they'd all been in jeans and cowboy boots the day before for the cookout and horseback riding.

With the eighties style Hazel seems to prefer in her clothing choices, Amy mused as Anthony's mom caught her eye while they were exiting the chapel to go to the area of the church where the shower was going to be held, *she actually reminds me of my mom.*

Amy had been raised by her mother, Andrea Lawton, who claimed her ancestry was a Heinz 57 mix of every race and nationality in the world, so she didn't look at race when picking her partners. Like Amy, Andrea looked more black than anything else, even though her father, Amy's grandfather, was white. Andrea's mother, Amy's grandmother, had strong African genes that she passed down to her daughter and granddaughters alike.

Amy still missed her grandparents, who'd passed away five years before when Amy was off at college. Her grandpa, Tom Lawton, had a massive heart attack while mowing the lawn and passed away at only sixty-three years old. His sixty-year-old wife, Amy's grandma, Shanae, followed him to Heaven less than six months later, with everyone claiming her cause of death was a broken heart from losing the love of her life. Their loss was the final straw that broke Amy's belief in true love.

Not wanting to shed another tear at the loss of her beloved grandparents in front of a whole town of strangers, Amy focused on Hazel's eighties-style dress and how it reminded her of her mother. Andrea Lawton still wore a mostly late eighties and early nineties style wardrobe, which was why Hazel reminded Amy of her own mother, since they didn't seem to have anything else in common. But unlike Hazel's obvious love of eighties fashion, Amy thought her mother's clothing style was more what she still owned from back then, more than an actual choice.

Leah Mae Wright

She didn't exactly have the funds to buy a new wardrobe when she was struggling to raise two daughters on her own. Amy was proud of how her mother had raised her. They might not have had much monetarily, but they had a whole lot of love.

"Amy, we're gonna have you sit over here." A blue-eyed, blonde woman, whom she thought she'd been introduced to the day before as one of Anthony's aunts, waved her over to a table full of Anthony's siblings and cousins. The realization of everyone else being seated at the various tables for the party to begin brought her out of her mental musings about her family and showed her just how out of place she was in the crowd of strangers.

Randi, Kay, their parents, and Deanna were the only people she really knew in the small town, and they were all sitting at the head table with Anthony's parents and the two groomsmen. She hadn't really thought about not being able to sit with them at all the events when she agreed to come on the trip. She could probably go sit with Kay's daughters, since they were the only other people she knew there, but they were seated with Kay's brother and sister-in-law and their children, and Amy didn't really know David and Diana any more than she knew the Burlesons. Now she felt like the outsider she was as she took her seat between two of the Burlesons she'd just met the day before.

It wasn't that she was the only person of color at the table, since that was common when she went anywhere with Randi's family, even though her darker skin tone was extremely obvious next to the lily-white Burlesons. It was more that she was normally shy and took a while to get to know new people.

It's not like you're the only person here who isn't white, Amy mentally chastised herself for her brief moment of self-consciousness. *This place actually looks like a meeting of the United Nations with such a diversified mix of races in the room. So, don't worry about how different you are from anyone else. Just enjoy getting to know Kay's new family like you did yesterday.*

Amy looked around the table and tried to remember all the names of the people seated with her. She knew they were Anthony's siblings and cousins, but other than the man to her immediate left, Justin, she couldn't put a name to any of their faces, since they weren't wearing name tags like the day before.

She couldn't forget Justin, no matter how hard she tried. He'd caught her eye the instant she'd stepped out of Mr. Lee's car the day before. While he was still over six feet tall, he wasn't as large and intimidating as the rest of the men on the ranch had been. His sandy, brown hair, blue eyes, and soft smile had made her heart go pitter-patter from the first moment she'd seen him across the field where the cookout was being held.

"How're you feelin' this mornin'?" Justin leaned over to whisper his question, the sandalwood scent of his cologne mixing with the mint of his breath causing flashes of memory from the night before to bombard Amy's imagination.

Surely, that was all a dream. Amy straightened in her seat, only slightly turning her head to answer Justin. "Fine, thank you."

"No headache from all the shots last night?" She examined his expression to see that his question seemed to come from pure concern.

How does he know how many shots I had last night? He was in the back room playing pool when the girls kept ordering another round.

"Don't mention the shots from last night," the blonde woman on Amy's right side groaned, placing her hand on her forehead like she was trying to massage away a headache.

"Sorry, Jen," Justin lightly chuckled. "Guess you should've had someone other than JJ take you home, so you'd have had someone thoughtful enough to leave you some ibuprofen and water on your bedside table this morning to help with that hangover."

Holy shit! He really did carry me to bed last night. Amy tried to cover her realization with a stoic expression, but judging from the gleam in Justin's eyes as their gazes met, he caught her shock at wondering just how much of the night before had been real and how much had been her dreaming. *Since I woke up still dressed, I know most of the making out, and definitely the sex, was all a dream. But were all those kisses just in my fantasies, or were any of them real?*

Amy didn't want to ask him while they were sitting there with an audience of his family. No matter how welcomed she'd felt by the whole lot of them, she didn't want to ask him about the night before in front of them. Even if he returned her attraction, she didn't think Justin would want to discuss it with his siblings and cousins listening to their conversation.

Leah Mae Wright

Thinking about the night before and when she could ask Justin about it distracted her from hearing the conversation going on around her for a few minutes. It wasn't until Justin leaned over and whispered, "Come on, Sweetheart, let's go get our food," that she realized the guests were all moving through a buffet line to get their lunch.

Sweetheart. He called me that last night, too. Amy struggled to focus to decipher the meaning behind the endearment as she went through the motions of filling her plate. *It must just be a Texas thing, right? Like some guys call everyone darlin' or babe, Justin just calls everyone sweetheart. It doesn't really mean anything. Even if we are both attracted, it's not like we'll see each other again after this week to do anything about it.*

Who am I kidding? It's not like I'd do anything about it even if we lived next door to each other and could pursue a relationship. Unlike Kay and Anthony, or Randi and James, I don't see a happily ever after in my future.

In addition to not wanting to die young of a broken heart like her grandmother, Amy had seen too many of her mother's failed relationships over the years to believe in the fairy tales her friends seemed to be trying to live out. She didn't begrudge her friends for their happiness, and she would never tell them how she feared they were setting themselves up for broken hearts, but she wasn't going to hold her breath for Mr. Right to sweep her off her feet, either.

"So, who all are our mothers trying to set up this week?"

Amy was brought back to the moment by the question posed by the man seated across the table. She really wished they were all wearing the nametags from the day before again, so she could put names to all their faces. Since that wasn't an option, she busied herself with eating while listening to their conversation to try and figure out who each of the people at the table with her were. *There are only nine of them, and I know they're all Burlesons, so it shouldn't be too hard to figure out who's who.*

"All us girls, for sure," the woman beside Amy declared.

Justin called her Jen. That's his sister, I think.

"The only reason we're not paired off with wrestlers right now," the blonde woman on Jen's right stated. "Is because they all sat together as a group with their coworkers and their families."

"Don't worry, Julie," the woman with light brown hair across the table replied, shaking her head. "As soon as our mothers realize they missed the opportunity to pair us up here, they'll fix it in time for Thanksgiving."

Julie is Justin's other sister, Jen's twin. So that means the two women on the other side of the table are Justin's cousins, Anthony's sisters, Charlotte and Becky. Becky was the one who came up with the most outrageous names for the shots last night, so I know that it must be Charlotte who said that about their mothers fixing them all up again at Thanksgiving.

"And if not by Thanksgiving, then by the rehearsal dinner," Becky chuckled and shook her head.

"I guess of us guys, it's just Justin they're trying to match up to marry off this week," the guy across the table, whose hair came closest to Justin's sandy brown, smirked.

At first, Amy was too focused on trying to figure out which of his cousins had spoken and almost missed what he'd said.

"Wait. What?" Amy dropped her fork onto her plate and looked around the table. The mix of hazel, green, brown, and blue eyes looking back at her fascinated her as she realized they were all alike and yet different as they acknowledged her confusion. "Your mothers are trying to match you all up with your future spouses this week?"

"Not just this week," the dark-headed Burleson, who was only slightly shorter than Anthony, grumbled.

"Why do you think you're sitting next to Justin?" Julie grinned.

"And with me on your other side, so none of the other guys here can get as close to you as Justin?" Jen added, giggling.

Amy's jaw dropped. She was sure she looked like a fish out of water with her mouth opening and closing again without her being able to come up with a reply.

Why on earth would they try to match him up with me? Don't they see he's completely outta my league?

"Oh, Amy, don't freak out. It's not that big a deal." Jen reached over and patted Amy's hand soothingly.

"The worst they're gonna do is make you sit next to Justin at every sit-down function this week," Becky assured her from across the table.

"And with ya'll both being chemistry geeks, ya'll should be able to fake a friendship long enough to keep them from tossing anyone else at ya. Right, Bro?" Amy assumed the man to Justin's left, who just punctuated his statement with a punch to Justin's shoulder, was his brother, JJ.

"I don't think Amy and I will hafta fake a friendship," Justin grumbled, shaking his head at his brother.

"But that's all it is," Amy asserted. "Friendship. That's it. I'm only gonna be here for a week. That's barely enough time for me to be able to remember all ya'll's names. So, it'd be silly to ever think any of us could ever be more than friends."

"I knew we should've worn the nametags again today," Charlotte remarked, looking around as if she was going to try to find some for them to put on at the table.

"Tell me you at least know you're sitting next to Justin," the biggest Burleson at the table laughed. "After seein' ya'll talkin' for so long last night, I trusted him to get ya home safe. So, he better have at least told ya his name before you were too drunk to remember it."

"Knock it off, Bobby," Justin growled at his cousin, who Amy vaguely recalled was the police chief for the small town of Heart's Destiny, Texas, where they were for the wedding events.

Amy wasn't sure it was wise of Justin to stand up to his cousin, Bobby, who was at least three inches taller and thirty or forty pounds of solid muscle heavier than Justin. But she couldn't deny that it felt good to have him defend her, regardless.

"Yes, I know who Justin is," Amy stated, hoping to diffuse the situation before it escalated to a shouting match, like it would have if she'd been seated at a table with one of her mother or sister's former boyfriends and their families. "I also remember Jen, Julie, Becky, and Charlotte." Amy pointed to each of the women as she said their names, before turning and giving Bobby a pointed look. "It's the rest of you who need to do a better job introducing yourselves."

"Damn, girl, way to put my brother in his place," the sandy-haired Burleson across the table grinned, standing and extending his hand to Amy. "I'm sorry for not properly introducing myself sooner. I'm Josh."

She had to stand, and they each had to bend to reach across the table, but she shook Josh's hand. "Nice to meet you, Josh. I'm Amy."

"We don't look it, but I'm Josh's twin, Jake." The dark-brown-haired, brown-eyed Jake was slightly shorter and thinner than his sandy-brown-haired, hazel-eyed twin.

Once Amy had shaken Jake's hand, which was easier than shaking Josh's hand since he was seated one seat closer with only Jen and Julie separating them, the clearing of a throat to her left caught her attention. As she took her seat again and turned to look, she noticed Justin's brother leaning across him and extending his hand. "And I'm Justin's brother, JJ. Nice to officially meet you, Amy."

"You, too," Amy smiled and shook his hand as well.

"Yeah, yeah, ya'll've made your point," Bobby scoffed, standing from his seat between Josh and Charlotte to walk around toward Amy. He stopped between her and Jen and extended his hand. "I'm sorry, Amy. I meant no disrespect to you. I just hafta pick on these guys every chance I get."

Bobby's dimples popped out with the smile he gave her then, bringing a smile to Amy's lips as well when she placed her hand in his to shake.

"I'm also not a neanderthal like my brothers, which is why I walked around to shake your hand, instead of making you reach across the table." He winked at her then, making her have to stifle a giggle. While he was just as attractive as his brothers and cousins, Amy didn't feel the tingles of attraction she felt when she looked at Justin, but it was still nice to have him flirt just a little bit. "I'm Bobby, the oldest of these idiots. And also the police chief. So, if anyone gives you trouble while you're here in our fair city, please let me know, so I can toss 'em in jail for it."

"Thank you," Amy giggled. "But I don't think I'll need you to arrest anyone on my behalf."

"Are ya'll through flirting with my friend now?" Justin growled and glared at his brother and male cousins.

His tone of voice made Amy question whether or not Justin was truly okay with them only being friends, but she brushed it off as nothing to worry about. Since she wouldn't be in town for very long, it wouldn't matter if he wanted more than friendship or not.

"For now," Bobby teased, grinning once more before releasing her hand and walking back around to his seat.

They finished their meal, making small talk with only a little more teasing about the matchmaking antics of their mothers. When the tables were rearranged to set up for the newlywed game, Amy continued to sit with the Burlesons, even though their mothers seemed to have realized they'd missed a matchmaking opportunity and rectified it by mixing in a few of the wrestlers and some local women. She called Deanna over to sit with her as well, since she and Dean were the only ones at their table who weren't participating in the game.

At one point, Kay's daughters came over and pulled a couple of their new uncles away from the group to entertain them and several of their friends, who weren't interested in the adults playing the game. Amy knew she should be focusing on the activities that were planned for the shower, specifically how her best friend, Randi, was doing in the newlywed game with her new boyfriend, James. But she was enjoying getting to know the Burlesons too much to pay attention like she should, specifically Justin and his brother and sisters, who'd each somehow been paired with one of the wrestlers in town when the seats were rearranged.

Justin's siblings all worked at Burleson Incorporated and were very interested in the ideas Amy had discussed with Justin the night before. She felt a little bad about not remembering every detail of their conversation, but most of it quickly came back to her when he started telling his siblings about how he wanted to try to incorporate her ideas into his current projects.

Her boss probably wouldn't like her sharing her chemistry knowledge with the leaders of another company, but since the cleaning products she was working on back in Tulsa weren't in direct competition with the clean energy and automotive chemical projects going on at Burleson, Amy didn't see it as a conflict of interest.

By the time the party was over, she and Deanna had plans to go to work with Jen and Julie the next day, so they could show them around San Antonio over a long lunch break after a tour of the corporate offices. Justin had to spend a little time at the refinery lab Monday morning, but he specifically asked Amy to find him when she got back from her lunch plans with his sisters, so he could show her his lab in the afternoon.

Amy knew it was just the Burlesons' way of trying to keep her and Deanna entertained when they knew Randi and Kay had plans with their men. But she couldn't stop herself from being excited about spending more time with Justin, even if she could only ever consider him a long-distance friend.

~~~

Saturday, November 24, 2018

Justin wasn't sure what to feel as he sat beside Amy at his cousin Anthony's wedding reception. He'd had a great time getting to know her all week. Not just when they were matched together at the various wedding and holiday events that week by his mother and aunt with their matchmaking stunts, but also on Monday, Tuesday, and Wednesday when he'd gotten to spend time with her in his lab at Burleson Incorporated.

Her experience in developing environmentally-friendly household cleaners might not, at first glance, appear to be related to new product development at Burleson Energy. But once she realized that biofuels were only the tip of the iceberg of what he was working on in research and development, they both realized that her knowledge easily carried over to the other automotive chemicals he wanted to make in a greener way.

Justin had been trying to talk Amy into coming to work for Burleson Incorporated since she'd first stepped into his lab on Monday afternoon. Though he couldn't deny that part of his reasoning was because he wanted her to move to Texas, so he'd have a chance to date her, he also thought she would be an invaluable asset in the lab.

Her knowledge, experience, and creative ideas were the only reasons he gave his family when he pitched the idea of her coming to work for them. Justin knew better than to let any of his relatives know he wanted to be more than friends with Amy. Though his siblings and cousins would all be supportive of him finding love and wanting to settle down to start a family of his own, Justin didn't want to give his mother and aunt the satisfaction of knowing they'd picked the right woman for him.
~~~

Leah Mae Wright

The guys would never let me live it down if I'm the first to fall for one of our moms' matchmaking schemes.

But since Amy seemed more reluctant to dating than any of his siblings or cousins, Justin figured he'd be better off playing the long game in trying to win her over. Which meant nobody needed to know he was falling for her, until he finally convinced her to give him a chance at dating her.

The first step in even getting the chance for a more meaningful relationship with her was getting the two of them in the same city for a lot longer than the week of Anthony and Kay's wedding events. He knew if they worked together daily, they'd eventually give in to the overwhelming chemistry between them.

If she won't accept this job offer, then I guess I'll just hafta look at jobs with her company in Tulsa.

Justin's cousins, Charlotte and Becky, had been right when they'd told everyone at their table at the wedding shower how their mothers would be matching them up with wrestlers at the other wedding events. At the reception, Justin and Amy were seated with his sisters and female cousins, alternated boy-girl with four single male GWA wrestlers, much like they'd been at the rehearsal dinner the night before. He wasn't sure how his brother and male cousins had avoided the matchmaking mess their mothers were making of the girls' lives, but he wasn't disappointed that he was caught in their web with Amy.

Once the dinner and cake were all served, and the women he was related to all got up to go dance with their pseudo-dates, Justin motioned for his father to join him and Amy at their table. As much as he wanted to get Amy in his arms on the dance floor, he knew his obvious arousal at being so close to her wouldn't be considered friendly. Besides, he needed his dad to extend an official job offer, since she hadn't taken his more casual offers seriously all week.

"Having a good time?" Amy only nodded as Jon Burleson took a seat at the table and inquired about their evening.

"Yeah, Dad," Justin replied, so the silence didn't drag on long enough to become awkward. "But I'd be having a better time if I could convince Amy here to come work in the lab."

"What makes you reluctant to come work at Burleson?"

Though Jon's question was clearly directed at Amy, she turned to look at Justin instead of his father. "I, um, didn't really think Justin was serious about offering me a job."

"Oh, Sweetheart, I was very serious. I really need your help with the new carburetor cleaner and antifreeze projects." Though Justin had only started those projects with the hopes to make their manufacturing process more eco-friendly, Amy's insights in the lab had shown him that they could also possibly make them less toxic to the humans who used them, as well as the pets that might accidentally lick up a spill.

"Oh, well, okay," Amy sputtered, finally looking away from Justin to take in the information his father was sliding across the table to her. "I guess if you want to give me more details about the job, I'll think about it."

"When Justin and I talked earlier in the week and he told me about your ideas while touring our lab, I had Jen put together an offer letter for you." Jon finished pushing the folder containing the letter in front of Amy. "I realize you'll have to go back to Tulsa and turn in your notice where you're currently working, and will have to work out at least two weeks there. I'm assuming it'll take you a couple more weeks to get everything set up to move, so I put together the packet to reflect a start date at the beginning of January. That timeframe will still work if you want to take a week to think about the offer."

"Oh, okay, thank you." Amy opened the folder and perused the papers inside. Justin couldn't tell exactly what she was reading with the way she held the folder between them to look at the documents, but he hoped it was a good sign when her jaw dropped, and her eyes went wide. "Are these numbers right?"

"Yes," Jon asserted, smiling at Amy.

"Buh-but, that's more than double my current salary," Amy stuttered.

"That's because you're not currently in a managerial position. If you accept the job at Burleson, you'll be second-in-command in the lab. If you flip to the job description, you'll see that in addition to developing and testing your own products, you'll be supervising the various teams working on other projects in the lab as well."

Leah Mae Wright

Amy flipped through more papers, her eyes scanning them like she was speed-reading all the responsibilities and benefits of the job. "Wow. Okay, yes, I'll take the job."

"Amy, Sweetheart," Justin softly whispered, reaching out to take her hand to get her attention. Once her eyes met his, he continued. "You don't hafta give us an answer immediately. Take the week to decide. Go home and discuss it with your family. Make sure it's really what you want before you commit to moving away from your mom and sister."

As much as Justin wanted Amy to come to work at Burleson Incorporated, so he could see her daily to convince her to go out with him, he didn't want her to feel pressured into making a snap decision about it. He wanted her to be really sure she wanted to move to Texas because he didn't want to risk her getting so homesick that she wanted to move home within a couple months on the job.

"No, I don't need a week." Amy shook her head as she squeezed Justin's hand. "After working as hard as she did to raise Ashlyn and I on less than a quarter of this salary, my momma would whip my butt if I went home and told her I was only thinking about accepting this job offer."

Damn, I knew she'd had a hard life being raised by a single mom, but I didn't realize she'd had to survive living below the poverty line. I wonder if we can find jobs for her mom and sister, too, so they can move down here and not hafta struggle anymore either?

"Welcome to Burleson Incorporated," Jon smiled, extending his hand to shake Amy's and bringing Justin back to the moment.

"We should grab another glass of champagne to celebrate." Justin waved over a waiter carrying a tray of drinks, wanting to toast to the beautiful woman whose heart he hoped to earn in the new year.

Sunday, November 25, 2018

Amy couldn't believe how drastically her life was about to change, all because she'd agreed to come to her best friend's sister's wedding. She'd thought the trip was just a way to show her support to the Lees because they treated her like one of the family. She'd wanted to be there for Randi, who she thought of like another sister, when she finally told her family about her feelings for James and her desire to work and travel with him. Little did she know that going along to support her best friend would lead to her dream job.

It was late when she got back to Bob and Hazel Burleson's home after the reception the night before, so she hadn't called her mom to tell her the news yet. While she was getting dressed and then sitting in church that morning, she decided that it would be best if she told her mother in person, instead of springing it on her over the phone. So, Amy planned to go visit her mother as soon as the Lees dropped her off at home once they landed in Tulsa.

The excitement over her new job was eating her alive, though, so she was glad she'd have the chance to talk to Randi about it as soon as the service was over. She'd wanted to tell her bestie about it the night before, but every time she looked Randi's way at the reception, she was either on the dance floor with James or ensconced in a conversation with her family. Knowing what Randi had to say to her folks, Amy had stayed close enough that Randi could see her if she needed her, but far enough away that she didn't intrude on the tense conversation.

Justin had eventually insisted on dragging her onto the dance floor. But since they were only friends, they only danced to the faster songs, nothing slow that necessitated touching each other while dancing.

While Amy knew in her head that they could only ever be friends, in her heart she couldn't help but wish she'd at least gotten one slow dance with him to know what it would feel like to be held in his arms. She'd fought her attraction to him all week, knowing she'd only get her heart broken in the end when he left her. But now that she'd accepted the offer to work for him at Burleson Incorporated, she was even more determined to keep him strictly in the friend zone, so she didn't risk losing her dream job in a messy break-up if they tried for more.

But damn, it would've been nice to at least get a little taste of him before setting those boundaries. He may be the shortest and thinnest guy in his family, but he still has big hands and feet which means he's probably bigger than average where it really counts.

Leah Mae Wright

If we'd only have met another place, another time, when we could've hooked up for a one-night stand without the potential problem of him being related to my best friend, even if it's only by marriage. I'm sure I'd've enjoyed taking that cowboy for a ride.

Amy was brought back to the moment when the service was dismissed and everyone around her stood to leave the chapel. *Yeah, I probably shouldn't've been headed toward fantasies of sex with my new boss while sitting in church anyway.*

"We're not gonna be able to stay for the potluck," Charles Lee informed everyone around them, reminding Amy that she needed to send Randi a text message to meet her at the Burleson Ranch, since she and James hadn't attended the services that morning.

Amy pulled her phone out of her purse and fired off a text while walking out to the vehicles with both the Lee and Burleson families.

> **Amy: We're leaving the church now to go to the ranch. Meet me there in 10. Need to talk before flying to Tulsa.**

> **Randi: K see you soon.**

Amy put her phone back in her purse without turning the sound back on, knowing she'd just have to put it in airplane mode when they got to the airport in San Antonio anyway. The only person who might try to call her before her flight was her mother, and Amy wanted to miss that call if it came in, so she could tell her mother her news in person.

"I know it wasn't mentioned in the new hire paperwork Dad gave you last night," Justin started, catching up to her as they got outside the church. "But you're welcome to stay on the ranch when you get back, so you can actually go look at what's available before you sign a lease or anything."

"Oh, um, thanks," Amy stuttered, smiling shyly at him. "I'll, uh, let you know if I end up needing to do that."

Amy wasn't sure exactly where Justin was implying she could stay. *Does he mean in the room I've been in all week at his aunt and uncle's house? Or in a room in his home? Unless Bob or Hazel offer me the room I've been staying in, I'm probably gonna be better off if I talk to*

James about staying at his mom's bed and breakfast until I can find a place of my own.

"Okay, well, you've got my number, so just call or text me if you need anything set up for you here while you're in Tulsa. Or just to keep in touch with your new best friend." Justin's light blush as he awkwardly asked her to keep in touch for the next few weeks was almost too cute for Amy to resist leaning in to give him a quick kiss.

"Sure thing, Boss." Amy smiled at Justin as she got into the car with the Lees, using the moniker to remind herself of the boundaries between them, so she didn't give in to her desire for him. "See you in a few weeks."

"Boss?" Deanna looked at Amy quizzically as she buckled her seatbelt.

"Yeah, I accepted the lab manager position the Burlesons offered me last night." Amy wouldn't have normally discussed anything about her new job with Kay's best friend, who Amy wasn't really close to. But she knew the Burlesons had also been trying to get Deanna to come to work for them, so she thought they might become better friends if the older woman also accepted a job and moved from Tulsa to Heart's Destiny.

Before Deanna could say anything about her own job offer, Mary Lee started asking Amy all kinds of questions about her new job and how she planned to handle the logistics of moving.

Amy barely had time to tell them about the job before they were on the ranch and getting out of the car. Luckily, Randi and James pulled up beside them, so she was able to deflect the moving questions by saying she needed to talk to Randi about the house they were currently splitting the rent on in Tulsa before she could figure all that out.

"I figured I'd just do a bank transfer to you for my half of the rent and utilities while I'm on the road," Randi offered, not realizing they had more to discuss than just Randi not being physically at the house with her new job.

"Yeah, that won't work," Amy chuckled. "Because I'm not gonna be living there anymore."

"What?" Randi's shouted question caused everyone in the vicinity to turn to look at them.

"I'm moving down here." Amy shrugged before looping her arm through Randi's and dragging her inside the big white house to the bedroom where she'd been staying, so they could talk in private.

Well, as private as they could be with James following Randi around like a little, lost puppy. *More like a huge, lost puppy,* Amy inwardly chuckled at her own thoughts. The man couldn't go five minutes without touching Randi in some way, even if it was only holding her hand while they sat and listened to Amy telling them all about the job she accepted and how much better the pay and benefits were than her current job.

"And is Justin included in those benefits?" Randi grinned sassily.

"No!" Amy shook her head vehemently as she started packing her things to fly back to Tulsa. "Justin's my new boss and a friend, with no benefits." *No matter how much I might wanna enjoy a few of those benefits with him.*

"You might wanna tell him that," James snickered.

"Look, I know I've been distracted with James this week…"

"And Kay's pregnancy mix-up and telling your parents about you and James and your dreams of being a wrestler." Amy interrupted Randi's words to fill in everything else that had her best friend distracted all week. "And I completely understand all that. That's why I've tried to be here if you needed to talk, but outta the way by touring the Burlesons' lab, so ya'll could have some time alone. But I really didn't need you to help me make the decision to take the job. I just need to talk to you now about the house, so we can get our deposit back and I'll know where you want me to have your stuff stored, since you won't be there to need the place either."

"Yeah, we'll get to that," Randi deflected, grabbing the dress from Amy's hand to stop her from continuing to pack. "But as I was saying, I was distracted this week, but not so distracted that I didn't notice how you and Justin were looking at each other constantly. So, spill, Sister, why are you not trying to hook up with him?"

"Because it wouldn't be appropriate to date my boss." Amy knew her best friend would see that as a cop-out, but she didn't really want to get into the reasons why she didn't think she'd ever have a long-term relationship with Justin or anyone else.

She had to hurry and get packed to fly out in a couple hours. She didn't have time to go through the therapy session she'd get from

Randi on why she couldn't judge all men based on the death of her father or the actions of any of the other men her mother had dated over the years.

"Okay, that's a valid point," Randi sighed, plopping her ass back down on the bed beside James. "Today. But why did you friend zone him immediately when we got here, when the offer of a job wasn't even on the table?"

"I didn't friend zone him immediately," Amy protested, going back to packing, so she didn't have to look her best friend in the eye while she lied. "I was feeling things out to see what might develop, but as soon as he started talking about the possibility of a job, I knew it couldn't be more than friends."

"How soon was he talking about you moving down here for work? And why didn't you mention it to me when he first mentioned it to you?"

"He said something Monday, the first time I went to the lab," Amy answered her best friend's questions. "And then you had plans with James on Tuesday, and your interview on Wednesday. With everything else going on, it just didn't seem important enough to mention until the official job offer last night."

"Yeah, I guess after Thursday, it was easy to forget a life-changing job offer when we were shopping on Black Friday."

Amy burst out laughing at the easy way Randi glossed over the screaming scandal of Thanksgiving. Randi and James joined in with the laughter for a few minutes before they finally got to discuss the house in Tulsa and the schedule of Amy's move.

"So, I don't actually start work here until the beginning of January."

"Does that mean you'll still be in Tulsa for Christmas?"

Amy nodded, just as realizing she'd have to leave town immediately after celebrating the holiday with her family caused a lump to form in her throat.

"Okay, we can do this," Randi reassured, reaching out to clasp Amy's hand comfortingly. "I'll come to Tulsa when the GWA breaks for the holidays to pack up my stuff and help you clean out the house. I probably won't be able to get a storage unit until the twenty-sixth or twenty-seventh, but I should still have enough time to move everything out, so we can turn in the keys by the end of the month."

"Are you sure you wanna move your stuff to storage? I mean, I can still pay my half of the rent until you find another roommate if you need me to." Amy hated feeling like she was forcing her best friend to give up their rental by moving away.

"Oh, yeah, I'm sure. I'm gonna be living in hotels for the foreseeable future, so I was only leaving my stuff there to keep you from having to get a new roommate. This'll actually save me money over paying half the rent and utilities on a house that I'm not actually living in." Randi seemed adamant in her statement, easing Amy's guilt over causing her friend to have to move.

"You could save even more money each month." James wagged his eyebrows at Randi suggestively. "Since Amy's gonna already hafta rent a truck to move her stuff down here, why don'tcha split it with her and move your stuff into my house instead of a storage unit?"

"Daddy's already freaked out enough about me traveling with you while working with the GWA." Randi shook her head. "We have to give him a little time to get used to the situation before we cause him to have a coronary by me moving in with you down here."

Amy walked into the bathroom off the bedroom she'd been staying in to make sure she had all her toiletries, giving Randi and James some privacy to discuss their future living arrangements.

"Do you have a place lined up to stay when you first get down here?" Randi inquired as soon as Amy was back in the bedroom to put her shower supplies in her suitcase.

"No," Amy admitted. "But I wanted to ask James about the bed and breakfast as an option until I can find someplace closer to work."

"Sure, you can stay at the B and B if you want," James agreed, his eyes cutting to Randi before moving back to look at Amy. "But I have a ton of space in my garage for all your furniture and a guest bedroom you're welcome to use. We'll only be here a few days around the holidays, so it'd be nice to know the house is being used while we're on the road for the first five months of the year."

"Ya'll don't have any breaks the first five months of the year?" Amy didn't think she'd ever be able to do a job like James and Randi, where they traveled constantly and only got to go home for a week around the major holidays.

"No, we'll fly out on New Year's Day and won't be home again until Memorial Day weekend." James shrugged as if it was no big deal.

"Wait, we'll be here in town the weekend before Valentine's Day," Randi objected. "I know it's not really a break since that's not one of the holidays the company takes off, but the pay-per-view is in San Antonio that weekend, so we'll be here for a couple days then."

"Sorry, Angel." James pulled Randi into his side to kiss her temple. "I forgot about that, since it's not a holiday the whole company takes off and goes home."

"But, even still, it's only a weekend we'll be here." Randi brushed her lips over James's beard before turning back to Amy. "So, you'll mostly have James's house to yourself with no rush to find your own place."

"Okay, yeah, that should work," Amy relented. She wasn't sure how comfortable she'd be with moving her stuff into James's house if Randi wasn't also moving her things there at the same time, but staying at his house would be less uncomfortable than staying on the Burleson Ranch when she was working for them.

Chapter One

Tuesday, December 25, 2018 — Christmas Day

Amy had accomplished quite a lot in the last month since flying home to Tulsa. She'd turned in their notice to her and Randi's landlord, so they could get their deposits back when they moved out in a couple days. She'd given her resignation to her employer and worked her last day there on the fourteenth. She'd gotten everything she needed to the bank the following week to get preapproved for a home loan, so she could purchase a house in Texas, instead of having to find someplace to rent. She also had almost everything at the house she'd shared with Randi for the last few years packed up and ready to be loaded into a truck to take to Texas. Now all she had to do was get through the day celebrating Christmas with her mom and sister before she and Randi went to pick up the rental truck on the twenty-sixth to load up and make their move on the twenty-seventh.

Randi would be moving her things to James's house in Heart's Destiny, too, having given in to his persuasion a couple weeks ago. While having Randi moving in with James eased some of Amy's discomfort at staying at his house, she still hoped to find a place of her own before they got home for the pay-per-view in February.

Who knows? With this much of a bump in income, maybe I'll be able to afford to buy a house with spare bedrooms for Mom and Ashlyn to have a place to stay when they come visit. If that's the case, I might even be able to convince them to move with me. Lord knows, my salary will be enough to support all of us until they can find jobs down there. I bet they'd be able to find better jobs in Texas than what they've got here, too.

"What's that whimsical look for?" Amy's mom, Andrea Lawton, tilted her head at her daughter as they worked together in the kitchen to prepare the holiday meal.

"Just thinking about possibly finding a house down in Texas big enough that you and Ashlyn could move down there with me." Amy smiled at her mother as she mashed the potatoes.

"Really?" Andrea questioned, giving her daughter a knowing smile as she put together the green bean casserole. "You sure that look wasn't from thinking about a boy?"

"Seriously, Mom, I was thinking about how much better life could be for all of us if you and Ashlyn moved to Texas with me." Amy knew her mother didn't understand her aversion to relationships, so she didn't bother trying to explain that she would never get a whimsical expression on her face from thinking about a guy. *My O-face when I think about Justin while using my vibrator doesn't count.* "Besides, I'm twenty-five. I don't think about boys anymore. I fantasize about men."

"I stand corrected." Andrea raised her hands in surrender, her face lighting up with humor as she laughed with her daughter. "So, tell me about these Texas men you met last month and are now fantasizing about."

Glad her sister hadn't arrived yet to embarrass her with really raunchy comments, Amy indulged her mother. But she tried to keep it all to generalities and not specific to one man in particular, whom she shouldn't be so attracted to and couldn't stop thinking about, no matter how hard she tried. "You know that saying about everything being bigger in Texas?"

Andrea nodded. "Please tell me it's true."

"Well, I didn't test out the goods or anything." Amy laughed and thought about how different her and Randi's conversations about sex were with their mothers. While Amy wasn't as outspoken as her sister, she was way more open about discussing sex than her best friend because of how different their families were when it came to openly discussing all aspects of life. "But I didn't meet a single man who was under six feet tall, so I can only assume that everything's bigger in Texas."

"Oh, girl, we definitely might hafta talk more about us moving down there with you." Andrea fanned herself after putting the casserole dish in the oven. Amy wasn't sure if it was from the heat of the oven or from the thoughts her mother was having about looking for her next boyfriend. "Did one of those sexy Texans catch your eye?"

"Not anybody I can actually date." Amy shook her head, knowing her mother would probably argue the point. "I'm sure there's a no-fraternization policy that'll keep my new boss off-limits."

"Oh dear, maybe you shouldn't've taken this job." Andrea's expression showed concern, but also curiosity. "If your new boss is the one who put that dreamy expression on your face, you should've kept your options open for dating him. Maybe look for a different new job down there, instead of taking the one he offered you."

"I wasn't exactly looking for this job," Amy protested, shaking her head at her mother once again. "And it's a dream job. One I didn't think I'd be qualified to get until I had another ten years' experience in the lab. So, there was no way I could turn it down when it was offered because I know there's not another company on the planet that'll give me the same deal right now."

"Nonsense," Andrea countered, stepping away from the counter to grasp Amy by the shoulders. "Big businesses don't get to be successful by giving away dream jobs to unqualified people. You're most definitely qualified, or they wouldn't've made the offer. And if they're willing to give you a good salary and benefits, so will the next company."

"Maybe." Amy reluctantly saw her mother's opinion as valid, but a little part of her still thought her job offer might've had more to do with the Burleson women and their matchmaking than her qualifications. "I just can't shake the feeling that Susan and Hazel had more to do with my job offer than Justin thinking I'm qualified for the job."

"You're gonna hafta explain a little better for me to know who these people are." Andrea grinned, hugging her daughter tightly before quickly releasing the embrace, so they could get back to work on their Christmas dinner. "I can't help you figure out what's causing your doubts if I don't know the whole situation."

"Burleson Incorporated is Kay's new husband's family business. Bob and Jon Burleson are the co-CEOs, and their ten kids are all on the board of directors. Bob is married to Hazel, and they have six children, the youngest of whom is Anthony, Kay's new husband. Jon is married to Susan, and they have four children. In addition to being on the board of directors, Jon and Susan's children all work at Burleson Incorporated full-time. Their son, Justin, is the vice president of research and development, and my new boss. All week while we were in Texas for Kay and Anthony's wedding, Hazel and Susan were trying to play matchmaker for their other kids. Like actively pushing them to sit with specific people at the various wedding events. Justin and I were seated together at every event, which is how we got to talking about our shared interest in chemical engineering."

"So, now you're wondering if the job offer actually came from your talks with Justin or from his momma and auntie still playing matchmaker between the two of you?"

"Exactly." Amy nodded her head at her mother while stirring the butter, cheese, sour cream, chives, and bacon bits into the potatoes.

"Hmm?" Andrea had her thinking face on while she put the rolls on the pan to brown. "I suppose it could be possible. Have they sent you an employment contract? Or company handbook?"

"No, not yet. I'll get those things when I report for my first day of work on January second." Amy didn't look at her mother as she answered, she was too focused on pouring her potato mixture into a baking dish, so she could cover it with more cheese and put it into the oven to warm through before dinner.

"Well, I guess you need to read those closely on your first day. If there really is a no-fraternization policy, then you got the job based on your qualifications."

Amy only nodded to acknowledge her mother's advice. They worked silently for a little while longer, getting everything else in the oven to finish browning before dinner.

When they were done with everything but the waiting, they sat down at the table that was already set for dinner. That's when Andrea finally broke the silence.

"So, how are you gonna handle it if your new job is really a matchmaking plot?"

"Try to do a good job, so I don't get fired for not being qualified," Amy guessed with a self-deprecating chuckle.

"There's no chance you're gonna fall for your new boss, is there?" Andrea gave Amy a knowing look as she asked the question.

Amy struggled with how to answer her mother. While she was adamantly against relationships and risking her heart by being involved for more than one night with any man, she could see how easy it'd be to fall for Justin.

"I don't want to," Amy finally admitted. "But I can't say it's completely outta the realm of possibility."

"So, tell me about Justin and why you don't wanna fall for him." Andrea placed a hand over Amy's reassuringly.

"You know why I don't wanna fall for him, or anyone else." Amy really didn't want to get into the same old argument with her mother that they'd had for years.

Andrea wanted her daughters to find love and settle down to give her grandchildren. While her sister, Ashlyn, was more than willing to put her heart on the line regularly trying to find true love, Amy didn't think the very slim chance she'd find her soulmate was worth the beating her heart would take from trying over and over like her mother and sister. Not to mention her fear of losing her soulmate if she ever did find him.

"Oh, Amy, how many times do I hafta tell you that love really is worth the risk before you'll finally believe me?"

"How can you say that, Mom? Have you forgotten all the times you've gotten your heart broken over the years?"

"I've only had my heart broken once," Andrea proclaimed with a sigh. "And yes, the time I had with your father, the love we felt for each other, was worth every ounce of pain I've felt since we lost him. That love is what brought you and your sister into this world, and I wouldn't wish away a second of my heartache at losing him if it meant I'd also lose out on all I've gained from the love we shared."

"I know that, Mom." Amy turned her hand over, so she could lace her fingers with her mother's. "I also know that Daddy didn't choose to leave us. But I don't think that's the only time you've had your heart broken. What about with Sam? Or Darren? Or Tray?"

Andrea took a deep breath and blew it out with a huff before refuting her daughter's beliefs about her previous relationships. "None of those men broke my heart. I wasn't in love with any of them. I was in like with them at most, maybe in lust, but never in love. What you saw as heartache was actually anger. Mostly at myself for being weak and needing to take comfort from men, who weren't capable of giving anything more than a hot hookup."

"Oh, Mom, you shouldn't've been mad at yourself. You didn't do anything wrong. They did." Amy wanted to comfort her mother, but she didn't want to list out the infractions her former partners had committed against her. She knew there would be nothing good to come from going over who cheated and who drained her mother's bank account before leaving.

"Maybe I wasn't wrong in the same ways as them, but I was still wrong in dating them and letting you grow up thinking any of those relationships were love matches. I'm afraid that instead of inheriting my natural tendency to wanna find love, you've learned from their bad influence to guard your heart because you're not sure you're capable of loving and being loved."

"That's not it, Mom. I know I'm capable of loving and being loved. I love you. I love Ashlyn. And I know you both love me, too. I also love my friends and my work. I'm just not gonna risk my dream job on the off chance my boss and I could fall in love. The reason I'm not willing to risk my heart willy-nilly is because the real lesson I learned from those losers is that not all men are capable of love. So, I have to be really picky before I, eventually, risk my heart on love with the right man."

"Okay, as long as you're willing to admit that there is a right man out there for you." Andrea's eyes were glassy looking as she held back tears from the emotional conversation with her daughter.

"I know I haven't believed he's out there for a while," Amy admitted, smiling sheepishly at her mother. "But after seeing Kay and Randi both meeting their soulmates, I'm starting to believe that there are still men capable of love."

"And could yours be Justin?" Andrea blinked a few times to clear her eyes as she smiled at Amy.

"Could what be Justin?" Amy's twin sister, Ashlyn, interjected, finally making an appearance when she knew all the cooking was completed. "Justin who? Do I know him? Have I dated him?"

Amy and Ashlyn looked identical, but they were polar opposites in every other way. Where Amy loved to cook and spend time with their mother in the kitchen, Ashlyn could burn the house down by trying to boil water. Where Amy was studious and considered a bookworm in school, Ashlyn was boisterous and known to be the life of the party. And where Amy was leery of love, Ashlyn was boy-crazy.

"Justin Burleson, my new boss. No, you don't know him. No, you haven't dated him." Amy rattled off the answers to her sister's questions and didn't acknowledge the overwhelming jealous feelings she was having at thinking of her twin with Justin before turning back to her mother. "As for your question, Mom, I don't know. If there's a no-fraternization clause in the company paperwork when I start next week, then I won't even be able to explore the possibility."

"Ah, so Ames has the hots for her new boss, got it." Ashlyn dropped her purse on the floor as she took her seat at the table.

"That's not what I said," Amy protested.

"You didn't hafta say it. I'm your twin. I feel you, so I know the flutters when you said his name are because you have the hots for him."

Amy didn't believe for a second that Ashlyn could determine what she was feeling from a metaphysical twin connection because she'd never once had the same kind of flutters about Ashlyn. But she couldn't deny that her sister was right in saying she had the hots for Justin. She just didn't know what she was going to do about the undeniable attraction she felt for her new boss when she had to work with him every day.

"So, what does Justin look like? And does he have a hot brother for me?"

"Actually, he does have a brother, and three single cousins, who're all pretty hot." Amy chuckled as she fanned herself, heating up from the memories of how hot all the Burlesons were the month before when she met them. "Justin's the shortest at only six-foot-two and a little thinner than his brother and cousins."

"Let me guess, he's more brains than brawn?" Ashlyn nodded at her own question, not giving Amy a chance to reply before continuing to speak. "You always did go more for the brainiacs. Please tell me at least one of the others is buff and muscular."

"Yeah, his brother, JJ, and cousin, Jake, are both an inch taller and maybe a bit more muscular. His cousin, Bobby, is super tall, like six-foot-five, and in great shape. But he has to be because he's the police chief."

"Ooo, a cop! I wonder if he'd use his cuffs on me?" Ashlyn wagged her eyebrows at her sister.

"Ashlyn Danae!" Andrea shook her head at her daughter, but she couldn't stop the slight smile that gave away her own kinky side, which was probably where Ashlyn got her outrageous streak.

"Actually, I bet you'd like his cousin, Josh, better. He's a Navy SEAL. Six-foot-four and more muscular than the rest of the Burlesons." Amy hoped to deflect the conversation away from her sister's sexual proclivities, but she wasn't sure continuing to describe the Burlesons was the way to do it. "They all have brown hair, with Josh and Justin's being the lightest of the bunch. Well, of the guys anyway. Justin's sisters are both blonde with blue eyes like his. The rest of the family either had brown, green, or hazel eyes, but I can't remember which of the guys had what color eyes, other than Justin."

"I definitely need to plan a trip down to see you, Ames, so you can introduce me. It's been a while since I've had some white meat."

"Ashlyn Danae Lawton!" This time it was Amy's turn to call her sister by her full name as she cringed at how her twin was referring to her new bosses.

"Amy Edwina Lawton!" Ashlyn shouted back before they both burst out laughing.

It'd been a few years since they'd acted goofy together, not since they were teenagers and Amy got serious about her school work to be able to earn her scholarships to pay for college. But back when they were kids, they would spend hours going back and forth shouting each other's full names in a bad imitation of their mother reprimanding them before breaking down in a fit of giggles. They may have only shouted once each, but the laughter was still reminiscent of how close they'd been as little girls.

"I'm definitely gonna look for a house big enough for all of us," Amy decided as her laughter died down, realizing just how much she was going to miss her mother and sister after she moved. "And as soon as I have the space, both of you better move to Texas with me."

"Deal!" Ashlyn grinned.

"I don't know," Andrea hemmed and hawed, acting like she was weighing her options. "You haven't said a word about the single men my age there. I might hafta stay here if all the older men there are married."

Leah Mae Wright

"But, Mom, I only told you about the Burleson men." Amy gave her mother a conspiratorial smile. "I didn't mention the wrestlers that Kay's husband works with, or the bunkhouse full of single cowboys on the Burleson Ranch. I didn't talk to each and every one of them, but I can say from looking around while I was there, you'll definitely have a wide variety of men your age to choose from if you move to Heart's Destiny with me."

"Well, then, I guess we need to hurry up and get you fed, then go help you finish packing up, so you can hurry up and get moved and find us a house. And maybe you can get me Hazel and Susan's numbers, so I can get them started with planning who they wanna match your sister and me up with when we all get moved."

Oh, Lord, what've I done? If Mom starts talking to Hazel and Susan, she's liable to help them push Justin and I together. That is so not what I need when I'm trying to keep myself from falling for him already.

~~~

Saturday, December 29, 2018

"Hey, friend. How was the move?" Justin tried to play it cool as he took the seat beside Amy at the late Christmas celebration his family was hosting to be able to exchange gifts with their family and friends who hadn't been in town on Christmas Day. In truth, he was nervous about seeing Amy for the first time in a little over a month. He'd tried to keep in touch with her by sending a few friendly text messages, but she hadn't responded with much more than one-word answers. *Hopefully, now that we're seeing each other in person, she'll hafta actually talk to me.*

"Tiring," Amy replied, smiling shyly at him. "Even with caravanning with Randi and James, and him having his brother and coworkers help us unload everything when we got here, I was so worn out I could've easily continued sleeping all weekend."

"You should've called me. I'd've come help, too."

"I know you said that before, but we already had more people than we really needed. It took James, Randi, and I all day Wednesday to
~~~

load the U-Haul. But when the GWA crew unloaded it, they had everything outta the truck and stacked in the garage within thirty minutes. I felt useless to do more than direct traffic at that point." Amy shook her head and let out a self-deprecating chuckle. "Who knew driving for twelve hours straight could be so exhausting?"

"Ya'll didn't take turns driving?" Justin wished he'd have thought to take a flight up to Tulsa, so he could've helped her drive at least.

"No, it was just the three of us." Amy shook her head again. "And with moving both my car and Randi's and also having the U-Haul truck, we each had to be behind the wheel of a vehicle."

Justin knew that hindsight was twenty-twenty, but he still wished he'd have gone to Tulsa to help Amy move. If he had, he could've towed her car behind the truck, and then only he and James would've had to drive while the girls were able to rest. Knowing sharing his hindsight ideas would only show Amy the inner caveman he feared would scare her off, Justin kept his thoughts to himself, letting the conversation drop as the rest of the people in attendance took their seats.

"Oh, let me introduce you," Justin's mom, Susan, announced as she directed a couple with a small child to sit between his cousins, Charlotte and Jake, across from where Justin and Amy were sitting. "Family, this is Ian Campbell, his sister Cait, and his son, Brody. Beside you, Ian, is my niece, Charlotte, and across the table is my son, Justin. Beside Justin is Amy Lawton, she's starting work with Justin in the lab next week. On his other side is my other son, JJ. Then we have my nephew, Josh, and across the table from Josh, and seated next to Cait is Josh's twin brother, Jake."

"Nice to meet you all." Ian looked around the group to acknowledge each of them as he took his seat with his son on his lap. Justin thought he saw a smirk on Jake's face when he made eye contact with the newcomer, but he wasn't sure what it meant.

He didn't get a chance to reflect on the fleeting look of recognition on Jake's face because Amy leaned in toward him to whisper, "I see your mom's still playing matchmaker."

"Yeah," Justin chuckled and whispered his reply to Amy, taking an extra moment to lean in close enough to appreciate her beachy scent. "I don't think that'll stop 'til we're all married off."

"I recognize the wrestlers she has your sisters sitting with, but who're all the new people? And did their plotting actually pay off with Bobby and the girl he's got his arm around?"

"Yeah, that's Brie. Aunt Hazel hired her to clean a few of the houses on the ranch and moved her into Bobby's house. Less than three weeks later, they let us all know they're together."

"Wow, who thought Bobby would be the first to fall prey to the matchmaking plots?" Amy giggled as she voiced the rhetorical question, making Justin's cock harden at the soft, sweet sound.

"None of us. Guess it's a good thing we never placed bets on it. I'd've said it'd be one of the girls for sure." He tried to use leaning in to whisper in her ear to cover how he had to adjust himself.

"Yeah, I'd've said Julie with the way she's looking at Dion." Amy nodded her head in Julie and Dion's direction where they were seated on the other side of Jake before turning back toward Justin and the newcomers across the table from them. "So, what do you know about Ian and Cait?"

"Nothing, but we can change that right quick." Justin grinned at Amy as he straightened in his seat and raised his voice to direct his next words across the table. "What brings ya'll to Heart's Destiny?"

Cait's eyes darted up to Justin like she was shocked to hear him speak so loudly before moving back down to the little boy beside her, who was demanding his aunt's undivided attention by crawling from his father's lap to hers.

"I'll be starting a new job in town in a little over a week," Ian replied to Justin's inquiry.

"Oh, what do you do?" Amy carried on the conversation Justin had started.

Justin wasn't sure how to feel about how she'd stepped in and asked about Ian Campbell. On the one hand, he liked that she seemed to be following his lead by continuing the conversation. But on the other hand, he felt the unmistakable twinge of jealousy at Amy asking about the other man, when she hadn't inquired about anything that had happened with him in the month since they'd seen each other last.

"I'm a middle school English teacher," Ian replied curtly.

"Of course you are," Charlotte grumbled under her breath, just loud enough to barely be heard, shaking her head. The Burlesons all knew that their mothers had intentionally put Charlotte's new coworker beside her at the table in the hopes of them starting a romantic relationship outside the school.

"What about you, Cait?" Justin hoped his quick question to Ian's sister would be enough to keep anyone from pointing out why Charlotte wasn't happy about the seating arrangements. "Are you just visiting your brother for the holidays or are you moving to town as well?"

"I'm, uh, moving here, too." Cait didn't lift her eyes from her nephew as she replied.

"Cait helps me out by taking care of Brody while I'm working." Ian reached over to pat his sister on the shoulder, obviously trying to calm her anxiety at interacting with so many strangers.

"Looks like you've definitely got your hands full with that little cutie." Amy waved at Brody, who was shyly looking up at her from across the table. "How old are you, Brody?"

Brody held up four fingers before burying his face in his aunt's shoulder, but he never uttered a word.

"Sorry, he's shy around new people." Ian tousled his son's hair as he smiled at Amy. "He's four, but it'll be an hour or two before he'll tell you that himself."

"Oh, I understand that," Amy laughed, wiggling her fingers at Brody who was twisting on his aunt's lap and peeking out at Amy shyly. "I was the same way when I was a kid."

"Susan said you're starting a new job next week," Ian stated, looking at Amy in a way that made Justin want to put his arm around her to stake his claim. "What do you do?"

"I'm a chemical engineer." Amy's smile beamed at Ian before she turned to direct it to Justin. "When I was here last month for Anthony and Kay's wedding, Justin told me about all the R and D projects he has going on to try and make Burleson Incorporated into a more environmentally-friendly company, and I couldn't turn down the opportunity to help make that happen."

Justin returned her smile as he looked into her amazing obsidian eyes. The twinge of jealousy he'd felt at seeing her smile directed at Ian dissipated once her focus was solely redirected to Justin. "Don't let Amy fool you. It took me a whole week after she schooled me on how I could do more than I already had planned in the lab before I convinced her to move here and implement her ideas to improve our projects."

"No, you were only vaguely hinting that I should come work at Burleson. Once there was an actual offer on the table, I accepted immediately."

Justin's enjoyment of the playful banter and flirtatious look Amy was giving him was short-lived when his cousin, Charlotte, spoke up and severed their moment.

"Ya'll need to stop with the lovey-dovey eyes and fussing at each other like an old married couple, or our mothers will let their matchmaking success go to their heads and keep trying to set the rest of us up."

"Oh, no, we're not," Amy sputtered, motioning between Justin and herself while looking across the table at Charlotte. "There's no lovey-dovey anything with us. We're just friends. And, um, coworkers starting next week. Or I guess, technically, Justin's my boss starting next week. So, we can't ever be anything more than friends."

Thanks a fucking lot, Char, for ruining the moment I was having with Amy. Justin fumed, but he knew he couldn't actually say anything without risking making the situation worse. *As if I wasn't already fighting the friend zone with Amy, now I'm gonna hafta overcome the obstacle of being her boss. I should probably check with Jen to make sure there's nothing in the HR paperwork that says I can't date my lab manager, just to make sure the only person I hafta convince we're a good idea is Amy.*

"Is that why we were seated here instead of with the Hunters, who actually invited us to this dinner? So your mothers could play matchmaker?" Ian looked pointedly at Charlotte before turning to glare at Jake, who was seated beside his sister.

"Technically, it was our aunt who seated you between my sister and I," Jake pointed out, smirking at Ian. "But, yeah, I'm sure Ma enlisted the help of her best friend, Mandi Hunter, and our Aunt Susan to try to pair us up."

"They've been doing it for years," JJ chuckled. "They've just stepped it up a notch with any new people in town, since Anthony found his new bride outside of Heart's Destiny."

"Most of the time, we just laugh it off and appreciate making a new friend, like Justin and Amy." Josh motioned to them before pointing across the room at Bobby and Brie. "But since Ma's matchmaking seems to have worked with Bobby and Brie, she and Aunt Susan are hoping that success snowballs into marrying us all off. But unless lightning strikes the instant you meet someone in our family, you don't hafta worry about a trip down the aisle. It's either love at first sight or not at all for the Burlesons."

Cait's eyes shot up to look at Josh when he said that last sentence, making Justin wonder if there'd been a spark for them when the Campbells first sat down. It'd certainly been instant for him when he first saw Amy over a month before, so he knew Josh was right in how he described the family's way of falling in love. *Too bad Amy doesn't seem to feel the same for me.*

"You all really believe in love at first sight?" Ian first looked at Josh, then at Jake, and finally at Charlotte. Charlotte just shrugged, not really giving Ian an answer to his question.

Justin didn't want to be the one to try and explain it to the newcomer, knowing if he tried he would only scare Amy off even more by admitting how he already felt for her, so he shifted uncomfortably in his seat and surreptitiously watched her reaction as his brother and cousins discussed their family history.

"I've never felt the tingles myself, but it's common knowledge that our family tends to know immediately when they've met their mate." Jake shifted in his seat as he met Ian's stare while he spoke. *Damn, Jake looks awfully uncomfortable. Is that because he's lying about not feeling those tingles before? Or because he's feeling them for Ian's sister and doesn't want the guy to know?*

"For as long as there've been Burlesons on this land, they've fallen in love at first sight." JJ took over for Jake in explaining the history of how Heart's Destiny got its name. "Our third-great-grandfather, Jonah Burleson, saw Emma Rogers on the train out of San Antonio goin' to Laredo, declared her his heart's destiny, and followed her off the train to settle here. Twenty-some years later when there were finally enough people here to form a town, he named the town Heart's Destiny to honor her and their love."

"Their son, Joshua, who I'm named after, fell in love with our second-great-grandma, Sarah, the first time he met her at a cattle auction in Dallas."

"Joshua and Sarah's son, Robert, who our dad and brother are named after, met our great-grandma, Sylvia, while on a business trip to the east coast. He stayed a little longer than planned on that business trip and had her moved home and married to him within six months." Jake grinned before continuing. "I know he fell in love at first sight, but since it took him a little while to seal the deal, I hafta wonder if she took a little convincing before she fell for him."

Damn, I wonder if Jake's right? Maybe I'm just gonna hafta do like our great-grandfather and show Amy that we're meant to be together.

"Our Pappaw Jerry told us stories about how he had to keep making several trips to Oklahoma to court Memmaw Judy," JJ added, nodding his head at Jake. "While he knew the moment he met her, it took him almost a year before he won her heart."

"And of course, there's our parents," Josh continued where JJ left off, motioning between himself and Jake.

"And our parents," JJ took back over explaining, motioning between himself and Justin. "They all fell in love at first sight, too."

"Not to mention Anthony and now Bobby in this generation," Jake added.

"Gracious, did the Burlesons only have boys until the current generation?" Amy's eyes widened at hearing all the love-at-first-sight stories in the family tree.

"No, there were a couple of girls before us," Charlotte replied. "Our great-grandpa, Robert, had a sister, Elizabeth, who died during a flu outbreak when she was fourteen. And Jonah and Emma had a daughter, Mary, who my house was originally built for, but we don't have a clue what happened to her after she left the ranch to serve as a nurse during World War I."

"She went off to serve and never came back?" Cait's eyes widened as she looked at Charlotte. "Do you think she died in the war?"

"No." Charlotte shook her head. "I found boxes of her stuff that were sent home at the end of the war, including a stack of love letters. I think she fell in love with someone she met while serving in France, and either stayed there to marry him or went back to his home after the war."

"So, ya'll could have some distant cousins out in the world and not even know it." Amy's face was practically glowing from the thought of his second-great-aunt possibly finding true love a hundred years ago and producing a line of descendants that could still be alive and not know they're related to the Burlesons.

"Yeah, I think so." Charlotte nodded her head. "When Tia was staying with me a couple weeks ago, she suggested we all do one of those online DNA tests to see if we can find our long-lost family. I've been thinking about it, but I don't want to be the only one doing it, ya know?"

"I'll do it with you, Char," Justin volunteered, thinking it would be cool to find some long-lost cousins.

"Yeah?" Charlotte looked at Justin quizzically, like she couldn't believe he'd volunteered to submit his DNA for testing.

"Of course." Justin grinned at his cousin before turning to look at his brother and the other cousins sitting close by. "We should all do it, don'tcha think?"

"Sure, why not?" JJ chuckled.

"Absolutely," Josh exclaimed before pointing to his brother. "Maybe it'll explain how we're twins but nothing alike."

"We'll probably find out you were switched at birth," Jake joked with his brother. "What about ya'll? Any of you wanna spit in a tube with the rest of us to see if you can find any long-lost family?"

Cait looked over at Ian with an expression Justin couldn't read. Ian shook his head at his sister before looking back up at Jake and saying, "I know all I need to know about our family, but thanks anyway."

"Whaddaya say, Amy?" Justin turned his attention to the woman beside him, who was looking back at him with an expression that appeared nervous, but her eyes were lit with excitement. "If I order a bulk lot of DNA tests, will you take one with me?"

"I, uh, I don't know," Amy stuttered. "I mean it'd be kinda cool to find out about my dad's side of the family that I don't know anything about, but it's kinda scary to think of what I might possibly find that I don't really wanna see."

"Like what?" Justin couldn't stop himself from asking the question, even though he knew he probably shouldn't pry into something so personal when they were still barely getting to know each other.

"I mean, those things don't just tell you who you're related to." Amy's expression turned extremely tentative. "They also give you a detailed racial breakdown. And while I know I'm mixed with both my dad and grandpa being white, I'm not sure I wanna know if the mixing started back when one of my Black ancestors was raped as a slave. Things don't always go well for Black people on **Finding Your Roots**, ya know."

Fuck! I didn't think about how far back that stuff could actually go. And it would absolutely gut me if we did these tests and found out one of my ancestors was a slave owner, who could've hurt one of her ancestors.

While the Burlesons had always been anti-racist as far as Justin knew, he couldn't be certain the family Jonah left behind when he moved west to find work as a cowboy were abolitionists when he was born right before the Civil War.

"Yeah, I've worried about what we'll find in our family history before Jonah and Emma started this branch of the family, too." Charlotte reached across the table and placed her hand on Amy's. "Since Jonah was born in eighteen-sixty, we could find that he was the product of one of those rapes and given the last name of the man who tortured his mother, which would taint the Burleson name as being on the wrong side of our American history. Or his parents could've been plantation owners, which would still put them on the wrong side, even if his father wasn't a rapist. But even as hard as all that will be to learn, I still want to know how much of Memmaw Judy's Native American ancestry flows through my blood, and if I have a Black fourth great-grandma that I would be proud to claim in my family tree for the strength she showed to live through that horrible time in history and raise a man as good as our third-great-grandpa, Jonah. Not to mention all the possibilities on the Rogers side of the family that we know nothing about."

Wow, I never thought of those possibilities. Justin reached over and clasped Amy's free hand in his. Her eyes were glassy when she turned to look at him. Before he could reassure her that she didn't have to do the DNA testing with him if she didn't want to, his Aunt Hazel was calling everyone to line up to fix their plates.

"Okay, I'll think about it." Amy squeezed both his and Charlotte's hands before releasing them both and standing to join everyone else in filling their plates.

And I won't bring it up unless she mentions it, so I don't risk upsetting her again.

~~~

Amy couldn't believe she was being dragged to yet another party by her best friend. She'd felt awkward at first when Randi insisted Amy had to attend the late Christmas celebration at the Burleson Ranch two days before. She initially panicked about gifts for everyone, only calming down when she realized that in order to keep from moving the raw ingredients, she'd made more than enough bath bombs and bottles of lotion to make up a couple dozen gift sets to take. She tied them together with red and green ribbons, but she didn't label them since she wasn't going to be the only outsider there and didn't know who all to address them to before the party. Once the party started, she'd been able to maintain her friendly distance with Justin, even though they were seated side by side yet again. She just hoped to be able to continue to keep him in the friend zone, if he was also attending the formal New Year's party that James's mother was hosting in the ballroom at the bed and breakfast.

Maybe he won't be here? He seemed to prefer the atmosphere at Tully's for the bachelor and bachelorette party last month, so maybe he'll go there, instead of having to dress up to come to the ballroom party. As hard as Amy tried to tell herself that Justin was more likely to celebrate on the other side of town, she knew he'd probably be at the bed and breakfast, if only to be there after midnight for Tia's surprise birthday party.

Regardless of the fact that she hoped to avoid seeing Justin that night, Amy still dressed up and made sure she looked her best in case she couldn't avoid him. She wore a yellow, knee-length, cocktail dress, knowing the color would highlight the warm undertones in her golden-brown complexion. She tamed her black hair in a sophisticated updo and only wore the minimum of makeup to conceal a couple blemishes and make her eyes pop since she was wearing contact lenses, so they could be seen without the encumbrance of her glasses.
~~~

Leah Mae Wright

I'm not dressed up because I expect to be seated beside Justin at the party like at every other event I've attended in town. I'm dressed up because I feel more self-confident when I look my best.

Or maybe I'm just so delusional that I'm even lying to myself about how I feel about Justin Burleson. Amy mentally shook her head at her inner ramblings.

Or maybe, if I keep telling myself, along with everyone else, that I'm not attracted to him and only wanna be friends, then one day it'll actually be true, so I don't risk my new job or my heart by acting on the sexual chemistry I feel whenever he's around.

Amy decided to believe the latter as she followed Randi and James into the packed ballroom to ring in the new year after dropping off Tia's birthday presents in the library, where they would all meet after midnight to celebrate Tia becoming a teenager. Though there were more people there than at the wedding reception, it only took a moment before Amy spotted Justin from across the room. Sure enough, just like at every other event and activity she'd attended in Heart's Destiny, Amy ended up seated next to Justin, even though he and Anthony were the only male Burlesons at their table.

So much for thinking sitting at the same table as Randi and James would mean I'd end up sitting by Dean Hunter instead. Amy had thought her best friend might've been trying to set her up with her boyfriend's brother, or one of the other single wrestlers Randi now worked with daily, especially after they'd had a discussion about which wrestlers Amy was most attracted to back in October. *I guess Randi could tell that even though I said I was interested in Liam Connery, Josh Parker, or Dean Hunter, Justin was the only guy who gave me goosebumps, butterflies, and tingles when we met last month, so now she's on the same page as the Burleson matriarchs with their matchmaking plans. As much as I love her like a sister, maybe it's a good thing she'll be going back to work tomorrow, so she won't be here to push me toward Justin even more than I'm already feeling drawn to him.*

"Only about thirty-six hours now," Justin announced, bringing Amy out of her mental rambling.

"No, Uncle Justin," Maria protested from her seat beside her parents on the other side of the table. "It's only four hours 'til midnight."

"I wasn't talking about the new year." Justin chuckled at his cousin's daughter.

"Then what are you counting down to that's thirty-six hours away?" Tia examined Justin curiously from her seat next to her sister.

"My new best friend, Amy, coming to work in the lab with me." Justin gave Amy a goofy smile as he leaned over and poked her shoulder playfully. "Ain't that right, bestie?"

"Are you drunk? Did you get started on the champagne early?" Amy was confused by the overly jovial antics she was seeing from Justin for the first time.

"Nope, just high on life, Sweetheart," Justin replied, grinning like a loon.

"Amy, I trust you'll clean up the lab when you start work on Wednesday." Anthony chuckled and shook his head at Justin. "Because I think my cousin's been inhaling some things in there he probably shouldn't."

"Dude, don't even joke about that!" Justin pointed at his cousin Anthony, and straightened up into his normal, serious self. "You know some of the chemicals we work with could be deadly if improperly handled and inhaled."

"Sorry, Cuz." Anthony held up both hands in surrender. "I didn't mean to make light of the risks of your job. I was just jokingly agreeing with your girl that you're acting like you're under the influence of something."

"I'm not his girl!" Amy realized too late that shouting made her statement sound more like a lie than it was, so she lowered her voice before explaining. "We're just friends, who don't mind hanging out together to keep from being matched up with anyone else by your mothers."

"The Matchmaking Mommas," Kay interjected, giggling. "That's what Brie and I have nicknamed their group. Now I'm trying to get Brie to collaborate with me on a series of romance novels based on the mischief of the Matchmaking Mommas of Heart's Destiny."

"You'd better include your own story in there, Sis." Randi pointed her finger at Kay. "'Cause you can't tell the world all about the antics at your wedding to start the series with them matching up James and I without telling your story first."

Leah Mae Wright

"Oh, I hadn't thought of that!" Kay's face lit up with excitement. She turned to Anthony and cooed, "You wouldn't mind if I wrote a modern-day fairy tale about us, would you?"

"How about we hit the dance floor to avoid hearing how Kay might wanna include us in her book series?" Justin leaned over to whisper in Amy's ear, as the rest of the people at the table discussed Kay's book plans.

"Yes," Amy agreed, practically jumping out of her chair to avoid any discussion of her love life, whether real or in Kay's imaginary book world.

Just as they got to the middle of the dance floor, the music changed from an upbeat rock song Amy could almost fake her way through knowing how to dance along with to a slow country song that was clearly meant for couples.

"You know how to two-step?" Justin reached for her hands to pull her in close to his body.

"No, the best you're gonna get from me to this song is swaying back and forth like back in junior high." Amy couldn't help but laugh at the look of mortification that crossed over Justin's face.

"Well, we're gonna hafta change that, Sweetheart." Justin placed her hands on his shoulders and settled his hands on her waist. Even through the material of her dress, the feel of his hands on her sent tingles throughout her body. "Now that you live in Texas, you've gotta learn how to two-step. But don't worry, it's not that hard and I'm happy to teach you. Just step back with your right foot, then bring your left foot back to meet your right."

"Yeah, I'm more likely to step on your toes," Amy joked, though it really wasn't as hard as she expected to follow his lead.

"I'm wearin' boots, Sweetheart, so if you'd rather just stand on top of my size twelves, I'll dance for both of us."

Size twelves? If what I've heard about size correlation is true, then yep, everything's definitely bigger in Texas. Amy felt herself blush at her thoughts. When Justin winked at her, the heat in her cheeks increased, giving her even more of a reason to look down at their feet than just to watch the steps. "No, I think I can do this. What's next?"

"You just keep steppin' backwards, twice with the right foot leading and then once with the left foot leading."

"That's it?" Amy looked up into Justin's bright blue eyes and basked in the glow of his smile.

"Yep, that's it. The only hard part about it is remembering the two-to-one rhythm."

"Wow, this is a whole lot easier than I thought it'd be," Amy admitted, though she wouldn't mention the way he was tapping the rhythm on her waist was doing more for making her panties wet than directing her which side to step back with as they moved around the dance floor.

As she continued to match her steps with Justin's, he started to sing along with the song about it being her *Last Night Lonely* before telling her that was the name of the song playing. When the song changed, Justin kept singing as they continued to dance.

Though she wasn't really in his arms like a lot of the other couples who were dancing much closer together, the way Justin kept singing to her, with one song about getting together as a couple blending into the next song about learning all about each other, made her feel like she was part of a couple, instead of staying in the friend zone like Amy knew she needed to with Justin.

When the song changed once more, to what was very clearly a love song, Amy couldn't handle dancing with Justin any longer. Needing some space, she made up an excuse about having to visit the ladies' room, so she could get out of the ballroom where she knew he wouldn't follow her.

She beelined off the dance floor to their table, so she could grab her handbag on the way to the restroom just outside the ballroom. Not recognizing any of the ladies in there, who were apparently already done with their business and washing their hands, Amy locked herself in a stall, so she could be alone to take a few deep breaths.

Amy hiked up her skirt and pulled down her panties to sit on the toilet, even though she didn't think she really had to go. *Not that I can be a hundred percent sure of anything right now.*

Her breath was coming out in rapid pants and her heart felt like it was about to beat its way out of her chest. *What the hell is wrong with me? Is this what a panic attack feels like? Or am I so freaked out about being too close to Justin that I've thrown myself into a heart attack? Geez, I hope it's a panic attack, 'cause I really don't wanna*

Leah Mae Wright

die while sitting on the toilet, too freaked out to show my face in the ballroom right now.

Amy felt her purse vibrate on her lap and was glad for the distraction of her phone signaling an incoming text. It was already easier to breathe as she pulled it out to check the messages.

Randi: You okay? Where'd you go?

Amy: Fine. Ladies' room.

**Randi: Don't tell me fine. I know better than fine.
What's really going on?**

Shit! Why can't she let me fake my way through this, whatever it is, before demanding I talk to her?

**Randi: Justin is worried there's something physically
wrong. Like bowel or feminine issues. Do I need to call
an ambulance or bring you a tampon or something?**

**Amy: No, there's nothing physically wrong with me.
Unless a panic attack can actually bring on a heart
attack.**

**Randi: I don't think so, but they do feel a little alike.
Talking it out helps & I'll gladly listen just like you have
for me.**

Damn it! Why does she have to throw my being a good friend back at me right now? I can't very well tell her that I don't wanna talk to her after listening to all her issues with her parents and James a couple months ago.

**Amy: Dancing with Justin felt too much like being a
couple. I can't let myself feel that way about my new
boss. So I'm hiding in the bathroom until my freak-out
passes & I'm back in the friend zone in my own head.**

Randi: Maybe you should give up fighting your attraction
    to him before you make yourself crazy. From what I've
    gotten to know of the Burlesons, I don't think you'll be
    risking your job if you give it a shot with Justin, even if
    it doesn't work out.

Randi: Though I think it'll work out for you 2 if you just
    get out of your own way & let it.

            Amy: Thx for the vote of confidence, but I'm not like you
                    & don't see it working out in the long run.

Randi: Is this a race thing? Is that what you mean about
    not being like me?

            Amy: No, I mean I've seen too many of my mom's failed
            relationships to believe in happily ever after for anyone
                                    in my family anymore.

            Amy: It's not even just her failed relationships.
            Supposedly, my dad was her white knight & they'd
            have lived happily ever after if he hadn't died. But
            even people who might not want to leave eventually
            do, like my dad, my nana, & my papa. And I don't want
            to go through the hell of heartbreak when it happens.

"Oh, Ames," Amy heard her best friend, Randi, sigh from outside
the stall she was still sitting in.

Randi: Nothing is guaranteed in life. But trust me when I
    say it's much better to have the good memories of time
    with someone you love than regrets when they're
    gone, & you never gave them a chance. Is it possible
    that he could be killed in a freak accident tomorrow?
    Yes, but wouldn't you rather have memories of being
    in his arms tonight than regrets of not knowing what

**his lips feel like on yours if it happens? It's also
possible that you could die tomorrow & leave him with
a broken heart full of regret at not taking his chance
with you.**

Amy sobbed at the thoughts Randi was filling her head with before standing up and righting her clothing, so she could walk out and face her best friend and her infinite wisdom. She walked to the sink and washed her hands out of habit before turning to Randi.

After looking around the room to make sure they were alone, Amy finally spoke. "Is it the therapy you've been doing or the month you've been traveling with James that's made you so wise all of a sudden?"

"Both," Randi replied, grinning. "I'm living my fairy tale every day, and talking to my therapist every week helps me to see and believe that it's all real. I'll happily give you her number if you think you need someone other than me to convince you that you can have the fairy tale, too."

"But what if I give in to this attraction and it makes things awkward at work? Or worse, we have a nasty break-up and I have to find another job? I doubt I'll be able to ever find something that pays as well as the Burlesons do, so I'd just end up back where I started, struggling to make ends meet."

"Look, I know some of the losers you've told me about your mom dating would make it awkward at work or fire someone they broke up with," Randi admonished. "But from what I've seen of the Burlesons, I don't think either of those things are scenarios you have to worry about if you and Justin become more than friends."

"You're probably right," Amy reluctantly admitted. "But I'm still scared. He's rich and powerful and gorgeous. He could have any woman in the world he wants. Why would he want me, when half the women in that ballroom are giving him longing looks to let him know they're ready to give him their bodies at the drop of a hat?"

"I normally don't like the *what ifs* but since you asked me a couple, how 'bout I throw a couple back at you?" Randi smirked before pulling Amy over to a sofa in the small room just outside the ladies' room. "What if he's not interested in any of those other women?

What if he's already figured out you're *The One* and by not giving him a chance you're dooming him to a life alone?"

"We barely know each other," Amy protested. "There's no way he's decided I'm *The One* in the last six weeks when we've only spent one of those weeks in each other's proximity."

"Did you not listen when I told you how I knew James is *The One* the instant our eyes met for the first time? Or when Kay told you about her and Anthony? Or to any of the other stories about the Burlesons and pretty much everyone in Heart's Destiny? This is, like, the love-at-first-sight capital of the world." Randi waved her arms around to indicate she was referring to the small town they were in at that moment. "You even told me you felt the butterflies and tingles when you first saw Justin within minutes of us arriving on the ranch for the first time. So, how can you not believe he'd feel the same about you?"

"I don't know that those butterflies and tingles mean as much as you seem to think." Amy was shaking her head, trying to convince herself as much as Randi that she hadn't already fallen in love with Justin. "That could just be a chemist recognizing another chemist and having a feeling that he'd be instrumental in helping me land my dream job."

"Fine, keep lying to yourself and fighting it." Randi threw her arms up in exasperation, shaking her head at her friend before turning to look Amy square in the eyes and pointing at her. "But I'm already calling my spot as your maid of honor when you finally lose the battle to keep Justin in the friend zone and end up marrying him."

"Oh, no," Amy playfully protested, trying to deflect from the possibility of her bestie being right. "You and James will be married long before I ever walk down the aisle. So, if it ever happens, no matter who I eventually marry, you'll be my matron of honor."

"Deal," Randi laughed as she hooked her pinky finger with Amy's, and they sealed the pact like they had when they first met as freshmen in college.

Amy joined her best friend in laughing as they made their way back to the ballroom. Randi may think she was closer to convincing Amy to give dating Justin a shot, but Amy was still resolved to just be friends with her new boss.

Leah Mae Wright

That's my new year's resolution this year — keep Justin Burleson in the friend zone. And that's gonna start now with making sure I'm not close enough to be tempted to kiss him at midnight.

Chapter Two

Wednesday, January 2, 2019

Justin tried to appear busy while sitting in his office waiting for Amy to finish going over all the new hire paperwork with his sister, Jen, and watching the employee orientation videos Jen had set up for her in the human resources department of Burleson Incorporated. He was far too anxious about Amy's first day at work to be able to safely work in the lab, so he spent the morning in his executive office instead. But as much as he tried to focus on reading his email, his mind kept wandering back over the last few days.

Though Amy was foremost on his mind, he wasn't just thinking about the two times he'd gotten to see her since she'd moved to town. He was also thinking about the conversations he'd had with his brother JJ, cousin Bobby, and friend James, when Amy wasn't in his presence, getting their advice on how to handle his feelings for her when she clearly wanted to keep them in the friend zone.

After the way she'd adamantly declared they could only be friends at the late Christmas celebration on Saturday, and then seemed to be caught up in her own thoughts in her head after the love at first sight and DNA testing conversations, Justin had pulled JJ aside after church on Sunday to ask what he remembered of Pappaw Jerry's stories about his time courting Memmaw Judy. While being part Black and part Native American were fairly different experiences, both Amy and Memmaw Judy's ancestors had been subjected to the worst atrocities at the hands of the American government and white people of their times. So, Justin had to wonder if there was anything in Pappaw Jerry's playbook that he could use to show Amy that their racial differences didn't have to be a divide between them.

Leah Mae Wright

Damn, I guess Memmaw Judy's ancestors would be my ancestors, too. Maybe our ancestral experiences aren't as different as our skin tones make them appear?

Having only been fifteen years old when Memmaw Judy passed away, Justin didn't remember the stories she or Pappaw Jerry told about the early years of their relationship. Since JJ was a year older than him, Justin hoped he'd have listened to their grandparents in hopes of using some of their romantic ideas to get a date or two in high school. When JJ wasn't much help, he'd called Bobby over to ask him if he remembered anything helpful, since he was a year older than JJ. After Justin had recapped the conversations from Saturday for Bobby, his cousin had shaken his head and told Justin not to bring up their racial differences at all.

"While we're probably not a hundred percent white, anything else we have mixed in happened so many generations ago that it's not obvious to just look at us," Bobby'd elaborated on Sunday. "So, even if we do these DNA tests and find a little Native American, or Black, or Asian, or whatever mixed in a couple hundred years ago, we still walk down the street looking a hundred percent white. With that comes white privilege that even with a white father and grandfather, Amy won't have no matter how unfair it is. So, if she brings up ya'll's racial differences, then you tell her how beautiful you think she is for her mixed heritage, but don't demean her or use your white privilege against her by saying the differences don't matter."

"But us being different races doesn't matter to me," Justin had protested.

"I know it doesn't matter to any of us," Bobby'd agreed, motioning around to include all the Burlesons in his statement. "Because we've never been discriminated against. Unfortunately, as much as we hate that it still happens and wish to eradicate discrimination, I imagine Amy has had to deal with racist, bigoted idiots more than once in her life. So, saying race doesn't matter might make her feel like you're trying to negate her experiences or whitewash it to make her fit into your life."

"That's not what I wanna do," Justin had sighed, shaking his head in confusion at how to deal with their differences to make it where they could be together without race dividing them.

"I know." Bobby'd slapped a big hand on Justin's shoulder reassuringly. "That's why I said, don't bring it up unless she does. And when she does, make sure you point out that you like her because of your differences, not in spite of them. And as for trying to get her outta the friend zone, just bide your time. If it's meant to happen, it'll happen."

"Ya think? Is that what you did with Brie?"

"My situation with Brie is a little different, but yeah. I followed a piece of advice my dad's given me a few times since I first started noticin' girls. Friendship is the best foundation for a forever relationship. He's varied the wording a little over the years based on the situation at hand, but the general gist of it is that you can't have a good long-term relationship with anyone if you don't start out trying to be a good friend. So, be the friend Amy needs now, and once that's strong, you can build the rest of your relationship on that foundation."

"I think I remember Pappaw Jerry giving us that advice as teenagers," JJ'd commented.

As Justin thought back to the conversation with his brother and cousin, he realized that in a roundabout way he'd gotten the advice he needed from his grandfather after all.

He'd thought he was being a good friend to Amy by getting her away from the romance talk at their table on New Year's Eve. But after she rushed off the dance floor and avoided him for the rest of the night, Justin wasn't so sure.

Dancing with Amy had been the sweetest torture Justin had ever endured. He'd tried to keep it friendly, holding her an arm's length away with his palms resting on her waist and her palms resting on his shoulders, instead of pulling her in close to his body like he really wanted to hold her. But even now, a day and a half later, he could still feel the searing heat where she'd touched him just by closing his eyes and imagining it.

I wonder if she felt the same heat where my hands were on her waist? With the way my palms were tingling from being allowed to feel the slightest of her curves through the material of her dress, she had to have felt something there, too. Fuck! I hope all this sexual chemistry isn't what scared her off the dance floor Monday night.

Justin had wanted to follow her to make sure she was okay, but he didn't get the chance when Randi and James stopped him to find out what was going on. After Justin had explained to them what she'd said right before taking off, Randi had pulled her phone out of her purse to text Amy to make sure she was okay. After only a few texts, Randi left Justin and James at the table while she went to make sure her best friend was indeed as fine as she indicated in her first text response to Randi.

"How well do you know Amy?" Justin had asked James while they were sitting alone at the table.

"Not super well," James'd replied. "But I got the impression over the last week that she's reluctant to let new people in to know her too well."

"Did she say anything while ya'll were packing and moving to give you an idea of why she might've freaked out while we were dancing?"

"Not really. Or maybe, just not this last week." James'd scratched his head like he was deliberating on whether or not to share something. "But while she and Randi were first talking about her moving down here, back in November right before Amy flew back to Tulsa..."

James's voice had trailed off, making Justin exceptionally nervous about what Amy had mentioned to Randi about him back in November. "What did she say?"

"Randi asked why Amy hadn't acted on the attraction we all noticed between you two, and Amy said she'd been feeling things out to see what could possibly develop, but then you started talking about the job. She seems to think that as long as you're her boss, ya'll can only be friends." James'd shrugged and looked toward the door like he was making sure the ladies weren't on their way back before continuing. "Maybe the dancing, on top of the matchmaking, and Kay talking about writing romance novels about all the couples that are being set up by our moms was too much for her to keep compartmentalized to friends and coworkers? So, she needed a breather."

"So, what am I supposed to do? I thought I was being a friend by getting her away from all the romance talk, when I know she's not ready for that from me. I wasn't trying to be flirty or anything while we were dancing. But now I have no idea what to do to, at least, be able to be friends with her until she's ready for more."

"Dude, you were singing to her," James'd lightly chuckled and shook his head. "Granted I don't think any of the songs that played while ya'll were dancing were super romantic or anything, but she probably still sees being serenaded while dancing as more than friendly."

"I was just trying to keep us from having an awkward silence when I couldn't think of a safe topic to talk about."

"So, next time, talk about work, or ask her about her hobbies or whatever. And maybe stick to activities you can do with her without touching her, at least until she finally gives in to her attraction to you and touches you first."

"Ya think she will?"

"Yeah, just bide your time, man. She looks at you the same way you look at her, so it's just a matter of time."

"Fuck, I hope James is right," Justin wished aloud to his empty office. "It's gonna be hard as hell to keep my hands to myself when we're working closely in the lab. But if he's right, then it'll be just as hard for her. And maybe she'll act on our mutual attraction soon."

"Mr. Burleson," the voice of Justin's executive assistant, Amanda Lewis, came through the intercom on his desk phone. "You have a Ms. Lawton here to see you."

Finally! Justin thought as he leaned over to push the button on his phone to reply to Amanda. "Send her in please."

Amy looked amazing as she walked into his office. She was wearing a brown and white striped top with brown slacks a couple shades darker than her golden-brown complexion. Instead of the heels that most of the women in the office wore, Amy's feet were adorned with a pair of loafers that were much more appropriate for wearing while working in the lab, where there was a risk of chemicals spilling. She had the top half of her hair pulled back in a clip to keep it out of her face and her rectangular-style glasses were large enough to act in place of safety goggles in the lab.

She's as sensible as she is adorable. And with as young as she looks in no makeup, adorable is definitely the best word to describe her.

"I see you survived the hard part of the day." Justin stood to greet her as Amy walked across the office and took a seat across the desk from him.

Leah Mae Wright

"The hard part of the day?" Amy raised a single eyebrow as she questioned him.

"Yeah, staying awake during Jen's coma-inducing orientation videos." Justin chuckled at his own joke while retaking his seat.

"Yeah, those weren't really that bad." Amy smiled as she looked around his office. "Sorry, I'm late for our meeting. I didn't realize you had a different office than the lab, so I went there first."

"Oh, don't apologize. If anything, it's my fault for not telling you where I'd be or showing you this office when you visited the facility back in November. I've been so busy in the lab that I haven't spent nearly enough time up here lately. But, hopefully, now that we have you to manage the lab, I'll be able to do more of the executive tasks of my job I've put on the back burner the past few months."

"Okay, so where do you want me to start, Boss?"

Justin cringed at her calling him Boss, hating how it felt like a brick being added to the wall between them.

"First, you can do like everyone else in the lab and call me Justin. I prefer a more casual environment where we're all part of the same team, hence the reason I wear jeans most of the time. Using a moniker like *Boss* or being too formal like the rest of the executives in the company puts people too on edge when I'm in the lab. And I don't wanna risk anyone getting nervous and dropping a beaker or spilling something hazardous."

"Oh, sorry, Justin." Amy's cheeks turned that hot-as-hell terracotta shade as she blushed.

Yep, fucking adorable. Justin couldn't stop himself from wondering if her whole body would blush like that in the bedroom. *Too bad that blouse has such a high neckline, preventing me from seeing her cleavage while she's blushing now.*

"Nothing to be sorry about, just one of the things I wanted to point out to you before we go down to introduce you to everyone in the lab. Technically, you're the one in charge in the lab now, so I wanna make sure you understand the reasoning behind my management style, in the hopes that you'll adopt a similar one."

"Oh, yes, absolutely. First name basis, casual environment to promote teamwork is absolutely what I prefer in a manager."

Justin couldn't help but grin at how cute she was when she rambled. "With that being said, there are a couple people on the team who might be upset that we hired you from outside the company, instead of promoting from within. They gave me a little pushback when I first started changing things up in the lab when I took over R and D a few years ago. I've already explained to everyone that you got this job based on your innovative ideas and how your outside experience gives you a perspective of our products that nobody in our company has seen before, which is exactly what we need. But I can't guarantee they'll all play nice, when they don't wanna change what they've done for years. If you have any problems with anyone, please let me know so I can handle it."

"Oh, okay." Amy looked apprehensive, biting her bottom lip in a way that was really affecting Justin's cock.

I might hafta start wearing my lab coat outside the lab to cover my inappropriate erections when Amy's in the building. Or at the very least, finding some slacks that aren't as confining as these jeans.

"Don't worry, Amy, I doubt it'll be as bad as I think you're envisioning. They're not gonna be openly hostile or anything like that. They just might try to convince you to let them do things their own way, instead of experimenting with more environmentally-friendly chemicals and procedures, like I hired you to push us all to do in the lab. If you put your foot down and set them straight from the get-go, then they should be fine. But if they argue too much or don't listen after you've told them a time or two, let me know so I can hit them with the tough love that's needed to get them in line once in a while."

<div align="center">~~~</div>

What've I gotten myself into? Amy wondered as Justin warned her of possible problems she could have come up while interacting with her new coworkers. *How am I supposed to have a casual, teamwork-based managerial style, while also putting my foot down and being stern enough to keep people, who resent me for taking the job they feel like they should've gotten, in line?*

Am I even capable of being an aggressive, takes no lip, manager like he seems to think I need to be? Did he not realize I'm more of an introverted, people pleaser before he hired me?

Leah Mae Wright

"Okay, um, I'll try, but I'm not really the put-my-foot-down type." *Maybe I can call Ashlyn to get some advice on how to be more assertive, since she got all the attitude when our egg split in utero.* "I'm more the kill-'em-with-kindness type."

"Yes, I know." Justin grinned at her from across the desk and set off the swarm of butterflies inside Amy that she was desperately trying to ignore. "It's one of the things I adore about you, and why I think you're ultimately gonna be very successful in winning everyone over in this job. But if anyone mistakes your kindness for weakness and tries to steamroll you into their way of thinking, let me know, so I can deal with them."

"Okay, I can do that." While Amy still wasn't certain she was fully prepared for dealing with unruly lab techs, she was ready to move on to the next part of her discussion with Justin, so she could hurry up and get to the lab. Being alone with him in his office was doing funny things to her female parts that she didn't think she could handle for much longer.

Thankfully, Justin moved on, handing her the company-issued tablet she needed to be able to login to the network and access the project specifications she was now responsible for. Once he was assured she knew her way around the software they used, he ushered her out of his office to go down to the lab and make formal introductions, even though she'd met almost everyone in the lab back in November when she'd visited the company.

"I'll be in the lab the rest of the day, Amanda," Justin casually mentioned as they passed by his assistant's desk.

"Oh, but, Mr. Burleson, I thought we were gonna review the quarterly budget this afternoon?" Amanda's question caused Justin to stop in his tracks, and Amy to barely stop fast enough to keep from running into him. The way Amanda's eyes roamed possessively over Justin's body made the green-eyed monster inside Amy roar to life.

Eyes off my man, Bitch! Amy recognized the jealous thought for what it was, even as she hated that she couldn't stop herself from feeling the dreadful emotion when she saw the other woman eye-fucking the man who should be off-limits for both of them, regardless of there not being a no-fraternization policy at Burleson Incorporated, as Amy had learned that morning in reviewing the company handbook while down in human resources.

"No, you're supposed to have it ready for me to review this afternoon, but I'm not actually gonna have time to review it until after hours." Justin barely turned to look at his assistant as he spoke, so Amy couldn't read his expression to know how he felt about the way Amanda was blatantly flirting.

"Do I need to stay late, so we can go over it? I can order-in dinner if you let me know what time you'll be back up here."

"No, Amanda, reviewing and making changes to the R and D budget is not part of your job. I only asked you to compile the numbers into a spreadsheet for me because I was too busy with other things, and I need them to go over with Amy as I'm getting her acclimated to her new job." Justin turned back toward the exit of the office and continued walking, effectively dismissing his assistant without giving her a chance to reply.

Amy wanted to ask about the budget spreadsheet to find out if it was something she should actually be the one compiling in her new role in the company, but with the curt way Justin had just spoken to his assistant, she wasn't sure she really wanted to broach the subject and risk overstepping their boundaries on her first day on the job. Based on the way Justin poked the button for the elevator with more force than necessary, Amy feared speaking to him at the moment would redirect Justin's irritation at her.

While that could be a good thing to help her keep him in the friend zone, Amy rather liked knowing that his assistant was the one he was aggravated with at the time. *It's all kinds of wrong that I don't want him to be with her when I have no claim on him. But at least if he's pissed at her, then I don't have a reason to be jealous of her, so maybe I won't be tempted to step outside the friend zone to stake that claim.*

As she tried to get her thoughts focused back on work, instead of on how her body was protesting her maintaining a professional relationship with her boss, Amy realized that Amanda had addressed him as Mr. Burleson, instead of Justin. *Is that some kind of sexretary role-play thing? Does she only call him Mr. Burleson as a signal for him to bend her over the desk and spank her for not getting her job done correctly before fucking her?*

"I thought you said everyone called you Justin at work?"

Justin raised an eyebrow as he looked at her from across the elevator. Not realizing she was showing her jealousy, Amy elaborated. "You told me to call you Justin like everyone else, but Amanda called you Mr. Burleson. Do ya'll have something going on that makes her special to be able to call you Mr. Burleson, when the rest of us are supposed to call you Justin?"

"No," Justin chuckled. "Absolutely not. The exact opposite, actually."

Amy was confused by Justin's reply and wasn't sure what he thought was funny about her inquiry, so she zipped her mouth shut, not wanting to say anything to make the situation even more uncomfortable.

Before she could internally berate herself for putting her foot in her mouth, Justin explained further. "I said everyone in the lab calls me Justin. I prefer the more relaxed comradery in the lab to the formality of the executive floor, where there are too many Mr. Burlesons to make it easy to figure out who's being addressed when we're in an executive meeting. But I learned rather quickly that some people can't behave appropriately in a more relaxed environment. Being more formal with my assistant keeps her from thinking there's more between us than a professional association. I'm bad about forgetting to stick with that formality when I'm on the executive floor, which is why you probably heard me call her Amanda instead of Ms. Lewis, as I should stick to all the time."

"Oh," was all Amy could say, unsure how else to respond.

"Even with four-and-a-half years in my current position in the company, I still can't make myself call my dad anything but Dad. Same with my Uncle Bob, my siblings, and my cousins, I always use the same names I call them at home." Justin shrugged nonchalantly. "So, I tend to use first names for everyone else, too, even when I shouldn't."

I don't think even using a more formal form of address would keep Amanda from eyeing Justin up and down like a tasty snack.

Amy just nodded her agreement, knowing anything she thought of to say in response to Justin at that moment would be inappropriate for the workplace. Luckily, she didn't have to suffer through any uncomfortable silence in the elevator, since the doors whooshed open for them to exit on the lab level.

Justin reintroduced Amy to the rest of the people who worked in the lab, going over all their projects and how they were divided into teams for each of them. She was able to follow along on her tablet, putting faces to the names on the project specs to make it easier for her to memorize the names of all her new coworkers.

Like I'll be able to forget the names of the women flirting with Justin constantly.

As the introductions were being made, Justin also informed all the team leaders that their proposals and supply requests and everything that they normally sent to Justin, or his executive assistant, would now be sent to Amy.

I guess that budget will be my responsibility from now on, along with a lotta other things I'm not sure I'm qualified to handle. Yep, I'm definitely in over my head.

<p style="text-align:center">~~~</p>

Monday, January 7, 2019

Amy was looking forward to her first full day in the lab at her new job. Wednesday, Thursday, and Friday of the previous week, she'd spent all her time at work going over all the administrative tasks of her new position with Justin. While she'd needed his hands-on approach to teaching her the specifics of the duties she'd never had to handle in her prior place of employment, spending basically two-and-a-half days in close proximity to his intoxicating sandalwood scent, while cramped in her small office beside the lab, was almost more than her libido could withstand without climbing him like a tree and begging him to ease the ache between her legs.

Though Amy never believed in true love like her mother, sister, and friends, being raised by the open-minded Andrea Lawton and her forever frisky grandparents taught her how to take care of her own needs from an early age. She'd had more than her fair share of one-night stands and even a few weekend flings since college; she just didn't ever go all in for the whole boyfriend-girlfriend thing. And when she was too busy to go out and find a one-nighter, she had her favorite vibrator to take care of herself.

After spending so much one-on-one time with Justin the previous week, she'd had to recharge her purple Voodoo Beso Plus vibrator multiple times, so she could use it every night. It was her favorite toy that she'd bought from her sister's side business as an It's My Pleasure consultant because it stimulated her G-spot with internal vibrations while the external sucker worked over her clit.

When Justin had been super friendly and invited her to hang out with his family over the weekend, Amy had used the excuse that she still needed to sort through all her belongings to find a few things she was missing after the move. But she'd actually spent most of the weekend using her favorite adult toy multiple times a day while fantasizing about her hunky boss.

She felt like a total perv for lusting after Justin, when she knew she couldn't even indulge in a one-night stand or weekend fling with him. *It's just because it's been a while since I've gotten laid. Once I get into my own house and get totally settled in here in Texas, I'll be able to go out in San Antonio to take the edge off with a random dick. And then it won't be so hard to be around him without imagining how good he'd be in bed.*

Yeah, keep telling yourself that, Amy heard her sister say in her head. *If you've met* **The One**, *then any dick but his won't do a thing for you.*

Shaking off the inner voice that Ashlyn swore was their twin connection, Amy grabbed her lab coat to put on over her clothes and got to work setting up her workstation in the lab. She'd spent her free time the previous weekend, when she wasn't lusting over Justin, reading up on the various vegetable-based antifreeze products that were being integrated into the marketplace in Europe. Her first project with Burleson Incorporated was to experiment with the various extracts from soya, rapeseed, sugar beets, and corn to determine the best ratio of each to go into a new environmentally-friendly, non-toxic antifreeze. Once she finished her experiments and determined what was needed to make the most effective product, then she'd get with Justin to determine if there were already production facilities in the company, which would be able to transform the raw materials from the fields, where those crops could be grown, into the extract components and ultimately the final product to put it out for sale to customers.

She got so focused on setting up her workstation and ordering the plant extracts from outside suppliers for her first experiments, she almost missed lunchtime. She was proud of herself for not thinking about Justin once all morning, until he poked his head into her office at noon.

"How's the first day of actual lab work going?" Justin's smile showed through the twinkle in his bright blue eyes.

"Good," Amy replied, unable to stop herself from smiling back at him. "Already have my first few plant extracts ordered to test, so we can hopefully get away from both ethylene-glycol- and propylene-glycol-based antifreeze."

"Excellent! I was just headed down to the cafeteria for lunch. Wanna come with and give me a heads-up on what you're thinking we might be able to plant in some of our dormant fields to bring that extract production in-house?"

After going to lunch with Justin and his sisters the previous week, Amy had brought her lunch on Monday, thinking she'd avoid the temptation of another meal with Justin. But since he wanted to talk about work, she couldn't really tell him no, so she grabbed her soft-sided lunch box out of her bottom drawer and followed him down to the cafeteria.

Amy found a seat and unpacked her salad and fruit, putting a couple strawberries in the infuser section of her water bottle before going across the room to fill the bottle at the water cooler. By the time she was settled back in her seat and ready to start eating, Justin was able to get through the line and sat down across from her with a tray full of more food than she would eat in two days.

In addition to a salad twice the size of the one Amy had brought to eat, Justin's tray also held a plate piled at least three inches high with chicken fried rice and half a dozen egg rolls, four different desserts, and two cans of soda.

"So, tell me more about this vegetable-based antifreeze you think we should switch to." Justin started digging into his food, clearly considering eating together as a working lunch.

"I looked up more details about the European products I was telling you about last week," Amy stated, no longer sidetracked by Justin's gluttony. "They all seem to be based on glycerol, betaine, or bioPG. Since betaine and bioPG are proprietary formulations derived from sugar beets and corn, I know we can't use them specifically for our new product. So, I talked to a few of the suppliers you already use for other products to order a couple gallons of the various extracts and by-products of processing those crops to experiment with to determine what might work best. Everything I read about the glycerol-based products said they were either derived from soybeans, rapeseeds, or cattle, so I also ordered a couple gallons of glycerol made from soybeans and rapeseeds. I figured since ya'll already have cattle on the ranch, you might already have a supply of glycerol from the beef processing part of the company that we could experiment with. In fact, I was about to call you to see who I needed to talk to in the company to find that when you popped into my office."

"Uncle Bob is the point person for Burleson Beef, but I'm not sure who he has in charge of the various by-products over at the slaughterhouse. I've only really gotten to know Manuel Garcia on the ranch as my contact person for getting the manure collected and processed for methanol production, but I don't think he'd handle the tallow-to-glycerol process, since the slaughterhouse is a separate facility."

"So, you haven't used any of the other beef production by-products in the lab?" Amy was surprised that Justin hadn't used the non-edible portions of the cattle that were raised on his family ranch in his prior research.

"No, when I first started with research and development, we were primarily focused on what we could do with the crude oil and finding additives that would improve our gasoline production. Before my brother, sisters, and I started working here, it all rested on my dad, Uncle Bob, and Pappaw Jerry's shoulders. While they did great with the oil and beef businesses, they didn't have great luck in diversifying the business or transitioning to greener energy sources. They were just stretched too thin and didn't hire enough executives from outside the family to be able to expand the way we have in the last few years."

Justin paused in his explanation to finish off a couple of his egg rolls and a few bites of his fried rice. Not wanting to interrupt him, Amy continued to eat her salad, silently waiting for Justin to finish telling her about the transition that had taken place in the company.

"With most of my cousins having interests outside the family business, things didn't start changing until a little over five years ago, when JJ was the first of us to graduate from college and start working here. He mostly stuck with the status quo that first year, learning everything he could about the oil business from Dad and Pappaw

Jerry. Then, when I took over R and D in twenty-fourteen, it was a division of Burleson Oil. We've pretty much left it that way, focusing on the oil industry and fuel production for the first couple years. Then I started working on other automotive chemicals and biofuels when JJ pushed for Burleson Oil to become Burleson Energy. With you now coming up with ideas that require more agricultural derivatives than just the beef by-products, I'm sure we'll end up with a Burleson Ag department soon. And if you do like I expect and start coming up with other innovative products outside the automotive industry, we'll probably turn R and D into its own division of the company eventually, instead of staying under the Burleson Energy umbrella."

"You really expect me to expand the product line that much?" Amy couldn't fathom how much Justin seemed to believe in her ability in the lab, when they'd only really spent a couple weeks getting to know each other over the last couple months.

"Absolutely. Especially if our team meetings go as well as I expect this week. Once we get our current product line switched over to more eco-friendly alternatives, we'll hafta come up with new product lines to keep everyone in the lab busy."

Amy was still a little nervous about the meetings coming up with each of the teams working in the lab. She and Justin were scheduled to meet with them to brainstorm ways to tweak their current projects to make them more sustainable than what they were currently attempting to experiment with, and Amy knew these meetings were when Justin expected the pushback to come from the employees who weren't as open to change.

Obviously seeing her trepidation at mentioning the meetings, Justin changed the subject. "So, what else did you get up to this weekend besides sorting through your stuff and researching the antifreeze options?" His sly smile as he posed the question relaxed Amy a little, even though she worried he was trying to push her out of the friend zone.

"I started looking at house listings." Amy shrugged like it wasn't a big deal, even though it was a major life change for her. "I thought I wanted to live closer to the office to cut down on commuting time, but I don't know my way around San Antonio enough to know if any of the listings I'm looking at are actually closer than Heart's Destiny."

Leah Mae Wright

"Do you have any of the listings with you?" Amy shook her head in the negative, since she'd been looking them up on her laptop that was back at James's house in Heart's Destiny. "Well, I'll be glad to look them over with you to help you figure out which ones to seriously consider. You can either bring them one day this week, when we can look at them over lunch, or we can get together this weekend to look them over."

"Oh, I wouldn't wanna interfere with your family time over the weekend." While Amy appreciated his offer of help in finding a house, she worried that looking at houses with him could easily feel more like couple-time than an only-friends activity like she needed to keep things with Justin.

"You aren't interfering with family time." Justin waved off her objection as if it didn't matter even a tiny bit. "Besides, I already have orders to make sure you know you hafta be at Aunt Hazel and Uncle Bob's house on Sunday evening for Charlotte's birthday party. Though we probably shouldn't go over house listings during the party, so it'll hafta be either at lunch here at work or on Saturday."

Fuck, shit, damn! Why do the Burlesons have to be so freaking nice that I can't decline a birthday invitation?

"Oh, okay." Amy struggled with what else to say, wishing she could come up with a good excuse to avoid hanging out with Justin other than when she had to work with him. "I'll try to remember to bring my laptop with me to work one day this week."

Justin just smiled as they continued to eat their lunches in quiet comradery.

When their silence started to feel a little awkward, Amy finally broke it. "So, what did you get Charlotte for her birthday? I need some ideas for what to pick up before her party on Sunday."

"Oh, um." Justin fidgeted in his chair, his cheeks pinkening as if he was embarrassed about what he got his cousin. "I got her a year-long membership to an ancestry site and a few dozen DNA tests, so the whole family can be tested, and she can track it all online."

"Wow, that's a very thoughtful gift." Amy was confused about why Justin would be embarrassed by giving Charlotte the gift she'd expressed interest in at Christmas.

He's not embarrassed about bringing up the DNA tests after my reluctance to do one at Christmas, is he? Surely, he realizes that my brief trepidation was in no way being judgmental of him or his family wanting to know their heritage. In fact, after hearing Charlotte's reasoning for why she wanted to do the DNA tests, I'm actually less hesitant and kinda wanna do one, too.

"But other than a big pack of gum or something to help everyone increase their saliva production to be able to spit into the test tubes, it doesn't really give me any ideas of what to get her."

They both chuckled at Amy's offhand comment, easing the tension Amy felt coming from Justin just as she'd hoped it would.

"The girls always tend to go for clothing as gifts for each other." Justin shrugged as he offered his suggestion.

Amy remembered back to Christmas, specifically to all the clothing gifts everyone seemed to receive, herself included, even though she hadn't expected to exchange gifts with the huge crowd of Burlesons, Hunters, and assorted guests. *Charlotte seems to have a classic style. Maybe she'd like a lightweight scarf that she could wear year-round as an accessory with the dressier blouses she seems to prefer. Maybe if it's lightweight enough she won't have the urge to use it to choke Ian, if he gets on her nerves at school the way he did at Christmas. Or her mother for pushing her toward the handsome new English teacher.*

Amy spent a few more minutes making small talk with Justin before they both headed back to the lab for their first of several meetings that week with the five teams of lab techs she now supervised.

Maybe it's a good thing I can't wear anything like that in the lab, so I won't get the urge to use it to choke out Amanda, or Megan, or Tara, if they continue overtly flirting with Justin this week like they did last week. I'd probably lose my job for assaulting Justin's assistant or the two lab technicians, who don't seem to understand that our boss is off-limits for all of us, no matter what the employee handbook says about couples just needing to disclose their status to the human resources department and promise not to make it into a company problem if they break up.

~~~
~~~

Justin was starting to feel a little bad about pushing Amy to have lunch with him in the cafeteria every day, especially when he realized that she kept leaving her laptop at home, trying to avoid looking at house listings with him the previous week, as if not having them to look at would get her out of having to eat with him. Though he wanted to have lunch with her each day as a friend, he'd resorted to asking her opinion on the changes the teams were implementing to the various projects they'd discussed in their brainstorming meetings to get her to step away from the lab for a private conversation, in order to get her to share a meal with him each day. They only spent a few minutes of the hour they were eating actually discussing work, though, so he felt they were at least spending more of their time together as friends than boss and employee.

Now if I can just get her to bring those house listings and let me help her look at them this weekend, maybe we can progress to closer friends, who at least hug once in a while, even if I know it'll be a while yet before she's ready for more than friends.

In their daily conversations the week before, they'd started getting to know each other much better than they had when she was in town back in November. They had a lot of things in common besides their chosen majors in college and career aspirations. They both preferred reading scholarly papers over popular literature and playing video games over watching television.

Of course, they also had their differences, specifically their taste in music, with Amy preferring more pop-rock and Justin preferring more country music.

At least we both agreed that we prefer more upbeat tunes with positive messages to the emo, woe-is-me stuff that was popular back when we were teenagers.

Justin was a little over two years older than Amy, with him being born in April of 1991, while she was born in June of 1993. But he didn't think that small of an age difference meant much, if anything, in the long run. Since much larger age differences didn't seem to be a problem for Anthony and Kay, or Bobby and Brie, Justin just made sure to memorize Amy's birthday and let the fact that he was a couple years older than her go.

Thinking of his cousins and their significant others made him think about how they'd each behaved so differently the night before when Charlotte started passing out the DNA tests to everyone at her birthday party. Anthony and Kay had made it a game with their daughters to see who could fill up the little tube they all had to spit into the fastest, while Bobby and Brie had set their kits aside to do the tests later.

Justin understood that Bobby was supporting Brie by waiting until she was out from under the issues with her father in Georgia to do their tests, so she could stay safely hidden until everything was all cleared up for her back home. But it still seemed strange to see his oldest cousin, who was normally the life of the party and the first one of them to instigate a goofy game, act so stoic, as if he was at work as the police chief instead of hanging out with his family.

Justin was certainly glad to see how Anthony had come out of the funk he'd seemed to stay in after losing his high school sweetheart and their unborn child to act like a kid again with his new daughters. Kay and their girls had certainly done a lot in the last few months to bring back the fun-loving cousin Justin remembered from their teenage years.

Amy had also surprised Justin when Charlotte tossed her one of the DNA tests and then Tia and Maria had pulled her into their speedy spitting game. After the way she'd reacted to talking about the tests at Christmas, he didn't think she really wanted to do one with everyone else there.

But when they all started talking about what they expected to see of their racial breakdown, she explained how her mother believed they were a Heinz 57 mix because their lighter-skinned African ancestors had blended in with the Native Americans, who walked the Trail of Tears to escape a life of slavery, and intermarried with every other race of people who were adopted into the tribe for whatever reason, and she wanted to prove her mother's theory correct.

After Tia had confirmed that Amy's mother's theory was plausible by giving them all a lesson in American, and specifically Oklahoma, history that none of the Burlesons had ever heard before, Justin certainly hoped Amy's results proved there were areas in the United States where race relations weren't always contentious.

And maybe our results will show that Memmaw Judy's Native American ancestors passed the ability to accept all races and nationalities into the family down to all of us.

Just hearing how several tribes adopted people of color into their ranks to protect them during that horrible time in American history made Justin proud of his grandmother's bloodline running through his veins, even if he now mostly resembled the white men they would've scalped to save them.

Amy pulling her laptop out of her bag to put it on the table as soon as he sat down brought Justin out of his mental memory lane of the last few days, which he'd been traveling down while going through the line in the cafeteria. *Maybe I should start bringing my lunch, too, so I don't hafta waste time in line when I could be sitting here with her a few minutes longer.*

"Before we go through the listings, tell me what you're looking for in a house." Justin picked up his fork to start eating, while Amy brought up the computer to show him what she'd been looking at for the last week.

"Three bedrooms, at least two bathrooms. I'd rather have three bathrooms, so if Mom and Ashlyn move down here I won't have to share a bathroom with either of them, but that's been hard to find with what I've been looking at so far." Amy shook her head with her lips turning up in the slightest smile as she focused on the computer screen, where it was situated between them and only half turned where Justin could see the screen. "Close to work and a safe neighborhood are most important, but I'm willing to do a little work to make it cute if it's not move-in ready. I don't need anything super fancy or modern."

The terra-cotta tint on her cheeks as she said the last sentence made him wonder if she thought the houses on the ranch were too fancy or modern for her tastes. His house certainly wasn't, even though his parents had it updated right before he moved in when he turned eighteen, a little less than ten years ago. It also barely met her minimum requirement of three bedrooms and two bathrooms, since they'd taken half the space of the third bedroom to turn it into an ensuite bathroom for the master bedroom during that remodel. Justin wasn't even sure he could classify the small space left as a third bedroom since it no longer had a closet, so he used it as a home office.

"Okay, well, that shouldn't be too hard to find." Justin bobbed his head at the computer on the table between them. "Show me what you've seen so far that you wanna consider."

Amy turned the laptop around, so it was basically facing the space on the table between their trays, so they could both look at the screen as she scrolled through the listings.

"This one is my first choice. It's not the best looking, but as I said, I won't mind having to do a little painting or whatever. But it's the biggest and has the best price tag."

"Yeah, that's a no." Justin shook his head, pointing at the address with his fork. "It's cheap because it's in one of the worst neighborhoods in town."

Amy's smile faltered, making Justin feel guilty for being the one to give her the bad news. "Besides, it's also on the opposite side of San Antonio, so you'd have just as far of a commute as coming from Heart's Destiny, and you'd also hafta deal with downtown traffic."

"I really wish they had these listings on a map so I could figure out which ones are actually in the southwest part of the city. I've seriously thought about going driving around after work to see if I see anything with a sign in the yard that isn't too far from here."

"Yeah, that's probably not the best idea." Justin shook his head again as he turned her laptop to where he could type on the keyboard to change her search parameters. "But we can still work with this. We just need to put in a few neighborhoods to help narrow the search."

Justin turned the computer back toward Amy when the new listings started populating the screen. He almost regretted making the adjustments to her search when her eyes bugged out as she scrolled through the new list of housing options.

"Maybe I should look at rentals instead of trying to buy until I can save up more of a down payment," Amy muttered under her breath, making it hard for Justin to make out her words.

Or maybe you could just move in with me, or let me buy you a house if you don't like my place on the ranch.

Justin knew Amy would balk if he suggested what he was thinking out loud, so he quickly offered another option. "You could do that. Or you could look a little farther out to find something you'll like that's more affordable."

"I suppose I have to choose between the commute from Heart's Destiny or spending three times my original budget, huh?" Justin only nodded, not wanting to mention the other little towns between his hometown and the office.

They sat in silence eating for a few minutes, until he couldn't handle the dejected look on her face a moment longer. "How about I set us up an appointment at Walker Realty on Saturday? While most of what they have listed with them is in Heart's Destiny, they'll probably be better suited to help you find something in between here and there, too."

"Okay," Amy replied, her lips barely turning up on the sides.

Justin was unable to stop himself from reaching over and patting her hand, where it was resting beside her laptop from her earlier scrolling. Even that brief contact was enough to send a lightning bolt of lust straight to his cock. Knowing he couldn't keep touching her for long without popping a boner that would be completely inappropriate for the workplace, he pulled his hand back as soon as she looked up at him. "Don't worry, Sweetheart, we'll find you the perfect house."

"Thank you."

"No problem. Oh, I forgot to ask you about bowling this weekend." Justin could tell by the way she blanched that she was definitely not ready for him to ask her on a real date. *Good thing this is just a friendly get-together with a big group.* "After you left last night, Charlotte and Becky were talking to Brie, and they started planning a trip to the bowling alley on Saturday evening. It'll be us and a bunch of our friends from town that I'm not sure if you officially met back in November or not. I promise it's not one of my mom's matchmaking things. Just a way for you to meet some new people, mostly the girls' friends and maybe a few of the Walkers. But we'd all just be hanging out as friends; I'm not asking you out on a date or anything." *Fuck me! I really need to learn to shut up when I'm nervous.*

"Oh, yeah, that sounds like fun. You think we'll have time to meet with the realtors and maybe look at some houses beforehand?"

"Definitely. In fact, let me call Walker Realty now." Justin pulled his phone out of his pocket and dialed the number, putting it on speaker, so Amy could hear both sides of the conversation.

"Walker Realty," Tully Walker announced when he answered the phone.

"Good afternoon, Mr. Tully." Justin smiled at Amy who looked a little more hopeful about her house hunt now that they were talking to a realtor. "It's Justin Burleson. I'm sitting here at work with our new lab manager, Amy Lawton. She's in the market for a house since she's new to the area, so I suggested we schedule an appointment with you for Saturday if you're available."

"Yeah, I'm available." Tully sounded like he was shuffling papers on his desk through the phone. "Is she there where I can find out what she's looking for, so I can have some listings ready to look at on Saturday?"

"Yes, sir, I'm here," Amy smiled at the phone as if Tully could see her. "I'm looking for a three-bedroom, two or three-bathroom house in the hundred-thousand-dollar range, somewhere between Heart's Destiny and the Burleson corporate office in San Antonio."

"In that price range, you're gonna be in Heart's Destiny," Tully chuckled. "You won't be able to find a three-bed, two-bath for under one-fifty-to-two-hundred-thousand, even in the other small towns between here and there."

"But you have some houses in Heart's Destiny in my price range?" Amy looked nervously up at Justin as she posed the question.

"Oh yeah, at least a dozen on the west side of town between Beefmaster and Hereford, another half dozen off Brahman and Clydesdale in the subdivision across from the high school fieldhouse, and a few in the subdivisions off Quarter Horse and American Paint near downtown. I'll have pictures of all of them for you to narrow down your choices on Saturday. Say ten a.m.?"

"Yes, thank you. Ten o'clock Saturday morning will be perfect."

"Think we'll be able to see enough to pick a place before we're meeting your boys at the bowling alley at four?" Justin thought it sounded like plenty of time to look at houses around Heart's Destiny, but he wanted to be sure, since he'd never actually gone house hunting before.

"Maybe. Depends on how long it takes for the paperwork to go through and if Amy wants to look at everything available before making a decision. We might have to spread the viewings out over a couple weekends to give her enough time to really look at everything I have available right now."

"That's fine." Amy smiled brightly at Justin, like she was grateful for him asking the question she hadn't thought of before. "I don't mind spending a few Saturdays looking."

"Excellent. See ya Saturday. And don't let my boys get ya'll into any trouble on the trails when you go hang out with them."

"That I can do," Justin laughed. "I can't guarantee your boys won't get into any trouble, but Amy and I won't go on the trails this weekend."

They said their goodbyes to Tully Walker before Amy asked what he'd meant about them getting into trouble.

"Um," Justin hummed for a moment, stalling while he figured out how to tell Amy about the Walkers and the trails on their property across Clydesdale Street from Lover's Lanes, the bowling alley in Heart's Destiny. "The trails are some dirt roads cut through the north side of the land the Walkers still own that used to be another ranch. Back when we were kids, Tully and his brother Wyatt cleared them out for their sons, and us as their son's friends, to ride four-wheelers. But once Luke and Bobby got old enough to drive, they turned them into the spot in town for all the teenagers to go parking. The gate to get onto their property where the trails are is right across the street from the bowling alley, which was ironically named after them, Lover's Lanes."

Amy giggled, covering her mouth as she almost choked on the last bite of her salad from not being finished chewing and swallowing it before her giggles started. It took her a moment to swallow her food and wash it down with a big gulp of her water.

Once Justin knew she wasn't in danger of choking again, he continued. "Anyway, a few years ago, right after Bobby started working at the police department, Becky came home from college with a boyfriend in tow. Bobby was on patrol and caught her out on the trails and made the Walkers put up gates to keep the kids from going parking, specifically his sisters."

"But if they wanted to go parking with one of the Walkers, couldn't they still?"

"Technically, yeah, but we've all made it clear that our sisters are off-limits, so none of the girls have ever dated the Walkers or anyone else from Heart's Destiny." Now that he was an adult, Justin realized it was a horrible double standard that kept his sisters and female cousins from dating until they went off to college, when all the males in the family had spent more than their fair share of time parking on the Walkers' trails while in high school. But there wasn't anything he could do about it now. He wouldn't let himself think about how he'd probably still want to reinforce that double standard if he ever had daughters.

Shaking off those thoughts, he finally explained the trouble portion of Tully's earlier statement. "But what Tully was referring to was how his two youngest sons, Hayden and Hudson, didn't like having to deal with the gate when they were still in high school. So, they protested it by throwing a party on the trails. They passed the gate code around to the whole school, so half the high school was out there when their bonfire got outta control and damn near burned the woods down."

"Oh my gosh! Were you there? Was anyone hurt?" Amy covered her mouth in astonishment as she excitedly shouted her questions.

"No, thankfully, nobody was hurt." Justin answered the most important question first. "I was already off at UT. In fact, it was Becky's freshman year in Austin and Bobby was the only Burleson living in Heart's Destiny, while the rest of us were either off at college or in the Navy. But it was such a big deal at the time that even my cousins who were in the Navy heard about it before they came home on leave. Anyway, that's what Tully was talking about. Though I doubt Hayden or Hudson will ever pull another stunt like that again, their dad still points it out to reprimand them once in a while to make sure."

"Yeah, I suppose that's a good deterrent." Amy chuckled and started packing up her lunch. "Did you ever do anything crazy like that?"

"Naw, the craziest thing I ever did was go parking on the trails and be late for curfew. What about you?" Justin hated that it was almost time to head up to their separate offices for the rest of the day, wishing they could continue their conversation since they were finally veering into more date-like, deeper getting-to-know-each-other questions than their normal friendly banter.

"No, even in college I was more likely to get locked in the library while studying than to miss curfew for any other reason. Ashlyn was the wild child, who would've been at the party with the Walkers if we'd lived here back then."

Amy continued to tell him about her twin sister and how different they were, even though they looked alike, as they made their way to the elevator. Unfortunately, their conversation was cut way too short for Justin, when Amy had to get off a couple floors before him to go to the lab, while he had to go spend the rest of the day in his executive office.

Chapter Three

Saturday, January 19, 2019

Amy didn't understand why Justin insisted on picking her up to drive from James's house to the realtor's office, instead of just meeting her there. Yeah, they had plans to meet his siblings, cousins, and a whole slew of their family friends to go bowling later in the day, but it wasn't like she couldn't drive herself to the bowling alley either.

It's not like I'll be drinking and will need a sober ride home. This makes it feel more like a date than one friend helping another friend find a house, or hanging out with a group of friends later.

Even worrying about them seeming more like a couple than the new friends they were didn't stop her from making sure she looked her best when Justin arrived to pick her up at fifteen minutes before ten on Saturday morning.

I didn't put on my best jeans and semi-dressy blouse for Justin. Nor did I do my hair and makeup for him. This is all so I look casual, but still able to afford the payments on the houses I'm looking at today. Amy tried reassuring herself as she walked out the front door to Justin's waiting truck.

Yeah, keep lying to yourself, Sis. Unfortunately, she couldn't quiet the inner voice that sounded like her sister. *You look hot. And the only person you care about noticing how hot you are is Justin.*

Amy shushed her inner Ashlyn voice as she climbed into the passenger seat of Justin's truck. Thankfully, Ashlyn's influence stayed quiet while she made small talk with Justin on the way to the realtor's office.

Amy wasn't sure what she expected when she met the realtor for the first time, but Tully Walker was definitely not it. She guessed he was in his fifties based on the lines around his eyes, but she couldn't tell if he'd naturally gone bald or if he shaved his head. The black hair of his goatee held no signs of graying, so it was no help in estimating his age any closer. But since Justin had mentioned he was the father of a couple of his friends, Amy knew he had to at least be in his late forties or early fifties.

"Morning, Mr. Tully." Justin extended his hand to shake the hand of the man who was at least a couple inches taller and fifty or sixty pounds heavier than him.

"Good to see you, Justin." As they shook hands, Amy noticed the tattoos on the older man's arms, where he had the sleeves of his dress shirt rolled up to just below his elbows.

If it weren't for the slacks and dress shirt, I'd say he looks like he'd be more comfortable at Tully's Roadhouse than in the real estate office. Wait! Tully's. Tully Walker. Does he also own the bar?

Amy was brought out of her mental rabbit hole when Mr. Walker extended his hand to her, and she realized that Justin had made introductions. She knew she was probably blushing from being embarrassed to have been lost in her own head, instead of paying attention to what was being said around her. "Nice to meet you, Mr. Walker." Amy shook his hand, trying to hide her lack of attention with a bright smile.

"Please, call me Tully," he grinned. "Justin said you're working with him in the lab at Burleson, but I think I remember seeing you at Anthony and Kay's wedding."

"Yes, Tully." Amy returned his smile as he directed them to his office to sit and talk. "It was when I was down here for the wedding that I met the Burlesons and learned about the lab opportunity at Burleson Incorporated."

"Amy is Kay's sister, Randi's, best friend." Justin clarified why she was at the wedding.

"Randi? The same girl who's now dating James Hunter?" Tully looked at her with scrutiny, tilting his head as he posed his questions.

"Yes," Amy squeaked, not sure why she felt so deeply examined by the older man, who was either of mixed race or spent a lot of time out in the sun to maintain his swarthy complexion.

"I didn't know you were so up to date on all the town gossip." Justin chuckled and lightened the moment.

"Not really," Tully snorted, shaking his head at Justin. "But my wife's been sucked in on your momma and Aunt Hazel's matchmaking plans, so I've heard a few things. Between James and Randi, then Bobby and Brie, and now the two of you, I'm almost afraid for my boys when the womenfolk run outta Burlesons to match up and start workin' on finding them wives."

"Oh, we're not a couple," Amy protested, motioning between herself and Justin. "We're just friends, and now that he's my boss, there's no way we can ever be more."

I knew this was too much like a couple's activity this morning, Amy thought as Tully barked out a laugh.

Amy looked to Justin to back up her statement, since it looked like Tully Walker didn't believe her. Justin just shrugged and shook his head, like he didn't know what Tully was laughing at.

"Yeah, okay," Tully finally chortled as his laughter died down. "I'll go along with that for now. But when you finally admit what everyone else can see whenever they look at the two of you together, you'd better come to me to put the house you're about to buy on the market, so you can move onto the ranch with Justin."

Amy's protest died on her lips as Justin answered for her.

"Deal. But don't expect it to happen too soon, because we can't let the matchmaking mommas feel too successful by starting to date immediately."

"Agreed. Not wanting any of them to get a big head about being right about who to match with whom is why I didn't mention to Lisa that ya'll have plans to go bowling today with our boys and all your cousins."

Amy wasn't sure what he meant by that statement until he explained that his wife, Lisa, was the principal at Heart's Destiny Middle School, where Charlotte worked, and she was working with Hazel and Susan to match Charlotte up with the new English teacher, Ian. He also went into a little of his family history, telling them about how he'd met Lisa at his bar back when he was working with his parents in the realty office during the day and running the bar at night. He also talked about his oldest son, Aiden, who also had his realtor's license, even though he spent most of his time working for Tully's brother, Wyatt, in the construction side of their family businesses. And how he'd turned the everyday management of Tully's Roadhouse over to his nephew, Leo, because he was the only one of the Walker boys who was interested in the bar, and also had the head for business to be able to handle the day to day operations and not drink away the profits. Tully's other sons also worked for the construction company, with Dalton specializing in plumbing, Hayden focusing on drawing up the architectural plans, and Hudson focusing on the landscape around the buildings, though he was hoping to convince them to get their realtor's licenses, too, one day.

His openness made Amy feel more comfortable as their conversation progressed. Their talk led to Amy opening up to give him a little of her family history as they filled out the paperwork to get started on the home-buying process. In addition to telling him about her mother and sister, she also explained how she'd applied for the home loan while she was still in Tulsa because of having a long history with her bank there. While she might eventually open a local bank account, she knew she'd be less likely to be approved for a home loan with the local bank, since she wouldn't have a long, positive history of dealing with the local lender.

They eventually got everything set up, so they could start looking at the houses he had available, even though it would be Monday before Tully could verify her loan approval through her bank in Tulsa. Amy couldn't believe the selection of houses for sale in Heart's Destiny. With almost three dozen that looked too much alike in the photos for her to decide on which ones she wanted to look at, Amy believed they were definitely going to have to break the tour of homes into more than one Saturday.

They started looking at the ones closest to downtown, where the Walker Realty office was located. When they barely got through all those before they had to leave to grab a late lunch before meeting everyone at the bowling alley, they scheduled another day of house hunting the next Saturday to look at the ones on the west side of town, closer to the refinery and the other production facilities owned and operated by Burleson Incorporated.

Instead of driving away from the realty office as Amy expected, Justin walked her across Longhorn Lane, and then Mustang Lane, to get to Kara's Kakes, which was diagonally across the intersection of the two streets from where Walker Realty was located on Longhorn behind the Bank of Heart's Destiny, which faced Mustang Lane.

"Ya'll got here just in time," the woman behind the counter greeted them. "I'm closing in five minutes, so I can rush home and clean up before meeting you at the bowling alley."

"Sorry, Kara," Justin apologized, sheepishly ducking his head. "I was hoping you had enough time to fix us a couple sandwiches on your homemade bread since we missed lunch."

"Yeah, I can do that." Kara pulled out a tray of bread from behind the counter. "But it'll have to be chicken salad or tuna salad because everything else is already put up for the weekend. And you'll have to introduce me to your lady friend while I'm making them instead of waiting 'til we get to Lover's Lanes."

"Sorry, Kara, this is Amy. Amy, this is Kara."

"Nice to meet you, Kara." Amy smiled at the beautiful mixed race brunette in front of her, who looked to be around their ages of mid-twenties.

"You, too, Amy. I've heard a little about you from the other Burlesons and look forward to getting to know you better this afternoon. But now I need to know whether you want chicken or tuna."

"Chicken, please." Amy smiled at the rushing woman.

"Same for me," Justin agreed, already getting his wallet out to pay for their sandwiches as he walked over to a cooler and pulled out two cans of Coke. "And a couple sodas. Amy, what would you like to drink?"

"Water's fine," Amy replied, not sure how to broach the subject of paying for her own meal. Justin grabbed a bottle of water out of the cooler along with his sodas before setting them all on the counter by the register. Amy moved over to where he was standing and pulled her own wallet out to pay for her meal, when Justin stopped her by putting a hand over hers, blocking her from getting her money out.

"I got lunch," Justin declared, smiling at her. Before she could protest that she could pay for her own lunch, Justin continued. "Since Kara's closing, we'll go next door to eat, and then you can get dessert from Nana Marie."

Giving her something else to pay for eased her guilt at him covering lunch, but it didn't distract her so much that she missed his mentioning a nana she hadn't met before. "Nana Marie?" Amy gave him a quizzical look as she put her wallet away for the time being.

Leah Mae Wright

"Yeah, she owns the Creamarie next door. She was best friends with my Memmaw Judy and kinda adopted all of us as honorary grandkids." Justin explained the way the older woman had acted as another grandmother after the Burlesons lost theirs, while Kara finished making their sandwiches and rang them up. Once he'd paid for their meal, they grabbed their sandwiches and drinks and hurriedly walked next door, so Kara could lock up her bakery.

After getting to know the Burlesons in her brief time in Heart's Destiny, she felt a little bad for being surprised to find that the woman they considered an honorary grandmother was an eighty-something-year-old Black woman, who reminded Amy of her own Nana Shanae. *Damn, this family really is all-inclusive when choosing their friends and loved ones, just like mine.*

"Nana Marie," Justin exclaimed, walking behind the counter to hug the older woman, who was a couple inches shorter than Amy's five-foot-five. "Did you meet Amy at Anthony's wedding?"

"No." Marie shook her head while returning Justin's embrace. "But I saw your momma and Aunt Hazel matchmaking the two of you, so I figured I'd wait it out and see how long before you gave in and introduced me to your future bride."

Amy was glad she hadn't started eating yet, because if she had, then she would've surely choked on her food at Marie's comment. As it was, she just stood there with her mouth opening and closing like a fish out of water, while she floundered for something to say to refute the possibility of her ever marrying Justin.

"Now, Nana Marie, don't be startin' rumors like that." Justin grinned conspiratorially at Amy. "Amy and I are on the down-low, telling everyone we're just friends, so Ma and Aunt Hazel don't get too full of themselves with their matchmaking."

What the… What did he just say? I know he did not just tell his honorary nana that we're a couple on the down-low. Why? Why would he say something like that to anyone? But especially to someone who's close with his family?

Amy was so shocked by Justin's declaration that she mentally checked out for a moment to contemplate his words and missed what he said to lead to them all sitting at a table to eat. She vaguely registered that she was interacting with the people around her, including Marie's son, Jackson, who helped his mother at the ice cream shop on weekends, when he wasn't working at the refinery owned by the Burlesons. But Amy was too dumbfounded by how out of character her body responded to Justin's claim of them being a secret couple to really focus on the rest of the conversation.

I should definitely not be getting tingles in my heart at the thought of one day marrying him. I mean, I can understand why my pussy is wet and my nipples are hard at thinking of the things we'd do if we were really a couple. But I don't do heartfelt feelings or think about forever with any man. And I really shouldn't with my new boss.

~~~

Justin was afraid he'd screwed up with Amy by claiming to be a couple on the down-low with Nana Marie. He'd tried to play it off as a joking line, so Amy wouldn't be uncomfortable with the lie he hoped to make real one day soon. But he knew Nana Marie would see his feelings for Amy written all over his face, so he couldn't throw out one of their *only-friends* lines without her calling him on his bullshit.

The way Amy hadn't really reacted to his statement one way or the other confused him as to what she might be thinking. *Does her non-reaction mean she's open to more with me? Should I try putting my arm around her while we're sitting here side by side at the bowling alley? Or maybe attempt to give her a kiss goodnight when I drop her off after? Or does she really think it was a joke meant to keep us from having another person in town tell us about how we're meant to be together? If that's the case, I might ruin any chance I have at even being her friend if I try either of those things tonight.*

Fuck! I wish she'd have had some kind of reaction other than to say how nice it was to meet Nana Marie and start asking questions about the rest of the Milton family to change the subject. Even if she'd have openly objected to our secret coupledom, I'd at least know she's not ready for me to ask her on a date to start moving us in that direction.

As much as this friend-zone stuff sucks, I'd at least like a hint about how much longer I hafta suffer in it before I make a move on her. I can handle only having sex with her in my head for a while, but it'd be
~~~

a lot easier to handle if I knew there was a possibility of us actually being together in the near future.

I can tell by the way she looks at me when she doesn't think I see her that she wants me as bad as I want her, so I know it's gonna happen eventually. I'd just like to know if it's gonna at least be this year, preferably in the next few months.

"You're up, Jus," his childhood friend, Aiden Walker, announced, bringing him out of his mental musings.

"Dude, are you sleeping in the middle of this rowdy bunch?" Aiden's cousin, Leo, teased Justin.

"Just a quick power nap, so I can whup ya'll's asses in this next game," Justin replied to the friends he'd known since they were all toddlers together. Aiden was just a couple weeks older than Justin and Leo was three months younger. They'd never had a choice but to be friends, since they'd had every class together from kindergarten through twelfth grade.

Aiden and Leo gave him shit while he walked over, picked up his bowling ball from the ball return, and lined up to toss the ball down the lane. Amy giggled along with Kara and Lexi, the other girls assigned to their lane to bowl. Apparently, Amy remembered meeting Lexi, Kayla, and Cassidy when the women were all getting ready for Anthony and Kay's wedding, so when they were splitting up into six people per lane, having Lexi join them meant she kinda knew more than just him in their group. Not that they were limited to only conversing with the people bowling in their lane, since most everyone else in their large group of two-dozen people were wandering around between lanes when they weren't up to bowl.

Justin liked seeing how Amy was coming out of her shell and interacting with all the women there that evening. Even though she had two-and-a-half weeks in at work, she was still pretty reserved with their coworkers. The only times he'd noticed when she wasn't one-hundred percent professional on the job were when they veered toward more friendly conversations at lunch. And that was only when it was just the two of them, or if his sisters had lunch with them. Any interactions with the lab techs, team leaders, or administrative staff were all polite but professional, not showing any of her personality like she was while hanging out with his family and friends.

She may think her sister is the outgoing one, but Amy's not really as introverted as she thinks, or as she acts at work. And fuck if it isn't sexy as hell to watch her having fun and making new friends. Justin smiled at his thoughts as he walked back over to sit down beside her after knocking down nine of the ten pins with his first turn bowling that game.

"Good job, Boss." Justin basked in Amy's praise, even though she was using the moniker to put distance between them.

Guess that's her way of telling me to back off and stay in the friend zone.

"Yeah, but you're gonna hafta start throwing some strikes if you wanna win a game." Aiden slugged Justin in the shoulder as he got up to take his turn bowling. Since Aiden threw a strike with his first frame of the game, Justin had to agree with him.

"Might as well give it up, Jus." Leo sauntered over to get his ball from the ball return as he spoke. "You know Aiden's been throwing nothing but strikes since he struck out with Cassidy on prom night."

Leo lined up and tossed his ball down the lane, knocking down seven pins.

"Then why can't you get a strike?" Kara smirked. "We both know you struck out on prom night, too."

"I didn't strike out on prom night," Leo protested while waiting for his ball to come back for his second chance of knocking down the rest of the pins in that frame. "I got a kiss goodnight, which was all I was expecting."

"That wasn't all you got that night." Justin chuckled as he brought up the memory. He wasn't the only one mentally reliving their prom night and finding it funny. Since everyone in their group but Amy were in the same grade in school, they were all laughing at how Kara's dad had shot Leo in the ass with a BB gun as he was walking back to his car after dropping her off for the night. Well, all of them except Leo.

"What's so funny?" Amy looked around in confusion at the raucous laughter.

"Nothing!" Leo threw up his hands in exasperation before he grabbed his bowling ball that had returned, so he could take his next shot at a spare. He obviously wasn't too mad at the memory since he was able to focus to knock over the last three pins.

"Aww, don't be mad, Cuz," Aiden mocked when his chuckles died down. "Not everyone gets to brag about getting anal on prom night."

"Oh, Aiden, we really need to reeducate you on a few things if you think getting shot in the ass and anal are the same thing," Lexi chortled.

"You got shot?" Amy's outburst was accompanied by her covering her mouth with her hand in shock.

"Don't worry, Sweetheart, it was just a BB gun." Justin reached over to pull her hand down and gave it a reassuring squeeze.

"And thankfully, that's the only time Daddy actually hit him," Kara added, still giggling. "I still can't believe you had Bobby arrest him on New Year's. You know he's gonna come after you every time he gets drunk, so you shouldn't've served him that much."

"Yeah, well, I wasn't the one who called the cops. He was waving his gun around in the parking lot after closing and someone else called it in while I was still inside cleaning up. And it was a packed house that night, so I wasn't the only one serving," Leo admitted, plopping down into his seat. "After that, I made sure everyone knows to limit him to one beer if he comes back in Tully's."

"Wait!" Amy held up the hand Justin wasn't holding. "So, he just tried to shoot you again a couple weeks ago?"

Lexi got up to take her turn as Kara explained. "Yep, and it wasn't the first time since prom night. Daddy's memory seems to be stuck on prom night anytime he gets drunk. So, he's gone after Leo at least a dozen times in the eight-and-a-half years since then."

"I'm just glad he's only called me to take him in to see Doc the one time." Aiden shook his head as Lexi took her seat and Kara got up to bowl.

"Dude, is that why you struck out with Cassidy?" Leo grinned like he was proud to be a cock blocker that night.

"Naw, Cass and I just went to prom as friends. I knew I wasn't getting any that night before it even began."

"Okay, so if Leo and Kara went to prom together and Aiden and Cassidy went to prom together, does that mean that you went to prom with Lexi?" Amy didn't let her eyes meet his as she posed the question, making him wonder what she was thinking.

Could she be jealous of my prom date?

"No, I went to prom with Justin's cousin, Jake, who was also in our same grade." Lexi answered before Justin could, giving him a moment to think about what he wanted to tell Amy about his first sexual experience the night of his senior prom.

Fuck! Don't tell her you lost your virginity on prom night with the preacher's daughter. At least not right here, right now. We'll discuss our first times when we finally get to moving toward a sexual relationship, but that's not something she needs to hear about while we're just friends.

"I actually went to prom with Fiona Harrison," Justin admitted. "You might've met her at the wedding. She's the English teacher that just started working with the GWA, so Randi, Kay, or the girls might've mentioned her to you."

"You went to prom with the preacher's daughter?" Justin couldn't quite read Amy's expression as she asked the question.

"Yeah," he admitted, knowing he couldn't lie to her, even if he didn't want to tell her all about that night right then.

"Your turn, Amy," Kara announced, sitting back down beside Lexi, effectively taking Amy's attention off Justin for the moment.

"Oh, yeah," Amy mumbled as she got up and went to take her turn bowling.

Thankfully, after Amy's turn, it was Justin's turn again. He used that time trying to come up with something else to talk about. He managed to get the spare even though he had no idea how to avoid any more prom night talk. He was thankful to whoever changed the subject because, by the time he got back to his seat after the second frame, the rest of the group was talking about the houses he and Amy had looked at earlier that day.

Kara and Lexi were offering their opinions about the houses they liked best around town, while Aiden mentioned that anything she bought through Walker Realty would be in tip-top shape with anything found in the inspection being fixed by Walker Construction before it was ever put on the market. They continued to have pleasant conversation for the rest of the game, until Leo mentioned the time and how he needed to get to the bar for work.

When they realized Leo was going to open up the bar, pretty much everyone else decided to move the group gathering to Tully's Roadhouse for the rest of the night. Justin was even in favor of the move at first, thinking it might be a good opportunity to get Amy in his arms on the dance floor. Then he had a flashback to her fleeing from him on New Year's Eve and decided it was still too soon to try for more.

He ended up playing pool with the guys while the girls were all up front line dancing and gossiping. His pool game was thrown off almost as much as his bowling had been earlier by him worrying about what the girls might be telling Amy about him. He wasn't as much of a player as some of the guys in the room, but he'd had his fair share of short-term girlfriends in high school and college and a few flings and one-night stands since then. With not knowing Amy's sexual history, he didn't know if she would consider him too promiscuous and be revolted by anything the ladies might share of his past.

It ended up being a long night with so much weighing on his mind. Even after taking Amy home and leaving her with a friendly wave instead of the kiss he so desperately wanted, he couldn't shut his mind off to go to sleep. He tossed and turned for hours, contemplating how to broach the subject of dating with Amy.

As nighttime turned into the wee hours of the morning, Justin's lack of sleep made him feel slightly delirious. Giving up on solving the problem of how to get out of the friend zone with Amy, he finally gave in to his fantasies of her instead. Knowing he didn't want Bobby's girlfriend to have to wash the mess off his sheets any more than he'd wanted his mother to, Justin got out of bed to masturbate in the shower, where he could wash the evidence down the drain like he'd learned to do as a teenager.

He slipped off his sleep pants and boxer briefs as he made his way into his ensuite bathroom and turned on his shower to warm up. He stood under the spray for only a moment, imagining Amy in there with him, before he was squirting a dollop of his bodywash in his hand to use as lube and palming his cock.

Fuck! I bet her lips would feel amazing around my dick, especially that plump lower lip that I always wanna suck on whenever I see it, Justin thought as he stroked himself up and down his long length.

As much as I would love to have her here sucking me off, I'm sure I'd be the one on my knees if she were really here with me. I wonder if she tastes as sweet as the coconut in whatever products she uses to

*make her smell like a trip to the beach? Or if she shaves her pussy?
Or waxes it? Or just trims her natural curls?*

*Yeah, I'd definitely be the one on my knees worshiping her. I'd
spend hours, hell, days, with her laid out on my bed while I lick and
suck every inch of her to show her how much I adore her. I wouldn't
stop eating her pussy until she's come so many times, she doesn't think
she can come again. Then I'd finally sink balls-deep inside her and
show her how many more times she can still get off on my cock.*

Justin squeezed tighter around his shaft as he sped up his strokes,
trying to envision how Amy would feel around him. The thought of
her clamping down on him as she came brought him over the edge.

"Fuck, yes, Amy!" Justin shouted as his orgasm washed through
him. He continued practically chanting her name, saying, "Amy" with
each jet of his white, sticky cum that exploded out of the head of his
cock. "Amy. Amy. Amy. Amy. Amy. Amy. Amy!"

He leaned against the wall, catching his breath before rinsing off
and getting out of the shower. After the intense release, he was finally
able to shut his brain off for a few hours to fall asleep. He spent the
rest of the night enjoying dreams about Amy that closely resembled
the fantasy he'd had in the shower. Dreaming about making love to
her was going to have to get him through for now, until he could
finally make his dreams come true.

<div align="center">~~~</div>

Saturday, January 26, 2019

Amy had struggled through the last week of work, and her struggle
had absolutely nothing to do with her job. She was desperately
fighting her growing feelings for Justin. No matter how much she
tried to only think of him as a friend, the more time she spent with
him, the more she wanted to rip his clothes off and ride him like she
was a cowgirl, and he was her stud. She was using her vibrator more
than she'd ever needed to in the past, especially on the nights when
Amy spent the whole day with Justin.

He'd apparently completed whatever executive tasks he'd had
keeping him up in his fancy office with his secretary (or sexretary as

Amy often referred to the flirtatious woman in her head), and had spent practically every working hour in the lab with her for the last week.

While Amy had mostly tempered her jealousy over Amanda after their brief conversation about the other woman on Amy's first day of work, she still had some latent twinges of envy whenever Justin left their meetings with the various teams in the lab to go back upstairs during her first full week on the job, and especially when he spent all his time, except for the hour they talked at lunch, up there during her second full week in the lab. But those small sightings of the green-eyed monster inside her were nothing compared to the roaring beast she'd been after hearing about Justin's high school girlfriend while they were out with their friends the previous Saturday, and in response to Tara and Megan blatantly flirting with him in the lab for the last few days.

She'd tried to hide her overwhelming jealous feelings, especially in front of her new friends on Saturday night when she'd worried one of them had been with Justin, but she wasn't sure she'd completely covered them up. Actually, after Kara had pulled her aside when they got to Tully's to reassure her that Justin hadn't ever looked at another girl like he looked at Amy, even his high school girlfriend, Fiona, she was pretty sure she hadn't concealed her emotions behind the mask of friendship she was desperately clinging to every time she was in close proximity to Justin.

She'd been elated to hear Kara's opinion that Justin returned her affection, but also devastated to know that they couldn't act on their mutual attraction. Although, when she really thought about it, Amy wasn't certain Kara's observations were accurate. That whole day they'd spent together, Justin had only touched her one time, when he took her hand and gave it a reassuring squeeze when she was shocked by hearing that Leo had been shot by Kara's father. He hadn't even given her a hug goodbye, like he'd given a few of the other women when they left for the night, Kara included.

When she thought back to the week at work while they were touring houses for the second Saturday in a row, she couldn't recall even an incidental contact between them, even though he was either in the lab or eating lunch with her every minute of the past five days.

Not that I was willing to brush up against him or touch his arm every chance I got like Megan or Tara. I wonder if he's been with them, and they're angling for another time in his bed? Or if they're like Amanda, and take his polite, friendly attitude to mean more than it does?

Crap! Maybe I'm like Amanda and am taking his friendship outside of the office to mean more than it is for him? Am I projecting my sexual attraction onto him when he's not really feeling it for me?

"So, do you have any favorites?"

Tully's question brought Amy back out of her head to focus on the task at hand, which was picking a house now that they were back at the realty office. She mentally ran through the list of houses she'd seen both earlier that day and the previous week.

Amy just thought the houses she'd looked at the previous weekend on the east side of town were similar. After touring a dozen cookie-cutter copies of the same layout on the west side of town, she realized there were definitely differences in the houses she'd previously toured. Specifically, the east-side houses might have all been older Victorian-style homes, but they varied in layout and whether they were two or three stories.

The ones on the west side were all single-story homes that had been built in the 1920s, when the Burlesons' refinery brought in a lot of jobs to the small town. Because they had to house so many people who moved there in a short period of time to fill those jobs, Walker Construction had picked a simple floorplan that they could build quickly to accommodate them.

The only real differences in the houses were whether or not they'd been renovated in the last almost ninety years. Or rather, how recently they'd been renovated, and if the renovations had included upgrades to higher quality materials like granite countertops and hardwood floors, instead of the standard laminate and carpet.

As much as she liked the big, beautiful Victorians, she was also drawn to the smaller bungalow-style homes that reminded her of the house she'd shared with Randi in Tulsa. When she struggled to decide which one she liked best, she narrowed it down to the three that were most recently updated with granite countertops, hardwood floors, and stainless steel appliances.

Leah Mae Wright

Just because I told Justin I didn't need anything fancy or already updated, doesn't mean I don't appreciate the work already being done without me having to pay extra for it later.

That narrowed her choices to a two-story Victorian on Roper Road in the subdivision off Brahman Boulevard between Clydesdale Street and Galiceno Street, a three-story Victorian on Saddle Street in the subdivision off Angus Avenue between American Paint Road and Quarter Horse Drive, and a single-story bungalow on Wildcatter Way in the subdivision off Hereford Road between Quarter Horse Drive Extension and Walker Road.

"Which of these three do you like best?" Amy wanted Justin's opinion after flipping through the files to pull out the ones she liked best but couldn't decide between.

"They were all nice." Justin ran a hand through his hair like he was undecided on which one he'd pick. "The one on Wildcatter is about the same size as my house on the ranch, which is perfect for me, but might feel cramped if your mom and sister move in with you."

"Yeah, I liked that one because it reminded me of the house I shared with Randi in Tulsa, but you might be right about the space. While it was fine with Randi and I, Mom and Ashlyn will definitely be much more in my face than Randi was when we roomed together." Amy pushed aside the folder for the house on Wildcatter Way and looked at the two Victorians again.

"If you're wantin' to have some separation between your bedroom and your mom and sister's rooms, then I'd pick the one on Saddle Street," Justin finally advised, breaking the silence. "With the way the attic space was turned into a master suite, you'll have a floor between you and the other two bedrooms."

"You could convert the attic on Roper to do the same thing but with bigger bedrooms," Tully asserted, pointing to the other file in front of Amy. "We could call my son, Dalton, to give you an estimate on the cost and time frame for putting in a bathroom up there to make it more like the Saddle Street property."

"No." Amy shook her head as she made up her mind. "I'm sure it'll cost more than the difference in price to renovate an entire floor, especially with putting in a master bathroom comparable to Saddle Street. And I'd like to move in as soon as possible without living in a construction zone, so I'll go with the Saddle Street house."

"Very well, let's get the paperwork started." Tully turned in his chair to pull some forms from a desk drawer beside him. "With getting all your loan paperwork earlier this week, we can push for a quick closing, possibly as early as next Friday. Is that soon enough for you to move in?"

"Yes, that's perfect. I should be able to move all my stuff next weekend and be outta the way when James and Randi come back to their house the following week." Amy bit her bottom lip as she contemplated asking Justin to help her move, so she'd have someone to help her with the heavy lifting. *Is that too much to ask for a friend? Will I be able to resist pushing him down on my bed and riding that sexy cowboy if he helps me carry my bed in and set it up? This move would be so much easier if I knew who I could hire to move me. Or if I had all the help we had last month to unload the truck when we got here from Tulsa.* "Or maybe I should wait until they're home to help me move my heavy furniture?"

"You don't hafta wait on James to help you move." Justin's voice came out almost like a growl, unintentionally making Amy's nipples harden in her bra. "I have a truck and a brother to help me with any extra heavy lifting that you don't need to do, Sweetheart, so I'll help you move next weekend."

"Oh, um, okay," Amy stuttered, more flustered by her arousal than planning her move. "If you're sure JJ won't mind helping, too."

"If he's got other plans and can't help, then I'll call Aiden or Leo, if any of your furniture is too heavy for you and I to carry." Amy relished the way Justin reached over and squeezed her hand reassuringly as he presented his backup plan, unable to fight the tingles he caused with his innocent touch.

"I don't think there's anything super heavy. Just my mattress is probably gonna be difficult to get up to the third floor." *And I'm gonna be in so much trouble if it's just the two of us who carry it up there.*

"Then we'll be fine. And we can double-check to see if anyone else is available to help on Tuesday at Brie's birthday party." Justin pulled their joined hands up to kiss the back of hers before turning back toward Tully, who was asking questions about the paperwork.

Amy was grateful that Justin was able to help fill in the blanks on the forms while her brain short-circuited for a moment, soaking in all

Leah Mae Wright

the flutters she was feeling from the brief brush of his pillow-soft lips against her skin.

Yeah, it doesn't matter who helps me move. I'm in trouble because these feelings for Justin aren't going away. If anything, they're getting stronger and harder to resist.

<p style="text-align:center">~~~</p>

Tully hadn't been joking about Amy being able to close quickly on the house on Saddle Street. She'd put in her offer on Saturday, and it was accepted before Tully hung up the phone from calling the previous owners to tell them there was even an offer. They finished up all the paperwork before Justin insisted on taking her to dinner to celebrate. Amy initially refused, thinking it would feel too much like a date. But when he invited a few of their friends to meet them at Millie's Diner, she gave in since there wasn't anything date-like about a casual dinner with friends.

She'd been surprised that his sisters and cousins weren't at the diner, but still had a good time with JJ, Aiden, Leo, Landon, Dalton, Kara, Cassidy, Lexi, Kayla, and Sierra joining them. It was nice getting to know a few of the people she hadn't spent as much time with the previous Saturday when the group had split up some while bowling.

Once Brie's, or rather, Brooklyn's press release hit on Monday, Amy figured out why Bobby and the female contingent of the Burleson family had been busy on Saturday evening. Then when her birthday party was interrupted and the family rallied around to determine who all would be accompanying her back to Georgia to deal with her family and legal issues, Amy had opted not to ask anyone else in the Burleson family to help her move. They had more than enough to deal with for the next few weeks, so she didn't want to infringe on their family time, when she knew Randi's boyfriend would gladly help her if she couldn't move the big stuff before they came home for their pay-per-view weekend. She could move the small stuff in her car, even if she had to wait another week for her furniture.

100

It won't be the first time I've made a pallet on the floor to sleep instead of having a bed.

As crazy as the situation with Brooklyn had been earlier in the week, Amy was glad to see there were no longer any reporters camped out on the road in front of Burleson Incorporated as she left work early to go close on her house. It'd been difficult to pull out of the parking lot around them for a couple days after the press release went viral, both there in San Antonio and on Rogers Road in Heart's Destiny, when she tried to go in the side entrance to the Hunters' property to get to James's house, where she was still staying.

The Heart's Destiny Police Department had stepped up patrols, and mostly had the roads around the Burleson Ranch cleared of reporters by Tuesday. But the San Antonio Police Department only came out to deal with them at the business headquarters when they received a call complaining of them blocking traffic. It wasn't until the reporters got wind of the fact that Brooklyn was back in Georgia that they quit showing up at Burleson Incorporated.

I hope the security guards Bobby hired are able to keep the vultures outta Brook's face while she's there.

Amy tried to distract herself from thoughts of Justin by thinking of her other friends and what they were going through as she made the hour-long drive back to Heart's Destiny to the realtor's office. Between the breaking news of Brie Brooks being Brooklyn Barns and having to go deal with the legal issues her father was causing her, and remembering back to her text conversations with James to help plan sneaking all their family and friends into the arena for his proposal to Randi at the upcoming pay-per-view, Amy had a lot of things to let her mind ponder. Unfortunately, they still weren't enough to keep Justin out of her head for the full hour she was driving.

Her phone ringing over the Bluetooth in her car really didn't take her mind off him because she knew as soon as she saw "Mom" on the radio display that her mother would be inundating her with more questions about her hot boss. They'd talked a couple times a week since Amy had moved, and Andrea Lawton never failed to ask about Justin on any of their phone calls or video chats.

"Hi, Mom," Amy greeted her mother when she pushed the button on her steering wheel to accept the call.

Leah Mae Wright

"Have you signed the papers yet? When are you gonna send me a picture of your new house?" Amy's mother didn't bother with pleasantries when she was excited and needed information.

"No, Mom, I haven't signed the papers yet. I worked this morning and just took off half a day to go to the closing. I'm on my way there now."

"Oh, okay. Is Justin with you?"

Wow! Less than a minute into the conversation and she's asking about Justin. I think that might be a record for the fastest she's asked about him.

"No, he's still at work." *And I didn't ask him to take off work to come with me.*

"Really? I thought he'd be with you since he went to look at all the houses with you."

"Mom, he's a vice president in a multi-billion dollar corporation. He has more important things to do than take off work to watch me sign some papers." Amy shook her head at her mother's ridiculousness at thinking Justin would blow off work to go to her house closing, even though she knew her mom couldn't see her through the phone.

"Yes, well, even vice presidents take time off work for the women they love," Andrea grumbled.

"We're just friends and coworkers," Amy objected.

"Friends and coworkers who obviously wanna be a whole lot more to each other. I saw the way you two were looking at each other last weekend. Love was written, plain as day, on both ya'll's faces."

"Mom, please." Amy didn't want to argue with her mother, but she wasn't ready to admit to her growing feelings for Justin to herself yet, much less to her mother.

"Don't *'Mom, please'* me," Andrea chided, placing special emphasis on the words "mom" and "please," mimicking the way Amy had said it first. "I know what I saw when you introduced me to that boy."

"I knew I shouldn't've answered your Skype call while we were looking at houses last week."

"Nonsense! If you hadn't, then I wouldn't've gotten to meet him until I come down for a visit and that's way too long for my daughter to be dating someone without me meeting him."

"I'm not dating him," Amy protested. "We're just friends."

"Oh, Amy, you may not think you're dating him, but having lunch with him every day at work, and then spending your days off house hunting and going out with friends together is dating. He's just sneaking in those dates because you're too stubborn to agree to a more traditional date with him. Mark my words, by this time next year, he'll have finally worn you down to the point you'll be married and knocked up with my first grandbaby."

"Geez, Mom, can you pick a better term than knocked up? You sound like Ashlyn." Amy laughed at the crass terminology and hoped mentioning her sister would help change the subject. *Thank goodness we're not on Skype for her to see my facial expression at the thought of getting married and having babies with Justin. She'd know she's on point with my secret dreams if she could see me now.*

"It's more like your sister sounds like me," Andrea chuckled along with Amy.

"Hey, speaking of Ashlyn, is she coming down with you when you visit me?"

"I don't know yet. We need to pick a week for me to take my vacation to come down, so she can see if she can get that time off too."

"Okay, well, I'm just getting the keys today. It'll take me at least a couple weeks to move my stuff and figure out what else I need to buy to furnish the other two bedrooms. So, the third week of February is the earliest I can have your rooms ready."

"Then let's plan to come down the twenty-third and go home on March third, if that works for you."

"Yeah, that should be fine," Amy agreed as she parked her car at Walker Realty. "I'm at the realtor's office, so I have to go. I'll text you pictures as soon as I have the keys."

"Congratulations, honey! I can't wait to see the pictures. Love you."

"Love you, too, Mom." They disconnected the call just in time for Amy to go into the realty office for her closing.

Amy met the daughter of the couple who'd lived in her new house for over seventy years. After sharing stories about her youth growing up in the home, how she'd fixed it up after her parents passed away, and then hadn't had time to come enjoy the home, even on vacations with her busy life in Houston, the woman finally signed the paperwork officially making Amy a homeowner.

While she imagined some of her earlier ancestors might have been landowners a few generations back, knowing her mother and grandparents had always rented made her feel like the first in her family to achieve this milestone in life. As soon as the paperwork was done, she snapped a picture of the keys with her phone and sent it to her mother.

Amy: Papers are signed. It's officially mine.

Mom: So proud of you! Can't wait to see pictures of the house.

Amy: I'm going to grab a few things to move before I go home, so it'll be an hour or so before I send them.

Mom: Maybe I'll have heard back from Ashlyn by then. ;)

Amy swung by H.E.B. on her way back to the Hunters' to pick up some cleaning supplies. Once she felt prepared to clean her new home from top to bottom, she loaded up her Kia Forte with as many boxes of her things as she could fit. Then she went to spend her evening cleaning and unpacking, feeling accomplished, even as her mother's prediction for her future with Justin dominated her thoughts.

As she settled on a pallet on her new bedroom floor to go to sleep for the night, Amy was glad she'd carried her box of adult toys with her in the first round of things she moved into her new home. *Even if I don't wanna admit that Mom's right about my feelings for Justin, I still need to be able to alleviate the ache for him in my pussy that my dreams about him keep causing.*

~~~
~~~

Justin was up bright and early on Saturday morning, looking forward to spending another day with Amy, even though he knew it was going to be a day of hard labor with moving her furniture to her new house. He spent extra time in the shower jacking off to thoughts of Amy, just as he'd done more times than he wanted to admit since he met her back in November.

"No, Amy, Sweetheart." Justin stopped the fantasy version of Amy, who was sinking to her knees in his shower. "As much as I love the feel of your mouth on me, I need your tight pussy more."

"But I wanna taste you," fantasy Amy cooed, her voice sultry as she reached for his hard cock with both hands.

"Next time," Justin replied, taking her hands in his to pull her back up to standing. As soon as she was on her feet, Justin released her hands to grip her hips and lift her up. "I need you too bad right now, Sweetheart."

"Oh, Justin," Amy practically purred, her arms going around his neck as her legs wrapped around his waist.

He lined up the blunt head of his thick dick with her wet cunt and pushed his way into heaven as their mouths collided in an almost frantic kiss. There was no room for talking as the strokes of his tongue matched the thrusts of his cock into Amy's sweet body.

Amy's passion matched Justin's perfectly. She dug her nails into his shoulders where she clung to him and used the strength of her legs to grind down on him every time he plunged fully inside her.

Needing to make her come first, Justin pressed her against the wall of the shower, so he could release his grip on her hips with one hand to rub his thumb over her clit to get her there faster. He alternated the pressure, setting a pattern to keep her stimulated constantly. He pushed down harder on her bundle of nerves as he pulled his cock from her cunt. Then as he thrust back in to rub the head of his dick on her G-spot, he lightly circled her needy nub, so the stimulation was constant, but it wasn't too much all at once.

Amy pulled back from their passionate kiss to scream out his name as she came. The intensity of the contractions of the inner walls of her pussy as she squeezed down on his cock milked him of his own orgasm.

"Fuck, yes, Amy!" Justin shouted as he painted the tan tile wall of his shower white with his cum, envisioning filling Amy's womb. He slowed the strokes of his hand as his euphoria ebbed, taking a few moments to allow his heart rate and breathing to slow down to normal.

"Fucking hell! Did imagining making a baby with Amy just make me come harder than usual? Talk about putting the cart before the horse." Justin berated himself as he rinsed off the wall and finished his shower. "I can't exactly make babies with her, when I can't even figure out how to ask her out as more than a friend."

Once he'd finished getting dressed for the day, Justin made sure the dolly he'd bought at the hardware store on his way home the night before was strapped down in the back of his truck, so it wouldn't rattle around again before heading out.

He took the ranch road south from his house to the South Rogers Road gate on the ranch, so he didn't have to drive through the middle of the rest of the family houses on the north side of the ranch. It was a longer way off the ranch, taking him past several pastures, the south bunkhouse, and Bobby's house before exiting out to Rogers Road. But it was worth the extra mileage to keep from being spotted by someone who would inevitably insist he stop for breakfast. Since he knew Bobby and Brooklyn were still in Georgia, he kind of wanted to check on their house, too, since they'd had reporters trying to get to them all week.

Once he exited the family ranch, he headed north on Rogers Road, and almost immediately turned right into the Hunters' property to go to James's house, where Amy had been staying since moving to town. He was surprised to find that she wasn't there, thinking she'd have had to sleep there the night before, since her bed hadn't been moved to her new house yet. He briefly thought about going in the usually unlocked house to see what he could load up to take to Amy's new place. But he decided against it, since he wasn't sure what all would be ready to load that wouldn't require a second person to help with the lifting, and he didn't want to move boxes without Amy with him, in case he got confused and accidentally moved some of Randi's things.

Instead of going straight to Amy's new house, he first swung by Kara's Kakes for a dozen donuts for breakfast, then to the Caffeinated Cowpoke for his morning java and the caramel macchiato Amy preferred. Once he had their morning treats from the center of town, he headed back south on Angus Avenue to the subdivision between American Paint Road and Quarter Horse Drive, and weaved his way through to Amy's new house on Saddle Street.

He parked in the driveway behind her Kia and carried their breakfast up the three steps to the porch where he rang the doorbell. It took a while before he even heard anyone rustling around inside. Just as he was about to ring the bell a second time, he saw Amy rushing down the stairs through the window in the front door.

He thought she was sexy as fuck, regardless of what she wore to work and when they hung out together on the weekends. But when she answered the door wearing a pair of fuzzy black shorts with yellow fairies on them, a yellow tank top that revealed more of her curves than it concealed, and had her hair wrapped up in a yellow silk scarf to match, all Justin could think was, *She's fucking adorable.*

"Morning, Sweetheart." Justin held up the drink tray and box of donuts, hoping she focused on them and didn't notice the bulge in his pants from seeing her in the childlike, yet revealing, sleepwear. "I brought breakfast to make sure we're fueled up for the move."

"Oh, um, thanks." Amy backed up to make room in the doorway for Justin to walk in her house. "Sorry, I was up half the night cleaning and unpacking what I brought over here yesterday. I didn't realize you were still planning to help me move, with everything going on with Bobby and Brook, or I would've set an alarm to get up earlier. But, um, give me a few minutes to run back upstairs and get dressed. You can take that to the kitchen, and, um, I'll meet you in there in a few."

Amy practically slammed the door as soon as Justin stepped through it and ran up the stairs before he could formulate a reply to her nervously muttered words.

"Yeah, um, take your time," Justin uttered to the blur of Amy that disappeared up the stairs, chuckling lightly as he made his way to the kitchen through the dining room that was off to the right of the foyer.

Justin realized what had kept Amy up late when he saw the coffee pot and other small appliances already set up on the granite countertops. She'd also already stacked the dishes in the glass-front white cabinets, but he couldn't tell if she'd filled the rest of the cabinets, since there were only a couple with the decorative glass that he could see through.

He put the box of donuts and drink-carrier tray down on the island, taking his coffee out of the carrier to take a sip while he waited for Amy to get dressed. *Damn, it's too bad we can't stay here all day, so she didn't hafta change clothes.*

Justin took advantage of being alone in the kitchen to adjust himself in his jeans, trying to make his erection less obvious. And maybe a little more comfortable, instead of pressing into his zipper, since he figured he'd be sporting a hard-on all day while working with Amy.

His constant arousal whenever he was in the same room as her, or even thought of her, already had him wearing dress pants to work instead of his normal jeans. The more relaxed fit of his slacks gave him a little more room and provided better coverage for the boners he'd had every day in the lab, but he couldn't exactly wear them while moving furniture and doing anything where he might have to crawl around on the floor, like checking the water connections under the sinks, behind the toilets, and when he hooked up her washing machine.

He'd actually thought about wearing sweatpants when he started to dress for the day, but he noticed the tent in them as soon as he put them on and thought about Amy, so he had no other option but to wear jeans.

Maybe I should look into finding some jeans for men that have spandex in them like the ones Jen and Julie used to wear when we were in high school? They'd at least stretch to give me a little room, instead of squeezing my dick into an uncomfortable angle.

"Sorry that took so long," Amy apologized as she came bounding into the kitchen.

Holy fuck! Who needs fairy shorts when she's wearing yoga pants?

He might not be able to see the smooth skin on the long length of her legs, but he could certainly see the definition in her thighs and ass with the skintight black pants that were little more than tights. She'd paired them with an orange Under Armor t-shirt style top that stopped on her hips just before the globes of her ass flared out and the vee neckline gave him just the barest view of about an inch of cleavage.

Thank God Doc said those commercials that say to go to the hospital if you have an erection that won't go down after four hours are talking about the side effects of medication. Seeing Amy in those skin-tight clothes the whole time we're moving her stuff is probably gonna have me hard all fucking day.

"Why haven't you eaten yet?" Amy's question startled Justin into realizing he'd just been standing there staring at her the whole time she'd been in the room, which was apparently longer than Justin realized since she'd gotten down plates and had already put a couple donuts on hers.

"While I knew your coffee preference, I didn't know what kinda donuts you like." Justin shook off his Amy-induced stupor and moved to pick a couple of the ones she hadn't chosen out of the box of donuts. "I wanted to wait and let you have first pick from the assortment, so I didn't risk taking the only ones you liked."

"Oh, well, that's sweet, but I'm not nearly as picky about donuts as I am about my coffee." Amy smiled up at him as she lifted a chocolate frosted donut to her lips. "I'd eat any of the ones you brought today, so if we do this again, don't wait on me to eat your favorites."

"I'll remember that." Justin picked up the cinnamon sugar donut he'd gotten out of the box while Amy took her first bite.

The moan that escaped her throat as she chewed the chocolate-covered, yeast-style pastry would also be stuck in Justin's memory for years to come. *Fuck, I wonder if she'll make that same sound when I'm buried deep inside her?*

They didn't talk much as they each devoured their breakfast because their mouths were too busy masticating three donuts each. Justin was glad that she wasn't like some women who avoided carbs at all costs.

He'd worried about her eating enough when they first started eating lunch together and she stuck to mostly salads and fruit that she brought from home. But after that first day when he'd gotten one of each of the four desserts offered in the cafeteria and insisted she split them with him, he'd found out she had a sweet tooth and ate healthy most of the time, so she could indulge it daily.

"So, what's the plan for today?" Justin finished his coffee and tossed the cup in the trashcan she already had set up in the corner of the room.

"Well, I was just gonna keep moving boxes in my car." Amy rinsed their plates and put them in the dishwasher. "But since you have your truck here, we can move the furniture that's not too heavy for the two of us. We'll have to wait until someone stronger than me is available to help with the sofa, washer, and dryer."

"I've got a dolly in my truck, so I can probably still move those."

"Oh, yeah, that'll definitely help with the washer and dryer, but I don't know if it'll work for the sofa. We didn't have one for the move down here," Amy elaborated, as they walked toward the front door.

"How did ya'll move the bigger stuff without a dolly?" Justin stopped at the front door for Amy to grab her purse and keys.

"James had to bear hug the washer and dryer to move them," Amy replied, locking the front door after they walked outside. "And it took Randi and I on one end of the sofa with James on the other to move it because of it being so awkward. He actually suggested we turn it up on one end, so he could carry it the same way he carried the washer and dryer. But with him having to stop and set the washer and dryer down every twenty or thirty feet, we vetoed that idea to keep him from putting the end of the sofa down in the dirt once he got it outta the house. And it only took one of us to help him with the mattresses and box springs, since they really just needed to be guided through the hallway at our old house and are more awkward than heavy."

Maybe not heavy for James, Justin thought as they went to their separate vehicles to go back to James's house. His brain was already working on figuring out how to maneuver her queen-sized mattress up to the third floor with just the two of them. *But I have a feeling her mattress is gonna be the hardest thing we move today, if it's too big to strap onto the dolly. Maybe being too worn out from all this heavy lifting will keep me from getting a hard-on while picturing Amy laid out for me on her bed. Who am I kidding? I'm already sporting a half-chub from picturing her laid out naked on her bed while I lick and touch every inch of her delectable body. Hopefully, being worn out will keep me from freaking her out by suggesting it once we have her bed set up in her house.*

As the day went on, Justin felt like he was really getting into deeper conversations with Amy while they moved her furniture. As they moved her living room and dining room furniture, covering the end of her sofa with a tarp so he could use the dolly, they talked more about her family, with Amy telling him stories about growing up in Tulsa. As they loaded up her bedroom furniture, Amy told him how close she was to her grandparents before they passed away while she was in college. And as they moved her bedroom furniture into her new house and put together her bedframe, Amy told him all she knew about her father was what her mother had told her because he'd been killed in action in Somalia in October of 1993, without having the opportunity to come home to meet his daughters, who were born in June that same year.

"You think he was the love of your mom's life?" Justin wondered as they carried the box springs up to her third-floor bedroom. It wasn't really heavy enough for Justin to need her help carrying it. It was more that he didn't want the front end to run into a wall because it was too bulky to turn the corners without her guiding the way. "Like maybe she hasn't settled down with anyone else because nobody else can compete with her soulmate?"

"I don't know," Amy replied, sounding a little down about the change of topic. "She seems to think so, but I'm not sure there's only one person in the whole world for each of us. I mean, if he was really her soulmate, it kinda sucks to think she only got to be with him for a few months before he went off to war and died, and now she has to suffer the heartbreak of not being with him for the rest of her life."

"Yeah, I guess I can see your point," Justin reluctantly admitted, worried her thoughts on soulmates would carry over to them not being fated to be together. "Maybe she just thought he was *The One* when she hasn't really met her soulmate yet."

"Or maybe our family is just cursed when it comes to love, and she should just enjoy being single," Amy retorted.

"You don't really believe that, do you?" Justin didn't know how he could ever change her mind if she did.

"Maybe," Amy sighed, sounding skeptical. Or maybe Justin just hoped she was skeptical of her family being cursed to not finding true love. "With seeing Anthony and Kay, then James and Randi, and now Bobby and Brook, all finding what looks like fairy-tale love, I have to wonder if my belief that I'll never get married or find the mystical *One* is wrong. But I'm still not holding my breath for him to find me. I'm happy being single and don't have any plans for a serious relationship anytime soon, if ever."

Justin didn't know how to respond to her statement about possibly never being in a serious relationship, so he just put the box springs down on her bedframe and ran back down the stairs to get her mattress next from the back of his truck.

Leah Mae Wright

Amy was quiet as they carried the mattress in, probably because she was struggling with the weight at her end, since it was much heavier than the box springs. When she had to take a break to rest on the second-floor landing, Justin tried to joke to lighten the mood.

He leaned against the mattress that was propped up against the wall, and quipped, "I bet I'm the best-looking guy to ever lay his head on your bed."

"You're the only guy to ever lay your head on my bed," Amy responded, laughing. Justin didn't know if she was laughing at his joke or the goofy face he was making, but he was happy to hear her mood improve.

"Oh, even better!" Justin wagged his eyebrows at Amy. "I haven't popped a cherry since senior prom."

"Yeah, well mine was popped in college, so you're not popping it…"

"I was talking about your mattress, not you." Justin cut her off. "Though I find it hard to believe you've never shared your bed with a boyfriend."

"I've never really had a boyfriend," Amy admitted as they picked up the mattress to go up the next flight of stairs. "I lost my virginity after a frat party in college with someone who could best be described as a friend with benefits. And since then, I've just had hookups or maybe a weekend fling, but never anything serious enough to bring home, where he could track me down later when I was ready to be done with him."

I guess her lack of belief in relationships started young, Justin thought while trying to figure out how to respond to her statement about her sexual history.

"I've only had a couple girlfriends," Justin finally admitted, thinking telling her his sexual history was appropriate since she'd just told him hers. "Though I'm not sure the first one in high school really counts since we didn't ever do more than hang out as friends. I lost my virginity on prom night my senior year. It was Fiona's first time too, but our relationship didn't survive past our first semester of college. I had another girlfriend later in college, but when I found out she was more interested in the family business than me, I pretty much gave up on dating anyone seriously. It's just been too hard to trust anyone to be into me for me, and not my last name or bank account.

Since then, it's been like you described after college, hookups and weekend flings."

"But you still believe you'll find your soulmate one day?" Amy's question came out just as they got to the third-floor landing, so he took advantage of her not being able to see his face around the bulky queen-sized mattress to answer.

"Yeah. Can't be a Burleson without believing in one day finding true love." *And you're it for me, Amy.*

Chapter Four

Justin stared at himself in the executive floor men's room mirror at Burleson Incorporated while he practiced what he wanted to say to Amy at lunch. After struggling with himself to keep from pulling Amy into his arms and kissing her all weekend while he helped her move, he knew it was time for him to step up and ask her out before his baser instincts took over and pushed him into skipping a few steps that were required to make her his.

The physical activity of moving her furniture had provided them just enough distance to let down their guards and delve deeper into getting to know one another. They'd talked about their family histories and what they each saw for themselves in the future.

While he hated hearing her doubt she'd ever find true love, it was easier to talk about their romantic histories when they had a mattress between them that was a struggle to get up a couple flights of stairs than when they were seated and looking into each other's eyes while having lunch together. So, Justin had gone there to try and push them out of the friend zone just a bit, in the hopes of proving her wrong about finding her one true love, since he thought she was it for him.

After their first confessions about losing their virginity and only having hookups and weekend flings since college, Justin told her about also never bringing a woman home to his bed. They'd taken a break in moving for Amy to make her bed and delved deeper into why their years since college had been similar with the occasional fling or one-night stand to scratch an itch, finally admitting that neither of them had ever felt like they'd connected with someone who they wanted to be with long term.

Justin wished he'd confessed his feelings for her then, but he'd chickened out, since he wanted to be able to look into her eyes to see her true response when he asked her to be more than friends. He couldn't blurt out his feelings while watching her perfect ass as she was bent over to put the sheets on her mattress.

Now he was thinking about revisiting that conversation while having lunch with her, wanting to see if she'd give him a chance to take her out on a date or two at least, even though he wasn't sure he could convince her they could be more.

"Hey, uh, Amy," Justin spoke to his reflection. "You remember the other day when we were talking about not ever feeling like we've met *The One*? Yeah, I, uh, wasn't exactly honest when I said that. I do think I've met the woman I'm meant to spend my life with, and I honestly think you're her. I know you just wanna be friends, but will you please give me a chance to see if we can be more by going on a real date with me?"

"Oh, fuck, Bro." Justin's brother, JJ, shook his head as he walked into the men's room. "Don't ask her like that. She'll say no for sure."

"What was wrong with that?" Justin turned away from the mirror to look at his older brother.

"Well, for one, it wasn't confident enough." JJ leaned against the frame of the stalls. "And for two, if you tell her you think she's *The One*, you'll freak her out by moving too fast."

"You don't think I should be honest with her and tell her how I've felt since the first time I saw her?" Justin wasn't sure how he felt about not being completely honest with her when he asked her out.

"Not yet," JJ replied, shaking his head. "Save that for once you're outta the friend zone, and she's starting to fall for you."

"Is that your plan for Deanna?" Justin wondered if JJ would ever act on the obvious feelings he had for Kay's best friend.

"It's what I wish I'd done with Deanna," JJ mumbled, no longer making eye contact with Justin. "Trust me when I say it's a mistake to declare your undying love too soon."

"Fuck, man, is that what happened between you two?" Justin was blown away by the revelation his brother had just inadvertently delivered.

"Something like that." JJ avoided answering by stepping into one of the stalls, but Justin waited him out by turning back to the mirror and running through some scripts in his head of what to say to Amy while JJ did his business.

When JJ stepped out of the stall and up to the sink beside Justin to wash his hands, Justin caught his brother's eye in the mirror. "You ever gonna actually tell me about the first time you met her?"

JJ took a deep breath, blowing it out through his nose as he finished washing his hands and stuck them under the hand dryer. "I met her in the hotel bar at an energy conference in twenty-fifteen," JJ confided when the hand dryer cut off. "I knew the first moment I saw her that she's *The One* for me. We hooked up and ended up spending every night together the week we were there. On the last day of the conference, I told her how I felt, thinking we'd do long distance for a while until she was ready to move here." JJ hung his head when he quit speaking.

Too impatient to withstand the silence while his brother collected his thoughts, Justin inquired, "And how did she respond to that?"

"She told me that our week-long fling was just a hookup for her." JJ's voice was low, sounding almost defeated. "That banging a younger man was one of the things on her bucket list. And while she thanked me for checking that off for her, a long-term relationship with me didn't fit into her future plans."

"Fuck, man, that's brutal." Justin hoped and prayed that Amy wouldn't be so cruel to him if she shot him down when he asked her out. "Did she even give you a hint into her future plans, so you can figure out how to worm your way into them?"

"Oh, yeah," JJ sneered with a self-deprecating chuckle. "She was using me to make her boss jealous in the hopes that he might stake his claim and walk her down the aisle."

"Since she's still not wearing a ring, I'm guessing her plan didn't work?"

"Nope." JJ's lips spread into the slightest of smiles. "And every time I've seen her since, she's struggled to not act on our connection, so I know it's just a matter of time before I figure out how to make her mine."

"Ya know, if her goal is to marry her boss, maybe we should look into buying out her company so you're her boss," Justin suggested, grinning at his brother.

"Damn, Bro, you're starting to sound as bad as Mom and Aunt Hazel with the matchmaking plans." JJ pointed at Justin as his grin spread to match his younger brother's. "Maybe you should ask them for advice on how to ask Amy out?"

"And clue them in that they're right in picking Amy for me? No way. That'll just make 'em more confident in their schemes for everyone else."

"You're right." JJ scratched his head. "And with Deanna being back in Tulsa, they might try to push someone else at me, so we definitely don't want them to think their work is done with you two yet. Okay, so we need to come up with a way for you to ask her out, and maybe date her without the matchmaking mommas figuring it out."

"Yeah, I've already got a list of dates to take her on that are here in San Antonio. And if things progress to sleepovers, we'll do them in hotels here, or maybe at her house for as long as possible." Justin had to laugh at the way his stoic, suit-loving, serious businessman brother was nodding his head comically as he plotted out ideas in his head.

"I'd suggest sending her flowers or something, but if you send them here, one of the girls will invariably leak the info to Ma. And if you send them to her house, you'd hafta get them at Flora's and…"

"Ma or Aunt Hazel would find out from her," Justin finished his brother's sentence as JJ's words faded out. "Yeah, I'd already ruled out something like that for those reasons. And I plan to buy flowers from somewhere here instead of Flora's to take to her for our first date. If she says yes."

"She'll say yes," JJ reassured Justin. "How'd she respond to increasing the flirty conversation last weekend?"

"Pretty well." Justin ran his hand through his hair as he remembered the way they'd playfully transitioned into talking about their sexual histories from him teasing her as they carried her mattress up to her room. "We were halfway up the stairs with her mattress when she needed to set it down for a break. I laid my head on it and made a joke about being the best-looking guy to lay his head on her bed, which led to her telling me that I was the only guy to ever do that."

"Whoa! She told you she's a virgin?" JJ turned toward Justin with a shocked expression on his face.

"No," Justin quickly corrected. "Just that, like all of us, she doesn't normally bring anyone back to her place. I know we do it because we live so close to the rest of the family, but as much as I wanna think she was trying to be respectful of her roommate, I think it was more to keep her space safe from creepy clingers. Anyway, the rest of the trip up the stairs with the mattress between us, we kinda went over our sexual histories, and our conversation continued to be flirty the rest of the night. More flirtatious than it's ever been before."

"Well, that's good." JJ ran a hand through his hair while looking in the mirror to make sure it was perfectly coiffed. "So, while ya'll're eating lunch together, just go back to that flirty conversation, and then maybe reach over and hold her hand to ask her to go on a real date."

"That's kinda what I was planning to do." Justin pointed at the mirror to reference the speech he'd been practicing when JJ walked in.

"Yeah, well, quit practicing it and go do it." JJ turned toward the door. "Just don't mention any of the love-at-first-sight stuff until after she says the L-word first."

As JJ exited the restroom, Justin looked down at his watch and noticed it was time to head down to have lunch with Amy. "Fuck, I hope she says yes," he groaned to his reflection in the mirror as he washed his hands one more time before going to meet her in the cafeteria.

<div align="center">~~~</div>

Amy was surprised to see that Justin wasn't already in the cafeteria when she got down there. Usually, they either walked down together when they were both working in the lab, or he was already there waiting for her when she got focused on an experiment and he'd been working in his executive office for the day. He'd been acting a little more awkward this week, more like the way he was the week of Kay and Anthony's wedding, since their conversation on the weekend had turned flirty and sexual.

Probably because I was the one who blurted out my sexual history first, and he's worried I went there because of being like the women he told me about, who were more interested in his money than in him as a

118

person. I know I'm not a gold digger, but he doesn't know me well enough yet to realize that, or completely trust me not to be.

I still can't believe I told him he's the only man who's ever laid on my bed, Amy thought as she filled up her water bottle and got her lunch set out on their usual table. *Or about losing my virginity and not really feeling a connection with anyone I've ever been with.*

At least I didn't give him a play-by-play or tell him how they each ranked in how bad they were at it, like Ashlyn would've if she'd been the one having that conversation. Who am I kidding? If Ashlyn had met him back in November when I did, she'd have already slept with Justin, not just given him a complete sexual history right down to performance reviews. If only I were a little more like Ashlyn to be able to risk my heart a little by acting on my attraction to him.

Amy pulled her phone out of her pocket and reviewed the last text thread she'd had with her sister while drizzling dressing over her salad.

Ashlyn: Have you banged your boss yet?

Amy: No, & I'm not going to.

Ashlyn: Why not?

Amy: Because he's my boss. We have to keep things professional between us.

Ashlyn: But you said there's not a no-dating policy at your new job. And you're already hanging out with him every weekend, so why not get the benefits with the hot friend?

Amy: I don't do friends with benefits.

Ashlyn: I thought that's all you did.

Amy: That was just until I realized it didn't really work for me.

Ashlyn: So date him then.

Amy: I don't date. You know this, so why are you bugging me about it?

Ashlyn: Because I want to see my sister happy. And whether you like it or not, being happy requires finding your person. With everything you've said about Justin, he could be your person. But if you don't give him a ride or 2, you'll never know.

Amy: And if he isn't my person, are you going to pay my mortgage when I can't work here anymore?

Ashlyn: No, but I'll sign you up as a Pleasure consultant. Even if the income isn't enough to pay the bills, you'll need the employee discount for your next B-O-B, since that's the only way you'll be getting the big O.

"Who're you texting?" Justin nodded at her phone as he sat down across from her at the table.

"Nobody," Amy squeaked, quickly backing out of her text thread, and hoping Justin hadn't read any of the texts from Ashlyn that she'd been reading. Amy stuck her phone back in her pocket while begging the universe for her golden-brown complexion to be dark enough to cover the heat in her cheeks. *I shouldn't've opened that thread when I knew he'd be walking up.* "Just looking back through my text thread with my sister, so I can put a note on my calendar for when I need to go pick her and Mom up at the airport."

"That's right, you said they're coming for a visit later this month." Justin smiled, sending the swarm of butterflies in her belly into a frenzy. "When will they be here?"

"The twenty-third through the third," Amy replied, focusing on her salad, instead of looking up into Justin's sky-blue eyes.

"You'll hafta bring 'em along to JJ's birthday party on the first." Justin dug into his own food and, thankfully, did not bring up her texts again.

"Oh, no, they wouldn't wanna crash JJ's party," Amy lied, knowing full well her mother and sister would probably use any excuse to meet the Burlesons.

"They wouldn't be crashing." Justin reached over to place his palm on her free hand. "I'm inviting them. I'm not sure if we'll have anything else going on that week, but I'm sure my mom and Aunt Hazel will wanna plan something as soon as they find out you have family in town, just so they can meet 'em. Inviting your family to JJ's party takes away their chance to do something embarrassing to meet 'em the first day they're in town."

Amy's head popped up, her eyes locking with Justin's when he mentioned his mom and aunt doing something embarrassing to meet her mom and sister. "You think they'd do something embarrassing?"

"With the way they're scheming against Charlotte lately, I wouldn't put anything past them." Justin shook his head.

"What're they doing to Charlotte?" Amy was glad for a change in subject, so she didn't have to contemplate the level of embarrassment that would be reached if Ashlyn met the Burleson women on her first day in town and convinced them to host a Pleasure party for their daughters and friends. It was best nobody found out about her sister's side business doing home parties for an adult toy company, especially the upstanding members of the community that ran the corporation where Amy currently worked.

"Well, you know how they moved Brook in with Bobby and were planning to do the same with the other housekeeper they hired to fix up either JJ or I."

"Yeah." Amy felt her inner green-eyed monster making an appearance at the thought of another woman moving in with Justin, but she tried to keep her facial expression blank, so it didn't show.

"Well, they hired Cait, Ian's sister that we met at Christmas, but since she lives with her brother to be able to take care of his son, she wasn't willing or able to move to the ranch. So, in addition to what Tully told us about how they've been working with his wife, Lisa Walker, the principal at the middle school, to have her push Charlotte and Ian together at school, they've started taking advantage of Cait having Brody with her when she works on the ranch. When Char gets home, if Cait's still working, they've been sending Brody to Char's house, trying to get Char to fall for the kid, as well as the dad."

"Is it working?" Amy couldn't stop herself from asking.

Justin shrugged. "Char claims Ian's too much of a pain in the ass for her to ever fall for him, but she sure does seem to enjoy teaching Brody all about the horses. And of course, Aunt Hazel had to invite Ian, Cait, and Brody to come to the ranch for a trail ride after church last weekend."

"And let me guess, Charlotte had to be the one to take them riding?"

"That's how Aunt Hazel was pushing it, but the rest of us took pity on Charlotte and went along for the ride, too. Well, those of us who were home, anyway." Justin's expression turned somber, and Amy knew it was because he was worried about Bobby and Brook still being in Georgia. His sister, father, and uncle had gone to help, too.

"Have you heard from anyone about how things are going with Brook and Bobby in Georgia?" Amy turned her hand over under Justin's, so she could squeeze it reassuringly as she asked the question.

"Yeah, apparently, her father was arrested yesterday, along with her former fiancé." Justin returned her comforting gesture.

"Well, that's good news, right?" Amy smiled at him, thinking it was probably what was best for Brooklyn.

"Yeah, but it's just the first step. They're going back to mediation today to see if they can settle anything with her family trust and the company, but it's gonna be a while longer before everything's settled, so they can come home. And even then, they'll probably hafta go back there from time to time to deal with Ashbury business."

They sat and ate in a comfortable silence for a little while before Amy realized they were still holding hands. "Wow, sorry." Amy pulled her hand back from Justin's grasp. "I didn't mean to hold your hand like that. I…" Amy's words trailed off when she couldn't figure out how to explain her inappropriate behavior.

"Nothing to be sorry for, Sweetheart." Justin reached over and pulled her hand back into his. "I like holding your hand."

"But it was just supposed to be a quick comforting gesture when you looked worried about your family." Amy tugged again on her hand, but Justin didn't let go. "Anything more is inappropriate for friends and coworkers."

"And what if I wanna be more than friends and coworkers?" Justin's eyes filled with so much emotion that Amy couldn't deny his sincerity in wanting more with her.

She'd been lying to herself for months now, using the excuse that her attraction to him wasn't reciprocated to justify not acting on it. Seeing his normally baby blue eyes darken to a bright sapphire, showing more feelings for her than the lust she was willing to acknowledge, made it impossible for her to keep hiding behind the façade she'd tried to put between them.

"How much more than friends and coworkers?" Amy was grateful her words sounded strong and didn't show the jitters she was feeling inside.

"I don't know." Justin placed his fork down on his plate and wrapped both of his hands around hers in the center of the table. "I think we'll hafta take it day by day and see just how far we're both comfortable goin' together."

"Oh, okay," Amy stuttered, not really sure what she meant by the words tumbling uninhibited from her mouth. "I can be comfortable with holding hands with a friend."

"Good, then I'm gonna hold your hand every chance I get." Justin gave her a beaming smile as he squeezed her hand in his. "How 'bout goin' on a date with me?"

"I, uh, I don't date." Amy shook her head, trying to clear it of the crazy mix of emotions fluttering through her.

"No?" Justin tilted his head inquisitively. "Then what did you call the outings you had with the guys you told me about on Saturday?"

"Those were short-term arrangements to fill a need with no strings, no attachments."

"So, friends with benefits?" Justin's raised eyebrow made Amy feel uncomfortable with what she was about to say.

"No, I might've called my first a friend with benefits, but looking back on it now, I wouldn't consider any of those guys friends and the benefits were sorely lacking."

"So, all you're willing to do is fuck buddies?"

Amy's blush had spread from her cheeks to cover her whole face, neck, and chest at his crass description.

"I'm okay with that if that's what you want." The right side of Justin's mouth lifted up in a half-smile. "I think our instant attraction and easy friendship connection means we should be more than that, but I'm willing to keep things as casual as you need them to be comfortable."

"I'm not really comfortable with any of this." Amy waved her free hand back and forth between them, not realizing she was flinging salad dressing over both their dishes because she was still holding her fork with a bite on it.

"Why not? What makes us acting on the attraction we feel for each other different than what you've had with other guys in the past?"

"That easy friendship connection you mentioned." Amy realized just then that she'd only glossed over her feelings about not having a long-term relationship in her future during their conversation the previous weekend, and she hated that she was going to have to explain it in detail now. "I told you, I've never felt a connection with anyone in my past. I've also told you a little about my family history, how I lost my dad right after I was born, and then watched my mom date a bunch of losers."

"That's made me very skeptical about relationships lasting. Even if it's more than a fleeting lust, people die and leave whether they want to or not. And I don't wanna suffer through a broken heart if it doesn't work out, or die of a broken heart like my Nana did after losing my Papa. So, I don't date or do relationships, and I only sleep with guys I know I'll never fall in love with."

"And our connection is already more than I've ever felt with a guy before, so I'm scared of what being more than friends with you could mean. If it ends like all my mom's bad relationships have, then I'll be out of a job on top of having a broken heart. I'm not willing to risk that."

"Oh, Sweetheart, you won't…" Justin's words trailed off as he ran his free hand through his hair and looked at Amy like he was trying to figure out how to word his next statement. "I can't guarantee that we'll both live to be a hundred years old and go peacefully together in our sleep, so neither one of us will hafta live with a broken heart after one of us dies. But I can guarantee that I'm not like one of your mom's former loser boyfriends. Death would be the only thing that would take me away from you, if you'd just give me a chance to see what we can be together. I can also guarantee that if you get tired of me and wanna end things between us, it won't cost you your job. You might get sick of me trying to win you back by spending all my time in the lab if you ever tried to break up with me, but your job will always be secure here."

"Did you just tell me that if I break up with you, you're gonna sexually harass me at work?" Amy had to laugh at Justin's mortified expression.

"No, absolutely not. Though I might need to check with Jen to make sure sending you flowers daily with cards declaring my undying love would be classified as sweet, boyfriend behavior, and not pushing the line of sexual harassment." Justin's expression changed to more of a goofy grin as he tried to lighten the mood between them with the joking line, even though he covered her hand with both of his to deepen their connection.

"So, if I say I just wanna be friends, are those flower deliveries gonna start tomorrow?"

Justin pulled one hand back from holding Amy's to look at his watch before locking his eyes back on hers. "I think it's still early enough in the day that I can have the first bouquet here this afternoon if I have to."

Amy just shook her head at Justin's outrageousness.

"Seriously, Amy, I understand why you're scared." Justin gave her a tentative smile. "And if you're not ready for more than friendship, then we'll stay friends for as long as you want. I'll wait as long as I have to for you to be ready for more with me. I won't harass you, with flowers or otherwise, until you tell me you're willing to go on a date with me. And even when you're ready to date, we'll take things as slow as you need. I just want a chance with you."

Oh Em Gee! Why does he have to be so sweet and sincere and give me that look that makes him so freaking hard to resist?

"If I agree to go on a date with you, what exactly am I agreeing to?"

"Dinner. A movie. Maybe a trip to SeaWorld or Six Flags. There's a really cool Japanese Tea Garden here in San Antonio where we could walk and talk. Or maybe a museum or art gallery, if that's what you'd prefer. There's also the River Walk, the Alamo, and the Tower of the Americas that you might like to see. I have a whole bunch of ideas of places we can go to just spend time together and get to know one another without the prying eyes of my family making it uncomfortable for either of us."

"Those all sound like things we could do as friends." Amy wondered if she was worried about progressing to a sexual relationship prematurely. "I thought you were talking about the, uh, benefits when you were talking about us becoming more than friends."

"Oh, Sweetheart, I definitely want those benefits." Justin wagged his eyebrows suggestively. "But friendship is the best foundation for any relationship, so I'm willing to focus on strengthening ours before we move on to the bedroom."

"Oh, wow, okay. That sounds like a plan I can live with." Amy wasn't really sure how long she'd be able to withstand doing more and more friendly outings with Justin before she'd give in to her desire to drag him to her bedroom, but she was starting to think she'd regret it if she didn't try to have a more meaningful relationship with him. "When do you wanna do our first date? I know it can't be this weekend because I wanna spend as much time with Randi as I can while she's in town."

"And we can't count goin' to the GWA show to watch James propose to her because your whole family will be there. I know you were just deflecting with Nana Marie when you said we were on the down-low, but if we're gonna do this dating thing, then we definitely need to be on the down-low with your family if this progresses to more than friendly outings."

"We probably shouldn't do anything when my mom and Ashlyn are in town either. So, that basically leaves us next weekend, right? Friday or Saturday?"

"Actually," Justin interjected when Amy finally stopped talking and took a breath. "Bobby's birthday party will be next Friday, the fifteenth, if he's back in town then."

"Oh, so, Saturday the sixteenth, then?"

"Or Thursday the fourteenth? I know we're just starting to date, but I'd kinda like to take my girlfriend out for Valentine's Day."

"Girl-girlfriend?" Amy was shocked at how Justin seemed to already want to label them. "Isn't it, um, too soon for labels like that? We haven't even gone on a date yet, or had our first kiss, or done anything that leads to labels like that."

"Relax, Sweetheart." Justin patted her hand reassuringly. "I'm not saying we need to announce it to the world or anything. And I completely agree with keeping things on the down-low with my family, that's why my date suggestions are all in San Antonio and not in Heart's Destiny where they'll get wind of anything. But that's only because I don't want them to start planning our wedding before we're ready to do more than holding hands."

Although Amy felt completely overwhelmed by the prospect of dating and maybe doing more with Justin, she couldn't stop herself from giggling at his statement about his family, knowing how true it was for his mother and aunt.

"But I believe in starting things the way we intend to go, and I intend for us to be a couple, so we should start getting used to the labels, even if we only use them with each other for now. So, I'm gonna think of you as my girlfriend. I'm gonna treat you like my girlfriend and act like your boyfriend, even if I'm only allowed to do those things when we're alone on our dates. If you're not ready to use the labels yet, I just ask you to have an open mind and think about them on occasion to see how they feel. And if you feel like I've picked the wrong labels and have better ones you wanna use, please tell me about them."

Better labels? Like what? Lovers? No, that sounds like something from a soap opera or porno. But boyfriend and girlfriend sounds like we're back in high school. Surely, he doesn't think I'll eventually suggest we switch to labels like husband and wife. Right?

Or maybe he means we should pick some better terms of endearment than him calling me Sweetheart and me calling him Boss?

"Don't think too hard on it right now, Sweetheart," Justin advised, bringing Amy back to the moment and out of her own head. "Just plan on me picking you up at seven on Valentine's Day and taking you to dinner."

"Oh, okay," Amy stuttered as Justin lifted her hand to his lips and brushed them across the back of her hand. She felt tingles where his soft lips made contact with her hand that quickly spread throughout her body. Her nipples tightened and her core clenched as his innocent kiss aroused her more than she could ever remember being turned on by any of the men she'd actually slept with in the past.

"I have a meeting I hafta get to, but I'll call you tonight if I don't make it to the lab to see you again this afternoon." With that, Justin cleared his tray of empty dishes from the table and left Amy sitting there dumbfounded as to how she'd sat down as his friend and was apparently going back to work as his girlfriend.

I wonder if he's gonna fill out the form with his sister in HR? Or do I need to do that? I'll have to remember to ask him when he calls tonight.

~ ~ ~

Saturday, February 9, 2019

Amy enjoyed the morning at the GWA Fan Expo at the Alamodome in San Antonio, even though she missed Justin since they were keeping their distance at any event his family might witness. On Thursday night when they'd talked on the phone, he'd told her not to worry about the human resources form for dating couples. He planned to take care of it by talking to someone other than his sister in the HR department, so word wouldn't get back to his family just yet. They also planned to continue to act as friends if they were seated together at any point when his family had a get-together, just as they'd been at every Burleson event since November, hoping nobody would get suspicious that things had changed between them.

It's not like they've really changed yet, Amy thought as she made her way through the crowd to where she was supposed to be meeting Randi when her commitment at the expo was completed. *Other than talking on the phone the past two nights, it's been business as usual since our lunchtime conversation about progressing our relationship past friendship.*

Amy contemplated talking to Randi about the strange turn of events, but she wasn't sure if she should before anything happened between her and Justin that was different than the status quo. *Maybe one of her therapy sessions masked as a pep talk can help me feel less anxious about going on a date with him?*

Amy really didn't have a chance to talk to Randi alone to worry much about confiding in her friend. As soon as Amy got to their meeting point, Randi dragged her out of the arena to have James and Dean move the furniture of Randi's that she didn't need for James's

128

fully furnished house over to Amy's house to fill one of her spare bedrooms.

"You sure you don't wanna keep all this?" Amy double-checked with her bestie as the guys were loading up Randi's bed, dresser, and bedside tables into their trucks to take them to Amy's house. "I already feel bad for taking the living room and dining room furniture and the washer and dryer when we'd split the cost of buying all of it."

"I'm sure." Randi shook her head, which seemed like a contradiction to her statement in Amy's opinion. "I told you when we were packing before Christmas that I didn't need any of it, since James has already furnished his house. Besides, I'd much rather know that your sister or mom are gonna be able to use it than it just sitting around, gathering dust in the garage, until I'm home long enough to sell it."

"I still feel like I should pay you for it." Amy felt guilty for taking Randi's furniture when she feared her friend might end up needing it if things didn't end up working out with her and James in the long run. Though if she were really being honest, after basically emptying her savings for the down payment on her new house the week before, Amy was going to be cutting it close to use her paycheck from the day before to furnish two bedrooms before her mother and sister came to visit. She'd originally planned to furnish one room out of this paycheck and the other on her next payday, which was February twenty-second, but she'd been worried about it being possible to have the furniture delivered the same day she bought it to set up the second spare bedroom. Randi giving her the bedroom set would save Amy a good deal of worry as well as a hefty chunk of change.

"Consider all the times you had to help me out when I was short a few bucks at the end of the month as payment in full." Randi gave Amy a one-armed hug as they stood in the garage watching the guys load up the furniture.

"Well, at least, let me cover lunch after we get this stuff moved." Amy returned Randi's embrace.

"Deal," Randi agreed as they made their way to their vehicles to drive to Amy's house.

As soon as they arrived at her house, Amy called Pistol Pete's Pizza to place their delivery order. She couldn't fathom how each of the

Hunters could put away two large pizzas each, when she and Randi couldn't finish off one combined.

And I thought Justin could eat a lot!

"Have you picked out what you're gonna put in the other bedroom yet?" Randi queried in between bites of pizza as they sat at her dining room table.

"No, but Brook's friend, Heather, was telling me about her parents' store a few weeks ago when we went bowling, so I'll be going as soon as I have time off when they're open."

"We can go as soon as we're done eating," Randi announced, looking over at James lovingly. "These two have plans to go fishing with their PopPop this afternoon, so we can go shopping, then maybe get our nails done or something."

"Whatever you wanna do." Amy swallowed a drink of her tea. "I didn't make any plans for this weekend, so I'd be free for some bestie time whenever you were."

As soon as the furniture was in place in the second-floor bedroom and the pizza was devoured, the guys left for their afternoon with their grandfather. Well, Dean left after the pizza mess was cleaned up. James gave Randi a very long, almost inappropriate for their audience, kiss goodbye first.

Amy averted her eyes as her best friend made out with her boyfriend. She wasn't sure if it was because she was trying not to be rude by staring at them, or if she was trying to keep them from seeing the flash of jealousy in her eyes because they had the type of relationship she secretly wanted.

"See you soon, Angel," James told Randi when their lips finally parted, and they started for the front door.

"Make sure you shower off the fishy smell before Amy drops me off later." Randi gave James one last peck before they went their separate ways.

Amy locked her front door before joining Randi at her car. Once Amy was behind the wheel with Randi in her passenger seat, they took off for Heart of the Home, since that was the only place they'd specifically mentioned for going shopping.

"Now that they're gone, I need all the deets on how things are going with working with Justin every day."

I guess I don't have a choice in confiding in my BFF, since Randi wasted no time in asking about my relationship with Justin, Amy thought as she turned out of her neighborhood onto Angus Avenue to go north to the center of town.

"It's, um," Amy started, not really sure how to describe her relationship with Justin at that point. "Confusing."

"Confusing? How?" Randi turned in her seat to watch Amy as she drove, leaving her no place to hide her emotions as she talked to her best friend.

"Well, we've been getting along great, staying in the friend zone, just like I wanted. But…" Amy's voice trailed off as she pondered how to explain the conversation she and Justin had at lunch on Thursday.

"But?" Randi drew the word out to multiple syllables trying to prompt Amy to keep talking. When she didn't, Randi pushed for more answers. "But you're having a hard time not climbing him like a tree and humping him every time you see him?"

"Oh, yes, that's it," Amy laughed, surprised at Randi being the one to word her question that way, instead of her sister, Ashlyn. "Getting some on the regular from James has certainly been good for you in being able to talk about sex."

"Yes, yes, it has," Randi boasted, nodding her head, and grinning like a loon. "But we're discussing your sex life right now, not mine."

"Unfortunately, the only sex life I have right now is with my B-O-B." Amy shook her head, unable to believe she was discussing her vibrator with Randi.

"Where did you find a place here to get a B-O-B? I need to get James to take me shopping again for Valentine's Day, since one of the toys we bought back in November wasn't as waterproof as we thought."

"What?" Amy almost missed her turn on Appaloosa by being so shocked at Randi's admission.

"Like you said, being with James has been very good for me." Randi wagged her eyebrows suggestively, surprising Amy.

Amy parked her car in front of Heart of the Home and stared incredulously at her best friend.

"I'll tell you all about it later." Randi waved off Amy's obvious question about her friend's surprising admission about using sex toys with James. "Tell me about you and Justin, and why you're not getting any Burleson beef stick on the regular yet."

"Who're you and what've you done with my sexually repressed best friend?"

"I'm still me." Randi held her hands up in surrender. "I've just learned to embrace my sexuality and not be embarrassed by it anymore. Well, at least, with people I trust anyway. I probably won't ever be okay talking about going sex toy shopping with my boyfriend with anyone other than a few select friends like you, but I'm not the prude my parents tried to raise me to be either."

"Well, good for you," Amy praised her friend. "And I didn't buy any of my toys in a store. I ordered them from Ashlyn's It's My Pleasure catalogue back when she first got started with her side business and was trying to get Mom and I to host a party for her."

"Oh, yeah, I forgot your sister was doing that." Randi unbuckled her seatbelt and got out of the car. "You'll have to send me a link to her online store."

Amy unbuckled her own seatbelt and followed her friend into the store. As soon as they were directed to the furniture section and were relatively alone, Randi continued her quest for information about Amy and Justin. "Okay, enough stalling, why haven't you exited the friend zone with Justin yet?"

"Honestly, I'm not sure if we're still in the friend zone or not." Amy looked around to make sure nobody was within earshot and there were no Burlesons in the store before expounding. "We've been having lunch together every day, and you know he helped me find my house and move."

Randi nodded, but she didn't say anything to interrupt Amy's explanation of her changing relationship with Justin.

"Well, on moving day, our conversation turned a little flirty. We were halfway up the stairs with my mattress when I had to take a break and set my end down. He leaned his head on the mattress while we were resting and made a joke about being the best-looking guy to lay his head on my bed."

"Wow, what a cheesy line," Randi laughed.

"Yeah, well, it worked on me. And when I told him he was the only guy to ever lay his head on my mattress, we ended up basically telling each other our full sexual histories while we finished carrying the mattress up to the third floor. Then, once it was in place on the bed frame, he laid down on the bed saying he wanted to be the first to fully lay on my bed, too. It took all my willpower to walk outta the room and not jump him while he was laying there. Thank goodness, he'd gotten up by the time I got back in there with the sheets, or I might not have been able to resist joining him in the bed." Amy felt her body heat once again at the memory of how hard it'd been to resist Justin when he was laying on her bare mattress.

"Ugh, I can't believe you're still fighting it when ya'll are so obviously perfect for one another." Randi shook her head at Amy while sitting down on a queen-sized sleigh bed.

"Yeah, well, he's apparently tired of me fighting it, too," Amy admitted, plopping down on the soft mattress beside her bestie. "Thursday at lunch, he actually asked me on a date."

Did he really ask me? Or just declare us boyfriend and girlfriend? No, he asked me at first and didn't slap a label on us until after I agreed.

"And? What did you say?" Randi looked at Amy with excitement dancing in her bright green eyes.

"I gave him all my reasons for not dating or doing friends with benefits."

"Oh, Ames!" Randi flopped back to lay across the bed dramatically.

"But he started in on a long speech about how he'd never be like my mom's loser ex-boyfriends, and how I'd always have job security at Burleson, and how he'd send me flowers every day to try to win me back if I ever broke up with him. He even said something about us living to be a hundred years old and dying together, so neither of us would ever suffer a broken heart by losing the other. His confidence that we're meant to be more than friends broke down my walls, and I finally agreed to go out with him, but only as long as nobody in his family knows, so they don't start planning our wedding when we might not ever make it there."

"Yeah, I can see why keeping it from his mom and Aunt Hazel is a major priority," Randi laughed, sitting back up and motioning to the bed. "Whaddaya think of this one?"

"It's nice." Amy actually looked at the bedroom set around them for the first time. "I think my mom will like it."

Leah Mae Wright

"Excellent, then let's get it scheduled for delivery and you can tell me all about your first date while we're next door shopping for lingerie for your next one."

"We haven't gone on our first date yet," Amy admitted as Randi was pulling her up off the bed.

"Seriously?" Randi looked shocked.

"Seriously." Amy shook her head as they walked to the register to place her furniture order. "We're going out for Valentine's Day as our first date."

"Wow, talk about pressure for a first date! We're definitely going next door to find you some new sexy undies for that date!"

Amy couldn't believe that her formerly shy, sexually repressed friend had just announced they were underwear shopping loud enough for the whole store to hear. *Thank goodness, I don't see anyone in here I recognize, who might tell the Matchmaking Mommas about my date with Justin, or what I'll be wearing that he might see at the end of it.*

~ ~ ~

Sunday, February 10, 2019

Justin couldn't believe how well everyone was getting along when the Lees returned to Texas to witness James proposing to Randi in the middle of the GWA wrestling ring at the end of the pay-per-view. After the Lees, Hunters, Burlesons, and several of their friends overflowed the ring to offer their congratulations to the happy couple, they'd all made their way to a twenty-four-hour diner, which they promptly filled to capacity for an impromptu engagement party.

Had anyone suggested back at Anthony and Kay's wedding that Charles Lee would be all smiles as he shook James's hand to welcome him into the family only two-and-a-half months later, Justin didn't think anyone who'd witnessed his outburst at Thanksgiving would've believed it was possible. But as he watched from a couple tables over, that was exactly what Justin was seeing.

When his eyes locked with Amy's from across the room, he couldn't help but wonder what her family would think of him when they met later in the month. Knowing that her family was down to just her mother and sister, Justin knew he wouldn't have to worry about an overprotective father trying to keep him and Amy apart, like James'd had to deal with when he and Randi first got together. But he still wondered if Andrea and Ashlyn Lawton would resent him for convincing Amy to move so far away from them.

I really should see if we have any job openings for them to be able to move down here, too. Maybe I'll use that as the excuse for why I'm in HR when I take that form back to Jen's second-in-command if she catches me there.

It wasn't that he didn't want to tell his sister about his change in relationship status with Amy that had him working with Sofia Reyes instead of his sister to comply with the dating rules at work. He knew Jen would be happy for him and Amy. But he also knew his mother could get the information out of Jen, and he didn't want Amy to be scared off by his meddling mom, when he was still in the process of convincing her they were meant to be a couple.

Not wanting to frighten her away from giving them a chance was why Justin had sat with his family instead of with Amy, who was seated with the Lees as Randi's best friend. He knew if there was any wedding planning going on that night, Amy needed to be at the table with Randi, since she was most likely to be a bridesmaid alongside Randi's sister, Kay. Justin assumed Anthony and Dean would be James's groomsmen since the three had been best friends since birth.

Justin wasn't sure what to do about the pang of jealousy he felt at the thought of Dean walking Amy down the aisle at James and Randi's wedding. While he'd played with the Hunters when they visited the ranch when they were all kids, he wasn't nearly close enough of a friend to them for James to want him to be a groomsman, so he could be the one to escort Amy.

Fucking hell! Why am I so freaked out over her spending a few minutes on someone else's arm at her best friend's wedding? It's not like Amy's marrying Dean, or even having to spend the whole time seated beside him at the reception. I'm being a fucking idiot for wanting to claim her like a caveman and not allow another man to share even a moment of her time.

He tried to push the negative thoughts from his head and pay attention to the conversations going on around him. He listened in as

Bobby and Brook told everyone about their plans for the Madeline Ashbury Foundation and turning her childhood home into a safe haven for women and children escaping abusive relationships. Justin made a mental note to check in with his cousin later about how he could donate to such a worthy cause.

Charlotte informed everyone that she'd started getting their DNA test results on her Ancestry account, so they could login and look to see how they all compared as she traced back their family tree. Justin decided to look at his test results the next day when he had a few minutes free between meetings at work.

Charlotte talking about all the research she'd done on how much DNA they should share with their second-great-grandaunt's descendants to be able to track them down to release the trust that had been set up for them by Jonah Burleson when his daughter didn't return to the ranch after World War I, pretty much monopolized the conversation at their table. Talk of the trust for their distant cousins led to Justin's father, Jon, explaining to the rest of the family about how each generation had reinvested the funds to grow them into a sizable fortune for any third or fourth cousins they might find through their DNA matches that were descended from Mary Burleson. Charlotte had apparently been frantically filling in the family tree on the website, so the site could find common ancestors for them and their matches in the hopes they could finally release that trust a hundred years after it was originally created.

When their late meals were all consumed and the party started to break up, Justin walked over to congratulate the happy couple one more time before heading home. Unfortunately, Randi and Amy were pulled away from the Hunters to hug some of the women who were leaving, just as Justin walked up to where they'd been standing.

"Just wanted to say congrats one more time." Justin extended his hand to shake James's.

"Thanks, man." James grinned as he shook Justin's hand.

"Ya'll planning a long engagement, or are you gonna elope the next time you're in Vegas for a show?"

"As much as Randi and I would probably prefer that, our families would kill us if we skipped out on the big wedding." James laughed, shaking his head like he really wasn't looking forward to the big elaborate wedding his mom and future in-laws were pushing them to have. "We're not sure on the date yet, but it'll probably be here at home on one of our holiday breaks later this year."

"I'll look forward to attending then." Justin laughed with his friend.

"You gonna be okay with me walking Amy down the aisle?" Dean's question brought back Justin's earlier jealous feelings.

"I, uh…" Justin's voice trailed off as he struggled to come up with a response.

"Actually, I think Randi has three bridesmaids picked out." James slapped his right hand on Dean's shoulder and his left hand on Justin's. "So, I was thinking I'd ask Justin to be my third groomsman to walk Amy down the aisle."

"Dude, you don't hafta do that," Justin protested, hating that his feelings for Amy were making his friend feel put on the spot in such a way. "While I don't relish the idea of seeing her on someone else's arm, I'm really okay with Dean escorting her down the aisle."

"I know I don't hafta do that." James squeezed Justin's shoulder. "And I'm not a hundred percent certain that Randi will be able to convince Allissa to be in the wedding to make it work, so don't hold me to it just yet."

"Allissa?" Dean's eyes lit up as he said the name of the other potential bridesmaid. "Oh, fuck, yes. Definitely make that happen, Bro."

"Don't tell me. Tell Randi." James chuckled, shaking his head at his brother. "She couldn't even get her to come eat with us tonight, so it's gonna be a hard sell to get her in the wedding. But if anyone can do it, it's my Angel."

"Hey, Randi, my super sweet, favorite sister-in-law," Dean shouted as he walked off in the direction of the women who were still huddled together a few feet away.

"Seriously, if Randi doesn't kill me for whatever Dean says about this idea and gets Allissa to be in the wedding, will you be my third groomsman?" James grimaced at the way Randi grabbed Dean by the ear to pull him down to eye level and make him quit shouting as they talked.

"Are you sure? Wouldn't you rather have someone you're closer to stand up for you at the wedding?" Justin still felt like he was pushing his way into the wedding when he wasn't close enough to James to warrant the position. Not that he didn't think of James as a friend, but he knew he wasn't up there at best friend status with him like he was with Aiden or Leo, or like James was with Anthony and Dean and probably a few of the wrestlers he worked with regularly.

"Dude, if you can ever convince Amy to let you outta the friend zone, you'll realize that the things your woman wants are way more important than anything you might think you want. And after our Christmas break, Randi has been just as bad as our mothers when it comes to wanting to match up all our friends. Trust me, giving you the chance to have Amy on your arm at all our wedding events will make my Angel happier than asking one of the guys I work with daily to be a groomsman."

"Well, then, yeah. If you're sure, I'd be honored to be a groomsman at your wedding." Justin felt a little bad about not telling James that Amy had already agreed to go on a date to start moving out of the friend zone, but he knew Amy wasn't ready for anyone else to know yet, so he kept his trap shut.

They said their goodbyes and went their separate ways. On the drive home, Justin went over his plans for his first date with Amy. He'd made reservations at Biga on the Banks for dinner with plans to tour the River Walk beforehand. It was probably cliché to do a romantic dinner for two for their first official date, but it was also Valentine's Day, and he wanted to romance her a little bit.

Fuck! I hope she doesn't think I'm moving too fast with pulling out the romantic date first, instead of a fun, friendly trip to an amusement park.

Chapter Five

Monday, February 11, 2019

Justin wasn't sure how to make heads or tails out of the information on his computer screen while looking at his DNA breakdown. Unfortunately, since he was looking at the test results while at work, he couldn't call his cousin Charlotte to help him figure it out, since she was also at work teaching middle school English, and she wouldn't be able to take his call.

He'd known simply based on his hair, eye, and skin colors that the majority of his ethnicity breakdown would list regions of the world that were primarily Caucasian, but he expected to at least have a little bit of his DNA show his Native American roots, which he thought all the current generation of Burlesons inherited from their Memmaw Judy.

Other than one percent of his DNA that showed as Southern Bantu Peoples from Africa, he was listed as ninety-nine percent European. The report listed out percentages from Scotland, England & Northwestern Europe, European Jewish, Sweden & Denmark, Finland, and France to make up that ninety-nine percent, but there wasn't a listing for anywhere in North America, where Native American ancestry would be listed as originating if it was included in his DNA like he'd been led to believe his whole life. At a loss for how to figure it out, he sent a group text to his siblings.

At least if they're in the building, maybe they can come look at this report and help me figure it out, if they haven't already looked at their own reports to know how to explain it to me.

Justin: Hey, have ya'll looked at your DNA test results yet?

JJ: **No, why?**

Justin: **I'm confused by not seeing Native American since that should be showing up from Memmaw Judy.**

Jen: **I noticed that, too.**

Julie: **Didn't Char say the family tree was going to be the key to figuring out how we're related to our DNA matches on there? Maybe when she gets to Memmaw Judy's parents and grandparents, she'll figure out why we're not showing Native American?**

Justin: **Yeah, but I know she's in class & can't answer the phone right now to ask her, so I thought one of you might have a clue.**

Jen: **We don't know how far back in Memmaw Judy's bloodline we might have a Native American ancestor either. Once it gets to a 5th or 6th great-grandparent, we might not have enough of their DNA to show on the test.**

Justin: **We have an African ancestor close enough for me to have 1% Southern Bantu Peoples show on mine.**

JJ: **Mine shows 2% SBP.**

Julie: **I don't have that at all. Mine is 100% European.**

Jen: **I'm also 100% European, broken down to all over Europe, though.**

Julie: **Yeah, same, 60% Scottish. Wonder if I should start wearing kilts instead of skirts to work? LOL**

JJ: Just don't start trying to do the accent, Sis.

Justin: Am I the only one who thinks it's weird that our reports aren't exactly alike? I mean, I know we only share ~50% of our DNA & each inherited different parts of Mom & Dad's DNA, but it seems like if one of us has African then we all should, not 2 of us having it & 2 of us not.

JJ: Yeah, but remember what Char was saying about us only getting 1.5% of our DNA from each of our 4th great-grandparents. If they weren't 100% of something, then we could get our 1.5% from the part of their DNA we're not expecting. So, if Grandpa Jonah's mom was mixed like Charlotte seems to think, it's possible us guys might have gotten her African DNA while you girls got her European DNA.

Jen: How about we plan on going over all this on Sunday after church when Char can show us what she's found on the family tree? It might make more sense with the full picture.

JJ: Agreed.

Julie: Sounds good to me.

Justin: Okay.

Justin put his phone away, only slightly feeling a little better about his test results. Thankfully, he knew how to get himself out of the slight funk he fell into when he didn't see what he expected in his DNA. He shut down his computer and headed out of his office to go spend some time in the lab.

"I'll be in the lab the rest of the day," he informed his administrative assistant as he walked by her desk.

"But you have a conference call at two that you need to be up here for," Amanda Lewis snapped.

Fuck! I hate wasting time sitting and listening in on conference calls that don't really have anything to do with research and development. Can't they just send me an email with the information I need to get from all these damn calls?

"I'll call into it from my cell." Justin punched the down button for the elevator and checked his pocket to make sure he had his Bluetooth earbuds. Since he didn't have to actually participate in the discussion, he'd listen in with his microphone muted while testing the freeze-point for the newest mixture Amy had come up with for a new eco-friendly antifreeze.

As he rode down alone in the elevator, Justin couldn't figure out why he was so irritated by the DNA test results. It wasn't like they showed he wasn't really a part of his family. When he looked at the DNA match list, his parents, siblings, uncle, and cousins took the top nine spots. The only people with the last name Burleson that he didn't match up with were his Aunt Hazel, Kay, Tia, Maria, and the three cousins who hadn't taken the test yet. Justin was pretty certain, based on everyone else showing up on his match list, that Bobby, Josh, and Jake would show up when they finally took the tests and sent them in to be analyzed. So, not showing Native American didn't really mean much in the grand scheme of things, but it still irritated him.

Probably because I wanted to be more mixed to show Amy and I aren't as different as we look, Justin thought as he barreled off the elevator and toward the door to the lab. As he swung the door open, Justin had to stop short to keep from running over Amy, who was exiting the lab just as he was about to enter.

"Whoa, Boss, you okay?" Amy's hands came to rest on his biceps, where she was trying to stop her own forward momentum. The feel of her hands on him calmed more of his irritation than all the texts with his siblings, even though it also sent a bolt of lust straight to his cock.

"Yes," Justin initially replied, but then shook his head and vacillated his answer, "No. I don't know."

"How about we go to lunch early?" Amy lightly pushed him back out of the doorway leading into the lab. "It's already eleven, so it's not too early for lunch. Just let me grab my bag from my office, and then we can sit and talk about whatever's got you looking like you're ready to explode."

"Yeah, that sounds good." Justin watched closely as Amy stepped away from him to go into her office briefly, unable to take his eyes off the woman of his dreams.

A moment later she was back and clasping his hand in hers to drag him back to the elevator to go down one more floor. She surprised him by going through the cafeteria line with him instead of bringing her lunch as usual. They didn't say much more than pleasantries to the staff as they got their food. But as soon as they were seated, Amy immediately asked what was going on with him.

"I'm honestly not sure why I'm so irritated," Justin admitted, pushing his food around on his plate more than trying to scoop some up with his fork. "I was in a pretty good mood this morning when I got here. Then I got stuck on a conference call about overlapping interests between Burleson and Ashbury to take note of anything we might wanna work with their R and D department on. I guess my irritation probably started when I felt like it was a waste of time since they aren't working on anything remotely like what we're doing here. Then after that, I looked at my DNA test results, and they irritated me even more. So, I was already grumpy as I was headed down to the lab to clear my head, when Amanda pointed out that I have another conference call this afternoon that I really don't think I need to be involved in."

"Okay." Amy tilted her head as she took a bite like she was trying to figure him out.

Good luck with that, Justin thought, finally taking a bite of his own food, even though he couldn't really taste it in his current agitated state. *If I can't figure out why I'm in a pissy mood, I doubt you can, Sweetheart.*

"Since I'm the lab manager, can I do the conference calls for you?"

"I probably should've had you do the one this morning since it was sorta lab-related." Justin shook his head, though, since he knew she couldn't cover the next one for him. "But the one this afternoon has absolutely nothing to do with the lab. I only hafta be on it because of being on the board of directors and needing to take notes for my cousins about a potential acquisition that they'll need for our next quarterly board meeting."

"I don't understand. Why do you have to be on the call as a board member, but your cousins don't?"

"Ideally, anything like this, where the whole board will hafta vote on an acquisition, we'd all be on the conference call to discuss it. But with most of my cousins not working full time for Burleson Incorporated, they're not always available for the initial discussions. So, we get as many of us on the line as possible to be able to give them our different perspectives to help them decide how to vote. Or like last week, those of us who didn't go to Georgia gave our dads our proxy to be able to buy Ashbury immediately once the negotiations were done without having to wait until we could have a board meeting."

"So, this call today is just to do the initial negotiation, but ya'll will have to have a board meeting later to actually buy whatever it is ya'll are gonna buy?"

"Yeah, pretty much," Justin replied, smiling at Amy. "So, I've gotta be on the call to take notes for Char, who can't be there because she'll be in the middle of teaching a class, and probably for Josh and Jake if their jobs keep them from calling in. Bobby and Becky both said they'd be able to call in from Heart's Destiny, and Anthony said he'd be calling in from whatever arena they're at today. With as much interest as Tia was showing in the company at our last quarterly board meeting, he might even have her listening, too, so she can school us all in whether or not it's a good deal at the next board meeting."

"Okay, so I get why these calls are kinda annoying." Amy placed her fork down on her plate to look deep into Justin's eyes. "But they don't sound like anything outta the ordinary to have gotten you so off-kilter this morning. Was it the DNA test that bothered you so much?"

"Yeah," Justin huffed out a breath. "I just..." Justin trailed off, trying to collect his thoughts to be able to finish the sentence. "I only briefly looked at my matches to see my mom, dad, siblings, Uncle Bob, and my cousins who've taken the test are my top nine matches. I didn't look at the rest of the list of more distant matches before switching over to my ethnicity estimate. I thought when I looked at that, I'd see Native American from my Memmaw, but it's not there. So, either I'm not related to Memmaw Judy, or she wasn't Native American like she always told us."

"I'm sure you're related to your Memmaw," Amy reassured him, reaching out to pat his hand.

Justin turned his hand over under hers to interlace their fingers. "You're probably right. But not seeing it makes me feel like I've been lied to my whole life about that branch of my family. And I can't stand lying, ya know."

"One of our common pet peeves, I know." Amy smiled as she squeezed his hand. "But I doubt your Memmaw meant to lie to you. She was probably just passing down what she'd been told way back before DNA, when people of mixed heritage really had no clue what they were. Kinda like my mom telling me we're a little bit of everything when I'm actually thirty-five percent African and sixty-five percent European. And that sixty-five percent is split over fewer regions of Europe than the regions of Africa that make up the thirty-five percent."

"Really?" Justin was surprised that Amy's results weren't what she'd expected either.

"Yeah, most of my DNA is from England, Wales, and France, but I have like five different regions of Africa listed to make up the third of me that's Black." Amy shrugged like it didn't matter. "But there's no Native American. No Asian. No Pacific Islander. Heck, there's not even most of Europe. As much as I love Italian food, I was expecting to have at least a little Italian in there. But nope. Not a drop."

"And it doesn't bother you that it's not what you expected?" Justin wished he could take it in stride like Amy seemed to be doing when looking at her DNA results.

"I'm disappointed," Amy shrugged. "But it's not like my mom was intentionally lying about it. She was just telling me the stories that were passed down from my Nana and Papa and their parents before them."

"When I was talking to my brother and sisters earlier, they reminded me that the family tree research that Char's doing will give us more information on Memmaw Judy's family in Oklahoma to know if it's there, but just too many generations back to see in our DNA. Are you gonna do a family tree to look at all those old records too?"

"I don't know." Amy's usually happy face fell as she muttered the words. "I've gone back and forth with whether or not I wanna look into all that. Part of me wants to, if for no other reason than to figure out where the Native American stories originated. But considering the way my father's family rejected us after he died, I'm not sure if I really wanna see their history."

Justin nodded and squeezed her hand in his, trying to be supportive of whatever Amy wanted to do with her DNA results. *Hell, if I were in her shoes and had a whole branch of my family that denied even being related to me, I'd probably do the family tree just to shove it in their faces that I was related to them whether they liked it or not.*

"Our family tree linking us to our DNA matches is what we're hoping will tell us what happened to our second-great-grandaunt at the end of World War I. Char seems to think it'll help us find our third or fourth cousins to be able to finally release the trust that was set up for Mary and her descendants almost a hundred years ago." Justin hoped changing the direction of their discussion to finding his long-lost cousins would bring back Amy's smile.

"See, that's the kind of family mystery that's worth all the research to solve." Amy squeezed his hand and slightly smiled at him. "So, what happens when you find your long-lost cousins? Will they just get the funds in trust for them, or will they also be added to the Burleson board?"

"It depends on who all we find and what generation they are." Justin went on to explain how the company was set up with the division of the shares in the company being divided among the two oldest generations of the family. "If Mary's living descendants are the same generations as us and our dads, then all our shares will be split to include each of them. If there's a living descendant from my Pappaw's generation, then the fifty percent of the company that's currently divided amongst my generation will revert to the older generation and my dad and Uncle Bob will share their fifty percent with anyone in their generation on that branch of the tree. Or we may find that there aren't any living descendants from Mary's line, and nothing changes."

"If that happens, then what happens with all the money in the trust? Does it just sit there forever as unclaimed? Or does it revert back to the company?" Amy was asking questions that Justin hadn't ever thought about before.

"I have no idea." Justin shook his head. "I'll hafta ask Dad and Uncle Bob when we all get together this weekend to go over the family tree stuff after church."

"You'll have to let me know how easy that family tree stuff is to research after you do it this weekend. If you're able to figure out your family mysteries fairly easily, maybe I'll get brave enough to look into mine." Amy gave him a grin then, finally.

"Or you could just come over on Sunday and see for yourself," Justin suggested, thinking it would be nice to have Amy there in case he struggled with what they found.

"You don't think that would give us away to the family?" Amy's grin disappeared as she chewed her bottom lip in trepidation.

Damn, I wish I could be the one nibbling on her lip.

"Maybe if I'm the one who invites you to come over," Justin admitted, while thinking, *So, I'll hafta get one of the girls to do the inviting. I could have Jen or Julie do it since they work here and will bump into us during lunch at least once this week. Or I could say something to Char at Bobby's birthday party about Amy wanting to know more about how to do the family tree research, so she's the one who invites Amy, and it won't seem like I'm pushing the girls to ask my girlfriend to come over.*

~~~

Thursday, February 14, 2019

Amy felt bad about skipping Brooklyn's proposal to go to work early, but she wanted to make sure she had time to get everything done, so she could go home early to have extra time to get ready for her date with Justin. But declining Brooklyn's invitation to witness the proposal didn't make her feel nearly as guilty as she felt about lying to Kay the day before, saying she wasn't feeling well when Kay had called to tell Amy about the Sweetheart's Ball that her mother-in-law was pushing for Amy to attend.

I hope Justin and I both being absent from the event won't be too noticeable and make the Matchmaking Mommas suspicious that we're out together, Amy thought as she put the finishing touches on her makeup for the night. *Maybe we should've scheduled this for another night, when there wasn't a town-wide event going on that his whole family will probably attend. Although, Kay did say that she and*
~~~

Anthony had other plans and wouldn't be there. And Brook said she and Bobby had other plans as well when she called to invite me to her surprise proposal this morning. Maybe we won't be the only ones not there?

She didn't have much time to worry, though, because just as she was stepping out of her ensuite bathroom to complete her outfit of a red knee-length cocktail dress by slipping on her gold lamé peep-toe pumps, her doorbell rang.

"Crap, crap, crap, he's early," Amy complained to her empty room as she rushed to throw her phone, wallet, keys, and lipstick in her matching gold lamé clutch before descending the stairs.

Though she hated to make him wait on her front porch, she took her time walking down the stairs, not wanting to risk falling down them in the four-inch high heels. The shoes would only cut their normally nine-inch height difference down to five inches, but they made her feel a little more on an even footing with him than she felt every day at work, when she always wore flats.

Although, even the heels didn't make me feel prepared for dancing with him on New Year's Eve, Amy remembered as she got to the bottom of the steps. *But I wasn't ready to act on our mutual attraction back then either, so maybe they'll help give me the confidence to go through with this date tonight.*

"Good evening," Amy greeted him as she opened the door. She would've said more, but she was speechless at the sight of Justin in a charcoal gray suit with a crisp white dress shirt sans tie and holding a bouquet of red, white, and pink carnations. *How did he know my favorite flowers? I don't think that was one of the things we mentioned when we were talking about our favorite things last month. Was it?*

"Amy, you look…" Justin's voice trailed off as if he wasn't sure how to finish his sentence. "Wow. You're absolutely stunning."

"Thank you," Amy replied, hoping she wasn't blushing too obviously at his compliment.

"Oh, um, these are for you." Justin's cheeks pinkened slightly and made Amy feel less self-conscious of her own blush. It was okay to be awkward and shy when they were awkward and shy together.

"Thank you." Amy took the flowers from him. "Let me just put them in water."

She turned and walked toward her kitchen with Justin following behind her. As she was filling a vase and unwrapping the flowers from their cellophane to arrange them, her curiosity got the better of her. "Did I mention my favorite flowers and forget telling you about them?"

"No, I, uh, just picked the bouquet I thought was the prettiest." Justin shrugged as his blush deepened. "I don't even know what kind of flowers they are, other than they aren't roses."

"Well, you have excellent taste then." Amy smiled at him as she finished arranging the flowers in the vase of water. "They're carnations and they are my absolute favorite flowers."

"I'll remember that for the future." Justin extended his arm to lead Amy back to the front door, so they could leave for their date.

Once she locked up her house, Justin assisted her in climbing into the passenger seat of his truck before jogging around to get in the driver's side.

"You don't think your mom and aunt will get suspicious of us both no-showing the Sweetheart's Ball, do you?" Amy couldn't stifle her trepidation as they drove toward the highway, passing right by the entrance to the bed and breakfast where the ball was being held.

"No, I don't think any of my siblings or cousins are going either," Justin replied, smiling at her. "I know my mom and the rest of the Matchmaking Mommas pushed Mrs. Hunter into throwing the ball to try to set us all up, but I think it's turned into more of a dance for the older people in town and maybe a few of their grandchildren they're supposed to be babysitting for the night, like Tia and Maria. I know Anthony and Kay are flying down to Padre for the night, and Bobby and Brook are supposed to be goin' to a restaurant in San Antonio. If they don't end up staying home to celebrate their engagement in the privacy of their bedroom, that is."

"Did you talk to them to make sure they're not gonna be at the same restaurant as us?" Amy was worried that Justin was giving away their secret dating plans by checking in with his cousins.

"I just asked what their plans were." Justin reassured her by reaching over and clasping her hand in his much larger one. "I didn't mention us or our plans, but I did pick a different restaurant than the one Bobby mentioned taking Brook to, so we're safe to be a couple tonight without any family around as witnesses."

"Okay." Amy relaxed a bit, pushing her worries about someone seeing them leaving town for their night out to the back of her mind. "What about the rest of your family? How do you know they aren't going to the dance to make it obvious that we're the only ones not there?"

"The girls were talking about inviting over some of their single friends for a girls' night watching rom-coms and drinking copious amounts of wine." Justin shook his head like his sisters and cousins' plans sounded horrible to him.

"And they didn't ask you to join them?" Amy giggled at the incredulous look Justin gave her.

"No, though I did hafta turn down JJ's invite to a BDSM club mixer." Justin's smirk made it impossible for Amy to tell if he was joking or not about his brother's plans for the night.

Her jaw dropped as she floundered for a response to the possibility of JJ going to one of the clubs she'd only read about in romance novels. "Seriously?"

"Yeah, um." Justin's blush was back in full force, even though keeping his eyes on the road kept him from looking directly at Amy as he spoke. "It's something he got into back in college and joined his club in San Antonio when he graduated."

"Has he invited you to their mixers before?" Amy wasn't sure how she'd feel if Justin was using his brother's plans for the night to tell her he was also into BDSM.

"Yeah," Justin admitted, still not making eye contact with Amy as he continued. "I've gone to a couple in the past, but I stayed in the bar area. My curiosity wasn't piqued enough to risk seeing my brother's bare ass or what he does in the dungeon."

"Even the bar area is farther into one of those clubs than I'd ever brave going into," Amy confided with a self-deprecating chuckle. "No matter how intriguing some of the things I've read about happening in clubs like that seems, I wouldn't wanna do any of it with an audience."

"And what, pray tell, have you been reading that's intriguing enough you might wanna try in private, Ms. Lawton?" Justin actually chanced a glance in her direction as he posed the question, wagging his eyebrows suggestively before turning his gaze back to the road ahead of them.

"Nothing I'm gonna tell you about on our first date, Mr. Burleson." Amy grinned, enjoying their flirty banter.

"Yeah, you definitely shouldn't call me Mr. Burleson when we're talking about our sexual proclivities." Justin chuckled and shook his head as he pulled his hand back from hers to adjust himself. "I don't need to be popping a boner at work if you slip up and address me professionally, but maybe now's a good time for you to call me Boss. When we're talking about anything sexual and eventually when we make it to the bedroom, especially."

Between his words and the way he repositioned himself, Amy couldn't stop her gaze from dropping to his crotch, causing his reference to calling him Boss to completely go in one ear and out the other. *Holy! Wow! I guess everything really is bigger in Texas. Either that or his pants are way too loose and bunching up in a weird way to make him look bigger than anyone I've ever been with before. That looks like something I'd expect to see in a pornographic cartoon because it's way too big to be realistic.*

"See something you like, Sweetheart?"

Amy's eyes popped up to Justin's face at his question, and he reached back over to wipe his thumb over her chin. *Probably to wipe off the drool,* Amy thought, closing her mouth where it was hanging open involuntarily. "Um, uh."

"Don't be embarrassed, Sweetheart. I like havin' you look at me like you wanna eat me for dinner. Hell, that's probably how I'm lookin' at you about half the time. But I'm not gonna push you to do more than you're ready for, ever. We're takin' it slow, remember?"

"Ye-yeah," Amy stuttered, not sure why she was so embarrassed to be caught looking at the bulge in his pants. *Sex is normal. Being sexually attracted to him is normal. I was never nervous and ashamed of my sexual desires with any of the guys I've been with in the past, so why do I suddenly feel like a shy virgin again with Justin? Hell, I wasn't even this awkward the night I lost my virginity.*

"While *The Anaconda* is obviously excited that you've noticed him, he doesn't get a say in when you meet him. We're going at your pace, and I don't expect more than a chaste goodnight kiss tonight. Okay?"

"The Anaconda?" Amy laughed at Justin's ludicrous reference to his penis, her embarrassment dissipating as the mood in the truck lightened. "Is that his official name?"

"Hey, don't laugh!" Justin was obviously fighting his own chuckles. "I was nine when I named him."

"How on earth do you come up with a name like *The Anaconda* at nine years old?" Amy couldn't stop laughing, thinking that even if she'd been a boy, she was too mature at nine years old to nickname body parts.

"We were all out playing one summer afternoon and rode our four-wheelers down to the creek to go swimming," Justin confessed, grinning at his childhood memory. "It was just the guys. The girls were too skittish to go swimming in the creek because Bobby convinced them all there were gators in it."

"Are there really gators in it?" Amy wondered if Kay knew about the potential alligators in the creek down by where she and Anthony were building their new home.

"I've never seen one." Justin shrugged as if it didn't matter if there were or not as long as he hadn't seen them. "I think we're too far west for gators. Everything I've read says they're only in the eastern third of Texas and we're closer to center, or maybe slightly west of the center of the state."

His answer alleviated Amy's fear for Kay, Anthony, and their kids being so close to the creek.

"Anyway, while we were swimming, I heard JJ and Bobby talking about naming their trouser snakes. Since they were calling it a snake, I thought of the biggest snake I knew of to name mine."

Amy couldn't help but giggle at the ridiculous childhood antics of the Burleson boys.

"I thought it sounded more accurate than Bobby or JJ's choices." Justin shook his head and lifted one shoulder in a half-shrug.

"Oh my, do I even wanna ask what they came up with?" Amy covered her mouth with one hand as she tried to stop the laughter from continually erupting.

"They went with their favorite Marvel superheroes, Thor and Ironman." Justin laughed along with Amy when she couldn't contain her bark of laughter. "Like I said, I thought mine was more accurately named since I at least picked a type of snake."

"Yeah, well, if and when I ever meet him, I won't be referring to him by name," Amy finally choked out when her laughter died down. *At least not that one,* Amy thought. *But I might have to come up with my own name for Justin's dick if it performs as well as that bulge is advertising.*

"Oh, Sweetheart, you're more than welcome to rename him." Justin chuckled as he pulled into a parking garage in downtown San Antonio.

Oh shit! Did I say that out loud?

Amy hoped the low lighting in the parking structure prevented Justin from being able to see how bright her cheeks felt as her embarrassment returned.

Luckily for her, Justin dropped the sexual innuendo as he parked, opting to tell her about the River Walk, which they walked through to get to the restaurant where he had reservations for the night. He was a perfect gentleman, helping her down from the truck and holding her hand as they strolled along the river. He even pulled out her chair and waited for her to be seated before sitting down across from her.

Dating Justin was a whole new experience for Amy. Prior to him, the closest she'd had to a date like theirs was back in high school when her prom date took her to dinner before the dance. Amy hadn't put out on prom night, and with the way Justin was talking as they enjoyed their steaks and the bottle of wine he'd picked to pair with them, she didn't think she'd be having sex on Valentine's Day either.

Looking around the restaurant to see the romantic ambiance of the establishment made her realize just how much Justin was going all out to make their first date special. *This is definitely a step or three above hanging out in the dining hall at OU with any of the guys I hooked up with in college. And lightyears better than the one-night stands I've met in bars, or the friends with benefits booty calls I had a couple years ago.*

As the night went on, they carried on with their normal easy conversation, only really turning flirty again when dessert was served. They ordered a Biga Sampler, which included sticky toffee pudding, chocolate pot de crème, and a warm apple blackberry crumble. It arrived as three separate dishes lined up on a rectangular plate that the waiter sat down between them.

"How are we supposed to divide three desserts between the two of us?" Amy batted her eyelashes at Justin in an overly flirtatious manner as she imagined them taking the desserts to go, so they could eat them off each other's bodies once they were back in the privacy of her home.

"Oh, Sweetheart, I'm sure we're more than capable of sharing." Justin picked up a spoon and dipped it into the dish closest to him before extending it across the table for her to taste.

As she closed her lips around the spoon, Amy swore she saw a flash of unbridled lust in Justin's eyes before she closed hers to savor the sweet explosion of fruit flavor on her tongue. She couldn't contain the moan in the back of her throat as she enjoyed the decadent dessert. "Mmm."

She opened her eyes to witness Justin taking his own bite of the apple blackberry crumble and realized that his lustful look hadn't dissipated in the slightest. She reached out and picked up her own spoon and dipped it in the dish closest to her, which she assumed was the sticky toffee pudding since the center dish was unmistakably filled with dark chocolate.

She waited for Justin to swallow his bite of the crumble before extending the spoon full of pudding over to him. The way he extended his tongue to take the spoon into his mouth made her wonder what else he could do with it if they were alone, possibly between her legs, like she'd only dreamed of in the past.

"Delicious," he declared after swallowing the bite. "But not nearly as delicious as the taste of your lips on the spoon before it."

Amy took her own bite of the pudding to give her time to think of how to respond to his flirtation. She barely had a chance to swallow before he had the spoon covered in chocolate held out before her. *I wonder if he realized I need more time to think of what to say?*

"Do you have a favorite?" Justin inquired before taking his own bite of the chocolate dessert.

Amy shook her head as she swallowed. "They're all excellent."

Justin smiled as they continued taking turns feeding each other bites of the desserts. They compared and contrasted the flavors as they finished off all three dishes, finally deciding that they couldn't choose a favorite, with Justin looking at her the whole time like he'd rather eat her for dessert instead.

Once he settled the bill, they took a longer walk around the River Walk area, noticing how much more romantic it seemed with the white lights strung over the walkway beside the river after dark. The drive back to Heart's Destiny was relaxed, with them holding hands the whole way while talking about everything and nothing, like they seemed to easily do no matter where they were or what was happening around them.

"I hate for the night to end," Justin sighed as he helped her out of his truck, and they slowly strolled toward her porch. "But I know we both hafta get up early for work tomorrow."

Amy was momentarily disappointed that he wasn't pushing to come in and extend their evening in her bedroom, but she tried to cover it with a soft smile up at him. She knew he wanted her as badly as she wanted him, but his intention to take things slow to build them up to a long-lasting relationship was what was keeping him from giving in and acting on their mutual desires.

She still couldn't believe she'd agreed to try a relationship with him, when she was still so wary of it ending in heartbreak. But after really getting to know him as a friend over the past few weeks, she knew if she didn't try with him, she'd regret it for the rest of her life.

If I have a chance at ever finding my soulmate, the perfect man for me, I have to try with him. Justin's the only man who's ever made me feel like it's even a possibility that I can have my own happily ever after.

"Yes, I was a little worried about being out too late tonight and having to call my boss to tell him I'd be late to work tomorrow." Amy playfully teased him as they stopped at her front door. "He's a bit of a stickler for punctuality, and I wouldn't wanna risk him having to punish me for being tardy."

"Oh, I don't know about that." Justin wrapped his left arm around her waist to pull her in close while tipping her chin up to him with his right hand. "I happen to know your boss pretty well. And I think he adores you way too much to ever punish you for anything."

"Is that so?" Amy pressed the palms of her hands to Justin's chest, right over the lapels of the jacket of his sexy charcoal suit. "Guess that means I should give up on my fantasies of him giving me a sexy spanking while I'm bent over his desk then."

Holy shit! Did I just say that out loud? That third glass of wine was definitely a bad idea! Loose lips and all that. But I just couldn't let that whole bottle go to waste when Justin stopped after one glass because he was driving. Now my good intentions are getting me in trouble.

"Fuck no, Sweetheart!" Justin shook his head briefly before pressing their foreheads together. "You keep that and every other fantasy you have for us at the forefront of your mind. And let me know as soon as you're ready to start living them out."

Before Amy could reply, Justin's hand slipped from under her chin to the nape of her neck, where he weaved his fingers through her hair to guide her lips to his. At first, it was just a feather-soft brush of his lips over hers, but as Amy melted into him, Justin deepened the kiss.

He sucked her bottom lip into his mouth before releasing it to tangle their tongues. Amy slid her hands up over the solid muscle of his chest and shoulders to wrap her arms around his neck. She weaved her own fingers through the short strands of his sandy-brown hair at the base of his skull, pressing her whole body into his as she pulled his head down closer to her own.

Justin slid his hand down from around her waist to cup her buttocks, pulling her in even closer to his body. She felt the hard evidence of his arousal pressing into her lower abdomen and prayed everything her mother had ever told her about a well-endowed man being more satisfying for a woman in bed was true. She couldn't be certain until she actually saw him undressed, but based on what she could feel as they made out on her front porch like a couple of horny teenagers, she thought he was definitely bigger than anyone she'd ever been with before.

Amy rocked her hips, seeking out the pressure against her clit from his erection that would alleviate the ache in her core. Justin responded in kind, thrusting against her several times as they continued kissing like they needed each other more than they needed air to breathe.

All too soon, he pulled back, breaking off their kiss and using both hands to still the movement of her hips.

"Fuck, Amy, Sweetheart, we hafta stop." Justin sounded as breathless as she felt as he pushed her back to hold her at arm's length with both hands on her hips.

"Wha-what?" Amy stuttered out the word as her brain slowly registered what he was saying.

"We hafta stop, Sweetheart." Justin released her and took another step back, effectively breaking her hold around his neck. "If we don't, then taking it slow is gonna go straight out the window. And as much as I want nothing more than to bury myself inside you right now, you deserve better than me giving in to my baser instincts. I wanna do this right, properly court you the way you deserve. I wanna take you on dates, and for us to really get to know each other."

"Oh, okay," Amy sputtered, not quite sure how to respond. She knew he wanted a long-term relationship, but she didn't understand why they couldn't have a quick screw along the way, too.

"When we make love for the first time, I want it to mean as much to you as it does to me. I wanna take my time, worshiping every inch of you. I wanna make sure that you really know you're ready, that you're one-hundred percent sure about us. Because once I have you, I'm never gonna be able to let you go. When we finally make love, it'll be because we're both ready to commit to forever together."

Holy shit! Is he for real? He's that serious about us? That one time in bed will mean forever for us as a couple?

Amy opened her mouth to speak, but she promptly closed it, not wanting to let him know how much she was freaking out. Talking about forever on their first date seemed beyond crazy to her.

"Don't worry about all that right now, Sweetheart." Justin leaned in to brush his lips over her forehead. "Just go inside and get a good night's sleep. We'll take everything else one day at a time. Tomorrow we'll be our normal friendly selves at work and at Bobby's birthday party. Then if it's okay with you, I'd like to spend Saturday on our second date at Sea World. Whaddaya say?"

"Sea World?" Amy wasn't sure how he'd changed the subject so fast.

"Yeah, someplace we can hang out and have fun." Justin ran a hand through his hair. "And I won't be tempted to push for more than you're ready for because of being surrounded by families all day."

"Oh, okay." Amy finally felt like they were somewhat back to their normal selves. "Sea World sounds good, but it'll have to be in the afternoon. I'm having Mom's bedroom furniture delivered Saturday morning."

"Sounds good." Justin smiled, slowly walking down the stairs off her porch. "Just text me when you're ready."

Amy pulled her keys from her clutch and turned to unlock her door. She looked over her shoulder one last time to say, "Goodnight, Justin," before opening it.

"Goodnight, Amy." Justin slowly walked backwards to his truck. "Sweet dreams, Sweetheart."

After stepping inside, Amy closed and locked her front door. She watched Justin through the window in the door until he got in his truck and backed out of her driveway.

Sweet dreams? More like a night of tossing and turning, trying to figure out whether or not I'll ever be ready for where you want our relationship to go.

~~~

Saturday, February 16, 2019

Justin still struggled to control his inner caveman, who wanted nothing more than to stake his claim on Amy by dragging her off to the nearest bed, even though it'd been more than thirty-six hours since their explosive first kiss. It'd taken all his willpower to walk away Thursday night with only one more brief peck on her forehead before going home and jacking off in the shower to alleviate his physical need for her. It was obvious to him by the way Amy responded that she wanted him as much as he wanted her. But he knew if they gave in to their mutual attraction too soon, then she'd see them as just another short-term sexual arrangement and not the forever relationship he wanted with her.

After Bobby and Brook announcing the night before that they're expecting their first child, Justin really wanted to move his and Amy's relationship along like his cousins had with their women. In the last five months, Justin had watched as both Anthony and Bobby had met and fallen in love with their perfect mates. Now Anthony was married to Kay, had adopted her daughters, and they were expecting their third child in July. And Bobby was engaged to Brooklyn, with their nuptials pending in less than two months, and their first child due in October. That meant there would be six new Burlesons added to the
~~~

family in approximately a year's time, and Justin desperately wanted to make Amy the seventh.

The first step to that even being a possibility was him keeping his inner caveman hidden while they were on a friendly date to Sea World. He'd realized Thursday night that the only time their interactions became awkward was when he tried to be more romantic, like when he gave her the flowers he'd picked up at a roadside stand on his way home from work, or when he talked about them being together forever.

Damn, I've gotta stop putting my foot in my mouth by saying stuff she's not ready to hear yet. I hafta rein it in and just be her friend today. Maybe a friend who holds her hand, hugs her a lot, and gives her chaste kisses whenever I get the urge to satisfy my inner caveman. Maybe that'll appease the beast inside me until I can really kiss her the way I want again, like we kissed Thursday night. But even if it doesn't feel like enough, for now I still need to act like more of a friend than her future husband, which is what I really wanna be.

His first test of whether or not he'd be able to keep things chaste and friendly was when he arrived at her house to pick her up. Before he could even get his truck turned off, she came bounding down the steps off her porch in a pair of figure-hugging khaki capris paired with a yellow off-the-shoulder sweater that had such an open weave it did very little to conceal the matching tank top underneath it. It was the first time he'd seen her in something she intended to wear outside her house that showed off her cleavage.

Though that yellow tank top looks a lot like the one she was wearing the other week when I got here before she'd changed outta her pajamas.

Wondering if it was the same one, he took a moment to adjust his dick in his jeans before getting out of the truck to walk around and help her up into the passenger seat. He took her hand, offering his as support while she climbed up into the tall vehicle. Once she was settled in the seat, he leaned in and gave her a peck on the cheek, needing to feel his lips on her if only for a moment.

"I like that outfit," Justin complimented as he settled in the driver's seat. "Yellow is definitely your color."

Leah Mae Wright

"Thank you," Amy replied, smiling as she buckled her seatbelt. "I got lucky that my favorite color doesn't clash with my complexion since I tend to wear it often."

"I didn't know that was possible," Justin mused aloud, buckling his own seatbelt and thinking Amy would look amazing no matter what color she chose to wear.

"Oh, yeah." Amy nodded her head as Justin started the truck and backed out of her driveway. "Much to my sister's dismay, we have warm undertones in our complexion, so we have to stick to wearing warm colors to look our best. Like the dress I wore Thursday, I had to pick an orange-red instead of a blue-red. Ashlyn's favorite color is purple, and since it's a cool color it clashes with her complexion every time she wears it."

Damn, hopefully, my purple t-shirt doesn't make her wanna distance herself from me today.

"Well, since I didn't know I even have undertones, much less what they are, I hope I haven't offended your eyes by wearing whatever I like without regard to whether it clashes with my complexion." Justin chanced a glance at her before focusing back on the road as he made their way to the highway headed into San Antonio.

"You most definitely haven't," Amy giggled. "In fact, all the blue, green, gray, and even the purple you're wearing today are cool colors that complement your cool undertones."

Great, another area where we're different. Why the fuck can't I find more stuff we have in common instead of all these differences?

"Now that I think about it," Amy pondered aloud, bringing him back to the moment. "Maybe I should suggest to Ashlyn that she should hang out with more people with cool undertones, so she can wear my yellow to look her best while complementing her cool friends in purple."

Justin gave her a quick quizzical look, not understanding what she meant, before turning his eyes back to the highway ahead of them. Apparently, Amy caught his confused expression as she smiled and reached over to clasp his hand in hers on the center console.

"Yellow and purple are complementary colors. They're opposites on the color wheel, but they go best together when they're paired up. That's why artists and marketing people tend to use them together a lot."

"So, the way we're dressed today is complementary?" Justin hoped Amy's explanation of the color wheel and complementary colors went for them as a couple, too. *Maybe that's why people say "opposites attract" when talking about couples?*

"Yeah, or like we're ready for a photo shoot to advertise a casual day out," Amy chuckled. "Actually, now that I think about it, we tend to wear complementary colors quite often."

Justin raised an eyebrow in question, not actually saying anything since he didn't know what other colors were complementary to know when they'd have done that in the past.

"Like at Christmas, I wore red, and you wore green. And when I've worn various shades of orange at work, you've worn complementary shades of blue. Even when I was in my orange-red dress the other night, your charcoal suit had undertones of blue in the gray. It's like we just naturally dress to go together."

Justin liked the sound of that.

"I guess that's our couple thing." Justin grinned at the thought. "But unlike Bobby and Brook, who we've all been picking on for dressing to match all the time, we're more subtle about it."

"Oh, speaking of Bobby and Brooklyn, I realized when I got home last night that my mom and Ashlyn will be in town next weekend when they're planning their wedding shower. Do you think they'd mind if I bring them with me? Or should I just plan to give them their gift early and skip the shower?"

"I'm sure they wouldn't mind you bringing your mom and sister to the shower." Justin was absolutely positive his family would welcome hers with open arms. "Though you might wanna give your family a heads-up about who Brook is beforehand, so they don't freak out if the paparazzi come back to town once they announce their engagement."

"Oh, I didn't even think about that." Amy looked pensively out the window as they exited the highway. "I'm sure Mom will be fine, but Ashlyn might go a little fangirl on Brook when they meet. She hasn't said anything about Brooklyn since Christmas, but she was following the story pretty closely between Thanksgiving and then. Maybe I should ask Brook to be sure, since my sister can be a little over the top when it comes to meeting famous people."

"I heard Char ask you to come over tomorrow when we're all getting together to go over the DNA stuff. Maybe you can ask her then if you want." Justin hoped Amy didn't see through his ploy to find out if she was coming the next day with his offhand mention of the family plans.

"Yeah, that's probably a good idea." Amy still looked contemplative as he parked the truck at Sea World.

"Or you could just not worry about it and bring them along without warning anybody, just to see how far your sister can push Bobby before he breaks out the handcuffs and arrests her," Justin joked, trying to bring back Amy's smile as he helped her down from the passenger seat of his truck.

"Don't even joke about that." Amy laughed and swatted at Justin's chest playfully. "Did I tell you what she said about him and his handcuffs at Christmas when I was telling them about all ya'll?"

"No-oo-oo," Justin drawled, making the short word into one with several syllables as he contemplated what might have been mentioned.

"I told you my sister has always been boy crazy and the more outrageous of the two of us, right?"

Justin answered with a nod of his head as he clasped her hand to lead her into the ocean-themed amusement park.

"Well, when I mentioned buying a house big enough they could move down here too, Ashlyn, of course, had to ask about all the eligible bachelors in the area. At the time, I only knew about your family, and I didn't know Brie had arrived in town and moved in with Bobby. So, I basically described you, your brother, and cousins to entice her to wanna move."

Justin pulled out his wallet and paid for their admission into the park as Amy continued telling him the story about her time with her mother and sister on Christmas Day.

"When I got to Bobby and mentioned that he's the police chief, Ashlyn actually asked if he might use his cuffs on her in the bedroom." Amy shook her head like Ashlyn's question was too outlandish for her to consider serious.

Damn, guess that means Amy's not up for any bondage games in the bedroom. Not that I'd ever wanna use anything as rough as handcuffs, but maybe some of my old ties, or a scarf like Amy gave Char for her birthday would be fun to try. Hmmm, with a blindfold and an assortment of things I could tease her with.

Amy's grin spread across her face like she had an idea about something she would enjoy. "She's gonna be so disappointed that she lost her chance to live out her kinky cop fantasies when I tell her Bobby's getting married."

Justin couldn't contain his laugh at seeing the ornery expression on Amy's face at thinking about taunting her sister. *Damn, maybe hanging around with my family is rubbing off on her, 'cause that sounds like something one of us would do to pick on our siblings or cousins.*

"Well, if she's super upset," Justin advised when his laughter died down. "Then we'll just hafta introduce her to Detective Dusty Deere, Bobby's second-in-command, or one of the other officers that work at the HDPD while she's in town."

"Maybe we should warn Bobby tomorrow to have all his eligible male officers wear their body armor to protect them from my sister while she's here." Amy giggled with glee.

Justin chuckled with her, not really laughing at what she imagined her sister might do with one of the town cops, but just because she was laughing.

I hope her mentioning warning Bobby tomorrow means she'll be on the ranch after church, Justin thought as they made their way over to the first orca exhibit. *Even if I hafta be more hands-off with the family around than I'm being today with constantly holding her hand, I can't stand the thought of going a day without at least seeing her.*

They continued enjoying the rest of the exhibits and sea-life shows with Justin dreaming about spending every day of the rest of his life adoring Amy.

Chapter Six

Sunday, February 17, 2019

Amy wasn't sure she really belonged at the Burleson Ranch when Justin's family was meeting to discuss such personal information as their family tree, but she couldn't bring herself to refuse Charlotte's invitation. *Maybe I can catch Charlotte first thing and have her show me how to fix the issues I'm having on my own tree, so I can focus on that instead of listening in on their private family matters?*

Not really being a religious person, Amy didn't normally attend the Sunday church services, except when she felt she had to because of other events coinciding with them, like when she was in town originally with the Lees for Kay and Anthony's wedding and the festivities surrounding it. But knowing the whole Burleson family attended every week, and she wouldn't know what time to go to the ranch for the DNA review that Charlotte invited her to if she wasn't also at the potluck dinner after church, Amy got up and went for the first time since moving into her house.

It wasn't that she didn't believe in God. She just didn't think He really cared if she was sitting on a church pew every Sunday. She was a good person; she prayed on occasion, tried to treat everyone she met with kindness, donated to various charities regularly, and even did some volunteer work before her move to Texas. She believed living a life trying to emulate a loving and benevolent God was much more important than picking a religion and expecting to get an automatic pass to Heaven by being in church every week.

Of course, that didn't stop her from taking a casserole to the potluck dinner, so she'd know exactly when to go to the ranch with all of Justin's family. Once she was there, she actually had a good time. She enjoyed the morning service and met a few more people from town at the potluck, even though she still ended up sitting with a couple of the Burlesons and the other women they'd been friends with for years that she'd recently met and really liked.

Unfortunately, having to get her empty casserole dish from the middle of the table where at least fifty other people were trying to get their dishes meant she was bringing up the rear when making her way to the ranch. By the time she made it to her car, she got hung up in a traffic jam of people leaving the church. When she finally cleared the logjam of people and got to the ranch, she was the last to arrive and the only vehicle she could see that didn't belong to a member of the Burleson family.

Maybe I shouldn't've come? I feel really awkward going up to knock on the door when they're all already inside.

Amy parked at the house Anthony and Kay were using until their new house was built. She knew they were out of town for work, but she wasn't sure which house everyone was meeting at, so she figured it best to park there since it was central to all the others around her. Instead of going door-to-door to find out where she was supposed to meet Charlotte and the rest of the Burlesons, she pulled out her phone and opened her text message app. Before she could pull up Charlotte's contact information to send her a text to find out where to meet, she was startled by a knock on her car window.

Amy dropped her phone as she squealed, looking up to see Justin standing beside her car.

"Sorry, Sweetheart, didn't mean to scare you." Justin held his right hand up in surrender as he opened her car door with the left.

Amy reached down and picked up her cell phone from her floorboard before putting it in the side pocket of her purse and grabbing her laptop bag.

"It's okay." Amy stood and shut her car door. "I probably should've been looking up to see where everyone seemed to be meeting, instead of looking at my phone to text and ask."

"We're meeting at Aunt Hazel and Uncle Bob's." Justin motioned with his hand in the direction of the huge white house she'd stayed in back in November. "We all end up here for Sunday supper anyway, so it's the most logical place to meet for anything we do as a family."

Amy walked alongside Justin, wondering if she was expected to stay for Sunday supper when they were done with the DNA discussion.

When they walked inside, she found they were all meeting in the dining room, so they had enough table space for several laptops to be set up at once. She sat down in a seat next to Charlotte, who was bringing up her own laptop, so she could ask her about what needed to be done differently on her family tree to be able to get some hints and trace her lineage.

Since Charlotte was in the middle of a conversation with her sister on her other side, Amy took the time to pull out her laptop and boot it up, while Justin sat on her other side and did the same with his. By the time she got set up with the Ancestry site open on her screen, Charlotte had finished her conversation with Becky and stood to direct everyone in the steps to authorize her to look at their DNA results to link them to the Burleson family tree.

Amy didn't think Charlotte's instructions pertained to her, since she wasn't a member of the Burleson family and wouldn't come up on their family tree. So, she pulled up the small family tree she'd started on the site that only contained six people.

Wow, my tree looks puny compared to theirs, Amy thought as she glanced between her screen and Charlotte's.

"You too, Amy." Charlotte pointed at Amy's computer when she took her seat.

"Me too, what?" Amy didn't realize what she'd missed Charlotte saying while focusing on her computer.

"Go in and authorize me to link your DNA to the family tree." Charlotte pointed at Amy's computer once more.

"But I'm not on your family tree," Amy protested, not understanding what Charlotte planned to do with the permission.

"Maybe not yet, but you will be." Charlotte shrugged and smiled. "So, we may as well go ahead and add you from the start since your DNA test is already linked to my account with Justin putting them all on my account when he bought them. And it'll save us from having to try and figure out how to merge our family trees later when ya'll get married."

"Ma-married?" Amy stuttered, looking around and wondering how many of Justin's family members already knew they were dating. "We, we're jus-just friends."

"Char, don't push," Justin commanded from beside Amy as he reached over and squeezed her hand reassuringly. "Amy already has her family tree started. She just wanted our help in learning how to link her DNA test to her tree and figuring out how to trace back through the branches to find ancestors she doesn't know about, not for you to join in with the Matchmaking Mommas before your time."

"Oh, no, don't even lump me in with our mothers!" Charlotte exclaimed, lifting her palms up in surrender.

Several people around the table laughed at Charlotte's abject horror at being compared to the Matchmaking Mommas before Char finally gave in and laughed along with them.

When their laughter died down, Charlotte walked Amy through the steps of linking her DNA test with her profile on the family tree she'd started.

"Okay, now that we got that fixed, what are you having trouble with on your family tree?" Charlotte queried.

"I'm not getting any hints to be able to trace back." Amy showed Charlotte the screen with the six-person tree and no leaves. "I think it's because I don't have enough information on my dad and grandparents. So, maybe once my mom gets here next week to give me full names with proper spelling and birth and death dates and locations it'll improve, but I'd kinda like to figure out how I'm related to some of my DNA matches before then."

"Oh, well, the best way to do that is to look at your matches and check out their family trees if they're public." Charlotte went on to show them all how to do that, since that was the main reason the Burlesons were meeting.

Soon, Amy felt herself relaxing as everyone began chatting about finding matches. Since Bobby and Brooklyn had just sent in their DNA to be tested, they were working on building Brooklyn's branch on the Burleson family tree with administrator rights to work on the tree that Charlotte started on her account. The rest of the Burlesons seemed to be focused on finding cousins that were matches with more than one of them, actively looking for their second-great-grandaunt's descendants with the hope of being able to pass on the trust fund that their third-great-grandfather had left them.

Amy was at a loss as to where to start with looking at her matches since her mom and sister were the only living relatives she knew of, and they hadn't submitted their DNA for testing. Looking at the long list of people that she was genetically related to was daunting, especially since she had no idea who they were or how she was related to them.

All I can do is look at them and see what I find. Amy clicked on the name of her first match, Donna Sinclair, with whom she shared twenty-eight percent of her DNA. According to the site, with that much DNA in common, Donna Sinclair was either her grandmother, grandchild, aunt, niece, or half-sibling.

Well, at least I can narrow it down to grandmother, aunt, niece, or half-sibling, since I don't even have children, much less grandchildren. Unless my grandchildren are gonna invent time travel and put their DNA in here for me to see them twenty or thirty years before they're born. Amy giggled at her thoughts.

"What's so funny?" Justin leaned in to look at her screen.

"Just a silly thought about my grandchildren inventing time travel and coming back in time to put their DNA on this site for me to see them as a match long before they're born." Amy pointed to the list where it noted her match could be her grandchild and Justin chuckled with her.

"Wow, that's a close match." Justin motioned to the amount of DNA Amy shared with Donna Sinclair. "That's like twice as much as I share with my cousins and slightly more than I share with Uncle Bob."

"Really?" Amy looked at Justin's screen to see if he had his match list up for her to see the amounts he shared with his known family.

"Yeah, see." Justin turned his computer, angling his screen toward Amy so she could see it better. He was on a page looking at how he matched up with a person with only initials listed, so he backed out to the main list of DNA matches to show her. Once he scrolled back to the top of the list, she saw he shared fifty percent with each of his parents, between forty-seven and forty-nine percent with each of his siblings, twenty-six percent with his uncle, and between eleven and thirteen percent with his cousins, Anthony, Charlotte, and Becky.

"Okay, so Donna is definitely closer than a cousin," Amy realized, her heart rate accelerating as she wondered if she was looking at a paternal grandmother, aunt, niece, or half-sibling. *Did our father have other kids before he met Mom? Or worse, while he was with Mom?*

With the match profile not giving her any information about the woman, Amy had no idea how old she was to be able to start to figure out how they might be related. *Maybe she's my paternal grandmother and used her maiden name on here?*

"Hey, you okay?" Justin reached over to rub his hand up and down on her back.

"Yeah," Amy replied, trying to shake off the anxious feeling she was having about finding her closest match on the DNA website. "Just overwhelmed by the possibilities. With so many private people listed on her tree and no personal information on her profile other than her name, I'm not sure how to figure out how we're related."

"You can send her a message through the site to ask about her parents and siblings to see if any names are familiar." Charlotte pointed out the message button on the page showing their DNA details.

"Yeah, maybe later." Amy smiled slightly at Charlotte, thinking she'd rather ask her mother if she recognized the name first. "Maybe Mom will recognize her name and be able to tell me how we're related. I know there was some animosity between my mom and my father's family, so I'd rather wait to see if any of my matches are people who still have hard feelings for Mom before messaging them."

"Yeah, okay, that's understandable." Justin smiled reassuringly before removing his hand from her back and pointing to her computer. "Let's move on to the next match then. Maybe the next one will have a tree with more people you can look at to see if you recognize any names."

Going back to the full list of DNA matches, Amy found her next closest match was Richard S., whom she shared twenty-five percent of her DNA with, so he was another close family member. When she clicked on his name in the list it brought up the page showing their match details and he also had a public tree she could look at to try and determine their relation. Unfortunately, when she did, she didn't recognize any of the names on it, though there was a whole line of

Sinclairs after a couple generations of "Private" being listed in the boxes for his parents and grandparents.

Amy focused on the Sinclair line as she looked through Richard's family tree, but she couldn't find Donna Sinclair. With the site displaying the word "Private" in any boxes on trees other than her own for living individuals, including the box Amy assumed was Richard, she presumed that was why she couldn't see Donna on Richard's tree.

When she didn't see any Lawtons or Andersons on Richard's family tree, she decided to go on to the next DNA match. She had several that were in the eleven to thirteen percent range, which indicated they were either first cousins, great-grandparents, grandaunts/granduncles, grandnieces/grandnephews, half aunts/uncles, or half nieces/nephews. With them only being listed with initials or monikers that looked like old-school screen names, Amy had no way of knowing any of their names to see if they were Lawtons like her mother's side of the family or Anderson's like her father's. A couple of them only had unlinked or private trees, so even when Amy tried to look at them, she couldn't see anything without paying extra for a subscription to the site or getting permission from the owner of the specific tree. And the few who did have trees linked were like her small tree with only a couple generations listed, and most of the boxes were marked "Private" to keep her from gleaning any information from them.

She spent a couple hours quietly going through what little she could see of the family trees for her DNA matches, going as far down the list as the first person listed as her third or fourth cousin. The Burlesons were doing the same all around her, only they were loudly discussing their shared matches while trying to figure out how they fit on their much larger family tree.

"Wait, did you just say you're looking at the Avington family tree?" Bobby jumped up out of his chair and shouted his question over to Charlotte, who was just discussing a shared match with Justin that the rest of their family was looking for in their shared match lists.

"Yes," Charlotte replied, looking at her brother questioningly. "Why?"

"You think it's the same Avingtons?" Brooklyn tugged on Bobby's shirt sleeve.

"Who are the Avingtons?" Jen popped her head over her computer from the other side of Justin to look over at Bobby and Brooklyn.

"Avington, that's the name of the security firm you hired in Georgia, right?" Julie nodded at Bobby from her seat across the table from her twin.

"Yes," Bobby confirmed, nodding to Julie before turning to look down at Brooklyn beside him. "I don't know if it's the same family, Brie-Baby, but it's certainly possible. Back when we were in training together, one of the things we learned about was how common certain last names were for trying to track people down. Being curious when neither of our last names were on the list of common surnames we reviewed, we looked them up. Burleson is like the two-thousand-seven-hundred-something most common last name in the US, and the twenty-nine-thousand-eight-hundred-something most common in the world. Blake couldn't find a listing for how common the surname Avington was in the US, but it was over a million down the list for the world. With it being that rare of a last name, I hafta wonder if Blake or his brothers are the common matches everyone's finding."

"Blake's that boy you brought home for supper a few times when you were training in San Antonio, right?" Hazel, Bobby's mother, chimed in, questioning her oldest son.

"Yes," Bobby agreed, nodding his head at his mother.

"Guess it's a good thing we didn't try to match him up with one of our daughters back then, if he's the one all the kids are matching up with now," Justin's mom, Susan chuckled at Hazel's mortified face.

"Goodness, I didn't even think about needing to check these DNA lists to make sure we're not trying to match our kids up with their distant cousins," Hazel gasped, covering her mouth with her hand.

"Yes, Mom, please make sure you get Ancestry usernames for anyone you want to push us toward dating," Charlotte glibly suggested. "So I can make sure they're on my DNA match list."

Amy giggled at how Charlotte was looking for a way of avoiding future dates set up by the Matchmaking Mommas. When several people noticed and turned her way, she decided it was best to turn the conversation away from the matchmaking and back to the DNA matches. She looked over at Bobby and offered what she hoped was a more helpful suggestion. "Why don't you call your friend and ask him if he's on the site?"

"Yeah, Bobby, call Blake and see if he or his brothers have done their DNA and are using these usernames." Justin pointed to his screen, where there was a list of shared matches with either initials or screen names that couldn't be deciphered into names.

Bobby walked around the table to look at Justin's screen as he pulled out his phone and dialed a number. He put the phone up to his ear as the call went through.

"Hey, Blake," Bobby addressed his friend through the phone. "Not much, just hanging out with the family and trying to trace our ancestry." Bobby paused, apparently so Blake could speak. "Yeah, have you or your brothers done one of those online DNA tests?" Another pause, combined with a chuckle. "Yeah, maybe. Most of the family did it last month, but Brie and I just sent ours in this last week, so we don't have our match lists yet. But there are several people linked to an Avington family tree that are showing up as matches to those of us who've gotten their results."

Bobby read off the list of usernames Justin pointed out to him before saying, "Holy shit! Seriously? Yeah, let me put you on speaker so you can talk to all your newfound cousins."

Bobby pulled the phone away from his ear and tapped the screen to switch it to speaker mode, holding it out between Amy and Justin and slightly above their heads.

"So, I guess it's a good thing I never broke Bro Code and asked one of your sisters to go out with me?" A deep chuckle rumbled out of the phone following Blake's question.

"I take it one of these usernames is yours," Charlotte interjected, leaning into Amy so that her voice could be heard through Bobby's phone.

"Yeah, I'm M.A.A.B.A.," Blake informed them, chuckling again. "And which of my new cousins am I speaking with?"

"I'm Bobby's sister, Charlotte. And according to what I'm looking at on here, you and I share fifty-four centimorgans on two segments of our DNA."

"Shit! Seriously? Let me pull my list up. I thought Bobby was joking around that we were matching up with ya'll."

"Dude, why would I joke around about being related to your ugly mug?" Bobby questioned, deadpan.

"Holy! Wow! You got a lotta Burlesons on this site." Blake exclaimed. "Bob, Jon, Anthony, JJ, Charlotte, Becky, Justin, Jen, and Julie are all showing in my match list. And we thought we were nuts when all six of us took the tests. How many of ya'll took it?"

"Yeah, well, our moms, Anthony's wife and daughters, Brie, and our friend, Amy, also took the test but none of them should show up as a match with you," Bobby elaborated into his phone. "And you'll probably see me show up on your list in a few weeks and then Jake and Josh whenever they come home on leave and take the test, too."

"Damn, I can't wait to tell Dad to look at his results again." Blake's voice was laced with excitement. "He's gonna flip to find out we're related. Now we just hafta figure out how."

"That's what we're wondering about most." Justin's excitement was showing in his eyes when Amy looked at him as he spoke. "Since you're not showing as related to us through our mothers, it has to be through the Burlesons somewhere further back."

Oh, wow, maybe this is the line they've been hoping to find, Amy thought, wondering if she should excuse herself from the conversation since she wasn't a part of the family, or if she should stay there to support Justin in case it wasn't the relatives he wanted to find most. *But can I really play the supportive girlfriend role when we're trying to keep anything more than our friendship hidden from everyone else in the room? No, I need to go and not push myself into the middle of his family quest like I'm one of them.*

While everyone was pushing in to see Charlotte's computer screen where she was looking at the Avingtons' family tree as they discussed with Blake who their common ancestor might be, Amy closed her laptop and slipped it into her bag. As she was slinking out of the crowd to leave, Justin reached out and took her hand.

"Hey, where're you goin'?"

"I, uh, just have some things I need to get done at home." Amy felt self-conscious for trying to sneak away. "I'll see you tomorrow at work."

"Oh, okay." Justin released her hand and let her go. "See ya tomorrow."

Amy watched as he turned back to his family and started talking about looking for the surnames of his various grandmothers in the Avington tree since they couldn't find a Burleson there. As she left the Burleson Ranch, she couldn't help but feel a little like a coward, running away before anyone saw how much she wanted to be a part of a big, boisterous family like theirs.

~ ~ ~

Justin wasn't sure what'd happened with Amy that she suddenly had to leave when he thought the plan was for her to stay for Sunday supper after they spent the afternoon looking at their ancestry. But he knew he couldn't push her for answers with the majority of his family in the room, so he let her go when she gave him a lame excuse for why she was running off.

Not that I can really push much tomorrow at work, either. Maybe I can convince her to go to dinner with me after work? But if we go out where we can sneak off without my family realizing we're on a date, do I really wanna risk messing things up for us when we're just getting started by asking about something that could be related to the DNA tests? Maybe I should just back off a little and let her tell me whenever she feels like we're close enough to talk about more sensitive issues?

Justin looked over to where Bobby was kneeling beside Charlotte with his arm around Brooklyn as the rest of their family members were searching through family trees to see if they could find any common last names between them to determine how they were related to the Avingtons.

He's obviously got this whole dating thing down, so maybe I should follow his advice and wait for Amy to bring up anything about our racial differences and whatever it is about our DNA tests that spooked her today.

"I don't understand why this says we both have Davis as a shared surname in our family trees, but I can't see it in the people I can see on your tree," Charlotte sighed into the phone laying beside her on the table where she was taking point in talking to Blake.

"That's because Davis is my aunt's husband's last name," Blake explained. "So, he's on the tree but we don't share any DNA with him. Once I get Dad to give you administrator rights on our tree, you'll be able to see him along with the rest of our living relatives."

"Yeah, that'll come in handy to get to know who all we're related to," Becky pointed out from her seat on the other side of Charlotte. "But with as little DNA as we share with each other, our common ancestors are more likely to be a few generations back and long dead."

"Yeah, well, it's obviously not on mom's side of the family, so we have fewer branches to look at since we've hit a few dead ends on the Avington side. You haven't been able to find any names you recognize on the Langston or Miller branches of the tree?"

"No, but I've just been searching the last names of our grandmothers since you don't have a Burleson on your tree." Charlotte clicked her mouse to expand the Langston branch of the Avington tree out a few more generations. "I need to pull together a list of all the surnames on the Teague, Davis, and King branches of our tree to search them in your tree."

"This is going to take forever," Jen whined, shaking her head as Justin squeezed in closer beside his sister to see the Avingtons' tree over Charlotte's head.

Bobby started calling out names for Charlotte to look for where he was in the Burleson tree since he and Brooklyn had been working on adding her branches to it. Charlotte jotted them down on a notepad beside her as she scanned the Avingtons' tree for them. When she couldn't find any of the names Bobby gave her on the Langston branch of the Avingtons' tree, she collapsed it back to Blake's grandmother, Carolyn Langston, who was married to his grandfather, Aaron Avington, and expanded the Miller branch that started with Blake's great-grandmother, Shirley Miller, who was married to his great-grandfather, Jack Avington.

"Wait," Justin shouted, pointing at the end of the Avington line of their tree, Benjamin Avington, who was listed as Jack's father, and was Blake's second-great-grandfather. "You don't have a second-great-grandmother listed on your tree. Do you know who was married to Benjamin Avington?"

"Dude, I only know my first-great-grandmother's name because Dad found it when he was putting together the family tree." Blake chuckled before continuing. "I'll hafta ask Dad if he didn't find anything on the second-great-grandma. Or if he just didn't get it added before his subscription expired. Maybe he knows who she was."

"Oh, wow!" Charlotte exclaimed, turning to look at Justin. "Are you thinking what I'm thinking?"

"Yeah." Justin nodded at his cousin when he noticed a flicker of hope in her eyes. "From looking at the birth years that are showing on this screen for Benjamin and Jack, and with us all sharing about the right amount of DNA to be fourth cousins, I think it's possible that Benjamin Avington married our second-great-grandaunt, Mary Burleson."

"Holy shit!" Justin's dad, Jon, shouted, jumping up from his seat on the other side of the room and running around the table to see Charlotte's computer screen. Justin was shocked to hear his father shout the expletive as he'd never heard either of his parents cuss before. "Bob, get over here. You've gotta see this. If our kids are right…"

It was an emotional moment when Justin watched his father tear up to the point he couldn't complete his sentence. Jon Burleson wasn't the only one in the room with tears in their eyes. Everyone who'd gone back to their seats after initially crowding Charlotte while she looked at the Avingtons' tree made their way back into a huddle. Justin even had watery eyes as he hugged his sister. *Damn, I wish Amy would've stayed to be here for this.*

There was a poignant moment of silence as it sank in that they might have just solved a hundred-year-old family mystery. Even Blake was quiet on the other end of the phone line until a few of the girls broke into sobs as the happy tears flowed.

"Hey, now, being related to me isn't so bad that ya'll need to start crying about it." Blake tried to lighten the mood with a little levity, not realizing that the Burlesons were all overwhelmed with joy at possibly finding the daughter that Jonah Burleson went to his grave missing.

"It's all happy tears, Cuz," Bobby promised, picking up his phone from the table beside Charlotte. "But you might wanna tell your dad to renew his subscription to verify how we're related. If it's really through our great aunt Mary, then life as you know it is about to change."

"Oh, man, sorry, I didn't realize this was such a big deal for ya'll." Blake sounded remorseful for his joking comment.

"Yeah, our family has been trying to find out what happened to Mary for the last hundred years," Bobby elaborated, hugging Brooklyn to his side as he spoke to his friend. "And if our hunch is right, your dad might just be able to finally solve the mystery of where she went after World War I when she didn't come home to the ranch."

"Wow, yeah, okay. How about I head over to Dad's now and see if I can get the whole family there for a Skype session to meet everyone?"

"Sounds good," Bobby replied, looking around the room to see the rest of the family nodding in agreement.

"How long do you think it'll take you to get everyone together?" Aunt Hazel probed.

"I can be at Mom and Dad's in about fifteen minutes," Blake replied. "But it might take an hour or two to get all my brothers there."

"Then let's plan the Skype for two hours from now, so I have time to get everyone through the kitchen and fed first."

Leave it to Aunt Hazel to focus on making sure our bellies are full before we dive in to what could be a DNA rabbit hole.

"That works for me. Maybe I can get a homecooked meal from Mom before we solve our DNA mystery, too."

They said their goodbyes and put away most of their computers before heading to the kitchen to fix plates.

"Hey, where did Amy go?" Charlotte questioned Justin as they sat back down at the dining room table to eat.

"She had some things she had to get done at home." Justin shrugged, not really sure how to explain his feeling that there was something about the DNA stuff that scared her away from continuing to hang out with the family.

"You don't think us connecting with some of our matches bothered her, do you?" Jen hypothesized from his other side.

Shit! That's probably it. Since she didn't even wanna message her closest matches, it was probably too much for her to see us not only messaging ours, but also calling one when Bobby recognized his friend's name.

"I don't know," Justin finally admitted, shaking his head at his own lack of sensitivity at how his family connecting with newfound relatives would make Amy feel. "She just said she had some things to do at home and she'd see me tomorrow at work."

"Oh, Justin," Jen sighed, reaching over to pat his hand. "If you ever wanna be more than friends with her, you're going to have to learn how to listen to more than just her words."

Justin ducked his head and focused his attention on his plate. He wasn't sure exactly what Jen meant. *But at least, if Jen thinks I'm still stuck in the friend zone, she doesn't know we've started dating. Maybe that means nobody else in my family has caught on yet either.*

When Justin didn't respond, Jen dropped the subject. The conversation around the table turned to how to figure out if Mary Burleson married Benjamin Avington, either during or immediately after World War I.

"I think I'm going to start by looking at Benjamin's profile on the Avington family tree." Charlotte pointed to her computer that she'd just moved into the chair beside her where Amy was previously sitting.

"I already texted Blake to give him Mary's full name, birth date, and what we know about her time as a nurse in the war." Bobby gestured with his fork between bites. "I figured if he's already at his parents' house, they might be able to look at the hints on Benjamin and see if her info lines up with his."

"Now that I have an idea of where she might've gone after the war, I can do a search for her in records from Georgia, too," Charlotte added. "Maybe I can find a marriage license or something to link them together."

"Did you not have any hints on her from the site already?" Becky inquired between bites.

"Yeah, but they were all from before the war," Charlotte replied. "With not knowing where she went after the war, I couldn't narrow down the search to a specific state, so all I could say for sure was that she didn't come back to Texas. Or if she did, she didn't leave any records for me to find when I searched. And I searched Texas' marriage records, birth records, census records, and even death records and couldn't find her."

Knowing they would get back to the discussion of Mary possibly marrying Benjamin when the Avingtons Skyped with them in a little while, Justin decided to switch the topic up to see if Charlotte could answer his questions about their lack of Native American in their ethnicity reports. "Have you had a chance to go over all the hints for Memmaw Judy's family branch on our tree?"

"Not all of them, but I've gone a few generations back there," Charlotte replied.

"Did you find anything in the paper trail about the Native American ancestry she told us stories about?"

"Oh, yeah," Charlotte laughed. "Apparently there were some not-so-scrupulous members of the Teague family back in the day. I found some Teagues on the Dawes Rolls, but they weren't in Memmaw's direct lineage. Memmaw's third- or fourth-great-grandpa apparently tried to claim he was Cherokee on his mother's side of the family, but was found to be lying about it, thinking they'd get free land in Oklahoma."

"Seriously?" Charlotte nodded an affirmative to Justin's question. "So, why did Memmaw think she was part Cherokee if they were proven wrong so many generations back?"

"I guess he was bitter about not being able to claim the free land and continued to claim his supposed heritage and later generations didn't realize it was all lies." Charlotte shrugged before continuing. "And her second-great-grandfather, Lorenzo Dow Teague, has a criminal record for liquor crimes in Arkansas, but he wasn't all bad since he fought for the Union in the Civil War."

"You've found records for our ancestors going back to the Civil War?" Uncle Bob looked surprised at how far back Charlotte was able to trace their family records.

"Oh, yeah, and way farther back than that," Charlotte answered her dad. "I haven't followed all the hints to verify everything, but the potential parent hints took me all the way back to England in the fifteen-hundreds on the Teague line and several of the lines that married Teagues to lead down to us. I think I went back as far as our fifteenth-great-grandparents on a few of them. And only back to the late sixteen-hundreds on the Burleson line."

"So you found Jonah's parents?" Justin's dad, Jon, arched an eyebrow, obviously curious about what she'd found.

"Yes," Charlotte confirmed once she swallowed the bite of food she'd just taken. She turned to her computer and clicked a few times, probably bringing up the specifics about their Burleson ancestors. "Jonah's mother's name was also Mary, and the census records I found for her listed her as mulatto. I couldn't find anything about her parents, but it appears she was born to a slave mother and later sold with her mother to a John Burleson who owned a farm in Alabama. I can't find anything for certain about his father, but knowing the atrocities of American history, I'm assuming Jonah's father was that John Burleson. It's his lineage that I traced back to an Aaron Burleson born in sixteen-ninety-five in Wales."

"So the first Mary Burleson is where we got our Southern Bantu Peoples listed in our ethnicity?" JJ voiced the question that Justin was thinking.

"I'm assuming, since she's the only person I've found in our tree that wasn't listed as white on the census records," Charlotte answered then grinned. "Well, and Jonah. He was listed as mulatto on the eighteen-seventy census records with his mom, but when he left Alabama and moved here, he started claiming white. I guess he was light enough to claim he was just tan from working outside all the time to be able to get away with the change in an area where nobody knew his mom."

"So, Memmaw's ancestors weren't the only ones who lied to the government about their race," Julie giggled.

"Yeah, but at least Jonah was doing it to avoid persecution and not for material gain." Jen giggled along with her twin. "I'm actually kinda proud of him for getting away with it."

Several heads nodded in agreement around the table, including Justin's. They finished their meal with Charlotte going through the family tree to tell them a little about the various ancestors she'd found fascinating in her first month of research. Once the table was cleared and the dishes were done, the laptops made a reappearance, though Justin mostly focused on what Charlotte was doing on hers.

First, she went to Mary Burleson's profile on the Burleson family tree to search for hints about her life. Once she put in the state of Georgia as Mary's possible state of residence after the war, the hints started showing up.

"Oh, yes, yes, yes!" Charlotte shouted, throwing her arms up in a V with each "yes" she screamed, like back in her high school cheerleading days, which was probably the last time Justin had seen his cousin act so excited about anything. "Marriage records, birth records, they're all popping up now!"

"Don't keep us in suspense," her mom, Hazel motioned for her daughter to continue speaking. "Tell us who she married."

"Give me a minute to look, Mom," Charlotte smiled and rolled her eyes at her mother before clicking the first record. "Okay, well, that's disappointing."

"What's disappointing?" Becky leaned in to look over Charlotte's shoulder at the record on her screen.

"The first marriage record is for a Mary Fulton who married a John Burleson in the eighteen-hundreds. I guess I should've narrowed down the years I was searching for before hitting the search button." Charlotte went on to click a few more records only to click the "ignore" button and move on to the next one.

They were all on pins and needles watching her go through the records when Bobby's computer chimed with a Skype notification.

"Hey Blake." Bobby accepted the video conference on his computer. "Or I guess I should say, hello to all the Avingtons. We're not all gonna be able to get close enough together to fit us all on the screen at once like that, so how about I walk around and introduce everyone before we start trying to figure out how we're related."

"Sounds good," someone chuckled from Bobby's computer.

Justin assumed it was Blake who was speaking, though he sounded a little different over the computer than he had over the phone a couple hours earlier. It took a few minutes for Bobby to walk around and make introductions multiple times and Justin wasn't sure he'd remember who was who with only a brief glance at the six faces on the screen. But luckily, Bobby invited them all to come to his and Brooklyn's wedding, so Justin figured he'd get to know his new cousins better then, even if they didn't end up being Mary's descendants who would inherit seats on the Burleson Incorporated board of directors.

Once everyone was introduced, Bobby took the seat between Justin and Charlotte, so Byron Avington could talk more with Charlotte about what they were finding when looking at the family trees they'd each started.

"When Blake first got here, he insisted on renewing my subscription, so I could look at the hints I hadn't followed yet." Byron poked the son next to him, whom Justin assumed was Blake.

Leah Mae Wright

"And were you able to find out who Benjamin was married to?" Charlotte probed.

"Well, yes, and no," Byron replied. "I found his marriage certificate, but it's in French. Though the names are handwritten in English, whoever filled out the paperwork had horrible handwriting, so I can't make out the name for certain."

"Why would the marriage certificate be in French?" Becky furrowed her brow in confusion.

"If they got married while they were both in France during the war," Justin answered.

"Oh, yeah, didn't think about that," Becky replied, shaking her head at herself for not seeing the obvious reason for a French marriage certificate. "Can you tell when they got married? Maybe that'll help us find it, too. If Benjamin married our Aunt Mary, then we should come up with the same certificate when we search for her records in France in the same year."

"Nineteen-nineteen," Byron replied.

Charlotte went back to the search screen for Mary and set the location for France and then adjusted the date range to encompass the two years prior and the two years after 1919, just in case it wasn't completely clear, or the search might also find a birth record for the couple's first child.

As soon as the parameters were changed, the marriage record showed up first in the search. "This is it!" Charlotte exclaimed as her eyes filled with tears. "Bride, Mary Burleson, groom, Benjamin Avington, married November seventh, nineteen-nineteen."

"You can actually read that?" Byron gave her a shocked look through the computer screen.

"Well, no, I can't read it on the actual document, but the citation for the document gives me the details in English."

"I must've missed that screen." Byron turned to fiddle with the laptop on the table beside him.

I guess they're Skyping on Blake's laptop so Byron can look at the site on his at the same time, like we're doing with Bobby and Charlotte's computers here, Justin thought as what they were saying sunk in. *Holy shit! That's the proof that the Avingtons are Burleson heirs.*

There was a lot of crying and more hugging and even a few squeals of delight at finally solving the mystery of where Mary Burleson went after the war before Justin's dad and uncle took over the conversation with Byron. Not wanting to make the Avingtons uncomfortable by seeming to listen in on the conversation about the trust and their interest in Burleson Incorporated, Justin scooted over closer to Charlotte and watched her as she followed the new hints that popped up and added the Avingtons to the Burleson family tree.

He couldn't believe they'd finally found their long-lost family all because he'd gotten the crazy idea to give Charlotte a subscription to a DNA site and tests for their whole family for her birthday. He just wished everyone in the family would've been there when they figured it out.

When he thought about who was missing from around the table as they celebrated this family milestone, it wasn't just Jake, Josh, Anthony, and his new wife and daughters that Justin was missing. He wished Amy had stayed to be there with him. He wanted to share everything about his life with her, especially the good times like this, because he wanted to be her family, too.

Hopefully, we'll get there. Soon. Though I'll wait a lifetime for her if I have to.

<div align="center">~~~</div>

Saturday, February 23, 2019

The last week seemed to have flown by for Amy. Everything was business as usual at work, but then after work, she and Justin had snuck off for nightly dates. Their goodnight kisses after their outings were always chaste since they were usually in the parking lot of wherever they'd met up for the dates, but Amy still felt like she was falling for Justin way faster than she ever expected.

To keep things from being noticed by his family, they left the office in their own vehicles each day. Then they met up at a restaurant, a roller rink, a mini-golf place, and even an arcade, but Amy's favorite was when they met up at the Japanese Tea Garden.

Since the garden closed at dusk, Justin had modified their work schedules, so they could both get off work at three in the afternoon to be able to walk through the whole place before it closed. It was nice to stroll hand in hand with him while talking about anything and everything they could think of, including both of their revelations about their DNA tests.

Justin had told her about the changes that would be coming to Burleson Incorporated with them solving the hundred-year-old family mystery about Mary Burleson's whereabouts after World War I. She still couldn't believe he was actually happy about losing one-and-a-half percent interest in the company to share it with his newfound cousins. He certainly wasn't driven by money like so many of the people she'd met throughout her life.

Amy had also confided in Justin about her concerns over not seeing some of the surnames she expected to find in her DNA match list. There were no Lawtons like her maternal grandfather and no Andersons like her father. And with her closest matches being named Sinclair, she was afraid she was going to find out that either her mother, her grandmother, or both had lied about who'd fathered their children.

Like the true best friend he'd rapidly become for her, Justin had listened as she'd poured out her emotions on the stone pavers throughout the Japanese Tea Garden. He didn't interrupt or offer platitudes to try and get her to move on and talk about a happier topic. When she veered off into grief over losing her grandparents and having never met her father, Justin found them a bench to sit on where he could hold her while she cried.

When she'd lifted her head from his chest and noticed the large wet spot she'd left on his navy blue button-down shirt, he'd shrugged it off as no big deal, telling her he would always be there to give her a shoulder to cry on if she needed it. He didn't make her feel guilty for being so emotional. He didn't even try to cajole her by telling her not to worry about the possibilities until she had all the facts, like Randi had when she'd called her after leaving the Burleson Ranch on Sunday afternoon.

Justin was supportive and made her feel validated in her belief that her life as she knew it was most likely built on a foundation of lies. He even offered to come with her to pick her mom and sister up from the airport and be by her side while she asked the hard questions she had for Andrea Lawton.

Amy had declined his offer, but she knew he was only a phone call away if things got to be too much for her and she needed his supportive presence to ground her after her talk with her mother. Amy sucked in a deep breath, then slowly blew it out as she walked from her car in the short-term parking lot at the airport in San Antonio toward the baggage claim area, where she was meeting her mother and sister. She repeated the breathing technique a couple times, hoping she wouldn't have to make that call to Justin because of the upsetting news when she showed her mother the DNA test results.

And hopefully, their excitement for being here will bring mine back out at having them here, so they won't notice how stressed I am about all this DNA stuff until we get back to the house to be able to talk it out.

Amy plastered on a smile that she hoped didn't look as fake as it felt, when she heard Ashlyn scream her name from across the terminal. As soon as she reached them, she was engulfed in hugs and not given a chance to get a word in edgewise with Ashlyn excitedly regaling her with tales of the trip down from Tulsa.

Somehow, they managed to get their luggage and load it into the trunk of Amy's car amidst the whirlwind of stories Ashlyn was going on and on about. When she finally settled down about halfway to Heart's Destiny, Amy finally got the chance to tell them about the wedding shower they were invited to the next day and the birthday party for JJ Burleson on Friday the first.

"I can't believe you're finally introducing me to the hot cop at his wedding shower." Ashlyn shook her head at Amy through the rearview mirror, since she was sitting in the back seat of the car. "I knew I should've come down with you when you first moved, so I could've had a shot with him."

"That still would've been too late to have a chance with Bobby. He met Brooklyn at Anthony and Kay's wedding reception." Amy filled the rest of the ride to her home with her explanation of who Brook was and how Bobby had met and fallen in love with her as Brie, which was why he still called her Brie when everyone else used her real name.

"If we're going to their wedding shower," Amy's mom, Andrea, supposed as they were carrying their suitcases into the house. "We should probably go buy them a little something as a wedding gift. I'm assuming you know where they're registered?"

"Actually, they did like Anthony and Kay and asked for donations to charity organizations in their names in lieu of wedding gifts," Amy replied, leading them up the stairs to show them to their rooms. "And since they each used a portion of their trust funds to start the Madeline Ashbury Foundation to help women and children escape from abusive situations, that's the charity I already donated to for all of us."

Amy actually wished the shelter they were opening for the foundation was local instead of being in Brooklyn's former home in Georgia, so she could spend some time there volunteering. But when she'd said as much to Justin, he told her about the youth center in town and suggested they talk to his aunt who ran it about starting a science club there as part of the next round of new classes in the fall. Amy zoned out thinking about how much fun it would be to volunteer there with Justin co-teaching a kids' chemistry class and missed whatever her mother and sister were talking about for the last few minutes.

"Earth to Ames." Ashlyn waved her hand in front of Amy's face. "You still with us or are you off in fantasyland with your hot boss?"

"Sorry," Amy replied, not elaborating on what she'd been off in her head thinking about. She led them back downstairs to the kitchen where they could grab a drink before having a seat at the dining room table to talk.

Amy already had her laptop set up on one end of the table, and she made sure to sit where she could wake it from sleep mode to show her mother the DNA test information.

"Mom, I actually need your help with something," Amy started, taking her time to login to the family tree and DNA website. "Remember I told you about how Justin gave his cousin those DNA tests for their whole family for her birthday last month?"

"Yeah," Andrea replied, nodding her head. "You said something about how everyone at the party took one whether they were related to the Burlesons or not."

"Yeah, well, I got my results back a couple weeks ago." Amy looked at her screen instead of at her mother, so she could take a moment to mask her emotions. "In addition to telling me that I'm thirty-five percent African and sixty-five percent European, it gave me a list of people who've also done the test that I share DNA with.

Apparently, we have a lot more family in the world than just the three of us, so I started a family tree to see how I'm related to all of them. But I'm having a hard time with it because I don't have enough information about Nana and Papa or Dad to get hints about their lives to learn about their parents or siblings to figure out how I'm related to my DNA matches."

"Okay." Andrea hesitated, looking at Amy with trepidation that Amy only caught because she finally looked up at her mother. "And you need me to give you more information for the family tree?"

"Yeah, I figured we'd start there and then maybe have you look at my match list to see if you recognize any names from stories they told you back in the day."

"Oh man, I wish I'd've done a test, too," Ashlyn mewled, scooting over closer to Amy to look at her screen.

"Yeah, well, with us being identical twins, your results would be exactly the same as mine, so you won't be missing out on anything by not actually having to spit in the tiny test tube." Amy giggled at the grossed-out face her sister made at the mention of how the DNA was collected for testing.

"Yeah, thanks for taking one for the team there, Sis." Ashlyn grinned and pointed at the screen. "Now explain our results to me, so I know what to list for race on any paperwork I fill out in the future."

Amy navigated to the ethnicity estimate page first, explaining their breakdown among the various European countries and African regions. Her mother was disappointed that they didn't have more of a racial mix like she'd always been told. Once Amy explained it, using what Justin had told her about the Burlesons learning about their lack of Native American bloodlines the previous Sunday as an example, and passed on what she'd learned about how misinformation was passed down back in the day when mixed-race people didn't really have any way of proving what their ethnic breakdown was before DNA tests, both Andrea and Ashlyn seemed to understand why they thought they were mixed with more than just black and white but actually weren't.

Once they all seemed to figure out that they, too, had been given a presumed history that their ancestors weren't really sure about, then Amy moved on to open the family tree for her mother to fill in full names, birth and death dates, and locations where her family members had lived.

Finally having enough information to recognize the deceased members of her family, the site started giving her hints about their lives. They spent about an hour following the potential parent hints for each of them, adding several generations' worth of grandparents that Amy hadn't ever heard about before from other people's family trees. Before they went through all their ancestors' hints, which would require subscribing to the site, Amy wanted to see if simply adding a couple dozen new people to her tree would show her how she was related to her closest DNA matches, even though none of the new people on her tree shared the last name Sinclair.

"Do you know how we could be related to anyone with the last name Sinclair?" Amy questioned her mother as she clicked over to the page listing her DNA matches.

"What?" Andrea paled as Amy said the name Sinclair.

"My closest matches on here are both Sinclairs, so I thought you might know how we're related to them, since that surname still didn't show up on our family tree." Amy pointed to the top two names on her DNA match list.

Andrea covered her mouth with her hand, her expression one of shock as she read the first two names on Amy's match list. "I was wrong."

Amy barely understood her mother's words as she whispered with her hand still covering her mouth. "Wrong about what, Mom?"

Amy watched, feeling helpless, as tears streamed down her mother's face. Andrea was speaking as she sobbed, but none of the things she was saying were intelligible.

"Mom, it's okay," Ashlyn consoled, moving around the table to wrap a comforting arm around their mother. "You hafta calm down, so we can understand what you're saying."

Andrea continued to cry for several long moments, wrapping an arm around each of her daughters, so she was sandwiched in between them. Amy and Ashlyn each embraced their mother and each other, turning Andrea's sobfest into a group hug.

"I'm so sorry," Andrea finally choked out as the wrenching cries subsided. "All these years, I was wrong. The doctors said you were a little early being born, so when I counted the months back, I didn't think there was any way anyone other than Eddie could be your father."

Amy wasn't sure what to think or how to feel as she learned that Edward Daniel Anderson, the man she'd been told was her dad her whole life, whom both she and Ashlyn got their middle names from, wasn't actually her biological father. *I guess it was a waste of time adding that whole branch of our family tree. Now I get to go and delete it all before trying to figure out who to really add to the tree as our father.*

"Who's our father?" Ashlyn saved Amy from having to voice the painful question.

"His name is David Sinclair," Andrea admitted, releasing her daughters, so she could wipe the tears from her face. "I dated him for about six months before I met Eddie. And we'd been broken up for over a month before anything happened with Eddie, so I thought our last time together was too far back for him to possibly be your father. But Donna is his older sister's name, so if she's showing as your match, it's probably because he's your biological father."

Amy remembered seeing on the list of possible relations with the amount of DNA she shared with Donna Sinclair that she could be her aunt, so she was convinced that David Sinclair was her and Ashlyn's biological father. She clicked on Donna's name to look over her family tree once more, but she was disappointed when she remembered that she couldn't see any information on the people on the tree that were alive and well, which meant she couldn't see anything about her father.

Ashlyn continued to ask questions about their father, but Amy was too numb to register what her mother and sister were talking about. She felt almost robotic as she navigated back to their family tree and started systematically deleting the Anderson branch that she'd just expanded with the false information her mother had given her.

Once that was done, she asked her mother for the correct information to add her father to her family tree, not really recognizing her own voice as she asked for it. Amy added David and Donna Sinclair to her family tree with the limited information her mother had for them, hoping it would be enough to give her hints for her grandparents and any other relatives she had on that side of the family.

She didn't have much luck since the site didn't give out personal information on living individuals, so Amy went back to Donna's family tree and added boxes to her own for each of the people she saw on Donna's that showed private because the people were alive. After that, she added the first few names that showed up as deceased grandparents, copying the information word for word from Donna's tree, until the site finally started giving her hints that she could follow to add the rest of those branches of her family tree easier.

When that was done, she went back to her match list and hovered her cursor over Richard's name. "Do you know a Richard Sinclair? With the amount of DNA we share, he could be our uncle, grandfather, nephew, or half-brother."

"No, I don't know a Richard Sinclair," Andrea denied adamantly, looking at the screen as Amy clicked on Richard's name.

When Amy scrolled down the screen to look at the preview of his family tree, she noticed they now had a common ancestor listed to the left of where the tree was displayed on the page. *David Michael Sinclair,* Amy read the common ancestor's name in her head. *We share our father as a common ancestor.*

Without even thinking about it, Amy clicked the words "View Relationship" under her biological father's name in the Common Ancestor box on the page describing her relationship with Richard Sinclair. That click took her to the ThruLines feature of the website, which showed a mini-family tree with her name and profile picture on the left under the box with their father's name in it and Richard's name on the right under that same box for their father. Instead of a profile picture for Richard, there was a circle with the initials RS. Underneath his name was the words "Half-Brother" with "1768 cM | 33 segments" under their relationship, the amount of DNA they shared.

"He's our half-brother," Amy croaked, her voice only half coming out because of how choked up she was. "We have a half-brother."

"Wait, how can you tell that?" Ashlyn squeezed back in close to Amy to look at her computer screen. "I thought the tree showed his father as private when you were back on that other page. How'd you get it to show his name here?"

"This is the ThruLines feature. It gives me common information on people in both our trees even if they're alive, but I can't see any information about living individuals on other people's trees unless they give me permission." Amy demonstrated by backing out to the other screen where Ashlyn had previously seen the boxes marked "Private" for Richard, his parents, and his grandparents.

She went on to show Ashlyn and their mother how she could only see the preview trees for her DNA matches if they had one linked to their DNA results, but if she clicked to look at the actual tree or any of the profiles from the preview tree she'd have to subscribe to the site to see more information, just like she'd have to subscribe to the site to follow the hints on the people on her tree, with the only exception being that she could add a potential ancestor whenever the site gave her one while looking at her tree builder portion of the site.

Amy still wasn't sure if she wanted to dig around in their ancestry enough to join the site with a full subscription, so she closed the subscription pages and went back to her list of DNA matches. When she looked through them, she saw that there were several other matches that had "common ancestors" listed on the preview on the main list now that she had a few generations listed on the various branches of her tree, but she was too emotionally distraught to click on them right then to see how they were related.

Her mother and sister were still discussing the Sinclairs, specifically that Andrea thought they all still lived in Tulsa, but she wasn't a hundred percent sure. They were planning the next steps for getting in contact with the girls' biological father and his family, since they weren't the family who'd shunned Andrea when she was pregnant and after the man she thought was the father of her babies died while serving overseas less than four months after her twins were born.

It was all too much for Amy to handle at the moment, so she closed her laptop, picking it up as she stood from the table. "I need a little time to process all this before I decide whether or not to contact him," Amy announced as she walked away from her mother and sister. "I'll see ya'll in the morning after I've slept on it."

She walked up to her third-floor master suite, dropping her laptop on her bed as she made her way to her ensuite bathroom and stripped off her clothes to soak in a hot bath. She wasn't sure how long she sat there crying in her bathtub, but the water was cold and her whole body was pruney when she finally got out.

She dried off, slathered on the coconut oil and cocoa butter lotion she made herself, and wrapped herself in a towel before walking back out of the bathroom into her bedroom. There was a knock on the bedroom door just as she stepped into the room. There was no more warning before Ashlyn opened the door and poked her head in.

"Your phone's been buzzing, so I thought you might wanna check your messages," Ashlyn explained the reason for her intrusion into Amy's room, holding out the phone Amy had forgotten downstairs in her retreat to solitude.

"Thanks, Sis." Amy took the phone and unlocked the screen to see they were all messages from Justin.

"It'll be okay, Sis." Ashlyn gave Amy a hug.

"Yeah, I know." Amy hugged her sister back. "It's just a little overwhelming to feel like we've been living a lie for almost twenty-six years."

"Yeah, well, sleep on it and maybe it won't seem so bad tomorrow." Ashlyn squeezed her tighter before releasing Amy from the embrace and leaving the room.

Amy flopped down on her bed and looked at her phone. Instead of reading through all the texts Justin had sent her, Amy swiped his contact name and called him.

"Hey, Amy, is everything okay? I've been worried sick when you didn't respond to my texts or answer my calls."

"Sorry, I've been hiding in my bathroom with my phone downstairs for the last couple hours," Amy replied, her eyes feeling watery as her tears returned. She closed her eyes and took a few deep breaths, trying to prevent them from falling once more.

"I take it your conversation with your mom didn't go as planned, if you've felt the need to hide out on their first night in town." Justin's voice was soothing, even as he tried to get her to talk about what was upsetting her.

"Yeah, I basically found out that Mom's been lying about my father for the last twenty-six years. She gave me the horrendous middle name of Edwina after the man she dated after breaking up with my biological father. All this time, I've been looking for Andersons in my DNA match list and dreading trying to contact them because of how they'd shunned her when she was pregnant with us and after our supposed father died. And there was no chance of finding them in my match list or having to deal with their animosity toward my mother because Edward Daniel Anderson isn't mine or Ashlyn's father."

A couple tears slipped down her cheeks as Amy relayed the story of finding out about her real father and realizing that her two closest DNA matches were her aunt and half-brother.

Justin quietly listened as she unleashed all her pent-up emotions that she hadn't felt comfortable sharing with her mother and sister earlier. She explained how finding out her father wasn't the hero she'd been led to believe he was all her life made her feel like she'd been lied to since the day she was born. She told him about how her mother had claimed to have counted back from the date she gave birth to her daughters to determine who'd fathered her children, and how that felt like a weak excuse at best in Amy's opinion.

"I mean, she was twenty-one years old when she had us," Amy ranted. "That's more than old enough to be able to look at a calendar and count back forty weeks, or thirty-whatever weeks, since she was told we were early, and realize that she'd been with two different men in the time period when she conceived us."

"Do you think it's possible she only counted back the thirty-something weeks since she was told you were born early, but you were actually born on time at forty weeks and just looked early because ya'll were smaller since you were twins?" Justin's calm manner in asking the question diffused some of Amy's anger, so she could really listen to what he was saying. "Maybe if she'd have actually counted back to the fortieth week, she would've realized the possibility of different paternity results."

"Maybe," Amy reluctantly admitted, not sure why she seemed to want to hang on to the anger at her mother over the mix-up. "I wasn't really paying attention to what she and Ashlyn were saying when they were talking about how things ended with David Sinclair and started with Eddie Anderson, so I don't know why I'm fixated on that to be mad about. I guess I'll have to ask her to explain again later to find out the whole story and apologize if I was rude or cold with her earlier."

"I doubt you were rude or cold with her, Sweetheart." Justin's smile was evident in his tone of voice, even over the phone. "And even if you were, I'm sure she'll understand that you were reacting to the shock of finding out the man you've mourned for years isn't really your father."

"Yeah, I'm sure she'll understand and forgive me for my distance this evening."

"Exactly." The cheerful quality of Justin's voice made her feel better. "So, are you gonna message your aunt and brother on the site? Or are you gonna track down your dad and call him first?"

"I don't know." Amy shook her head even though she knew he couldn't see her. *Since I'm laying here in my bed in just a towel, it's probably a good thing he can't see me right now.*

What was I thinking? Why on earth would I call him before getting dressed? Now all I can think about is whether or not he's dressed on the other end of the phone. And if he's not, why are we talking about my biological family when we could be having phone sex?

No, no, no, no! I can't be thinking about having phone sex with him, when we've barely shared a few innocent kisses and one scorching hot one. Amy fanned herself with the hand not holding her phone, trying to cool off from her carnal thoughts about the sexy man on the other end of the call.

"Um, I gotta go," Amy blurted, the words coming out in a rush and with a higher pitch than normal, making her sound excited when that wasn't the message she wanted to present to Justin at the moment. "I'll, um, see you tomorrow."

"Goodnight, Sweetheart," Justin barely uttered the words before she cut him off by swiping the screen to disconnect the call.

Amy dropped the phone on the bed beside her and picked up a pillow to scream into.

"What's wrong with me? I don't normally freak out when my thoughts turn sexual while I'm on the phone or in the same room as him. Why did I act like such a dork just now?"

Knowing that her empty room wouldn't answer her rhetorical questions, Amy shook her head at her odd behavior. After laying there a few minutes, thinking back to the conversation to figure out why she acted so strange, she got up long enough to make sure her bedroom door was locked before getting her favorite toy out of her bedside table.

If I'm gonna have visions of naked Justin running through my head, I don't want Mom or Ashlyn to walk in and interrupt me while I'm enjoying them.

Amy laid back down on the bed and turned on her favorite toy. She opened her towel and then closed her eyes as she ran the small suction section of her Voodoo Beso Plus toy over her nipples, imagining it was Justin's mouth lightly sucking on her breasts.

Knowing his soft, full lips would actually feel better than the toy, Amy moved it down her body, teasing through her slit with the tip of the vibrating end. In her mind, she was picturing Justin hovering above her, imagining the tip of the vibrator was actually the head of his cock.

As her juices flowed and provided the necessary lubrication, she slowly inserted the vibrator into her vagina. Once it was fully seated, she twisted it enough to settle the suction cup on the other end over her clit. Keeping one hand pressing and releasing on the bend in the toy to mimic the feel of her imaginary version of Justin thrusting into her and pulling slightly back out, Amy used her other hand to play with her boobs. First, she rolled one nipple between her thumb and forefinger, then she moved to the other side and repeated the action. She went back and forth rolling and plucking at her nipples while her hips undulated the way they would if Justin were actually there fucking her.

It only took a few minutes to have her orgasm crashing over her. She stopped playing with her breasts to grab the pillow closest to her. She bit down on the pillow to keep from screaming out Justin's name as her pussy clamped down on the vibrator inside her.

Somehow, while floating on the wave of bliss, she managed to move the little suction cup off her clit before it became too much stimulation. She drifted off to sleep with the toy still inside her, too worn out from her stressful day and the most intense orgasm she could ever remember to get up to clean it before putting it away.

Yeah, I'll clean it and put it away in the morning.

Chapter Seven

Amy wasn't sure what she was thinking when she agreed to bring her mother and sister to Bobby and Brooklyn's wedding shower. *Obviously, I never thought my sister would try to promote her sex toy business at an event in a church.* Amy inwardly fumed as she tried to figure out how to get Ashlyn away from Bobby and Brooklyn's table before his parents joined them. *I can't have Ash embarrass me in front of one of the Matchmaking Mommas. Even if we don't want them to know they were right about Justin and me just yet, I want them to still like me when we're finally ready to admit to our relationship to his family.*

"Oh, we're asking everyone to donate to the Madeline Ashbury Foundation in lieu of gifts." Brooklyn tried to politely decline the gift card to Ashlyn's online store for her It's My Pleasure business.

"Yes, but Amy didn't tell me that in time, so I thought I'd give you a little something extra and go donate to the charity online after the party," Ashlyn asserted, still trying to push the card into Brook's hand.

"And we thank you for that." Bobby plucked the card out from where it was hanging between Ashlyn and Brooklyn's hands. "We'll definitely enjoy picking out something from your website. Won't we, Brie-Baby?"

The look Bobby gave Brooklyn as he tucked the gift card into his jacket pocket was hot enough to make Amy blush.

"Yes, I'm sure we will," Brooklyn agreed, grinning at Bobby, even as she thanked Ashlyn for the lovely gesture.

Finally, Amy was able to get her sister to move on to the table where their mother was already sitting and talking to Justin and his siblings.

"Actually, Ashlyn," Brook added before they got more than a couple steps away from their table. "If you have business cards with your web address on them, my bridesmaids will probably become three of your most loyal customers."

Brooklyn pointed to the next table over where Kenzie, Heather, and Ashley, her three best friends, were sitting.

"Thanks for the referral." Ashlyn grinned at Brooklyn before walking over to talk to the younger women that Amy had talked to in passing while hanging out with the Burlesons the past couple months.

Unsure what else to do about her sister, Amy joined her mother at the table with Justin and his siblings, taking the empty seat between Justin and her mother, where her name was written in beautiful calligraphy on a place card beside the china they would eventually be eating from as part of the party.

I wonder who manipulated the seating arrangements this time? My mom? Justin? Or Justin's mother? Amy had to wonder if it was Justin's mother since JJ was sitting a space away from Andrea, leaving the space open where they probably expected Ashlyn to sit. *Though, if he's really into the BDSM stuff Justin was telling me about on Valentine's Day, then maybe he and Ashlyn will get along just fine. He might even become her top customer on her sex toy site.*

Amy leaned into her mother to whisper, "You should really have a talk with your youngest daughter about what is and isn't appropriate to discuss in a church."

"Oh, goodness, what did Ashlyn do this time?" Andrea at least had the decency to look worried about what her outrageous daughter might have said or done, though her slight smile gave away the fact that she was probably more amused by Ashlyn's antics than embarrassed like Amy.

"She gave the bride and groom a gift card for her website."

Apparently, Amy didn't whisper quiet enough that only her mother could hear her like she thought because Justin's next words made it clear that he'd overheard. "What kind of website does your sister have?" And he didn't make any attempt at whispering, so everyone at the table turned to look at Amy for her answer.

"Um, not one that should be discussed in a church," Amy confessed sheepishly.

Justin laughed as recognition dawned on the faces around her. Amy just shook her head at the giggles surrounding her.

"Good thing she'll be here for a week, so I'll have plenty of time to get a link from her when we're not in church," Jen chuckled, still grinning through her giggles.

"Don't worry about it, Sweetheart." Justin reached over and clasped Amy's hand under the table so nobody else could see his comforting gesture. "It's not the first time something of an indelicate nature was discussed in this church, as you well know from the last time we had a family wedding here."

"Yes, but my sister trying to sell, um, marital aids, is a far cry from Kay announcing her pregnancy during her rehearsal," Amy whispered back.

"Oh, Amy, I know I raised you not to be such a prude." Andrea shook her head as she admonished Amy. "You don't hafta use a euphemism like *marital aids* to talk about the sex toys and lingerie your sister sells just because we're in a church. The preacher's married for cryin' out loud. He knows about sex, and probably has it with his wife on the regular. It's a perfectly natural, normal part of life, so there's no reason to be ashamed to talk about it."

Oh my word! I knew I shouldn't've brought them here! Amy tried to cover her face with her hands to hide her embarrassment at her mother's outburst being as outlandish as her sister trying to sell sex toys in a church. She didn't get far with the hand still clasped in Justin's grasp, but she at least got the one hand up to cover her face.

"How about we go put in our guesses for the Kisses game?" Justin's question was more rhetorical as he used his hand holding hers to pull Amy out of her chair and away from the table.

Amy was grateful for the save, clinging to his hand for dear life as she walked as fast as she could to keep up with him on their way past the table with the canister of candy and out a side door of the church.

They didn't stop once they were outside. Justin continued walking, leading her across Quarter Horse Drive, past the Heart's Destiny Cemetery, and then across Brahman Blvd. to the park where there were benches and a playground set up. They sat on the first bench they came to before Justin finally spoke, breaking the silence surrounding them. "You okay?"

"Yeah, just mortified that my mom and sister can't behave like civilized people," Amy replied, looking at the kids playing on the jungle gym a few yards away instead of at Justin.

"They're not that bad." Justin squeezed her hand reassuringly.

"They were talking about sex toys in church." Amy shook her head, incredulous at the lack of decorum shown by her family the first time they met Justin's family. "Who does something like that? Especially when I specifically asked them beforehand not to embarrass me in front of the whole town where I now live. I get that they don't care what anyone else thinks about them, but I do. I have to live here and face everyone at work. How can I ever feel okay with finally letting your family know we're dating when they now know I'm part of the perverted Lawton family? Your Matchmaking Mommas are gonna wanna fix you up with someone else after an hour spent with my mom and sister. They're gonna wanna run me outta town to keep me from corrupting you."

"Naw, they're not gonna do anything like that." Justin chuckled, releasing her hand to wrap his arm around her shoulders and pulling her into his side. "If they didn't shun Brook for the actions of her psycho father, then they're not gonna judge you for whatever your mom and sister say or do while they're here this week."

Amy looked up at him skeptically as she slipped her arm around his waist. She wasn't sure the family situations were comparable.

"Seriously, Amy, it's not a big deal." Justin ran his hand up and down her arm. "If my mom or aunt have any reaction to hearing about your sister's business or what your mom said about sex at our table just now, it'll be to try to recruit them to help with fixing us up. We may not openly talk about sex around the dinner table or while we're sitting in church, but the Burleson women want all their kids in sexual relationships, so they can get all the grandbabies they want. They'll see your family's openness to talk about it as a good thing."

"Ya think?" Amy wasn't sure why she was asking, since she was pretty sure if that were the case, his mom would probably want to fix him up with Ashlyn instead of her. "It won't be a negative that I'm not like my family?"

"Whaddaya mean?" Justin's expression made it clear he didn't know what she was asking.

"If my mom and sister being so open about sex is a good thing in the eyes of your family, then they won't decide to start pushing you toward Ashlyn, instead of me, since I'm not as open as she is, will they?"

"No." Justin chuckled once more. "And even if they did, I'm not interested in Ashlyn. I'm only interested in you."

"But we're identical twins," Amy protested, shaking her head. "If we dressed alike and didn't speak, you wouldn't be able to tell us apart."

"Yeah, I bet I'd still be able to tell you apart," Justin grinned.

"Really? How?" Amy didn't believe his claim since nobody else had ever been able to tell them apart when they dressed alike. It wasn't until she started dressing a little more conservatively than her sister that the boys in school quit mistaking her for Ashlyn.

"Because I don't just see you with my eyes, Sweetheart." Justin leaned down and kissed the top of her head. "My heart and my soul see you too, and they recognize you even when my eyes are closed. I feel you when you enter a room, even if I've got my back turned toward you so I can't see it's you. My Spidey senses don't recognize Ashlyn."

"I thought Spidey senses recognize danger, not specific people." Amy pulled back from their sideways embrace to turn and look into his ocean blue eyes. "I'm guessing if you weren't into superheroes enough to name your dick after one, you don't have very accurate Spidey senses either."

"Hey, just because I'm smart enough to give The Anaconda a proper name and don't know all the specifics about superheroes and their senses, doesn't mean I'm incapable of understanding my own intuition." Justin gave her an incredulous look before reaching over to use both hands to tickle her waist. "In fact, I'd go so far as to say you could blindfold me and I'd still be able to pick you out of a lineup without you even saying a word to give me a hint of where you were standing."

"Whatever." Amy laughed both from the tickling and from the goofy look on Justin's face as he tried to lighten her mood from her earlier embarrassment. "You'd probably get confused like I read about in a book once and kiss the wrong wife in the husband games."

"What?" Justin finally relented on the tickling as he looked at her with a confused expression.

"It was a book about a wedding crazy town that held the husband games every year for all the newlywed couples," Amy explained, remembering back to one of the Pippa Grant books she'd read the year before. "In one of the games, they had the wives all lined up on the stage and the husbands were led out one at a time, blindfolded, and had to kiss their wife when they thought they got to the right woman. One of the husbands thought he knew his wife by her smell and picked the wrong woman who used the same soap."

"Yeah, well, as much as I love your beachy smell, Sweetheart, I don't hafta smell you to feel you walk into the room." Justin insisted, shaking his head. "Besides, that game sounds more like something a divorce lawyer would set up to gain customers."

"Well, it did end up with the woman getting divorced before falling in love with the guy who accidently picked her when he came back to town as a widow," Amy shrugged, not really wanting to recap the whole book.

"Exactly," Justin chuckled before pointing over their shoulders with his thumb. "We should probably get back in there. If your mom tells my mom that we snuck out together, they're liable to have our wedding planned for the first weekend in July by the time we get back in there."

"Oh Lord, you're probably right about that," Amy bemoaned as they both stood from the bench. She reached over and took his hand as they ambled back to the church. "Wait. Why do you say the first weekend of July?"

"Because Randi and James have already claimed the Memorial Day holiday week for their wedding." Justin smirked, lacing their fingers together as they strolled across the street. "So, the next time they'll be home when Randi can be in our wedding will be for Independence Day. Hence, the first weekend of July will be when my mom will wanna plan our wedding, if she figures out we're dating before then."

"Then we can't let your family find out about us 'til Thanksgiving." Amy giggled, not realizing that she was telling Justin her most secret dream. "Because if I ever get married, I want a Christmas wedding. Summer's too hot to have to wear all those layers in a wedding dress."

~~~

Amy wants a Christmas wedding! Is that actually on Christmas Day or just during the Christmas season? Justin wondered if asking her right then was too soon and would scare her off. Or if he could play it off as a lighthearted question with the way they were talking, and have the information to be able to start planning in advance for the wedding he hoped they'd have one day. *Only one way to find out.*

"So, is the Christmas wedding just so it's cool enough to wear the dress, and anytime in December is good? Or do you actually wanna get married on Christmas Day with a red and green color scheme if you ever do the deed?"

"Oh, it's just to not sweat to death in the dress," Amy replied, shaking her head like she couldn't believe she was discussing their future wedding plans. "Since I want yellow flowers and bridesmaids' dresses, an actual Christmas theme on Christmas Day wouldn't work for my vision of my dream wedding."

"Yeah, I guess not." Justin ran his free hand through his hair as he contemplated asking his next question. *Fuck it. In for a penny, in for a pound, right?* "And what would the groom and his groomsmen be wearing in your dream wedding?"

"Classic black tuxedos with the only pop of color being their yellow boutonnieres." Amy's dreamy expression as they crossed the final street to get back to the church told Justin that she was sharing a vision she'd had for her wedding for quite some time.

Damn, even when she wasn't sure it'd ever be possible for her to find true love, she still wanted it enough to plan for the possibility. And if this is her vision of her dream wedding that she's kept hidden for years, then I'm damn sure gonna give it to her. I just hope yellow carnations aren't too hard to find in the middle of winter when she wants her favorite color of her favorite flower for our wedding. Maybe I'll ask the florist the next time I go get her flowers before a date.

Justin dropped the topic of conversation when he opened the door to the church for Amy. He knew better than to be caught by his family talking about her dream wedding, even if he was trying to make it
~~~

seem hypothetical to keep from making Amy think he was talking about weddings too soon.

They stopped at the table where the jar of chocolate Kisses was displayed to put in their guesses for how many pieces of candy were in the jar before going back to their table. Justin wasn't surprised to see that Aiden, Leo, and Landon Walker were seated with them to make sure all ten seats were filled around the round table. Though he did feel a little sorry for his sisters having to be alternated boy-girl-boy-girl-boy between them.

Justin pulled out Amy's chair beside her mother as soon as they got to the table. Once she'd taken her seat, he took his between her and Aiden. He noticed that Ashlyn had finally made it to her seat between her mother and JJ and hoped she wouldn't make Amy too uncomfortable by mentioning her business again.

"How is it I ended up being the only woman at the table not seated beside at least one good-looking man?"

Guess it wasn't Ashlyn I had to worry about, Justin thought at Andrea's shocking question.

"Mom," Amy reprimanded at the same time Ashlyn replied, "You're too old for the Matchmaking Mommas to try to fix you up with their sons."

When Ashlyn's words registered, half their table barked out a laugh. The only reason Justin didn't join them was because he knew Amy was embarrassed enough by her mother and sister, and he didn't want to make her feel worse.

"Oh, well, I suppose you're right there." Andrea laughed off her daughter's statement. "While I don't mind a younger man, I should probably avoid dating someone young enough to be my son. How old are you boys anyway?"

Jen snorted from her spot at the table on the other side of Aiden from Justin.

"Did you just snort?" Leo pointed out from her other side, making Julie giggle from his other side.

Justin was too busy looking at the reaction of his sisters and friends to realize Andrea Lawton had focused her gaze on him to be the first to answer her question.

"Justin?" Andrea saying his name as a question drew his attention.

When he turned to look at Amy's mother with Amy between them, Amy mouthed, "I'm sorry."

Justin slightly shook his head, hoping Amy understood the movement to convey what he was thinking, *Nothing to be sorry for, Sweetheart.*

"I'm twenty-seven," Justin admitted, finally making eye contact with Andrea. "Same as Aiden and Leo." He pointed to the men seated between him and his sisters.

"Oh, yes, the three of you are definitely too young. I'd've been nineteen when you were born." Andrea shook her head before turning to look at JJ and Landon, who were seated between Ashlyn and Julie on her other side. "Please tell me at least one of you is older than the rest of the babies at this table."

"We're both twenty-eight." JJ half-shrugged, shaking his head.

"So, we're older, but not by much," Landon added.

"JJ will be twenty-nine on Friday," Jen interjected, giggling and pointing at their brother, who was suddenly turning red.

Justin knew it wasn't from embarrassment, more likely he was irritated at Jen trying to push his buttons.

"Yes, well, I could've still had him when I was a teenager, so no, that doesn't work. Any hot guys in town who're at least in their thirties? Preferably closer to thirty-five or thirty-six? I could handle a ten-year age difference or even a twelve-year age difference, but nothing in the teens."

"Yeah, but we don't really hang out in the same circles, so they're not here today," Julie grinned at Amy's mom. "When this is over, you'll have to get with our moms. They know everyone in town and will be able to help you find a hookup for while you're here."

"Don't listen to Julie if you're just looking for a hookup. Our mom specializes in marriage matches." Jen couldn't keep a straight face as she uttered the words, cracking up laughing at her own bad joke.

"Well, Amy did say she wanted us to move down here with her," Andrea grinned at Jen before turning to look at Amy. "But I'm not sure that's still the case after the whole DNA debacle yesterday."

"What DNA debacle?" Julie's expression turned serious as she picked up on Amy's trepidation at the mention of the family revelation she had the day before.

Justin reached over and clasped her hand under the table, wanting to support her when her family aired their dirty laundry that he wasn't sure she was ready to share.

"Our mom was a ho back in the day and told us the wrong name for our father for the last twenty-five years," Ashlyn stated, deadpan.

Amy turned to lean into Justin burying her face in his chest. He wrapped his arms around her to comfort her and enjoyed having her arms around his waist, even as her shoulders shook with her sobs.

"Wow, you don't sugarcoat anything, do you?" JJ shook his head at Ashlyn before locking eyes with Justin and softly asking, "Is Amy okay?"

Justin didn't know how to respond, so he gave his brother a half-shrug before dipping his head to whisper in Amy's ear. "It's okay, Sweetheart. I've got you. You can stay right here for as long as you want. And when you're ready, just say the word and I'll get you outta here, so you don't hafta deal with this until you're ready."

"I, I'm," Amy stuttered, still shaking as she cried in his arms.

"You're ready to go now? Okay, let's go." Justin pushed his chair back from the table with his feet to stand up, lifting Amy up with him.

"No." Amy shook her head against his chest. "I'm not crying. Not really."

Justin wanted to argue that she was indeed crying when she lifted her head and he saw the tears streaming over her cheeks. But when he looked closer at her expression, he could see that she was smiling, laughing even. One could even say she was laughing so hard she was crying.

"I might be hysterical, but I'm not upset." Amy pulled out of his arms to wipe her face with her hands, while still laughing so hard that she couldn't stop the tears from flowing. "It's just too ridiculous a situation to be anything other than comical. I mean, my sister just called my mom a ho in the middle of a church, while seated at a table with four of my bosses, who I specifically asked my family not to embarrass me in front of, while at another of my boss's wedding shower. This is the stuff that soap operas are made of, so how can I consider it anything but laughable?"

"Well, when you put it that way, it does sound pretty funny." Justin lightly chuckled along with Amy and the rest of the table.

They retook their seats with Amy reaching out to grab the napkin from around the silverware that was left at their seats, where they missed lunch by being out at the park when it was served as part of the shower.

"I'm sorry, Ames," Ashlyn apologized when they'd all regained some of their composure. "I didn't mean to embarrass you. But you know I just call it like I see it. Mom was twenty-one when we were born, and we all hoed around a little bit at twenty-one."

"No," Amy replied to her sister, adamantly shaking her head. "No, we didn't."

"Fine," Ashlyn exclaimed, throwing up her hands. "Maybe you didn't, but Mom and I did, so I understand how she could've gotten confused about who our bio-daddy is and named us after the wrong guy."

"Ashlyn Danae Lawton, enough!" Andrea shouted, holding up her hand to Amy's twin to get her to stop speaking. "I don't think your sister wants to discuss any of this right now, so just drop it." She then turned to look at Amy, reaching out to take the hand Justin wasn't already holding. "I'm sorry, Amy. I didn't mean to embarrass you either. Maybe it's best if your sister and I get an Uber back to your house and we can discuss all this in private later."

"There's no Uber in Heart's Destiny," JJ interjected, not really being helpful. "It's too small a town for things like that."

"No, you don't have to go." Amy shook her head at her mother. "Just try to behave like civilized human beings until it's time to go home."

Justin wasn't sure that was possible, but he didn't say a word to keep from making Amy feel worse than she already appeared to feel. He wished he knew what to do to make it all better for her, but giving her his shoulder to cry on was the only thing he could come up with for how to help her deal with her family drama.

"Well, I can try." Andrea smiled at her daughter.

"But we can't guarantee anything." Ashlyn made a goofy face at Amy that Justin hoped meant she was kidding.

"So, Justin was telling me last week that ya'll might wanna look into jobs at Burleson while you're here in town," Jen blurted, obviously trying to change the subject. "If you tell me a little about what you currently do in Tulsa, I should be able to figure out what positions we might have available you'd be interested in down here."

"I'm a receptionist at Bama." Ashlyn grinned across the table at Jen. "Well, that's my normal nine-to-five job. I'm also a sales rep for It's My Pleasure, doing Pleasure parties in the evenings and on weekends."

"Yes, I've already told Amy that you'll have to give me a link to your website for that when we're not in church." Jen grinned at Ashlyn before turning her attention to Andrea.

"I work in the cafeteria for Tulsa Public Schools," Andrea mumbled, her gaze dropping to the table like she was embarrassed about her job.

Amy squeezed Justin's hand, obviously picking up on her mother's discomfort. Hoping to help ease the Lawton women's unnecessary embarrassment, Justin decided to out himself for his childhood crush before his sisters could do it for him. "It's probably a good thing I didn't go to school in Tulsa then," he confessed, grinning in Amy and Andrea's direction. "Because it'd be really awkward to sit here if you were the lunch lady I had a crush on in school."

"You didn't," Amy gasped, covering her open mouth with her free hand that was no longer held by her mother.

"Oh, yeah, he did," his sisters and best friends chimed in unison. The rest of the table erupted in laughter.

"Justin was always flirting with Ms. Betty at lunch from first through fifth grade," Aiden expounded, shaking his head and chuckling.

"And Ms. Hannah all through middle school," Leo added, also chuckling.

"Oh, we know," Jen chorteled, motioning between herself and Julie. "Being his younger sisters and a year behind him in school, we heard all about how he flirted his way into an extra chocolate milk or dessert daily."

"Is that how you get four desserts every day at lunch now?" Amy giggled at her own question, her obsidian eyes twinkling as she looked over at Justin.

"Hey, what can I say?" Justin shrugged as he grinned back at Amy. "I know the lunch lady is still the most important person I'll speak with every day."

After everyone had another chuckle at Justin's antics, Jen turned the conversation back to Amy's mother and sister. "If you're both looking for comparable jobs to what you have now, we've definitely got openings at Burleson Incorporated. Or if you're looking for a change of pace, we have excellent training programs for jobs in other divisions that might interest you."

"Oh, I'm not sure," Andrea faltered, looking to Amy and then back to Jen.

"I am," Ashlyn practically shouted, raising her hand like a child wanting to be called on in school. "Where do I sign up to be trained to do something other than being a receptionist for the rest of my life?"

"Come into work with Amy this week and we can take you through some tests in HR to see what you might be most interested in at the company."

Before Jen could elaborate more on the aptitude tests and interest surveys she'd have Ashlyn fill out at Burleson, they were being directed to rearrange their tables to set up for the newlywed game.

While everyone else was getting into position to participate in the game or observe as the audience, Justin tugged on Amy's sleeve to pull her aside. "How about we sneak over to the kitchen and get a plate since we missed lunch?"

She nodded her assent, so they snuck off to find out if there was even any food left for them to eat.

"I feel kinda bad for not really paying attention to anything going on at the shower," Amy admitted as they entered the kitchen.

"Don't worry about that." Justin looked around the kitchen to see which of the women of the church would be most likely to allow them to raid the leftovers. "Getting outta there right now is more about self-preservation than not paying attention to the happy couple."

"Wow, you really can't miss a meal, can you?" Amy giggled as she poked him in the belly.

"I'm not talking about getting lunch." Justin retaliated for her poke by reaching over to tickle her ribs one-handed. "I'm talking about not being roped into being the fourth couple in the newlywed game like James and Randi at Anthony and Kay's wedding shower."

"Oh, goodness, I didn't even think about that!" Amy's expression could only be read as mock horror. "Yeah, we definitely need to hide out in here until they get the game started. And I'll make sure Randi knows not to even suggest it for her and James's shower."

"Didn't they say something about James's grandparents being the fourth couple at their wedding shower?" Justin hoped he remembered correctly as he finally narrowed his search down to Kathy Harrison, Pastor Dale Harrison's wife, and Justin's ex-girlfriend, Fiona's mother. Without giving Amy the chance to answer his question, he redirected her. "Let me introduce you to Pastor Dale's wife, Mrs. Kathy Harrison."

Hopefully, this won't get too awkward, Justin thought as they made their way across the room. *It's not too weird to introduce my girlfriend to my ex-girlfriend's mother, is it?*

~~~

Amy wasn't sure what to think as Justin led her over to meet his high school sweetheart's mother. *This isn't completely awkward at all,* she thought sarcastically.

"Mrs. Kathy, have you met Amy Lawton?" Justin inquired as he led Amy over to the older woman with a hand on the small of her back that was sending tingles to inappropriate places while they were in a church.

"No, I don't believe so." Kathy Harrison extended her hand to Amy. "I've seen you at church a few times since Anthony and Kay's wedding, but we've never been formally introduced. You're one of Kay's friends, right?"

"Yes," Amy replied as she extended her hand to shake the older woman's, but Kathy had other ideas, using the clasp of her hand to pull Amy in for a hug.

"We're huggers in Heart's Destiny. You'll get used to it if you stick around for a while."

"Considering I just bought a house here, I hope to be sticking around for a while," Amy giggled, returning the brief embrace. "And I hope to have a long tenure working at Burleson Incorporated, as well."

"Oh, well, I'm sure you will." Kathy released Amy to look back and forth between her and Justin. "So, what can I do for the two of
~~~

you that's got you finding me back in the kitchen, instead of staying in the fellowship hall for the shower?"

"Amy and I actually stepped out at the beginning of the shower to talk about some, uh, lab stuff." Justin barely stuttered, clearly not bothered too much by lying to the preacher's wife while standing in church. "And we missed lunch when everyone else was eating. I thought we might grab a quick plate while they're setting things up for the next game."

Kathy gave him an inquisitive once over before shaking her head at Justin's ridiculous grin. "I'm sure we can scrounge up something for you."

Kathy quickly pulled a few plastic containers out of the industrial-sized refrigerator and made them each a plate, directing them to the microwave to reheat the food before ushering them back out to the fellowship hall.

They stopped at a table in the back of the room to eat without interrupting the festivities at the front. Apparently, Justin's parents, Jon and Susan, had been recruited to participate as the fourth couple in the Newlywed game alongside Bobby and Brooklyn, Bob and Hazel, and Joe and Mary Turner, the couple Brooklyn credited with raising her.

I wonder what we'd do in place of this game if Justin and I ever got married? It's not like I can have my parents participate. Even if I'm able to track down my biological father and start a relationship with him, I doubt his wife would want him to participate with Mom. And with the way Mom goes through guys, there's no telling who she'd wanna pull up there with her as her partner if I had my father and his new wife take part as one of the couples. Yeah, this game is a definite no-no if Justin and I ever get married.

Holy cow! What am I thinking? I'm barely comfortable with dating Justin. Why on earth am I picturing marrying him?

Thankfully, Justin didn't seem to notice her trying to shake off her outlandish thoughts as they finished eating and disposed of the plastic plates and utensils they'd picked up in the kitchen instead of trying to track down the dishware everyone else had used earlier. They made their way back over to where their families were seated to watch as Bobby and Brooklyn got perfect scores to easily be declared the winners of the game.

Amy was grateful she was able to get through the rest of the party without her mother or sister embarrassing her again. Though she wasn't quite sure she was ready for the hard conversation they were about to have once they got back to her house.

She said her goodbyes to her friends, relishing the hug Justin gave her when he whispered in her ear. "I'm just a phone call away if you need me after talking more with your mom tonight."

Amy just smiled and nodded as they released the friendly embrace, hoping she wouldn't have to break down and call him for the second night in a row.

The ride home was quiet, mostly because it was only a few blocks and too short to get started on the deeper conversation she needed to have with her family. Once they arrived, they each went to their rooms to change into comfy clothes from their church dresses before reconvening in her kitchen.

Amy was pouring herself a glass of iced tea when her mom and sister joined her.

"Maybe we should go for something a little stronger before we have this talk," Andrea sighed, waving a hand toward Amy's tea glass.

"Sorry, Mom, I don't have anything stronger," Amy replied, taking a sip of her tea.

"Maybe we should've stopped at the store on the way home for a couple bottles of wine," Ashlyn interjected, getting down another glass and pouring her own tea.

"Can you even buy wine here on Sundays?" Andrea followed her daughters' lead in fixing a glass of iced tea.

"No clue." Amy shrugged. "I haven't tried. The only time I've had a drink down here was when I've gone out and at Kay's bachelorette party, rehearsal dinner, and reception."

"With Charles and Mary Lee being teetotalers, I'm surprised there was alcohol at the rehearsal dinner and reception," Andrea lightly giggled. "I guess the Burlesons aren't so straight-laced."

"I don't know," Amy replied, shaking her head at her mother. "The only time I've seen the older generation of Burlesons drink was champagne at the wedding reception and rehearsal dinner. Anytime I've been on the ranch for other get-togethers, they always serve tea and soda, but I didn't even see a single beer at the cookout they had the first day we got here for Kay's wedding week."

"Yeah, I don't think I could marry into a family that doesn't even have beer at a cookout." Ashlyn looked mortified at the lack of alcohol on the Burleson Ranch. "What about those cute Walker boys? Is their family just as anti-alcohol as the Burlesons?"

"Well, I haven't met all of them." Amy lifted a shoulder in a half-shrug, chuckling at her sister's way of fishing for information about the other bachelors at their table during the wedding shower earlier that day. "But Aiden's dad, Leo and Landon's uncle, owns the only bar in town, so I'm guessing they're okay with daily drinking. Leo actually manages the bar for his uncle."

"Yeah, we'll hafta plan a night for you to take me to the bar to get to know Leo a little better." Ashlyn grinned at the prospect of picking up her next man of the week.

"I suppose this uncle is married?" Andrea questioned, her interest piqued by a bar owner old enough to have sons in their late twenties.

"Yep," Amy grinned, taking a little too much pleasure in bursting her mom's bubble. "To the middle school principal. Tully's also the realtor who helped me find my house. And Luke, Leo, and Landon's dad, Wyatt, is married to the woman who keeps his construction office running smoothly."

"Well, I guess I'll just hafta keep looking for ya'll a stepdaddy, then." Andrea shrugged like it was no big deal.

Amy inwardly fumed, annoyed by her mother's lackadaisical view of relationships.

"How about you just tell us more about our bio-daddy instead?" Amy hated how hard her voice sounded as she asked the question, but she was having a hard time controlling her emotions surrounding the bombshell that her mother had dropped on her less than twenty-four hours earlier.

"Let's go sit down and get comfortable before we have this conversation." Ashlyn grabbed her glass and walked out of the kitchen.

Amy and Andrea followed her, settling in on the sofa and chairs in the living room before Andrea finally spoke. "Whaddaya wanna know?"

"Everything you can remember about him," Amy replied, putting her glass down on a coaster on the coffee table, so she didn't risk spilling the contents as she learned about her real father.

"I met David at a Saint Patrick's Day party in nineteen-ninety-two," Andrea began. "He's tall, six-foot-three, I think. Brown hair, brown eyes, olive complexion. He was really sweet. Smart. While we were dating, he took summer classes at T.U., so he could finish up his degree early. He graduated in August. Then in September, when he started what he called his first real job, he got too busy to go out like we had for the previous six months."

"So, ya'll broke up because he was working too much?" Amy couldn't fathom that being the reason her parents didn't stay together.

"Yeah, pretty much," Andrea shrugged. "We had fun all summer, got along with each other's families pretty well, but we both knew we weren't soulmates or anything like that. When he had to start schmoozing with his bosses, I didn't feel comfortable going with him."

"Why?" Ashlyn looked at their mom like she didn't understand.

"It wasn't like dating a Black waitress was gonna win him any brownie points with all his white bosses," Andrea sighed, shrugging once more. "And even though I knew I was half white, I still didn't look the part to fit in with all the Barbie dolls his bosses were married to, so we broke things off. It wasn't a bad breakup. In fact, I was out with his sister, Donna, at an early Halloween party a month later, when I met Eddie."

"I just don't understand how you could be so positive that Eddie was our father and never even thought it was possible it was David." It sounded to Amy like her mother had ample time to notice she skipped a period in the month between dating the two men, so she couldn't comprehend her mother's colossal blunder in identifying her daughters' biological father.

"Oh, Ames, you hafta understand, I didn't have the money for top-of-the-line medical care back then. I went to a Planned Parenthood clinic to confirm my pregnancy because I didn't have an extra ten bucks to buy a pregnancy test. And the only reason I did that was because I got sick at Christmas and my momma made me. There wasn't money for ultrasounds and all that fancy stuff to get an accurate date of conception. Hell, my version of prenatal vitamins were Flintstones."

"Oh Gawd, even I know better than to substitute Flintstones for prenatal vitamins," Ashlyn laughed, somewhat lightening the mood of the room.

Leah Mae Wright

"Yeah, well, when you can't work because you're spending all your time puking, you get what you can at the dollar store." Andrea leaned over from her seat in the chair across from the sofa to clasp one of each of her daughters' hands over the coffee table. "Since I didn't find out I was pregnant until Christmas, I just assumed Eddie was the father because I'd only been with him in the previous two-and-a-half months. I didn't think about the fact that he was only in town for a month on leave or that I'd been with David a month before that. We wrote back and forth the whole time he was deployed. He was excited to be a dad. And I honestly believe that if he hadn't been killed in action, he'd have come home to fix the situation with his family, so we could get married and raise ya'll together."

"What exactly was the deal with his family?" Ashlyn voiced the question that Amy thought no longer mattered.

"His father was a racist bastard who didn't think his son should fall in love with a Black girl." Andrea shook her head and made a face as she remembered her one, brief interaction with Edward Anderson, Sr. "I'll spare you the details of the way I was cussed and discussed the one time I went to his father the way Eddie told me to, in order to get help with doctors and such while I was pregnant. But when I told Eddie about it, he promised to talk to his father and fix things."

"Yeah, we've seen the letters to know how much he loved us and wanted to come home to be a family with us." Amy had tears running down her cheeks as she thought about the man she'd mourned for as long as she could remember, thinking her father had died at war before being able to come home to meet his newborn daughters. "But that still doesn't explain how you counted back wrong to not realize David could be our father."

"Well, like I said, I went to a Planned Parenthood clinic to confirm I was pregnant. They didn't do an ultrasound or anything to tell me how far along I was. They guessed based on what I told them about my last period, which was what I thought was a light period the first week of October right before I met Eddie."

Amy pulled her hand back from her mother's to wipe the tears from her face with the hem of her long t-shirt.

"I didn't even know ya'll were twins until you were born, and the doctor who delivered you said that most twins are born at least a month early. With you barely making the five-pound mark to be able to leave the hospital when you were born, he estimated you were born at thirty-six weeks. I counted back thirty-six weeks and it was the weekend I met Eddie, so I didn't think I needed to count back to forty weeks, since the doctor didn't think you were full term."

I guess that makes sense, Amy thought. *Even though everything I've read about twins lists five-and-a-half pounds as the average birth weight of full-term twin births, we weren't quite there at five pounds, four ounces, so I can see why Mom and the doctor might've thought we were earlier than we actually were when we were born.*

Too bad understanding why Mom was wrong about who our father was doesn't seem to be lessening the anger I feel about being lied to my whole life and missing out on twenty-five years with my real dad.

"So, now that we know who our dad is," Ashlyn said, bringing Amy back out of her own head. "What're we gonna do about getting in touch with him and getting to know him?"

"I could message Donna or Richard on the website," Amy half-heartedly offered, hugging her knees to her chest to self-soothe, as they talked about their options for finding their father. "But I don't feel right about telling them he's our father before we tell him. Ya know?"

"Yeah, I agree." Ashlyn reached over to pat Amy's knee comfortingly. "But how are we gonna find out where he lives to be able to contact him? The only David Sinclair I found when I tried googling him was an Australian biologist, and I don't think that's him."

"No, that's not him," Andrea chuckled, her lips turning up in a little grin. "Though if he'd have had a sexy Australian accent, I might've tried harder to stay with him."

"Mom!" Amy exclaimed as she burst out laughing at her mother's outrageousness.

"What? You can't tell me you wouldn't enjoy listening to a sexy accent talking dirty in the bedroom." Andrea pointed back and forth between her daughters.

"Oh yeah, I would agree with that." Ashlyn laughed with Amy.

"But it's gross to think of for our father," Amy admonished when her laughter died down.

"Then I guess it's a good thing your father isn't Australian." Andrea lifted one shoulder in a half-shrug.

Leah Mae Wright

"I'll ask Justin if his cousin can help us find him," Amy finally decided after a few minutes of sitting there in silence, while they racked their brains, trying to figure out how to hunt him down on their own. "Or maybe Randi can get her dad to look him up for us since he's the sheriff in Tulsa?"

If I still lived in Tulsa, I'd go ask Mr. Lee myself. But maybe Bobby Burleson has enough law enforcement contacts outside of Heart's Destiny to be able to help us? Not that I'm gonna call him up and ask him tonight after the humiliating experience of introducing him to my mom and sister at his wedding shower today.

Amy ended up ordering pizza for dinner and sat up half the night talking with her mom and sister. After reviewing all the gossip about their friends and neighbors back in Tulsa, they talked a little about job possibilities at Burleson Incorporated for both Andrea and Ashlyn before going back to the family tree. Amy ended up signing up for a subscription to the website to be able to look at all the hints about the ancestors they'd found so far. Unfortunately, that didn't allow her to find any more information on living relatives, so she still couldn't fill in their information on her tree.

Maybe tomorrow at lunch I can ask Justin for some better ideas for how to find my father, Amy thought as she made her way up to bed for the night.

~~~

Monday, February 25, 2019

Justin spent his Monday morning in meetings with his father, siblings, and cousins, Anthony, Charlotte, and Becky, along with half the legal department at Burleson Incorporated. Since Bobby and Brooklyn had to go back to Georgia to deal with more of her legal issues with her father and work on the foundation they were starting, Justin's Uncle Bob had gone with them to meet with the Avingtons to sign all the paperwork required to release their trust and restructure the Burleson board of directors. Jake was able to Skype into the meeting to verbally authorize his father to sign for him on the legal documents all the Burlesons had to sign relinquishing part of their ownership of the
~~~

company to the Avingtons. But Josh was off on a mission with his SEAL team, so Bob had to attach a copy of his proxy papers to show he was authorized to sign for him on the contracts since he was incommunicado.

Justin thought it was an awful lot of paperwork and dealing with lawyers when all he really had to do was sign his name. But apparently, his whole family had to review everything before signing to make it all legal. While he understood it was important to make sure every t was crossed and every i was dotted to transfer a couple billion dollars into their cousins' names, Justin would've much rather been able to go in that morning and sign his name first thing, so he could've spent the morning in the lab with Amy.

She hadn't called him the night before, like he expected she would after talking more with her mom about her biological father. And it was eating him alive to not know how that conversation went or how Amy was feeling over the whole situation. He was so frantic to see her that he wasn't sure the pen had even hit the table after he signed his name on the final document before he left the conference room to go downstairs and find her.

He checked his watch as the elevator approached the floor where the lab was and realized that it was already five minutes after noon, so he punched the button for one floor lower to meet her in the cafeteria. When the elevator stopped on the lab floor, he let the doors open just long enough to make sure she wasn't standing there waiting to go down before hitting the close-door button to get it moving faster to the floor he knew he'd find her on.

She was already seated at their usual table with her tray of food when he walked into the room. "Hey, Sweetheart," Justin greeted her as he plopped down in the chair across the table from her, where he always sat, before even going through the line to get his food. He was too anxious to know how she was doing after talking to her mom the night before to waste time getting his food before he found out.

"Aren't you eating?" Amy looked concerned when he sat down without a tray of food.

"Yeah, in a minute." Justin ran a hand through his hair nervously. "Since you didn't call me last night or text me all morning, I wanted to make sure you're okay first."

Leah Mae Wright

"I'm fine." Amy waved him off. "Go get your food before I trap you at the table talking."

Justin wasn't sure her expression conveyed that she was truly fine, but he followed her orders and went to get his lunch as quickly as possible, so he could hurry back to her.

"Alright, spill," he commanded as soon as he was back sitting down at their table with his usual trayful of food in front of him. "And don't say you're fine, because I know *fine* really means *not fine*."

"You were right about her only counting back thirty-six weeks instead of forty," Amy confided between bites of her own lunch. "And after hearing how rough it was on her back then between not being able to work while dealing with morning sickness and her boyfriend being deployed to a war zone, I understand why."

"Yeah, I bet that was rough," Justin agreed when Amy paused to take another bite of her salad. He couldn't imagine how hard that had to have been on Andrea.

"But regardless of understanding why she identified the wrong man as our father, I'm still struggling with being mad at her." Amy's expression as she spoke made it clear to Justin that she felt chafed by her conflicting feelings.

Justin could relate, having his own conflicting feelings about his own DNA revelations. "Yeah, I get it." He reached across the table to hold her hand. "I'm still a little pissed at Memmaw, even though I know she was just passing on stories her parents and grandparents had told her. I wish she would've gone to search for her family on the Rolls when she was in Oklahoma, so she could've found out it was all lies and quit perpetrating them further."

"You know I lived in Oklahoma and heard all the Heinz 57 mix stories from my mom and grandparents and never once thought to go look for their people on the Rolls." Amy shook her head. "Not even when I went with Randi to her parents' cabin just outside of Tahlequah."

"What's Tahlequah?" Justin had no idea what or where Amy was talking about.

"Capital of the Cherokee Nation, where all those Rolls are stored." Amy's smile seemed to brighten as she was thinking about a town she'd visited back in Oklahoma.

"Oh, well, no need now, since they're all online, just like all the other public records of births, deaths, marriages, etc." Justin returned her bright smile with one of his own.

"But it sure would've saved us all some grief if our grandparents would've done a little research the old-fashioned way before the invention of the internet. Not that the internet is really doing me any good at finding my biological father." Amy's smile fell as she looked down at her plate before taking another bite of her lunch.

"You've searched online for him?" Amy just nodded as she chewed. "And you haven't been able to find him?"

"No." Amy shook her head after swallowing. "Ashlyn found an Australian biologist with the same first and last name, but it's not him. I widened the search to social media accounts for him anywhere in Oklahoma in case he was still in the state, even if he moved outta Tulsa. I found a lotta Sinclairs, but no David."

"And the Ancestry site hasn't given you any hints for him?" Justin was curious about why she hadn't messaged her aunt or half-brother on the site to find him that way, but he wasn't sure how to ask without sounding insensitive. So, he only asked the one question before stuffing his face with more of his lunch.

"No, it doesn't give much information on living people. And I think that's mostly why I'm still mad at my mom."

Justin couldn't vocally ask for an explanation of Amy's thought process while chewing, so he raised an eyebrow inquisitively, hoping she'd understand his unspoken question.

"Her miscalculation of our date of conception meant she didn't think she had a reason to keep track of him after they broke up." Amy looked down at her mostly empty plate before setting her fork down and looking up into Justin's eyes. "If she'd have kept in touch with him or his family, since she was supposedly friends with my aunt, then maybe they'd have figured it out sooner. Maybe we wouldn't've spent our whole lives grieving for a man who wasn't our father. Maybe we could've been raised by two parents, even if they didn't get back together as a couple. Maybe I could've had a relationship with my dad."

"Oh, Sweetheart." Justin's heart broke for her. He squeezed her hand and wished he could pull her into his arms as a single tear slipped down her cheek. He dropped his fork to his plate and reached across the table to wipe it away without releasing her hand. "I wish those close matches really had been your grandkids inventing time travel, so we could go back in time and fix everything before you were born."

"Wow, you must really like me if you're willing to risk time travel to go back and give me my daddy." Amy smiled as she giggled a little.

"Yeah, I do," Justin admitted, smiling back at the woman he knew was the love of his life, even though he knew she wasn't ready to hear that from him yet. "I'm sorry I can't go back in time and give you the last twenty-five years with your dad, but I'm gonna do everything I can to help you find him, so you don't hafta miss him for very much longer."

"Yeah, I was gonna ask you if maybe Bobby has some way of tracking him down like he would a criminal." Amy's smile slightly dimmed. "But then I worried that he'd only be able to find him if he's actually a criminal, and I'm not sure I'd wanna find him if that's the case."

"Actually, I was gonna suggest goin' to my cousin Jake to track him down." Justin hoped his smile conveyed his confidence in finding her father that way. "If he's done anything on a computer in the last twenty years, Jake can find him, criminal or not. And he can go through his life with such a fine-toothed comb that you'll know everything about him to be able to decide if you wanna contact him or not."

"Is that legal?" Amy looked worried as she posed the question.

"Yeah," Justin laughed, knowing Amy was picturing Jake hacking into his email and bank accounts, like he did with Brooklyn's father to help bring him down. "I'll make sure to tell him to only look at public records, no hacking."

"Oh, okay." Amy chewed her bottom lip like she was still anxious about something.

As much as Justin wanted to soothe that pouty bottom lip with his tongue after she finished scraping it with her teeth, he hated seeing her looking trepidatious about anything. "What's wrong, Sweetheart?"

"Do you think I should reach out to my biological father?" Justin tried to interpret the meaning behind the look in Amy's eyes, but he couldn't figure out the strange glint that he'd never seen in her obsidian orbs before. "You don't think it's disrespectful to the man, who thought he was our father and would've come home to raise us as his own if he hadn't died, to reach out to a father, who didn't bother checking in with Mom to make sure she didn't have babies nine months after they broke up?"

"No!" Justin adamantly shook his head. "I understand how you can feel that way, but I don't think it's disrespectful at all. From everything you've told me about Eddie Anderson, he was a good man, who would've been a wonderful father. But if he'd have survived, came home to raise you, and was sitting here right now, I think the man you described to me would want you to reach out to your biological father. He didn't sound like a selfish man who'd wanna hoard your love all to himself. He'd want you to love your biological father as much as you've loved him all these years."

Shit, unless her biological father was an abusive asshole or something like Kay's ex, Justin thought, suddenly worried about what her mother had told her about her biological father the day before. *Maybe I should've asked more questions before I offered my opinion.*

"Unless…" he finally muttered, drawing out the word as he tried to plan the wording of his next statement.

"Unless what?" Amy questioned when Justin's voice trailed off.

"Unless your biological father isn't such a nice guy?"

Amy's eyes widened at his words which came out sounding like a question. She opened her mouth as if to speak, but then she promptly closed it without saying a word.

"What did your mom say about David Sinclair last night when you talked?" Justin rubbed his thumb over the back of Amy's hand, trying to comfort her as he posed the question.

"She said he was sweet and smart," Amy whispered, but she looked a little less worried. "That they broke up because she didn't feel like she fit in with the people he had to socialize with for his new job, but they parted on friendly terms because it was just having fun together, not a soulmate connection."

"Okay, well, that sounds like he was a pretty decent guy when your mom knew him. So unless Jake comes up with something horrible he's done in the last twenty-five years, I don't see any reason why you shouldn't contact him."

"What if he didn't keep in touch with Mom because he found out she was pregnant, and he didn't wanna be a father?" Amy's quivery lower lip was back until she bit down on it, a sure sign of her anxiety.

"Then you tell him what a jackass he is for abandoning you and never speak to him again." Justin was mad as hell at the thought of her father abandoning the beautiful woman across the table from him. "But you won't know if that was what happened without talking to him."

"I, I'm scared," Amy stuttered, squeezing his hand in a death grip. "I don't know if I can handle finding him just to be rejected by him."

"I know, Sweetheart." Justin stood to walk around the end of the table. He sat down in the chair beside her and pulled her into his arms, not caring if anyone saw them and thought it was inappropriate for the workplace. "But you don't hafta worry about what might or might not happen. If he turns out to be a jackass who doesn't wanna be your dad, then nothing about your life has to change after you talk to him. You'll still have the people in your life who really matter. Your mom, your sister, me. Hell, you have my whole crazy family in your corner. And I can guarantee that whether or not your sperm donor wants to step up and be your dad, my dad will always treat you like another of his daughters. Though, hopefully, he won't try to scare me away from you with his shotgun, like he did Jen and Julie's boyfriends when they were teenagers."

Amy laughed at Justin's truth-based joke. The sound was melodic and made him smile, but not nearly as much as the way she returned his hug. He could happily spend the rest of his life in her arms. Unfortunately, he glanced at the clock on the wall and realized that he couldn't stay cuddled up with her for another minute, much less the rest of his life.

"Okay, lunchtime, and worry time, is over." Justin dropped a kiss on the top of her head before releasing her to stand up and go deal with the trash on his tray. "I'm gonna go to my office and give Jake a call to get him started on looking for the right David Sinclair before coming to the lab to review the latest antifreeze tests. And when he finds him, I'll be by your side, if and when, you're ready to make the call."

"Thank you." Amy stood and cleared her own tray from the table. "I like to think I'm strong and independent and can handle anything life throws at me." Amy shook her head as they left the cafeteria, reaching out to hold his hand when they entered the elevator. "But I don't think I'd be able to deal with this mess without having you there to talk to about it."

"Anytime, Sweetheart, anytime." Justin grinned. He knew he couldn't really fix anything for her about the whole situation, but he was glad he could be there to support her as she dealt with the emotional fallout. He wanted to spend the rest of his life being the rock she leaned on whenever she needed someone else to help shoulder her load.

Chapter Eight

Sunday, March 3, 2019

Amy was exhausted after an emotional week with her mother and sister in town. After dropping them off at the airport, she opted for a light dinner of tomato soup and a grilled cheese sandwich before heading up to her huge clawfoot tub to soak away the stress of the week. She stripped out of her clothes and wrapped her hair up in a silk scarf, to keep it up out of the water while she bathed and protect it from becoming a tangled mess while she slept, as the tub was filling with water just hot enough to steam up the window and mirrors. She dropped in a bath bomb containing cocoa butter and lavender essential oil for the skin-softening and aromatherapy benefits as she settled in to soak.

She closed her eyes and rested her head back on the blow-up bath pillow she'd found on a shopping trip with her sister at Beautiful Destiny the day before. She let her mind wander, thinking over the events of the last week. While there had been some definite bumps in the road with the DNA revelations and not being able to see Justin after work every night with her mom and sister staying with her, Amy already missed her family now that they'd flown back to Tulsa to go back to their normal routines.

Amy really did wish her mother and sister would move to Texas, so they could spend more time together. But considering how having them staying with her had prevented her from going on any more dates with Justin, she wasn't going to push them to move immediately.

Both Andrea and Ashlyn had come into the office with Amy a couple days that week, when Jen had pushed them to meet with her about job opportunities at Burleson Incorporated. Amy thought Ashlyn would be moving down as soon as her lease was up in Tulsa, after her testing with Jen showed a high aptitude for a job as an executive assistant. Amy wasn't sure if it was the salary Jen quoted her or the fact that Becky was trying to recruit her to work in the entertainment division of the company that most excited Ashlyn about working there, but she was glad to see her sister motivated to move.

And waiting three months for her lease to be up gives me three months to date Justin before we have to tell everyone we're dating, so Ashlyn doesn't blab it for us.

Amy wasn't as sure her mom would be joining them in Texas at the end of the school year. Andrea had given the excuse of wanting to stay in her current job a couple more years to be able to retire with twenty years of service. But Amy worried her mother's reluctance to move had more to do with the tension between them surrounding Amy and Ashlyn's newfound paternity.

Amy had tried her best to be understanding of her mother's position and how her thought process was impeded by all the things going on in her life when she found herself pregnant with her boyfriend deployed to a war zone. But no matter how much her mind comprehended the situation to realize how easy the error was to make for her mother, her heart still felt like it'd been cheated out of a relationship with her biological father.

And Mom knows me too well for me to be able to keep that hurt and anger hidden from her, no matter how hard I tried while she was here.

Amy wasn't just angry at her mother for the whole situation, either. She was angry at her biological father as well. It takes two people to make a baby, or two babies in her and Ashlyn's case, so he should've been just as responsible as their mother when they were born.

Amy was struggling with dealing with the conflicting emotions she had for her biological father. Part of her wanted to find him and call him, so she could finally have the father-daughter relationship she'd always dreamed of having. Yet another part of her wanted to confront him in person, so she could slap him upside the head for not checking on her mother to make sure he wasn't a father before walking away completely.

She'd gone back and forth all week in trying to decide whether or not she would contact him if Jake was able to find him for her. One minute she wanted to call him up and beg him to be her daddy, and the next minute she didn't want to waste her time on someone who'd abandoned her before she was even born.

The more she thought about the whole situation while she was soaking in the tub, the more she cried. She'd mostly held her tears back all week, focusing on work during the weekdays, and spending time with her mother and sister every evening and while she was off work for the weekend. The only times she'd come close to breaking down was during her nightly phone calls with Justin after going to her room for the night, and the one time she'd discussed the situation with him at lunch.

After Monday, they hadn't been able to have any alone time at lunch because of either having her mom and sister, or his sisters, or both of their family members seated with them. So, there hadn't been any more hugs or hand-holding since Monday either. Amy realized she missed the easy affection he gave her as she finally grabbed a washcloth and her favorite handmade soap to wash her body now that her bath water was cooling down.

As much as she enjoyed their nightly talks, his soothing voice over the phone wasn't quite as calming to her overwrought emotions as a gentle squeeze of his hand on hers. That was saying a lot about how comforting she found his touch, since she'd started calling him the *Amy Whisperer* with how he was able to listen to her rant about whatever new revelations she found on her family tree each evening and talk her down from her angry, agitated state in just a few minutes.

And she'd had quite a few doozies of revelations on her family tree in the last week. In trying to keep from being angry at her mom about her father situation, Amy had subscribed to the site and started looking into the hints on her grandparents' profiles. She thought learning more about her mother's parents would bring them closer together and help heal some of the pain she was feeling from the dad discovery.

Unfortunately, she found out that Tom Lawton met and married Shanae Keaton and adopted her infant daughter, Andrea. That led to a whole new scandal as they tried to figure out who Andrea's biological father was by looking through Amy's DNA matches that weren't shared matches with her father's sister or her half-brother.

So far, Amy had only found some distant cousins that were related to her through Nana Shanae's siblings and parents. Amy hadn't even known her grandmother had siblings until her mother dropped the bombshell that Shanae's family had disowned her when she got pregnant with a half-white baby and then married a white man. And Amy didn't even want to get started on how she'd been named after Papa Tom's mother, whom she wasn't biologically related to in any way.

The only good news she'd found on that branch of her family tree was that her ancestors apparently immigrated to the United States in the early nineteen-hundreds and weren't in the country before the Civil War. Though when she found the immigration records and saw they came from various islands in the Caribbean, Amy assumed the generations before them had still been subjugated as slaves on those islands, with the boats that brought them from Africa not actually making it to America. At least it didn't appear that any of the women on her maternal line had been raped by a slave master, or if they were, they didn't bear children from it that were showing up on her family tree. *Or maybe I'm just not seeing the records of those instances, since I only subscribed to the US Discovery level of Ancestry membership.*

Jeez, I really need to go back to thinking about Justin and his calming touch, Amy thought as she got out of the bathtub, dried off, and slathered on her lotion. *Maybe start thinking about all the places I want him to touch me besides holding my hand while we're eating lunch. Now that Mom and Ashlyn have gone home, maybe we can figure out a way to go on another date, or at least sneak away from town, where he can touch me in more than a friendly manner.*

Just as she was slipping on the t-shirt and panties she would be sleeping in that night, her phone rang on her bedside table. The screen flashed with Justin's name prominently displayed as her caller. Amy quickly swiped her thumb over the screen to answer the call.

"Have you bugged my brain to know to call me right when I started thinking about you?" Amy quipped in lieu of a typical greeting.

"Naw," Justin chuckled. "You must've telepathically signaled me somehow."

"No, I don't have superhero abilities like that." Amy giggled along with Justin, loving their easy banter.

"Really? You seem pretty super to me."

"That's got to be the worst of your cheesy lines," Amy groaned.

"Yeah, that one was pretty bad," Justin agreed with a self-deprecating laugh. "So, how're you holdin' up after taking your mom and sister to the airport?"

"I'm doing okay." Amy adjusted the pillows on her bed, so she could get comfortable for their nightly chat. "I already miss them, of course. But with everything else going on, it's also nice to have a break from them being here twenty-four-seven, so we can all come to terms with everything on our own, too."

"Yeah," was all Justin said, letting her control the conversation. He'd been doing that all week, letting Amy talk as much or as little as she wanted about the whirlwind of emotions she was dealing with while learning all about her family history.

Appreciating the stoic support Justin provided her, Amy decided to go easy on the man, who'd quickly snuck past her walls to become her closest confidant, by changing the subject away from anything DNA drama related.

"So, now that I don't have a houseful of people preventing me from going out as more than friends," Amy started, only slightly tentative about being the one asking him out. "Would you like to plan our next date?"

"Absolutely, Sweetheart." Justin's voice sounded deeper than normal, the gravelly tone making her panties wet. "Dinner tomorrow after work? Or would you rather try something a little more interesting like a tour of the Alamo?"

"The Alamo?" Amy couldn't contain her giggles at his suggestion. "That has to be the most quintessentially Texan a date could ever get."

"Naw," Justin chuckled with her. "A rodeo would be the most quintessentially Texan a date I could take you on. And I haven't suggested that 'cause we'd probably run into some of my family, or friends, who'd tell my family about seeing us there."

"Well, then let's plan a trip to the Alamo for one night this week and schedule a rodeo when we can sneak off to the other side of the state for a weekend, so nobody will tattle on us to your family. I mean, I need the full Texas dating experience now that I live here."

"Deal." Amy heard Justin typing on his laptop in the background. "Just let me check the schedule for the Alamo to know when we can go there, and then we'll pick a different place to meet after work for every night this week."

After more typing and clicking coming from Justin's end of the phone line, he finally told her he had to book them a private tour for Thursday evening because it was the only way they could go after work. They planned a couple different restaurants for Monday and Wednesday and an escape room on Tuesday.

"How about Tower of the Americas on Friday night? In addition to the historical exhibit, they have a revolving restaurant that has a great view of the lights of the city at night."

"Oh, that sounds nice." Amy was excited about their plans, but she was also wondering if they had a hotel in the tower, so she could finally have some alone time with Justin to do more than chastely kiss him goodnight.

"Perfect." Justin didn't seem to notice the way Amy's voice quivered with her unspoken question. "I'll book the reservation."

"Is there somewhere private we could reserve for that night, too?" Not used to being the aggressor in any of her previous rendezvous with men, Amy's voice came out a little squeaky as she posed the question.

"Um, maybe," Justin replied, drawing out the word like he wasn't sure what she was asking. "Are you thinking, like, a private room for dinner? Or someplace we could spend the whole night alone?"

"Someplace we could spend the whole night alone," Amy answered, her voice sounding breathy to her own ears. "I mean, we can't exactly go back to your place without your whole family seeing my car parked there. And if you spent the night here at my place, they'd probably come find you here when they noticed your truck wasn't home all night."

"I take it this means you're ready for more than just a kiss goodnight in a parking lot before we go our separate ways after our dates?" Amy detected a hint of hopefulness in the tone of Justin's voice as he questioned her.

"I'm beyond ready for more than a goodnight kiss with you, Justin." *Holy shit! What's going on that my voice sounds like I'm a porn star? Is it normal to have a phone sex voice?*

Ever since she'd had thoughts of having phone sex with Justin the previous Saturday, Amy had been wondering if she could somehow work up the courage to ask him for what she wanted on one of their nightly phone calls. *Guess I'm skipping asking for phone sex and going straight to asking for hotel sex.*

"Yeah? Just how much more, Sweetheart?" When Amy moaned instead of answering, Justin inquired further. "Second base kinda more? Or maybe heading toward third?"

"Oh, I think you'll have to make sure you touch every base because I'm ready for you to hit a home run," Amy practically purred into the phone. Metaphorically pulling up her big girl panties, Amy decided to ask a more suggestive question to let him know just how far she was ready to go. "Do you have a big enough bat to hit a home run?"

"Fuck yeah, Sweetheart," Justin growled into the phone. "I definitely have a big enough bat. Though I might need to warm it up between now and Friday. Maybe take a few practice swings while we're on the phone. And have you make sure you're ready for me to slide into home."

Amy couldn't contain her giggles at the way he continued the baseball analogy. "Is that your way of suggesting we have phone sex, Mr. Burleson?" *Guess I don't have to ask for it after all.*

"Yes, Amy," Justin drawled, his voice deep and gravelly from arousal. "But you'd better call me Boss while we're talkin' dirty, so I don't get any inappropriate erections at work when I'm addressed as Mr. Burleson and flashback to picturing you touching yourself for me."

"Yes, Boss," Amy replied, putting her phone on speaker, so she could lay it on the pillow beside her head and have her hands free to explore her body. "Do you just want me to use my hands while I'm touching myself for you? Or would you like me to get one of my toys outta my bedside table and use it while we're on the phone?"

"Toys? Just how many toys do you have, Sweetheart?" Amy could tell Justin's interest was obviously piqued by the tone of his voice.

"Just three." Amy wasn't sure if she should describe them each in detail, so he could pick one for her to use, or just tell him about her favorite one. She didn't get the chance to decide before Justin started speaking, taking away her opportunity.

"Three? Sounds like you're hiding a little bit of naughty under your good girl persona, Sweetheart."

"Maybe just a little," Amy admitted. "But I'm being a really good girl right now and waiting for you to tell me how you want me to touch myself before doing it, Boss."

"That is being a very good girl, Sweetheart. You're much better behaved than me. I've been stroking my cock since you asked the size of my bat earlier."

They both chuckled and Amy couldn't ever remember a time when she was turned on while laughing in the past.

"But even though you're being such a good girl, I don't want you to play with your toys until I'm able to watch you," Justin ordered, sounding very commanding. "Bring them with you on Friday, Sweetheart, but just use your fingers on your sweet pussy now."

"Yes, Boss." Amy slipped her hand into her panties to slide through the slippery wetness of her sex.

"Tell me what it feels like, Sweetheart," Justin demanded, his breathing rate picking up from the way he was jacking off.

"Smooth and slippery," Amy cooed as she envisioned Justin's big hand wrapped around his dick. "I'm so wet for you, Justin."

"Are you just rubbing your fingers over the outer lips? Or are you fucking yourself with your fingers?"

"Just outside, especially over my clit," Amy replied, her own breath coming in short pants as her orgasm built inside her.

"Use your other hand on your tits. Pinch your nipples for me."

"Yes, Boss." Amy did as she was told. She'd never considered herself a submissive person, but she was surprisingly turned on by following Justin's commands.

"Fuck, Sweetheart, I'm close. Is playing with your clit gonna get you there? Or do you need a good finger-fuck to come with me?"

"I just need you to keep talking," Amy admitted, speeding up the circles she was making over her clit with her middle finger. "You telling me what to do is what's getting me most of the way there."

"Picturing you laying on your bed naked and touching yourself for me is what's got me most of the way there. Fuck, it's even better than picturing you in my shower every morning."

"Oh, whaddaya picture me doing in your shower every morning?" Amy wondered if Justin jacked off in the shower to some of the same fantasies about her that she'd had about him while masturbating and using her vibrators.

"I imagine *us* doing all kinds of things in my shower." Justin put special emphasis on the word "us" in a way that made Amy think he pictured doing things to her and her doing things to him. He wasn't going to be a selfish lover, expecting to receive pleasure from her with no regard to her enjoyment of the experience, like everyone else she'd ever been with. "I dream of the day I'll get to show you all the things I want *us* to do in the shower. Kissing, touching, licking every inch of each other before picking you up in my arms and sliding home between your thighs is my favorite fantasy."

Amy knew by the sensual way he described the fantasy that sex with Justin would be unlike anything she'd ever experienced before. Even his dirty talk was loving and affectionate. She gentled her strokes through her folds with her fingers, trying to mimic the way she imagined he'd touch her.

"I imagine being on my knees, worshiping you with my mouth 'til the water turns cold, turning it off, and continuing until you've come so many times on my tongue that the hot water is back, so we can start all over again."

"Oh, yes, Justin," Amy moaned as the tension built in her core. She knew she was getting close and wanted to hear him tell her about his dick to get her the rest of the way. "Would you let me get on my knees for you then?"

"Absolutely, Sweetheart, if that's what you want."

"I want you to describe it for me," Amy practically begged as she inserted two fingers inside her pussy and kept her thumb rubbing on her clit. "Tell me what you see when you picture me sucking your cock."

"I picture you naked with your nipples hard and begging me to play with them. Your knees are wide, so I can see your sweet, creamy cunt dripping for me. Your perfect pouty lips are wrapped around my dick, but you can only suck on about half of me because going any deeper would make you choke. You'd work the base with your hands until I tell you to use one on your pussy, so we could come together."

"Oh, yes, Justin!" Amy shouted as the first waves of her orgasm washed over her. The inner walls of her channel clamped down on her fingers as her whole body contracted in blissful spasms.

"Fuck, yes, Amy, come with me!" Justin's shouted words mixed with her own as they continued panting out each other's names while floating through nirvana.

"Fuck, Sweetheart, that was…" Justin's voice trailed off, or maybe Amy was still too floaty to comprehend what he said.

"Wow," was the only thing she could mutter as she felt like she was finally coming back into her own body.

"Yeah, wow sounds like an apt description," Justin chuckled. "That's the hardest I've ever come in my life."

"Yeah, me too." Amy was surprised she admitted that out loud.

"Does that mean I'm not the only one who's gonna hafta change the sheets before goin' to sleep?"

"No, I don't have to change the sheets, but I do have to change my panties," Amy giggled. "I guess you're messier than I am."

"Yeah, I probably should've gone to sit in my shower, instead of trying to lay in bed where I was comfortable talking to you." Justin chuckled as Amy heard him rustling around on the other end of the phone call. "Shit, I'm gonna hafta throw these sheets away before Ms. Mary comes over to clean my house this week."

"You don't have to throw them away, silly." Amy was desperately trying to hold back her laughter at the sounds Justin was making while apparently stripping his bed. "You can just run them through the washer and dryer."

"Amy, Sweetheart, please don't hold this against me," Justin beseeched, his tone turning serious. "But I don't even know how to turn on my washer and dryer."

Amy could no longer hold back the bark of laughter that escaped at picturing Justin's face as he admitted to his laundry room ignorance. It only continued as he laughed along with her.

"Good thing for you, I'm an expert at doing laundry," Amy told him when her laughter died down. "I can talk you through getting the washer started if you wanna carry your soiled sheets there now."

"You're a lifesaver, Sweetheart." Justin's footsteps sounded through the phone as he walked from his bedroom to his washroom. "Now I won't hafta be embarrassed by anyone else seeing the gallon of jizz on my sheets."

Amy had him describe his washer, so she could help walk him through the process of laundering his sheets. After a comical conversation about how the stain removal spray just looked like he was squirting more cum on his sheets, Justin was finally able to get the sheets in the washer with the liquid soap and fabric softener in the correct dispensers to start the machine. She even gave him instructions on how to start the dryer, so he wouldn't have to call and

Leah Mae Wright

wake her up in the middle of the night when the load was ready to be swapped before they finally said goodnight.

~ ~ ~

Friday, March 8, 2019

Justin was a nervous wreck as he paced the lobby of the Omni La Mansion Del Rio waiting for Amy to meet him for their date. He'd already checked-in to the presidential suite he'd reserved for them and was just waiting for her to arrive, so they could go upstairs and change for their night out.

After their first impromptu experience with phone sex the previous Sunday, and subsequent nightly variations of the same, he wasn't sure why he was so nervous. *We've talked about all the things we like and wanna do to each other, so why does it seem so overwhelming to move from only talking about it on the phone to actually starting to live out our fantasies in the flesh?*

It's not like we haven't even kissed or are planning to lose our virginity. Hell, I wasn't even this anxious back when I was a virgin and planning to have sex for the first time. It's gotta be because it's Amy and I know how special it's gonna be. The first time with the only woman I'll be with for the rest of my life.

Not that Justin was going to tell Amy that's why he was so nervous. Though she was much more relaxed on the dates they'd gone on earlier in the week than she was on their first few dates almost a month before, he could tell she still wasn't completely convinced that dating could lead to marriage, babies, and happily ever after. So, Justin was biding his time, biting his tongue to keep from saying those three little words every night when they hung up the phone.

Hopefully, I can keep from declaring my love when I'm balls-deep inside her tonight, so I don't freak her out by moving faster than she's ready for toward our walk down the aisle. Though we might not make it down the aisle if I can't find a florist who carries yellow carnations.

Justin shook his head as he remembered how he'd tried to go get her flowers several times that week without success. He'd been able to find white, pink, and red carnations, but no yellow. After the third florist he'd gone into told him they didn't carry yellow carnations because they symbolized disappointment and rejection, he worried he wouldn't ever be able to give Amy her favorite flowers in her favorite color.

If I can ever convince Amy that we're meant to be, maybe I can talk Florence into bucking the superstitious meaning and special ordering them for our wedding.

Justin hoped the way Amy had admitted to wanting him earlier in the week meant more than just sexually. Though he was enjoying how their flirty banter and secret touching had increased at work the previous week, Justin wanted more than just their sexual chemistry connecting them.

Justin thought back to how things had seemed to change at work in the last week. The first few weeks she worked there, Amy always sat across from him at the table when they ate lunch together and kept an arm's length of space between them in the lab. But after their first time mutually masturbating while on the phone together, Amy sat beside him at lunch, making it easier to hold hands the whole time. She even held his hand under the table when his brother and sisters joined them for the midday meal.

She'd also started standing or sitting closer to him in the lab. In addition to innocent, possibly unintentional, brushes of their arms or legs under the table, she'd started reaching out to touch his shoulder or arm where others could see. Justin suspected that had a little to do with the way some of the other women in the lab were the overly touchy types, and Amy was combating her jealousy over the way they'd innocently touched him in the past by staking her claim in front of them in a similar manner.

Justin knew Amy had nothing to be jealous over when it came to any of the women who were a little too flirtatious at work, but he didn't mind her feeling that way if it prompted her to act a little territorial and possessive of him. He never really noticed other women were in the room, much less flirting with him, whenever he even thought of Amy, whether she was present or not.

But, fuck, she's hot whenever she's acting jealous and making sure she's between me and any other women in the room. I wonder if she thinks the same about me sticking close to her to stake my claim, so none of the guys will try to hit on her? Or does that possessive behavior turn her off? Fuck, I hope my caveman tendencies don't scare her off or offend her in any way.

Justin didn't get the chance to reminisce long enough to try to figure out how Amy reacted to his past behavior when he'd felt jealous of any other man talking to her because she finally walked in the door.

She was still in the coral top and tan slacks she'd worn to work that morning, but nevertheless, she was more beautiful than any of the other women who were already dressed up for the night and making their way out of the hotel.

"Sorry I'm late." Amy unnecessarily apologized as soon as she got to within a few feet of Justin.

"No worries," Justin replied, reaching out to take her suitcase from her hand. "I've already got us checked in, so we can head upstairs and get changed before going out."

"I almost thought I was gonna hafta change before leaving the lab." Amy shuddered as she relinquished her bag to him, making Justin worry about what might have happened to cause such a strange reaction from her.

"Why?" Justin put his free hand on the small of her back to guide her toward the elevator.

"Because one of the techs bumped a table and sent a dozen beakers crashing to the floor." Amy shook her head as she reached out to push the button for the elevator. "Thankfully, they were mostly empty since we were cleaning up for the night. But I still had to stick around to fill out an incident report and clean up the mess."

"Was anyone hurt by the broken glass?" Justin didn't think there were any injuries since Amy didn't lead with telling him about them, but he asked just to make sure.

"No, but Megan wasn't happy about a drop of glycerol that landed on her Louboutin loafer." Amy made a face in disgust as they got on the elevator. "I don't know what made her think it was a good idea to wear a pair of thousand-dollar shoes to work in the lab. One of the first things I learned in school was to only wear clothes and shoes you wouldn't mind losing in case of spills in the lab."

Thousand-dollar shoes? Seriously? And I bet she's gonna expect the company to replace them because of this accident, Justin thought as he followed Amy onto the elevator. He pushed the button for their floor before turning to Amy to continue their conversation. "So, I should expect a bill for her expensive ass shoes on my desk Monday morning?”

“Nope!” Amy grinned as she popped the P.

“No?” Justin raised an eyebrow questioningly, wondering what Amy had done to settle the situation without a big bill for the company.

Amy shook her head, her smile widening. “Just one of the benefits of having a brand new lab manager, Boss. I actually read every line of the rules and regulations I was given in HR on my first day on the job. And I pointed out the fifty-dollar limit on the replacement cost of any single item if personal effects are accidentally damaged in the lab.”

“Damn, Sweetheart, I didn’t even realize we had that limit,” Justin chuckled.

“Well, now you know why I leave my cell phone in my office and only reply to intraoffice messages on my company-issued tablet when I’m in the lab.” Amy shrugged as the elevator doors whooshed open. “Maybe after me pointing out the replacement cost limit, and Megan not getting a new pair of Louboutins on the company’s dime, they’ll all start leaving their phones and other expensive items in their lockers. And I won’t have to start writing reprimands for wasting time on their phones when they should be working.”

“Has that been an issue when I’m not in the lab?” Justin put his hand on Amy’s low back once more to guide her to their room, where he’d already dropped off his suitcase.

“Not too bad.” Amy stopped for Justin to unlock the door to their suite, explaining more once they stepped inside. “And I completely understand people like Marla carrying their phones, so her kids can text her when they get home from school and if they have any issues while they’re home alone. It’s the ones who act like unruly teenagers, trying to sneak in playing games on their phones, when they should be paying attention to the experiments they’re running, that I’ve had to warn to put them away.”

Justin inwardly fumed at the thought of his employees acting like children and disrespecting Amy’s authority by continuing to ignore her warnings to play games when they should be working.

“Well, no more warnings.” Justin sat her suitcase on a table in the sitting room section of their suite. “If you catch anyone else playing games on their phone, shut down their experiment and send them up to me." *They can have all the time they want to play games while they're sitting at home unemployed.*

"Oh, okay." Amy looked around their room for the first time. "Wow, this is really nice."

Her expression told him she was expecting more of a typical hotel room instead of the opulence of the most expensive suite in the hotel. *Fuck, I hope I didn't make this feel weird for her by going overboard and insisting on only the best for our first night together.*

"I wanted to make sure our surroundings reflect how special tonight is for us, Sweetheart." Justin slipped his arms around her waist, finally pressing their lips together now that they were alone in their suite.

Amy ran her palms up his chest to wrap her arms around his neck as she returned his ardent kiss. Justin couldn't resist delving his tongue between her plump lips to explore her mouth.

Fuck, I love the way she tastes! Justin knew he couldn't spend much more time kissing Amy, though, or they'd miss their dinner reservations.

"Do you wanna change in the bedroom or bathroom, Sweetheart?" Justin gave her the choice when they broke the kiss to breathe. The bathroom in the suite actually had two doors, one into the bedroom and one into the sitting room, so they could go to separate rooms to get ready without one of them being trapped in the bathroom while the other was changing in the bedroom, so they wouldn't see each other naked until after their date when they returned to the room.

"Bathroom, since I have to do a little more than just change my clothes," Amy replied, her voice a little breathless from their kiss.

"Then I'll change in the bedroom and meet you back here to leave for the restaurant." Justin dropped one more quick peck on her lips before grabbing his garment bag and going to the bedroom. He double-checked the door between the bedroom and bathroom was closed, so Amy could be assured of her privacy while they got ready.

He was glad he'd guessed correctly which room she'd want to get ready in when he noticed the flowers he'd ordered earlier were already on the dresser in the bedroom. The large vase was filled with three dozen red, white, and pink carnations. The arrangement was reminiscent of the bouquet he'd brought her on Valentine's Day for their first date, but three times the size. He'd ordered this arrangement specifically for their special night, not bothering to bring her a smaller bouquet earlier in the week when he couldn't find the flowers in her favorite color.

Knowing Amy would probably want the bathroom to get ready in, Justin had taken special care to do all his manscaping that morning in the shower and had brushed his teeth and knocked down his five o'clock shadow with his electric razor when he dropped his things off in the room before going back downstairs to meet her in the lobby.

Now all he had to do was change out of the jeans and Henley he'd worn to work that day and into his navy-blue suit to be ready for their date. He paired the suit with a lighter blue shirt and medium blue tie for a monochromatic look, thinking it made him look a little more suave and sophisticated than he really felt.

It only took him a few minutes before he was seated in the sitting room waiting for Amy. He checked his watch and was glad he'd scheduled their reservation for eight o'clock to make sure the sun had set, so they could enjoy the lights of the city through the windows of the restaurant. It wasn't quite seven yet, so the hour Amy was delayed from leaving the office wouldn't make them miss their reservation time unless she took an extra-long time getting ready.

Hopefully, she doesn't need as much time to get ready to go out as my sisters. But if she does, I'll just have the horse-drawn carriage take us straight to the Tower of the Americas, so we don't miss our restaurant reservation, and we'll do the city tour after.

~~~

The last week with Justin had done wonders for Amy's confidence in herself and their relationship. Not only had he continued to be her sounding board when she was struggling with her erratic emotions, being the best friend she'd ever had, but he'd also stepped up the sexual side of their relationship.

In addition to their goodnight kisses after their dates getting almost too steamy for the parking lots in which they separated to go to their respective homes, he'd also insisted on a phone call every night once they got home to have phone sex. They ended up sharing several of their sexual fantasies on the phone each night and then teasing each
~~~

other with whispered innuendo and seemingly innocent touching every day at work.

Their sexual tastes seemed to align well, with both of them being mostly vanilla and only interested in lighter kinks. They'd briefly discussed soft bondage, but only so Justin could tease her with her toys before replacing them with his cock. They also both had several office sex fantasies.

The only reason they hadn't followed through on some of those fantasies in his executive office was because he insisted they wait until Friday night for their first time together. After all, he had plans to make it special. The way he treated her like a queen and controlled his desire to make their first time seeing each other naked into a romantic dream for her made him seem too good to be true.

If he's too good to be true, or I'm just dreaming how great we are together, then I hope I never wake up from the dream, Amy thought as she stripped out of her work clothes to do a quick rinse in the shower. She was careful not to get her hair wet, but she couldn't just change her clothes and run the risk of having missed a small sliver of glass or spot of glycerol that might have gotten through her clothing to her skin.

Thinking back to the accident in the lab dimmed her happy mood. She didn't have any way to prove it, but she really thought Tara had caused the accident on purpose. Her suspicions made her wish there were security cameras in the lab for her to be able to go back and watch the incident over and over until she figured out if it was really an accident or not.

While Amy had been feeling closer to Justin the last week, she wasn't so sure they were hiding their growing attraction as much as they should. She didn't think them sitting side by side at lunch and in meetings, so they could secretly hold hands under the table, was what gave them away.

No, it was me being a jealous bitch and making sure I was always between Justin and the lab techs who constantly flirt with him, Amy thought as she got out of the shower, dried off, and started slathering on her lotion. *Suddenly touching his arms or shoulders the way they used to do before I got between them is probably what gave us away to instigate their jealous fits. And if I were a betting person, I'd be willing to bet that Tara's jealousy over me getting closer to Justin is what caused her to intentionally knock those beakers over while I was standing right beside them.*

Amy wasn't sure how to tell Justin about her suspicions without sounding like a vindictive bitch. Without video or other tangible proof, she didn't want to say anything to him. Though she knew he would listen and take her concerns seriously, tattling about the mean girls at work to her boss boyfriend seemed petty and childish. Not to mention it would bring relationship drama to work which was a direct violation of the expectations on the relationship form she and Justin had signed and filed with Sofia Reyes in human resources.

Amy quickly freshened up her makeup and tousled her curls, glad she'd been standing when the spill happened, so there was no chance the broken glass could've landed in her hair. She slipped on a barely-there lace thong and demi-bra in a peachy color that was the closest she had to match her tangerine chiffon wrap dress. With the way the dress wrapped around her, it created a deep V, allowing her cleavage to show more than she normally preferred.

But I bet Justin will appreciate it, she thought as she tied the dress around her waist. Multiple layers of flowy material flared out at the hips and ended just below the knee, but it was far from conservative with the way the wrap created a slit that would reveal everything underneath if that knot at the waist came untied.

She accessorized the dress with a pair of black pumps and transferred the essentials into a matching black clutch before leaving the bathroom to meet Justin back in the living room area of the suite.

"Wow! You look…wow!" Amy giggled at Justin's words as he stood from his seat when she walked into the room. The way he ate her up with his eyes made Amy glad she'd opted to add the additional makeup to conceal her blush.

"You don't look so bad yourself, Boss." Amy took in the vision of him in his custom-tailored suit and noted how the shades of blue complemented the bright orange of her dress.

"We'd better go before I say 'to hell with our reservation' and carry you off to the bedroom." Justin looked her over from head to toe once more before offering her his arm to escort her out of the room. Amy felt tingles where she rested her hand on the crook of his elbow and flowing throughout her whole body, especially the sexy parts, from the seemingly innocent connection. "As much as I would prefer spending our whole evening in bed, I'd also hate to miss out on dinner and the special surprise I have waiting downstairs for you."

"A good surprise I hope." Amy smiled at Justin as they made their way back down the elevator to the hotel lobby. She hadn't had a whole lot of good surprises in her life, but she had a feeling Justin was going to change that for her.

"I think it's a good surprise." Justin's grin widened as he winked at her. "But you'll hafta let me know if you think so after we get outside."

Amy expected to head from the lobby to the parking garage, but Justin directed her straight to the street in front of the hotel, where there was a horse-drawn carriage waiting for them. Apparently, there were several in the area that could be flagged down by anyone wanting a tour of the downtown area, or they could be reserved, like Justin had done, to be their private taxi for the night.

"I should've known a Texas surprise would include livestock," Amy laughed as Justin helped her up into the carriage.

"I didn't even think of it that way." Justin laughed with her as he climbed in behind her. "I was thinking this would give you the whole Cinderella experience. One more way of making tonight magical."

Amy extended her leg to examine her shoe, twisting her foot around like she was really trying to get a good look at it. "Nope, definitely not wearing glass slippers, so we should be safe to not have the carriage turn into a pumpkin while we're at dinner."

"Nope, no pumpkins," Justin chuckled as he leaned over to give her a peck of a kiss. "Just our own real-life fairy tale."

He told the driver to take them to the Tower of the Americas and to save the tour of the city for after they'd eaten, so they weren't late for their reservations. Amy leaned into Justin's side as he wrapped an arm around her shoulders while they made the short trip.

Amy enjoyed the sights, though with this first ride being less than a mile, there wasn't a whole lot to see.

Their time at the Tower of the Americas made Amy feel like she was living in a movie. The romantic dinner was delicious. The view of the lights of the city was breathtaking. Their conversation was laced with innuendo and promises of what was to come when they got back to their hotel room. But kissing Justin on the observation deck was what really made it feel like she was living out the final scene of a romantic movie, where the hero and heroine reunited atop the Empire State Building and the credits rolled before the kiss turned too erotic for a PG viewing audience.

After a quick walk-through of the historical exhibits in the tower, they made their way back down to their waiting carriage for a longer trip around the city. As they cuddled in the carriage, they made note of several other places they wanted to go on their after-work dates in the coming weeks.

After what seemed like only minutes, but was probably closer to at least an hour, they arrived back at the hotel. Justin tipped their driver and thanked him for their rides before lacing his fingers with Amy's to walk back into the hotel.

The closer they got to their room, the more Amy could feel the butterflies flapping away in her stomach. It wasn't that she was nervous per se, but more that she was excited about what she knew was coming when they finally got there.

Me! I'm gonna be coming! And so is Justin!

Amy giggled at her giddy thoughts as they got into the elevator taking them up to their suite. She still couldn't believe that Justin had insisted on the presidential suite at the fanciest hotel Amy had ever stayed in for their first night together. He really was trying to make the night seem like a fairy tale come true.

"What're you giggling about?" Justin inquired as soon as they were alone in the elevator.

Shit! How do I explain my giggles without sounding like a silly schoolgirl?

"Just happy." Amy smiled, and hoped that was enough of an explanation.

"Me, too, Sweetheart." Justin pulled her into his arms and dipped his head to brush his lips over hers. It was a chaste kiss, even though it went on much too long to be considered a peck. It was nothing like the elevator sex scenes from some of Amy's favorite books, but it was still enough to get her panties wet.

Maybe I should've worn something with a little more coverage down there to keep from dripping down my legs before we make it to the bedroom, Amy thought as she squeezed her thighs together and wrapped her arms around Justin's neck. Apparently, that was his go signal because he deepened the kiss by sucking on her bottom lip before plunging his tongue into her mouth.

As Amy weaved her fingers through the short strands of hair at the nape of his neck, Justin pulled her tighter to his body, with one hand on her mid-back and the other on her butt. She could feel the evidence of his arousal pressing into her belly, even through the layers of fabric still separating them. Their tongues continued to tango in an ever more erotic dance until the elevator chimed and the doors started to open on their floor. Amy was breathless as they exited the lift and rapidly walked toward their room.

As soon as they were inside their room, Justin spun her around and pressed her back against the closed door to kiss her once more, dropping the keycard to the floor when he missed putting it in his jacket pocket. With both hands on her butt, Justin lifted her up, so he didn't have to bend as far to keep kissing her.

Amy's clutch joined the keycard on the floor as she wrapped her arms around his shoulders and her legs around his waist, grinding her core against his hard length, no longer able to hide her desire for him.

"Fuck, Amy, Sweetheart, we hafta slow down." Justin pulled his lips from hers to take a breath. "Otherwise, I'm gonna embarrass myself by coming in my pants before we even get naked."

"I don't think that's anything to be ashamed of, considering I was about to do the same," Amy admitted, grinding against him once more and enjoying the pressure against her sensitive clit.

Justin trailed his lips down her neck and growled just below her ear. "Fuck! Sweetheart, you're gonna hafta wait until after the first round to enjoy the flowers I have waiting for you in the bedroom."

"I don't need flowers, Justin, just you." Amy returned his ardent neck kisses as he carried her to the bedroom.

Amy's back hit the soft mattress with Justin coming down over her, since neither one of them was willing to release their hold on the other. They continued to kiss like teenagers making out in the backseat as their hands roamed, touching each other over their clothes until the barriers between them became too frustrating.

Amy tried to start undressing them by pushing Justin's jacket off his shoulders, but it didn't go too far since she hadn't unbuttoned it. Justin pulled back long enough to unfasten the jacket and toss it to the floor before pressing down into her once more and taking her mouth in a claiming kiss.

Amy loosened his tie and started working on the buttons on his dress shirt, needing to run her hands over the hard planes of his torso beneath it. Justin ran his hands over her body, cupping her breasts, and not seeming to focus on how to remove the dress that was keeping him from touching her skin to skin.

"Clothes. Off." Amy barely got the words out when their lips parted for them to momentarily breathe.

"Can't stop tasting you," Justin growled against her lips before diving into another possessive kiss.

Amy turned her face and scraped her teeth across the sensitive skin of his neck before whispering in his ear. "We can both taste a lot more if we get these clothes outta the way."

"Good point," Justin replied, pushing up off the bed. He made quick work of removing his belt and kicking off his shoes while Amy sat up to start working on removing her own clothing.

She watched in awe as he separated the ends of his tie, leaving it hanging around the neck of his shirt as he took it off. She fumbled with untying her dress as she took in the smattering of hair across his pecs, his chiseled six-pack abs, and that perfect, muscular V that guided her eyes back to his happy trail leading below the waistband of his pants. Amy was mesmerized as she watched Justin unfasten his slacks and drop them to the floor. He toed off his socks, leaving him standing there beside the bed in nothing but a pair of navy-blue boxer briefs that did absolutely nothing to conceal his extra-large erection.

Holy shit! I don't think he's gonna fit.

"Oh, I'll fit just fine, Sweetheart," Justin promised, moving her hands from the tie at her waist that she'd somehow fumbled into a knot when she was too focused on looking at the gorgeous man before her instead of untying it.

Did I say that out loud? Amy wondered as Justin deftly released the knot to unwrap her dress.

"Fuck, Sweetheart, you're gorgeous!" Justin pushed the dress from her shoulders, dropping to his knees beside the bed to start kissing his way down her body. With a flick of his fingers behind her back, Justin removed her bra. He licked and sucked her breasts as he used his hands to slide the straps down her arms. He took his time worshiping her breasts with his mouth while tossing the bra to the floor behind him.

"Oh, Justin," Amy moaned, running her hands through his short hair as he moved back and forth between her breasts, suckling each nipple in turn, kneading and squeezing the breast he wasn't sucking on with his big hands, so neither was ever neglected.

Just when she thought she was about to come from him only playing with her breasts, Justin pulled back, pulling her up to a standing position beside the bed with him kneeling at her feet. He slid a finger under each of the thin strips of lace at her hips and slowly lowered her thong.

Amy lost her shoes as she stepped out of her panties, reveling in the lustful look in Justin's eyes as he gazed at her bare mound for the first time.

"Lay back on the bed, Sweetheart," Justin commanded as he stepped away from her to go dig around in his suitcase.

Amy did as she was instructed, watching Justin intently as he pulled a brand new box of condoms out of his bag and tossed them on the bed beside her. When he got back to the bed, he lifted one of her legs, kissing his way from her ankle to her knee as he crawled on the bed with her.

Justin reached down and lifted her other leg, repeating the kisses from her ankle to her knee before moving up to her ticklish inner thighs. Amy couldn't stop the giggles as he alternated feather-soft kisses back and forth between her thighs.

"Harder, Justin," she begged between giggles. "Too soft is just tickly."

"How about I just focus on a less ticklish area?" Justin suggested as he reached the apex of her thighs. He ran his nose through her folds, inhaling deeply like he was savoring her scent.

Amy didn't have time to feel even the slightest embarrassment from having him sniff her before he was following the trail of his nose with his tongue. "Oh, yes," she cried out, enjoying his oral attention more than she'd ever dreamed possible.

He held her legs open with his shoulders as he licked, sucked, and teased her in ways she'd only imagined in the past. He alternated between suckling her clit and fucking her with his tongue until she couldn't hold her climax back any longer.

"Oh, Justin!" Amy screamed his name repeatedly as she flew over the edge to ecstasy for the first time that night.

Justin prolonged her orgasm by tracing his tongue in circles over her needy nub while slipping a finger inside her. The first finger was soon joined by a second and then a third until he was rubbing over that spot deep inside her that she hadn't even been able to find with her vibrator before.

Her first oral O was quickly surpassed by her second as he continued to work her over with his mouth and fingers. *Wow, multiples are a real thing. And we haven't even gotten to the main event yet. Maybe I'll find out tonight just how accurate those romance novels are about four or more in a single session. And based on the size of the bulge in his shorts, I bet he'll hit my G-spot with his dick, too.*

Amy lost all control of her body as her legs clamped down around Justin's head, her hands in his hair shoved his face further into her pussy, and her hips thrust up at him of their own accord. "Oh, fuck, Justin!" Amy continued to scream his name repeatedly as wave after wave of orgasmic bliss washed over her.

She wasn't sure if the gush of wetness between her legs was his saliva or her cream, but she hoped Justin didn't drown before her body relaxed enough to release him. He still had to show her just how well he would fit inside her.

As soon as Amy felt like she was finally coming down from her high, Justin pulled out of her grasp and ripped the plastic off the box of condoms. He spilled them out on the bed as he was getting the first one out. Using his teeth and one hand to open the condom, he used his other hand to push his boxer briefs down, freeing his gloriously long, thick dick.

Amy pushed up on her elbows to watch as he rolled the condom down his length before he crawled back on the bed and settled between her thighs.

"You sure you're ready for this, Amy?" Justin cupped her face in one hand, balancing over her on the same elbow. Amy nodded, still unable to form words from not having caught her breath after that last explosive climax. "I need the words, Sweetheart. Because you hafta be sure you're one-hundred percent ready for what this means for us."

"I want you, Justin." Amy wrapped her arms around his neck and pulled him down to her for a kiss, not comprehending his whole message.

"You know this means forever," Justin growled between kisses. "Right, Sweetheart? You know there's no going back after this. Once I'm inside you, I'm never gonna be able to let you go."

"Oh, yes, Justin!" Amy pressed her mouth to his for a fiery kiss. She might not have believed it just a few short months before, but after everything she and Justin shared recently, she now knew he was her soulmate. *I just have to trust that he's for real with all the forever stuff because I know I'll only end up with a broken heart if he ever realizes I'm not the one he wants to spend the rest of his life with.*

Amy didn't have time to let the negative thought affect her as Justin used his free hand to line up the blunt head of his cock with her opening and slowly started to push inside her.

"Oh," Amy moaned, not quite prepared for just how big Justin was. He was definitely bigger than anyone she'd been with before, but he was much more gentle, taking his time to slowly enter her and allowing her time to adjust to his sizable invasion before moving in a little further.

Justin swallowed her moan in a heated kiss as his hand slid up between them, over her belly, and up to cup her breast. He used light, teasing touches to relax and arouse her, so he could push the last couple inches in, filling her completely.

Amy wrapped her legs around his hips as her hands explored his upper body. She matched the softness of the way he was caressing her, though she didn't limit the areas she stroked to just his chest. Justin held still as he sank all the way inside her, making sure she was ready for him to move before he slowly pulled back and then pushed back in.

"Amy, Sweetheart, you feel so fucking good." Justin's voice was deep and gravelly as he trailed kisses down her neck. "So tight and wet."

"Oh, Justin," was all Amy could reply, too carried away by the sensations Justin's slow, sensual strokes in and out of her were causing to even be able to think, much less form words.

The first waves of yet another orgasm washed over Amy as Justin continued to whisper sweet nothings against her skin. With his mouth on her breasts instead of at her ear, Amy didn't quite hear everything he said, but she caught several snippets like "perfect" and "made for me" before her cries of pleasure drowned him out.

Amy chanted Justin's name as she reached the height of pleasure for the third time that night, her body uncontrollably writhing beneath him as he continued his languid lovemaking. At the same time Amy felt her whole body go into spasm during the most intense part of her climax, Justin pushed in all the way to the hilt and felt like he was swelling inside her.

"Yes, Amy, come with me!" Justin arched his back, rearing up before crashing his mouth to hers once more, swallowing both their cries of pleasure.

Amy floated in a cloud of bliss, not even realizing Justin rolled them, so she was resting on top of him as they each caught their breath. She wasn't sure if it was hours or minutes that she laid there basking in the afterglow while they were still connected before she raised her head to look into Justin's expressive ocean blue eyes.

Amy contemplated what to say, feeling slightly awkward because she knew it was considered bad etiquette to say the three little words that were on the tip of her tongue for the first time while still in a sexual stupor. But she didn't have to worry about thinking too hard over what to say since the slight movement of her body on top of his alerted her to the fact that he was still hard inside her.

"How are you still hard?" *And why did I just blurt out the first thing that popped into my head? Maybe Ashlyn rubbed off on me a little when she was down here last week?*

"Not still, Sweetheart," Justin chuckled as he rolled them to their sides and slid out of her. "Just already hard again. But I hafta go deal with this condom and put on a new one before we start on round two."

Amy opened her mouth to reply, but quickly closed it as she watched him walk toward the bathroom. Seeing his tight, milky-white ass gave her too many ideas of things she'd like to try for round two to formulate a sentence. Luckily for her, Justin had listened intently when she'd told him her fantasies earlier in the week to be able to fulfill a couple without her having to say a word.

And I thought romance books were lying that four O's were possible in one night, Amy thought as she drifted off to sleep in the early hours of the morning. *I never dreamed Justin would get me close to double digits on our first night together.*

~~~

Saturday, March 9, 2019

Justin woke the next morning laying on his side with Amy wrapped in his arms. He took a moment to savor the feeling of her naked breasts pressed into his chest, her head resting on his bicep, the feel of her back and ass under his palms, the weight of her leg thrown over his hip, and especially the heat of her pussy pressed against the underside of his hard-as-a-rock cock. He wanted to memorize everything about the first time they woke up together, hoping to retain the memories to tell her about them on their fiftieth wedding anniversary. *Though if I'm lucky enough to convince her to marry me one day, we'll have thousands of mornings just like this.*

He still couldn't believe he was finally with the woman of his dreams. *I guess if I was gonna wake up to find out it was just a dream, it would've happened when Amy pinched my ass last night.* Justin grinned at the memory of the night before when he'd come back from the bathroom after disposing of the first condom.

She'd sat up in bed to stare at his bare ass as he walked away to dispose of the condom after their first time making love. When Justin saw the lustful look in her eyes as he returned to her side, he couldn't resist asking, "See something you like, Sweetheart?"

"I don't know," Amy replied, twirling her finger to indicate she wanted him to turn around just as he got to the edge of the bed. "Turn around and let me get a second look, so I can decide if I like it or not."

Amy scooted over to the edge of the bed just as Justin turned around. She startled him by reaching out and pinching his right ass cheek.

"What was that for?" Justin spun around and almost poked her eye out with The Anaconda already standing at attention for round two.
~~~

"Just had to make sure you're real," Amy muttered before taking hold of his cock and blowing his mind.

Amy stirring in his arms brought him back to the present before he could relive the best blow job of his life or any of the other things they'd done the night before.

"Good morning, Beautiful." Justin bent his head down to kiss her.

"No, morning breath." Amy pushed back from him with one hand on his chest and the other covering her mouth. "Give me a minute to brush my teeth before you kiss me good morning."

"I don't care about morning breath." Justin kissed her forehead before letting her go, so she could scramble out of bed and into the bathroom.

Though if it bothers her, I should probably follow her to the bathroom to brush my own teeth. Or is it too soon in our relationship for us to be in the bathroom at the same time?

Shit, I didn't even think about her probably having to piss first thing in the morning. It's not like women hafta wait for the morning wood to go down to be able to. I should probably at least give her a few minutes to do that before going in there to brush my teeth in the sink beside her.

Justin listened intently for the toilet to flush and the water in the sink to turn on before getting out of bed to go join her in freshening their breath, so they could have the good morning kiss he really wanted.

"What're you doing in here?" Amy squealed the question as she finished washing her hands before grabbing her toothbrush from the cup beside the sink.

"Figured I'd better brush my teeth, too, so you'll let me kiss you." Justin smiled at her in the mirror as he got his toothbrush and toothpaste out of the drawer where he'd stored them the night before.

"Oh, um, okay," Amy sputtered as she fumbled with her toothpaste, dropping the cap as soon as she opened it. "Give me a couple minutes and I'll be outta your way. Um, in case you, uh, need to do anything else in here."

Fuck, she's adorable! Justin just smiled at her awkwardness at thinking he needed the toilet immediately. He quickly brushed his teeth while enjoying watching her do the same. As soon as they'd finished rinsing and spitting, Justin took her hand to keep her from fleeing the bathroom. "All I need to do now is you."

Justin pulled her into his body, using his free hand to tilt her chin up, so he could properly kiss her good morning. He released her hand to wrap his arms around her when she snaked her free hand up over his shoulder and pulled his head down further to deepen the kiss.

Fuck, I should've grabbed a couple condoms to bring in here with me, Justin thought as he lifted Amy up to carry her back to the bedroom to get them. Amy wrapped her legs around his waist as he stalked toward the bed without breaking their kiss.

Thankfully, he'd put the extra condoms on the bedside table closest to the bathroom door at some point the night before, so it would only take him a second to grab a couple before he could carry her back into the bathroom to fulfill his shower fantasies.

"What're you doing?" Amy pulled out of the kiss to ask her question when he removed one of his hands from her ass to grab the condoms.

"Grabbing supplies, so I can fuck you in the shower, Sweetheart," Justin replied, holding the handful of condoms up for her to see before carrying her back to the bathroom.

"Oh." Amy's mouth made a perfect O as she looked at him with lust and mischief in her dark-brown eyes. "Lucky for you it's Saturday."

"Why's Saturday lucky for me?" Justin sat her down and turned on the water to warm up.

"Because I wash my hair on Saturdays, so I won't get irritated if your shower fantasies cause me to get my hair wet." Amy turned and walked out of the bathroom.

"Where're you goin'?" Justin was confused about why she'd left the room when he'd just started the shower, until she returned with a plastic bag full of products that she opened on the counter to pull out her shampoo and conditioner.

"You might get away with using the stuff provided by the hotel," Amy started, pointing to the small bottles already in the shower. "But Black hair needs special care."

"Is that why you were grumbling something about needing your scarf in your sleep last night?"

"Yes, you've already messed up my hair enough with sexing me into a coma, so I couldn't properly wrap it up last night." Amy pointed at him and made a face like she was trying to act angry at him. "So, take this as your only warning. My hair gets wet on Saturdays when I wash it. And *only* on Saturdays. No funny business in the shower any other day of the week to screw up my hair."

"Understood." Justin held both of his hands up in surrender.

Amy couldn't maintain the gruff expression, giggling and shaking her head at him as she walked past him into the shower.

Justin didn't bother to point out that the only way he could share a shower with her on any other morning of the week was if they were at one of their houses where his family could find out about them. He just considered her statement to mean that she was planning for a future with him where that would happen.

"What about if I buy you a swim cap, so we can shower together without getting your hair wet?" Justin stepped into the now warm shower with her.

"You must have a lotta shower fantasies." Amy grinned as she turned to face him after setting her shampoo and conditioner down on the ledge in the shower.

"So many shower fantasies." Justin pulled her back into his arms. "Starting with washing every inch of you before getting you dirty again."

"And do I get to wash every inch of you, too?" Amy wrapped her arms around him.

"You can do anything you want to me, Sweetheart." Justin ran his hands over her delectable body as he kissed his way down from her lips while lowering himself to his knees. He paid extra attention to the sensitive spot at the base of her neck just above her collarbone before moving down to knead and suckle her perfect peaks.

"Oh, Justin," Amy moaned as he teased her nipples with his fingers and teeth. He soothed any discomfort from the gentle nips with his tongue before moving to repeat the process on the other breast.

As much as he loved worshiping her magnificent mounds, he couldn't wait a moment longer to lick the cream from her cunt. *Fuck, I hope she squirts in my mouth again like she did last night,* Justin thought as he kissed his way over her belly and lifted one of her legs over his shoulder to open her up for his oral onslaught.

"Fuck, you're so wet," Justin growled after swiping his tongue through her folds for the first time that morning. "And I don't think any of it is from the shower."

"No, Justin, it's all because of you." Amy weaved her fingers through his hair and pushed his head closer to the heaven between her thighs.

Justin couldn't say another word with his mouth otherwise occupied. He swirled his tongue through her lower lips, then sucked her clit before poking his tongue out to stiffen it, so he could fuck her with his tongue. He lost count of how many times he repeated the sequence alternated with lapping up her cream before she finally exploded.

"Oh, yes, Justin," Amy screamed as he swallowed down the gush of her orgasmic honey.

He licked her clean as she rode the waves of her release, gentling the strokes of his tongue where he knew she was almost too sensitive to touch, so she could come down from her high. He lowered her leg to the floor of the shower when she released her death grip on his hair, banding an arm around her waist to hold her up as he stood because she wobbled on her feet, having not completely recovered from her climax.

He reached out to grab a condom off the ledge of the shower with his free hand, opening it with his teeth.

"Let me help you with that." Amy took the condom from the package to roll it down his length.

"Fuck! I love the feel of your hands on me, Sweetheart," Justin groaned, slightly worried he'd come just from the way she teased him as she covered his cock. "But I need to be inside you now."

"And I need you inside me now." Amy placed both of her hands on his shoulders just as soon as she was done rolling on the condom.

Justin gripped her ass in both hands, lifting her up just as she jumped and wrapped her legs around his waist. The Anaconda was laser-focused on getting inside her tight pussy and slithered home almost immediately. With as wet and ready as she was, there was virtually no resistance as he shoved his cock balls-deep inside her.

"Oh, Justin," Amy cried out, wrapping her arms around him, her nails digging into his shoulders.

"Fuck, Amy!" Justin returned her excited shout before crashing his lips on hers, loving the feel of her marking him.

They only kissed momentarily before she was pulling back to beg, "Harder, please. Fuck me harder, Justin."

"As you wish, Sweetheart," Justin replied. He used his two large handfuls of her ass to move her up and down on his dick, timing the way he was bouncing her with the thrusts of his hips to pound into her like a man possessed.

The feel of her breasts brushing over his chest was amazing, but he had to get his mouth back on her, too. Not wanting to muffle her moans of pleasure, he moved his lips down her neck and across her collarbones, licking and sucking his way from one side to the other as they continued their primal mating.

When she exploded in his arms for her second orgasm of the morning, Justin fucked her through it, not letting up until she went lax in his arms. He slid one arm up behind her back to support her as she rested her head on his shoulder, holding still inside her to allow her to recover before starting over to bring them to a mutual release.

"You've gotta come one more time for me, Sweetheart," Justin demanded, pressing her back against the wall, so he could angle his hips to rub his pubic bone across her clit with each thrust.

"I don't know if I can." Amy panted out the words as her inner walls started to flutter on his cock once more.

"I know you can, Sweetheart." Justin captured her lips again, fucking her mouth with his tongue the same way he was fucking her pussy with his cock. The impassioned kiss was all it took to bring them both over the edge to heaven.

He swallowed their orgasmic expletives as he thought about how he wanted to spend the rest of their day balls-deep inside the love of his life.

Justin collapsed onto the bench in the shower, holding Amy in his arms while they caught their breath.

"Yeah, we might need to buy stock in swim caps." Amy's voice came out breathy against his shoulder. "With shower sex being even better than bed sex and balcony sex, we're gonna hafta do it more than just on Saturdays."

"I'll order a truckload as soon as we're done in here." Justin lightly chuckled at her sudden change of opinion. "But first, I want you to teach me how to properly wash your hair and anything else I can do to take special care of you, Sweetheart."

"Seriously?" Amy lifted her head to look him in the eyes, like she was trying to figure him out.

"Yeah, Sweetheart." Justin pecked her on the lips. "My new goal in life is to do everything I possibly can to pamper you and take care of you the way you deserve."

"Does that mean I can get you to give me a full-body massage while putting on my lotion after the shower?"

"Absolutely!" Justin wagged his eyebrows at her suggestively as he imagined rubbing her down from head to toe. "I'll enjoy that just as much, if not more than you will."

Chapter Nine

Monday, March 11, 2019

First thing Monday morning, Justin was on the phone with his cousin Jake to discuss reviewing the security footage of the lab accident on Friday. He would've asked his cousin Bobby, since he'd been the one to actually oversee the installation of the security cameras because of being local law enforcement, but he was back in Georgia with Brooklyn to deal with more of the legalities of her former life there and the charitable foundation they were starting together.

"Hey, Cuz, what's got you calling me so early in the morning?" Jake queried as soon as he answered Justin's call, sounding like he'd just woken up, instead of already being at work as Justin expected.

"We had an issue in the lab Friday after I'd left for the day and I'm hoping you can tell me how to access the security footage, so I can see exactly what happened," Justin replied, not beating around the bush.

"Oh, yeah, I can do that." Jake sounded a little more focused than his greeting. "I'm assuming nobody was hurt, or I'd've heard about it on Friday."

"Correct. The only damage reported was a dozen broken beakers and a spot on one of the tech's thousand-dollar shoes." Justin shook his head at recalling the asinine cost of the shoes Megan chose to wear in the lab. "But I'm still concerned because of the expression on Amy's face when she told me about it."

"Yeah, I'd be concerned about the sanity of a tech wearing expensive ass shoes in the lab," Jake chuckled, like he assumed that was the cause of Amy's trepidatious expression.

"That's a whole other issue I'm gonna hafta address with the lab techs this afternoon." Justin huffed out a breath. "But right now I'm more concerned with finding out which tech caused the spill and whether it was accidental or intentional."

"You think it was intentional?" Jake's tone turned serious, and Justin could picture his cousin straightening up in his chair as he clicked the keys on his keyboard to remotely bring up the security footage.

"I don't know." Justin ran a hand through his hair and scratched the back of his head. It was still a little tender from the way Amy had pulled his hair and dug her nails into his scalp over the weekend. Justin relaxed a little at the memory of all the things they'd done Friday night and all day Saturday that he brought back to his mind by running his hand over the slightly sore spot. "When Amy told me about it, she kinda looked uncomfortable. Like she wasn't sure it was really an accident, but she wasn't positive it wasn't to bring up the possibility of it being intentional."

"Okay, are you in the lab, your office, or the security room?"

Justin wasn't sure why his location mattered, since he just planned to write out the instructions he got from Jake to go to the security room to access the footage, but he answered the question anyway. "My office, but I'm on my cell, so I can go to the lab or security room if that's where I need to be to access it. I was just gonna write down the instructions from you, so I wouldn't keep you tied up on the phone while I searched through the footage."

"Naw, you don't hafta go anywhere." Jake was quiet for a few minutes, the only sound coming over the phone being his keyboard clicking. "Okay, I've given you access to the security cameras on both your office desktop and your laptop. If you reboot, you should have new icons on your desktop to access them."

"Oh, okay." Justin rebooted his desktop first before pulling his laptop out of the case he carried it in to reboot it as well.

"You'll probably have a better view on the big monitor on your desk, but I figured you might need to have portable access to review the footage with Amy as the lab manager and anyone else in the lab responsible for supervising the techs."

"Okay, both computers are coming back up from the reboot." Justin entered his password into his desktop to finish bringing up the system.

Once the desktop with the new icon was up, Jake walked Justin through the process of accessing the cameras, specifically the ones in the lab, and reviewing prior days' footage.

"Jeez, how many freaking cameras did ya'll put in here?" Justin was surprised when he saw the long list of cameras he could now access.

"Enough to make sure the only private areas of the building are inside the executive offices and the restrooms." Jake chuckled. "Why? You need to know where you and Amy can make out without getting caught?"

Yes! "No, I was just surprised by the long list of cameras I'm having to scroll through to find the ones in the lab."

"Sure, Cuz, whatever you say." Jake's light chuckle was soon replaced by flat-out laughing. "Just remember you can fuck her in your office, but not hers."

Fuck! How the hell does he know?

"Dude, I'm not…" Justin's voice trailed off as he realized he couldn't deny his relationship with Amy without it being obvious he was lying.

"Whatever, man, I'm just picking on ya 'cause I know you wanna be."

"Yeah." Justin chuckled along with his cousin, hoping it covered the fact that he'd actually gotten his wish to be with Amy.

"Speaking of Amy, I'll be emailing you the report on her bio-dad later this week. I'm just waiting for confirmation that the latest contact information I have is correct."

"Oh?" Justin straightened in his seat, no longer focused on looking through the list of cameras. "Anything come up that might make her not wanna contact him?"

"No, he seems like a good guy," Jake divulged, much to Justin's relief. "Kind of a quiet, family man. Actually has three kids besides Amy and her sister, not just the one on the Ancestry site. Worked his way up in the company where he started to work right before breaking things off with her mom, and transferred to the Houston office when he made VP. His only vice seems to be that he spends his weekends on the golf course, but that's not really a bad habit. Ya know?"

Leah Mae Wright

"Yeah, thanks, Cuz." Justin relaxed a bit since Jake's report didn't uncover any more bad news about Amy's family for her to have to endure. "I'm sure she'll be glad to hear all that."

"Cool. Okay, if you've got what you need on the lab footage, I'm gonna go and get back to my actual job."

"Yeah, I think I can find it from here." Justin went back to looking through the list of cameras until he saw the three labeled "R & D lab." "See ya on the twenty-seventh for the board meeting."

"Yeah, see ya then. Oh, and let me know if I need to remotely revoke anyone's access to the building or network while Bobby's in Georgia."

"Will do," Justin agreed just as they disconnected. "Let's hope it really was an accident, so I don't hafta make that call."

Justin spent the next hour looking over the security footage from all three angles in the lab before sending Amy a message through the intraoffice system, requesting her presence in his office for a meeting.

He was fuming as he watched the footage. And not just about the way Tara seemed to look around to make sure nobody was watching before she hip-bumped the table to send the beakers crashing down around Amy. When he saw that the first time, he decided to go back through the footage for all day Friday. He saw several instances of dirty looks aimed at Amy from both Tara and Megan whenever her back was turned to them, along with them and several other people horsing around and playing games on their phones whenever he or Amy weren't in the room.

Justin restarted the first camera from the beginning of the day on Friday and made notes of every infraction he saw while watching the events in the lab on fast forward. He'd just finished reviewing the first camera view and was about to start the second camera view to see if he caught any other instances when his intercom buzzed on his desk.

"Yes, Ms. Lewis," he snapped after pushing the button to speak with his executive assistant.

"Mr. Burleson, we seem to have a situation with employees who don't understand they need an appointment to see you." Amanda Lewis spoke in a rather snide tone of voice that put Justin on edge even more than he already was from watching the lab footage.

Justin didn't have a second to comprehend what Amanda was saying before he heard Amy speaking over her.

"No, what we have is a secretary who thinks she's a guard dog and can't comprehend that I was asked to report to the boss's office regardless of there not being an official meeting on her calendar."

Maybe I should review the video footage of my assistant's office as well as the lab's to make sure I catch everyone who's been behaving inappropriately toward my girlfriend at work. Justin blew out a frustrated breath before punching the intercom button once more. "Ms. Lewis, please accompany Ms. Lawton into my office."

Justin stood as the two women walked into his office. "Amy, please have a seat," he commanded, briefly enjoying the view of her curves in khaki slacks and a bright yellow blouse before turning his attention to his assistant. "Ms. Lewis, please consider this your one and only warning before termination for insubordination. Ms. Lawton does not, and never will, need to have scheduled a meeting with me to enter my office. She is to be given the same courtesy as any member of my family who might pop into my office to speak with me. Understood?"

"But she's not a member of your family, so I told her, just like I'd tell any other manager or department head in the company, to schedule a meeting," Amanda argued, slamming a hand on her hip indignantly.

Justin held up a hand to signal her to stop speaking as soon as the word "not" left her lips, but Amanda didn't shut up until she finished her tirade.

"Your opinion on the matter is not needed, Ms. Lewis." Justin leveled the woman with a glare before continuing. "Either treat her, and anyone else who comes to my office to speak to me, with respect, or your employment here will be terminated. Don't test my patience on this."

"Yes, Sir," Amanda sighed, looking down at the floor before slinking out of his office.

"And please close the door on your way out." Justin made sure his orders were obeyed before taking his seat and redirecting his attention back to Amy.

"Damn, you're really hot when you go into Dom Boss mode." Amy smirked up at him.

"Dom Boss mode?" Justin questioned, chuckling.

"Yeah, that commanding, deep voice when you're barking out orders and expecting them to be immediately followed just made my panties wet," Amy confided with a twinkle in her obsidian eyes.

"Well, it's a good thing we're in my office, so you can show me without being recorded." Justin's dick hardened at the thought of living out a couple of their office sex fantasies.

"Re-recorded?" Amy stuttered out the word, making it sound like a question. Her previously flirtatious expression was replaced with one of apprehension.

"Not in here, Sweetheart." Justin hoped the statement would reassure her. "But there are cameras in the lab and other areas of the building. That's actually why I called you up here."

"To let me know where we can and can't fool around at work?" Amy's flirty expression was back in full force.

"Well, that too," Justin chuckled. "But first to show you what I found on the footage from the lab on Friday, and discuss any other issues you've had with our other employees before taking all my findings to HR for disciplinary action and possibly a couple terminations."

"There are cameras in the lab? Thank goodness! I was wishing there were when the whole thing happened, but since the only ones I'd seen were in the parking lot and on the outside of the building, I didn't think there were any cameras inside to catch what happened." Amy waved her arms around animatedly as she spoke, confusing Justin about whether she was excited or anxious about what was recorded.

"Yeah, there are a lot more cameras in the building than I even knew about." Justin motioned for her to come around the desk so he could show her. "Three in the lab, one in your office, and two more in the hallway on the R and D floor. I've only gone through the footage from Friday on the three in the lab so far this morning."

"Oh, wow, guess it's a good thing we haven't tried to sneak any kisses in my office after lunch." Amy rounded the desk and stood beside his chair, so she could see his computer monitor to watch the footage. "Are these monitored all the time? Or just reviewed if there's an incident like Friday?"

"There's actually a security room downstairs where the security guards can monitor them, but I think they're more focused on the doors when people are coming and going. They only give a cursory glance at the rest of the cameras to catch something really out of the ordinary, like major equipment theft, or if someone enters the building who shouldn't, and we have a hostage situation." At least that was what Justin thought was the case, since he hadn't verified that with Jake when he talked to him that morning.

"Is a hostage situation really a possibility here?" Amy's bottom lip quivered as she asked the question.

Shit! I didn't mean to scare her, Justin thought as he reached out and took her hand to pull her down into his lap. Amy wrapped her arm around his shoulders as she sat sideways on his thighs. *Now, what the hell can I say to reassure her that she's safe here with me?*

"Burleson Incorporated has been in business for over a hundred years without a single incident like that." Justin hugged her to his chest and kissed her temple before explaining further. "I don't know if you've noticed it or not, but at least three of my cousins that you've met are so security conscious they're bordering on paranoid. Bobby, Jake, and Josh were insistent on putting in security cameras a few years ago, as well as security guards at all our facilities because, even though we're working to be a more environmentally-friendly company, we're still considered big oil. And I'm sure with the five new cousins we've found being in the security business, they'll probably wanna beef it up even more when they come to visit for the board meeting at the end of the month. So, I don't really think we hafta worry about there ever being an issue with someone coming here to harm our family or any of our employees."

"Oh, okay." Amy shook her head like she was shaking away her worries. "So, show me what you wanted to show me from Friday."

Justin pulled up the second lab camera that he'd just reset to the beginning of the day when his intercom buzzed earlier. "I was actually making a list of issues from the whole day and checking each camera to make sure I didn't miss one when you got up here." He pointed to the notepad beside his keyboard to show her the dozen or so issues he'd noted from the first camera view. "But I can go back to that after showing you the best angle of what really happened Friday evening."

He fast-forwarded the footage to fifteen minutes before five Friday evening before letting it play at normal speed for Amy to witness the events she hadn't seen as they happened. Amy was clearly visible putting away the chemicals she'd been working with all afternoon with her back to Tara, when the tech looked around to make sure nobody was watching her before making her move. Then, just as Amy started to turn back toward the space where she'd been working, Tara hip-checked the table to cause the rack of beakers and a glycerol jar to topple over, landing between Amy and Megan's feet.

"That conniving little bitch!" Amy jumped up and headed for the door, like she was ready to go kick Tara's ass.

Justin jumped up to follow her, barely grabbing her hand and pulling her back into him before she was able to round the desk to beeline toward the door. "Whoa! Wait, Amy, Sweetheart." Justin scooped her up in his arms to carry her back to his chair and sat back down with her in his lap. "As sexy as you are when you're pissed off, we hafta play this right, so we can fire her without risking a lawsuit or you goin' to jail for assault."

"You mean we can't just go down there and tell her to get her shit and get out?" Amy pointed at the monitor in exasperation as she asked her question.

"We can," Justin admitted while shaking his head to indicate that wasn't what he wanted to do about the situation. "But I wanna double-check that this isn't a criminal offense first. I also wanna look through the footage for the last couple months to make sure we have video evidence of every transgression to present to the authorities, so they can arrest her here. If we go down there all hot-headed and just fire her, she might skip town before she can be arrested for what looks to me like a clear case of assault and possibly corporate sabotage."

"Oh." Amy's previously aggressive state dissipated as her body seemed to deflate down into him.

"Can you think of any other incidents in the last couple months when you might've turned your back on your projects and then didn't have the reactions you expected? Or anything else you might've questioned as being odd in the lab when she could've been trying to mess with your work?"

"Maybe?" Amy shook her head like she wasn't sure. "I mean, I've had a couple experiments that didn't turn out the way I expected them to, but I'd have to go back through my lab notes to give you dates to look at the footage to see if you see sabotage. But none of those were anything that could've actually injured anyone in the lab."

"Yeah, well, if we can find anything that shows a pattern of behavior that just escalated to trying to cause physical harm to others in the lab on Friday, it'll still help build a case for the authorities," Justin contended.

"Okay, let me run down and get my tablet, so I can review my notes and give you dates to pull up on the cameras." Amy hopped up and took off before Justin could object.

He pulled up the security cameras on his laptop and split the screen four ways, so he could view the live feed of the three cameras in the lab and the one in Amy's office while she was on her way down there. He watched as she entered her office and grabbed her tablet and purse before exiting to head back up to the executive floor.

"Damn, I wish I'd've opened up all the hallway and elevator cameras between here and there to watch her the whole way," he muttered to the empty room before turning back to his desktop to review the Friday footage from the other two angles to note any other possible issues.

When Amy arrived back in his office, she ordered in lunch while Justin finished examining the footage from Friday. Once that was done, she started reviewing her lab notes from all the way back to her first day on the job to give him specific dates to look at the lab footage.

There were four dates, two in January and two in February, when Amy had gotten inconsistent test results with the effectiveness of the antifreeze and coolant she was trying to create with various agricultural forms of glycerol. Justin clicked through the video logs to find the first date and started camera one playing on fast forward. He caught several incidents of inappropriate phone usage, but nothing that stood out to appear as sabotage of Amy's experiment on the first date she mentioned. At least, not until he switched to one of the other camera angles later in the afternoon.

"Those are the only dates I can find that are questionable," Amy reported, coming back around his desk to watch the video over his shoulder. "Whoa! Is that live video of right now?"

When Justin turned to look at her to be able to answer her question, Amy was pointing at Justin's laptop, where he still had the cameras in the lab and her office open. "Yeah," was all he uttered before turning his head to look at the screen, which clearly showed that someone was in her office who shouldn't be. "What the fuck?"

"Can you tell who that is?" Amy pointed at the screen where a woman was rifling through her desk drawers.

"No, not with her head down like that." Justin shook his head before reaching out and picking up his phone to call the security guard to go handle the situation.

"No, wait!" Amy pointed to the phone in his hand. "We can't call down to catch her in the act. It'll alert everybody of the cameras before we have time to go through all the other footage to compile a case for the cops. We'll note this in with everything else we're finding."

"You're right." Justin put the handset back in the cradle of his desk phone. "But I'm not going back to watching the older footage until she's outta your office, so I know she's not done anything that could hurt you when you go back down there."

"Or I could just go back to my office right quick to catch her in the act without alerting anyone of the cameras." Amy took off out the door before Justin could even think of what to say to stop her. He was torn whether to keep watching the live feed to make sure the woman didn't leave the office before Amy got there or following her to protect her in case whoever was in her office was there to do her harm.

Fuck! If my gut is right and Tara was intentionally trying to hurt Amy on Friday, then there's no way I'm gonna stay here and watch the love of my life run headfirst into a dangerous situation.

Justin quickly jumped to his feet to follow Amy. He bypassed the elevator when he saw it was already a floor away and going down. *Fuck! I hope I don't freak out the security guys watching the monitors when they see me running through the stairwell.*

Justin bolted through the stairwell door on the lab floor at the same time the elevator doors opened, and Amy stepped out.

"Wow, Boss!" Amy exclaimed, grabbing his hand to slow his momentum toward her office. "Miss me that much that you had to run the whole way down here?"

"Something like that." Justin ran his free hand through his hair before taking the lead as they walked toward her office door. He kept Amy behind him as he opened the door to confront the lab tech still searching her desk. "Megan, what're you doing in here?"

Megan's head snapped up and her eyes went wide as she saw Justin and Amy walk into the small office. "Justin. Amy. I, uh, was just looking for the form to submit a claim for the damage to my shoes on Friday."

"That form isn't in my desk." Amy put her hands on her hips. "It's electronic, and I already told you where to find it on Friday."

"Oh." Megan's expression looked panicked for a second before she schooled her features. "I was so freaked out on Friday, I must've missed hearing that."

"That still doesn't explain why you're in the lab manager's office, rifling through a desk that contains information you aren't authorized to look at." Justin raised an eyebrow inquisitively at his insolent employee. "Regardless of the location of the form you're looking for, you should've waited for Amy to come back to her office to ask for it."

"I, uh, I'm sorry," Megan stuttered as she pouted like a child, her eyes filling with crocodile tears. "I didn't mean to do anything wrong. I just wanted to fill out the form while I'm on my lunch break."

Amy reached over, grabbed a Post-it note from her desk, and quickly wrote out the information for where to find the form on the company servers. "Then go here and do it electronically, like you were told to do on Friday."

Amy slammed the note into Megan's hand a little harder than Justin would have if he'd been the one to give her the information, but he didn't say anything as Megan scrambled past them to leave the room. Amy then opened and closed her desk drawers, like she was looking to make sure there wasn't anything out of place. She grabbed a set of keys from the last one before walking back toward him at the door.

"I'll make sure and lock my office anytime I'm not in it from now on." Amy held up the key as she sashayed by him out the door. He quickly followed, stopping just outside her office for Amy to lock it.

"Come on, Boss." Amy took his hand and led him back to the elevator. "Our lunch should be getting to your office any time now, and I have a feeling we'll need the sustenance for our long afternoon project."

Justin's dick twitched at her mention of a long afternoon project, giving him ideas for what he really wanted to do in his office with her all afternoon, instead of the video reviews she was innocently referencing. *Maybe we can lock my office door, too, and I can eat*

Amy for lunch before we start looking through the rest of the lab footage.

He was just about to suggest as much when the elevator doors opened, and they met the delivery driver bringing their Tex-Mex lunch. *Fuckin' cock blocked by barbacoa.*

~~~

Amy couldn't believe all the stuff they were finding on the security footage of the lab in the last couple months. There were a lot more incidents of people playing games on their phones than the few she'd caught. In addition to the proof that Tara had intentionally bumped into the table to knock over the rack of beakers Amy was in the process of cleaning up, there were also four other times when the woman was caught on tape messing with Amy's experiments.

Though Amy'd been reluctant to tell Justin about her gut instinct that the incident on Friday wasn't an accident, she was glad he'd told her about the security videos to have her help him go through them to prove her intuition correct. They both lost a full day of work on other projects, but they had sufficient evidence against Tara to turn over to the authorities and terminate her employment.

By four o'clock that afternoon, they had enough compiled that Justin called his dad and sister to meet with them to figure out their next steps. Amy wasn't sure she was comfortable being included in the meeting with his family, but Justin insisted.

"You've been the target of everything she's done, so you need to be included in the meetings discussing the repercussions of her actions." Without giving her a chance to object any further, Justin placed the hand not carrying his laptop on the small of her back and ushered her to the conference room where they'd be meeting.

"What's so urgent, Son?" Jon looked back and forth between them when they walked into the room.

"We're having an issue with a lab tech." Justin put down his laptop and pulled out a chair for Amy before he took a seat beside her.

"I guess I'm needed here to start the termination process?" Jen took the seat across the table from Justin and Amy.
~~~

"Yes, but we might also need to get our head of security up here." Justin reached under the table to discreetly take Amy's hand. "And figure out which law enforcement agency to call to have Tara arrested."

"We don't really have a head of security on site." Jen looked shocked at Justin's statement. "Bobby handles training the security guards on-site, and Jake handles the cyber security issues remotely."

"Yeah, I talked to Jake this morning," Justin admitted, before explaining how his cousin had helped by giving him access to the security videos. He then told them about the incident on Friday afternoon and the other issues he found while looking back at the older footage.

"So, she went from watering down the solution you were working on back in January," Jon started listing Tara's infractions, directing his statement to Amy. "To switching chemicals a couple times in February, and escalated to trying to injure you with a bunch of broken beakers on Friday?"

"Yes, sir," Amy answered even though she wasn't completely sure he intended to make the statement sound like a question.

"And you've got all this on video?" Jon redirected his gaze to his son. Justin only nodded. "Okay, first let's call Jake and see what we have to do to be able to export this video to the authorities. He'll probably know who we should call in law enforcement with Bobby being unavailable today."

Justin pulled his cell phone out of his pocket and dialed his cousin, swiping the phone to speaker mode before setting it on the table between them. As Justin was calling Jake, Jon pulled out his cell phone and called someone else, also putting it on speaker and placing it on the table where they could all hear the conversation.

"Hey Cuz, you get everything figured out for me to block someone's access already?" Jake inquired from Justin's phone.

"Avington Security, this is Byron," a deep voice barked from Jon's phone.

"Actually, Jake, let me catch you and our cousin, Byron, up on everything," Jon suggested before relaying everything Justin had just told his dad and sister. Justin helped with filling in the dates of when each act of sabotage had happened and giving Jake Tara's full name and departmental information before Jon continued. "Normally, we'd have called Bobby to handle this with the local LEOs, but I was kind of hoping he'd be there with you, Byron. Thought maybe you having more experience with corporate security could help us beef things up here in ways Bobby and Jake haven't thought of previously, so we don't have any future issues like this."

"Yeah, Bobby already asked me to review all the security protocols he and Jake put in place when we come down there in a couple weeks," Byron chuckled. "But he's not here today. A couple of my boys are actually with him and Brook in Macon for the start of her dad's trial today."

"That's right," Jon sighed, shaking his head. "I knew that was this week, but I didn't know exactly what day it was supposed to start. Regardless, I'd still like your opinion on who we should call to have the woman arrested before we start the termination process here. I'm guessing it'll be the San Antonio Police Department, since the incidents all appear to have happened in our corporate headquarters."

"Actually, Uncle Jon," Jake interrupted his uncle's discussion with their newfound cousin. "While ya'll were discussing Bobby's whereabouts and a corporate security review, I pulled all the videos Justin mentioned and forwarded them to my contacts in Homeland Security. Swapping out chemicals like that could've caused a toxic reaction and could be considered an act of domestic terrorism."

"I don't think it was anything more than swapping one type of glycerol for another." Amy shook her head, even though the men on the phones couldn't see her. "None of them are toxic unless they're ingested in large quantities."

While Amy didn't like Tara and agreed that her actions on Friday could've caused serious injury if one of those shards of glass had nicked an artery in one of the people standing close enough to get cut, she didn't think the woman was a terrorist or actually out to kill anyone. Being jealous of Amy's relationship with Justin wasn't grounds for prosecuting Tara as such either. Amy didn't get the chance to state that, however, as Jake explained his reasoning.

"We can't be sure that's all she did," Jake warned. "In at least one of the videos, she swapped your jar of glycerol with one she pulled outta her coat pocket, not another one on the shelf in the lab. We have no idea what could be in that jar that she altered elsewhere to make it look like the glycerol you've been working with recently."

"Shit! Do you think we need to evacuate the lab until the authorities get here to analyze it?" Justin squeezed Amy's hand under the table.

"If it was the jar I've been working with the last three weeks, they can't analyze it." Amy teared up at the thought of working with contaminated glycerol the last few weeks. "I disposed of it with the rest of the broken glass on Friday."

"Can you analyze the remaining inventory to make sure none of it is compromised?" Byron asked from Jon's phone on the table.

"No, we don't have the equipment to determine the chemical breakdown of a substance in our lab." Justin shook his head as he answered his cousin, even though the other man couldn't see him. "We trust that our suppliers are labeling everything correctly and haven't ever needed to verify it in the past. Most of what we do is come up with new solutions of the various chemical compounds and then test their effectiveness for whatever we're trying to develop a product to do. Like combining the various glycerols Amy's been working with but in different percentages and testing to see what temperature they freeze at or how effective they are at cooling an engine in the heat of the summer."

Jon, Jake, Byron, and Justin started discussing the options for having everything Tara touched in the lab tested to make sure she hadn't contaminated anything in a way that could make it dangerous to work with for everyone else who worked there. Jake told them he was already working through all the footage of the lab to review everything Tara had done for the last few months at least. Byron got in contact with the agents Jake had already sent some of the footage to and coordinated with them and the San Antonio Police Department to arrest Tara.

Since it appeared that she'd only targeted Amy and her experiments, they decided that it was safe to leave everyone else in the lab working on their normal projects until the arrest was made. But Amy couldn't work on any of the projects she'd started until they deemed all her remaining raw materials were safe for use.

That put her working with Justin and Jen to plan how they were going to retrain everyone else in the lab on the various rules and regulations they'd been caught on tape breaking. Not that she could even start working on that until the next day, after Jen had taken care of everything in human resources for terminating Tara.

When they finally adjourned the meeting so everyone else could deal with the legal stuff, Amy followed Justin back to his office. "I guess it's a good thing I left my stuff in your office," she sighed as they approached his door.

Justin held up a finger to indicate she should wait until they were in his office to continue speaking. *I guess he doesn't trust Amanda to overhear anything about that meeting either,* Amy thought as she watched Justin unlock his office door and walked inside when he opened it.

Once inside, Justin relocked the door before taking her hand and pulling her back to his desk. He leaned back against it before asking, "Now what were you saying?"

"I said it's a good thing I left my stuff in your office." Amy sat down in the chair in front of his desk. "So, I don't have to go back to my office and risk anyone in the lab figuring out what all is going on."

"Oh, Sweetheart, I doubt you'd give anything away by popping into your office to pick up your stuff." Justin stroked his hand over her cheek reassuringly.

"Maybe not." Amy shivered from the goosebumps Justin caused whenever he touched her. "But if I run into Tara, I might end up being arrested for assault right alongside her. Maybe show her some of the wrestling moves Randi's been telling me about learning. After watching the GWA shows for the last few months, I think I can figure out at least one or two of them without her having to train me."

"How 'bout we keep Ass-Kickin' Amy as our plan B," Justin chuckled. "And let me spend the rest of the evening with Adorable Amy instead."

"Are you seriously giving me alliterative wrestling names right now?" Amy couldn't stop the little giggle that escaped her at the way Justin could lighten the mood in such a silly way.

"Seemed appropriate." Justin shrugged one shoulder.

Gaw, he's just too cute sometimes, Amy thought, suddenly more focused on her attraction to Justin than all the craziness of the lab.

"What if I'd rather be a little inappropriate?" Amy scooted to the edge of the chair, so her face was only inches away from Justin's crotch. "Did I hear you right this morning when you said there aren't any cameras in here?"

"That you did." Justin smiled as he ran his thumb back and forth over her cheek again. "Why do you think I locked the door when we walked in here just now?"

"Because you're a wonderful boyfriend, who wants to let me live out some of my fantasies," Amy stated, reaching for Justin's belt and unfastening it.

"Not just your fantasies, Sweetheart," Justin replied, his hand weaving through her hair as she released the button and lowered the zipper of his slacks. "But we need to remove some of your clothes, too, not just mine."

"We'll get there." Amy pushed his pants and boxer briefs down to free his cock.

He was already hard, his dick reaching up almost to his navel. She reached out with both hands to pull the tip down to her lips, licking up the bead of precum already leaking out of him before taking him into her mouth as far as she could.

"Fuck, Sweetheart," Justin whisper-shouted while looking down into her eyes. "I love the feel of your mouth on me."

I love the taste of your cock, Amy thought, her mouth too full to actually say the words. She swirled her tongue along the underside as she bobbed up and down the half of his dick she could actually take into her mouth. She stroked the base with one hand while cupping his balls with the other.

She'd only gotten the chance to suck him briefly on Friday night before he pulled back to put on a condom, wanting to be inside her so they could come together. Considering he ate her pussy before every other time they fucked, and she came in his mouth every single time, she felt it unfair that she hadn't tasted his release yet.

Amy planned to do everything in her power to change that before removing a single piece of her clothing in his office. Not that she had all that much experience in giving blow jobs, but she hoped the tips she'd picked up at her sister's It's My Pleasure parties over the last couple years would be effective for making Justin come undone.

First, she tried swirling her tongue around, trying to find that super-sensitive spot where the shaft met the head. Justin moaned lightly, but he didn't seem to react as intensely as he had when she'd taken him as far back in her throat as she could and sucked hard. So, she went back to what he seemed to enjoy the most while gently squeezing with her hands to stimulate him everywhere.

"Fuck, Amy, Sweetheart," Justin growled in response.

Amy felt clumsy as she bobbed up and down on his shaft to alternate between the tongue swirl and deep throating, but Justin's continued moans and guttural words of praise for her actions made her feel like she was doing a better job than she thought.

"Fuck, Amy, you hafta stop, Sweetheart," Justin whisper-shouted, trying to pull back.

Amy released her hold on his shaft and balls with her hands to reach around and grip his ass, pulling him deeper into her throat than she ever realized she could handle.

"Fuck, I'm gonna…" Justin's whispered words trailed off as she felt his cock seem to thicken on her tongue. His hands tightened in her hair, not that he was using it to control her movements, more like he was trying to ground himself during the most intense part of his orgasm.

Yes, Justin! Come! Amy dug her nails into his tight, muscular ass, holding him so deep she didn't even taste it as he spurted the first few streams of cum down her throat. She had to back off when she started choking, but only far enough that she could control the flow as she swallowed the salty spurts he continued to release on her tongue. *Yum!*

She sucked him dry and licked him clean before releasing his semi-flaccid dick from her mouth. Justin released his grip on her hair to reach back and hold onto the desk he was half sitting on.

"Fuck, Amy, Sweetheart, that was amazing." He grinned down at her as she leaned back in the chair she'd barely stayed seated on the edge of during the blow job. "But you're gonna hafta give me a minute to get the feeling back in my legs, so we can fulfill a few more fantasies."

Before Amy could come up with a witty reply, the intercom on Justin's desk buzzed.

"Fuck," Justin groaned as he turned to look at the offending device before punching a button a little too forcefully. "Yes?"

"Mr. Burleson, I just wanted to check to see if you needed anything before I leave for the day," Amanda practically purred in her saccharine sweet, flirty voice.

Justin shook his head as he stabbed the button with his finger once more before speaking. "Only to not be disturbed as I requested earlier, Ms. Lewis."

"Oh, well, goodnight then," Amanda replied.

"I guess it's quitting time." Amy stood from her seat and pretended to gather her things to go home.

"Just because everyone else is leaving the building," Justin growled, reaching out to take her hand and pulling her into his arms. "Doesn't mean we hafta leave right now."

He dipped his head, covering her mouth with his. His arms around her tightened, allowing him to grind his growing erection into her abdomen as he deepened the kiss. Unable to resist a kiss from Justin, Amy wrapped her arms around his neck and returned his passion with fervor.

Good to know he's not turned off by tasting himself on my tongue, Amy thought as they made out like teenagers in his office. Words were no longer necessary or possible as they continued kissing. Clothing disappeared as if by magic, and soon, Amy found herself sitting on Justin's desk with her legs spread for him to lick and suck every crevice and fold of her pussy.

"Oh, Justin, you have the most talented tongue." Amy was breathless, feeling her climax building in her core. She gripped his hair, much like he'd gripped hers earlier. Again, it wasn't meant to be a way of controlling the action, but as a way to ground her, to feel connected to him as she floated through the waves of ecstasy he was causing deep inside her. "Fuck, yes, Justin!"

She continued to repeatedly chant his name as her orgasm washed through her, not thinking about being quiet in case there were still people on the executive floor who might hear them. Justin brought her back to earth gently before kissing his way up her torso. He paid special attention to her breasts before finally making his way to her mouth.

The kiss tasted like a mixture of the two of them, his salty and her tangy-sweet. *Wow, we actually taste really good together. Like the world's best salty-sweet snack.*

Amy ran her hands over the muscular planes of Justin's back and wondered why he wasn't touching her with anything but his mouth. Then she heard the unmistakable sound of a condom wrapper being torn open and knew it would only be a matter of seconds before he was touching her everywhere again.

She felt movement near her thighs and knew it was him sheathing himself. *How can he do that without even looking?*

Before Amy could even finish thinking the question, his hands were on her hips, and he was pushing the head of his cock inside her. As always, he was gentle, allowing her to stretch open for his sizable invasion without risking hurting her.

Amy moaned at the fullness, waiting for him to settle in all the way to the hilt before trailing kisses across his jaw to be able to whisper in his ear. "The fantasy is a dirty office fuck, Boss. As much as I love the slow and sensual with you, now's not the time for that."

"I'm trying to keep things quiet, Sweetheart," Justin whispered in her ear. "While I might be able to convince my family that you were screaming my name earlier because you were arguing with me about the protective measures I wanna put in place for you until Tara's arrested, I can't think of a cover story for the sound of me pounding you into my desk."

Amy pulled back to look Justin in the eyes, her own wide with worry as she realized how loud she'd been a few minutes earlier. "Was I really that loud?"

"Well, I don't think they heard you in the lab," Justin chuckled. "But if there was anyone in the outer office, they probably heard you."

Amy was mortified at the possibility of one of Justin's family members having come to talk to him and overhearing her cries of ecstasy from his oral attention.

"Don't worry, Sweetheart." Justin gave her a peck of a kiss. "With Amanda leaving earlier, I highly doubt anyone was out there to overhear us. In fact, I'm pretty sure we're the only people here this late."

Amy scanned the room to see the clock on the wall saying it was almost seven o'clock. *Surely, he's right, and there's nobody here to overhear us.* Thinking they were all alone in the building gave Amy the courage to think it was okay for them to make a little more noise.

"Well, if there's nobody else here," Amy cooed, rocking her hips to grind on Justin's cock that was still buried inside her. "Then there's no reason you can't pound me into the desk for that dirty office fuck we've been fantasizing about, Boss."

"Fuck, you're right, Sweetheart." Justin grinned wickedly as he pulled halfway out before slamming back inside her. "And I think you need to take a good hard pounding on your boss's desk for being a naughty girl at work."

"How've I been naughty, Boss?" Amy batted her lashes at him, trying to get into the role play as his sexretary.

"You didn't stop sucking my cock when I told you to," Justin reprimanded, his thrusts speeding up and intensifying. "And you know the rules, Ms. Lawton. I always make you come at least twice before I come. So, now I hafta make you come at least three more times before I can come in your tight, wet cunt."

"And what're you gonna do if I don't come as much as you want me to before you do?" Amy had to stifle her giggles, thinking three more orgasms didn't sound like a punishment at all. *Guess I gotta give him some better punishment ideas.* "Spank me? Leave my ass so sore I'll remember my punishment every time I sit down tomorrow?"

"If you don't start coming right now and keep talking like that, you'll find out," Justin replied, pounding into her harder. He pulled her legs up around his waist and squeezed her torso tighter against his, adjusting the angle, so he could grind his pubic bone on her clit with each thrust.

The new position felt amazing, causing her inner walls to flutter with the beginning of her second release of the evening.

"Still being naughty I see." Justin lifted her off the desk and lightly slapped her ass with one hand while bouncing her on his cock with his other hand guiding her up and down in time with his hip thrusts. "Guess I'm gonna hafta spank you while I fuck you to get you to come when I tell you to."

"Oh, yes, Justin," Amy cried out, the light smacking on her ass being all pleasure and no pain. It was just enough to take her over the edge.

"Fuck, yes, Amy," Justin growled, his voice deep and gravelly. "Show me what a good girl you are by coming on my cock when I tell you to."

He fucked her through the orgasm, massaging the globes of her ass, as if trying to alleviate the sting of a hard spanking, even though it was nonexistent.

As Amy came down from her high, Justin gripped her hips and lifted her off his dick. "Let go with your legs, Sweetheart," Justin whispered, setting her down on her feet when she did as he requested. "Turn around and put your hands on the desk, so I can see your ass while I give you the rest of your spanking."

"Yes, Boss." Amy grinned at him and released her arms from around his neck to get into position.

"Fuck, Sweetheart, you have the perfect ass." Justin kneaded her cheeks with his big hands.

Amy had always thought her ass was a bit too big, but if Justin liked it, she wouldn't complain about the size again.

"I wanna stick my dick in this perfect ass," Justin growled, one of his fingers trailing between her cheeks and circling her backside opening.

"I've never…" Amy trailed off, feeling herself blush at the forbidden images in her head.

"Me, either." Justin rubbed her reverently for a moment before smacking her ass and slamming his cock into her pussy. "But that's a fantasy for another day. Right now, I'm gonna fuck your hot little cunt 'til you come on command for your boss."

"Yes, Boss!" Amy could already feel her next orgasm building. She pushed against his desk to give her leverage to ram back against him every time he bottomed out inside her.

They settled into a hard, fast rhythm with Justin slapping her ass every time he pulled almost all the way out.

"Oh, please, Justin," Amy begged, not sure what she was even begging for, but she still felt the need to beg.

"Yes, Amy, come now!" Amy exploded on Justin's command. "Fuck, I love the way you squeeze my cock when you come. Like you're trying to push me out, but I'm not gonna let you keep me outta your perfect pussy."

"Yes, Justin, yes!" Amy wasn't sure if her cries of pleasure were coherent as fireworks went off behind her closed eyes from the intensity of her orgasm.

"You're mine, Amy! Every part of you is mine."

"Yes, Justin. And you're mine."

"All yours, Sweetheart. All, fucking, yours."

As Amy started to come down, Justin reached around to play with her clit with one hand and her nipples with the other. He never slowed the rhythm of his dick ravaging her pussy, continuing to impale her with abandon. The ongoing onslaught on her G-spot combined with the clit and nipple play brought her right back to the precipice.

Amy could only grunt and groan, no longer able to form words as Justin fucked her into oblivion.

"Fuck. Yes. Amy. Come. With. Me." Justin punctuated each word with a powerful thrust, holding still as far as he could get inside her with the last one.

Amy felt him swell inside her, knowing he was coming at the same time she felt like she was shattering from the inside out. The orgasm was so intense, she collapsed down onto his desk. She wasn't sure how long she floated in another realm, oblivious to everything around her.

It must have been a while. When she finally felt like she was waking up after passing out, Justin had disposed of the condom and was cradling her on his lap in his desk chair that had somehow been rolled into his private bathroom. Apparently, he'd taken her in there, so he could clean them both up, and he'd stayed in there to wet a second washcloth with cool water to revive her.

"You okay, Sweetheart?" Justin looked at her with concern.

"Wonderful," Amy replied, still too high on endorphins to understand why he looked worried.

"You sure?" His concerned expression was finally starting to break through Amy's orgasm haze. "You went completely limp and would've hit the floor if I hadn't had a hold of you. And it took a few minutes for you to come to after passing out."

"I didn't pass out." Amy cupped his jaw with her hands to lean up and kiss his perfect lips. "You fucked me so good, I had an out-of-body experience."

"An out-of-body experience, huh?" Justin chuckled and returned her butterfly kisses.

"Yes, I've been floating around in heaven for the last few minutes." Amy nodded, rubbing their noses together. "After the best orgasm of my life."

"As much as I love knowing that it was the best of your life, I don't think I like giving you orgasms that are so intense you pass out from them." Justin hugged her tight, like he was afraid if he let her go she'd pass out again. "Have you ever passed out like that before?"

Or maybe he's nervous about asking that question.

"No," Amy quickly replied, hoping to relieve his worry, or at least reassure him that he was the only person to ever make her come that hard.

"Then maybe we should take it easier?" Justin released his hold on her enough to pull back and look into her eyes. "At least until you can get in with your doctor to make sure there's no reason to be concerned."

"I, um, actually have to find a doctor down here still," Amy admitted, knowing it was on her to-do list since her birth control shot was due the next week.

"Well, then, we'll call Doc Hayes tomorrow and see when he or his nurse practitioner can fit you in." Justin smiled as he used his feet to walk his desk chair back into his office. "Now let's get dressed and go get some dinner before deciding where we're staying tonight."

Amy was so focused on figuring out how she felt about Justin making the decision about what doctor she'd go see that she almost missed his last statement. On the one hand, she liked the way she felt taken care of by the way he worried about her and put together a plan to make sure she didn't have an underlying medical condition that caused her to faint. On the other hand, she thought it was a bit high-handed and controlling to tell her what doctor to go to without giving her options to vet for herself.

"Wait." Amy stood from his lap to start getting dressed. "I'm good with getting dressed and going to dinner. But whaddaya mean about deciding where we're staying? I'm going home to my house and you're going home to yours."

"No, not now that I'm worried about you being Tara's target." Justin shook his head as he picked up his boxer briefs and slipped them on. "Remember I mentioned protective measures earlier?"

"Yeah, but what's that got to do with staying anywhere but our own homes?" Amy quickly slipped on her own underwear, not wanting to argue with Justin while standing there naked.

"Amy, Sweetheart," Justin cajoled, taking her hand, and preventing her from putting on her pants. "Until Tara's been arrested, I'm not comfortable with you going anywhere alone, even your own house, where she might go try to attack you again."

"She's not gonna drive all the way to Heart's Destiny to attack me at my house," Amy protested, pulling her hand from his to get dressed, so she didn't feel so vulnerable while they had this conversation.

"You sure about that?" Justin tilted his head quizzically while reaching for his own pants. "Because if you'd have asked me last Friday morning if she would sabotage your experiments or knock over a rack of beakers hoping you'd get cut by the broken glass, I wouldn't've thought it was possible either. Now I'm not sure what she's liable to do. Even though we've kept all talk of the security cameras up on this floor where she couldn't overhear us, knowing you've spent the whole day in meetings with me and my family might be enough to trigger her to go after you outside the lab."

Shit! I didn't think about that. Since jealousy over Justin is what I think is her whole motivation for targeting me, just me spending the whole day holed up in his office with him is probably a major trigger for her.

"Okay, I can see your point." Amy put on her blouse. "But I have to at least go home to pack a bag before going to a hotel or whatever."

"We can both pack a bag to go to a hotel if that's what you want." Justin put on his shirt. "But I think I'd rather have you stay with me on the ranch for the extra layer of security."

"Justin!" Amy shook her head in exasperation as she slipped on her shoes. "I can't stay with you on the ranch or your whole family will know about us."

"Not if we tell them what's going on with Tara," Justin argued as he, too, finished dressing. "We can put your stuff in my spare bedroom and leave the bed unmade every morning, so Mrs. Mary will report to my mom that we're sleeping in separate beds. They'll all think I'm just being a good friend and boss."

"I don't know." Amy double-checked that all her clothing was in place and gathered her things to leave the building.

"Trust me." Justin held out his hand for her to take. "It's our best option. And it'll only be for a few days until Tara's arrested."

"I do trust you." Amy took Justin's hand to head out to their separate cars. *I'm just not ready to commit to more than dating and sex when we can sneak it in.*

"Then come play house with me for a few days while we're waiting on the authorities to arrest her, so you're safe." Justin bent down and kissed her temple while they waited on the elevator. "Let's enjoy a few nights sharing a bed. And when it's safe, we'll go back to sleeping in our separate houses until you're ready to let the world know we're together. At which point, I'll probably move into your house since it's so much bigger than mine."

Justin winked, letting her know his last sentence was meant to be a joke. *At least I hope he meant it in a joking manner.*

~ ~ ~

Justin couldn't believe how hard it was to convince Amy to come back to his house on the ranch for the next couple days. She'd argued all through dinner that it wasn't necessary, claiming she was perfectly safe at home alone. It took Justin calling his Dad while they were at dinner to request a security detail for her to convince her to hang out on the ranch until Tara was arrested.

Thank fuck, she finally agreed to stay on the ranch and go to the lab in the new methanol production facility with me for the next few days, Justin thought as he followed her from her house in town to his house on the ranch. *And that call to Dad took care of notifying the family about why she's staying with me, so none of them should ask any questions when they see her car at the house all night. Though I still don't understand why she couldn't leave her car at her house and ride with me to and from work all week.*

If she hadn't agreed to stay with him, he'd planned to stay with her. The threat of armed guards shadowing her twenty-four-seven was a bluff, just his last attempt to get her to agree to let him keep her safe.

And that really is the whole reason I want her here on the ranch in my house. Sharing my bed with her for a few nights is just a bonus.

When they got to the gate to enter the ranch, Amy pulled over to the side and let Justin go ahead of her to put in the gate code. Though he wasn't sure why since he'd given her a code for the gate a couple months before when she was coming over for Charlotte's birthday party. And she'd used the code again in February to come to the ranch when they gathered to go over their DNA results.

She then followed him through the gate and around the pasture and other houses to his driveway. He pushed the button on his garage-door opener to pull into his normal parking space and wished for the first time that the other half of his garage wasn't the home to his four-wheeler and dirt bike, so Amy could park her car in the garage with his truck.

Thank fuck, we have extra space in the old barn, he thought as he got out of his truck. He left everything in his vehicle and walked back to Amy's car, where she'd already parked and was getting out.

"Give me a few minutes to move these over to the barn and you can park in the garage." Justin motioned toward the four-wheeler and dirt bike to let her know what he was moving and where to park her car when he was done.

"You don't have to do that," Amy protested. "I'm just gonna be here for a day or two. My car will be fine in the driveway, just like it is all the time at home."

"Sorry, Sweetheart, my house, my rules." Justin smirked at the adorable face Amy made at his statement. Not giving her a chance to argue anymore, he turned and walked through the garage to the door going into the laundry/mud room. He grabbed both the keys he needed from the hook by the door and went back to move the toys he'd not grown out of since childhood.

Amy continued to argue that it wasn't necessary to free up space in his garage for her car as he took care of moving things around. *Necessary or not, it still feels like the right thing to do. I just wish it was a more permanent arrangement.*

Justin didn't fight back when Amy continued to push. Her argument changed to more of a rant about all the stuff they'd uncovered in the videos of the lab and how annoyed she was with the "rude ass bitches" at work. *I think she might be talking about more than just Tara. But I don't think now's the time to ask for clarification about who all she's pissed off with at work.*

Justin just smiled and let Amy rant, knowing she needed to vent after the stressful events of the day. Once he had the space cleared out, he finally spoke, extending his hand to her. "Give me your keys and I'll get your car parked and suitcase carried into the guest room."

"I don't need you to park my car or carry in my stuff," Amy huffed, slamming her hands on her hips and not handing him her car keys. "I'm a grown woman. I'm more than capable of doing those things myself."

"I know that, Sweetheart." Justin smiled at her adorable show of independence. "I never said you couldn't do it all yourself. But since you don't seem to be making any moves in that direction, I figured I'd take care of everything for you, so you can continue ranting to get out all the stress of the day. You need to vent all that, so it doesn't keep you up all night."

If anything is gonna keep you up all night, it'll be me worshiping your body the way you deserve.

Amy opened her mouth as if to speak, but she didn't say a word. After several times of opening and closing like a fish out of water, which Justin thought was cute as hell, Amy finally barked, "Why aren't you arguing with me?"

"Because other than it not being necessary to park your car in the garage, I've agreed with everything else you were saying." Justin shrugged, slightly grinning at her. "And I know it's not necessary to park your car in the garage. I just wanna do that 'cause I like the idea of sharing my space with you, so I'm taking advantage of the opportunity to see your car in my garage for a few days."

"You're not mad at me for losing my temper and throwing a fit like a child?" Amy looked nervous as she posed the question. The way she was chewing her bottom lip was a dead giveaway of her anxiety.

"No, Sweetheart." Justin threw an arm around her shoulders to pull her to his side for a friendly-looking one-armed hug, in case his family was outside and saw him. If they'd have been at her house, he'd have pulled her in and hugged her properly, probably laid a kiss or two on her lips, too. Since he was cognizant of a potential audience, he leaned down to whisper in her ear, so there wasn't a chance of his family hearing what he was about to tell her. "I think your fiery temper is sexy as hell. So, rant and rave all you want around me. It just makes my dick harder."

"Justin!" Amy slapped his abs as she shouted his name, but she obviously wasn't too upset by his statement, since she was grinning from ear to ear.

"What?" Justin raised his hands in surrender, chuckling and fighting the urge to tickle her to make her laugh along with him. "I told you, I'll always be a hundred percent honest with you. I'm just tellin' it like it is."

Amy's eyes darted down to the bulge in his pants and widened when she saw how aroused he obviously was, which was probably more than he should be while standing outside, where any of his family could walk up and see.

"I guess we should probably go inside, so you can take care of that problem you seem to have, Boss." Amy smirked as she sauntered past him to get in her car and pull it into the garage.

Justin grabbed his laptop bag and coffee go-cup from his truck before walking around to take anything Amy was willing to let him carry for her into the house. Not that Ms. Independent would let him carry a damn thing. He still did his gentlemanly duty of holding the door open for her as they entered the house.

He paused in the mud room to push the button to close the garage door, grabbed his spare garage-door opener, and clipped it on one of Amy's bags as they walked through to the kitchen. He dropped his coffee cup in the sink before walking on through the house.

"What's that?" Amy pointed at the device with her head.

"Garage-door opener," Justin replied as he led the way through the dining room and living room to get to the hallway that led to the bedrooms and bathrooms. "So, if you end up having to drive your car later this week, you'll have a way to get back in the house when you get home."

Fuck! I probably shouldn't've referred to my house as her home. Justin was glad he was walking in front of her, so she couldn't see the grimace that crossed his face when he realized he'd used the word he wanted his place to be for her.

"Oh, so is that like the equivalent of giving me your spare key, since nobody on the ranch actually locks their doors?" Amy quipped, her voice sounding lighter and making Justin relax about his faux pas. "You realize that I could just walk in the front door, right?"

Leah Mae Wright

"Yeah, but this way you can park in the garage anytime you come over, too." He stopped in the middle of the hallway between the doors going to his office and guest bathroom, pointing them out to Amy before continuing to the end of the hall where the doors to the two bedrooms were on opposite sides of the hallway. "This is the guest bedroom, where we'll keep your stuff, so Mrs. Mary will think we're sleeping separately."

"You gonna help me mess up the bed to fool her before you carry me off to your lair for the night?"

"I like the way you think, Sweetheart." Justin winked as he walked past her into the room, putting his laptop case down on the dresser before removing hers from her shoulder to place it beside his.

Amy dropped the suitcase on the floor beside the dresser as Justin pulled her into his arms. "Finally," he groaned as he pressed his lips to hers. He deepened the kiss and savored the taste of the woman he loved.

"Whaddaya mean by *finally*?" Amy arched an eyebrow at him when they took a break to breathe.

"Finally, I get to kiss you again, Sweetheart." Justin trailed butterfly kisses down the column of her neck. "It's been almost two hours since I've had a taste of you, and that's entirely too long to go without my lips on yours."

"You'd better figure out how to go longer than two hours, Boss," Amy giggled. "Or you're gonna out us to everyone at work."

"I might can stretch it out a little longer if we start taking a private lunchtime in my office all the time, so I can get a taste of my favorite dessert in the middle of the day." Justin continued kissing her neck as he backed her up to the bed. He reached down to pull back the bedding before spinning them around, so he could flop down on the bed, pulling Amy down on top of him.

"I think that can be arranged, Boss, but maybe not every day." Amy pushed up slightly, so they could look into each other's eyes.

Seeing how tired she looked brought back his earlier concern after she'd passed out during their mutual orgasm. He didn't want to kill the moment by bringing it up again, but he made another mental note to call Doc Hayes's office first thing the next morning to see when she could be seen. As bad as he wanted her right at that moment, he knew he could only make love to her if he maintained control, keeping the actual act soft and sensual, instead of hard and intense like it'd been earlier in the office.

"You think this is enough to make the bed look slept in?" Justin was already moving to sit up in the bed.

"Yeah, I think so," Amy replied, looking at the bed around them.

"Then grab whatever you need to get ready for bed." Justin lifted her up off his lap, standing her beside the bed, so he could stand up. "Especially whatever toys you brought with you." He wagged his eyebrows suggestively as he picked up his laptop bag to take it to his room. "And meet me across the hall in my bedroom."

"You wanna play with my toys, huh?" Amy grabbed her suitcase from the floor and placed it on the bed to rummage through it.

"Most definitely." Justin walked across the hall to his bedroom, put his laptop bag down on the table by the window, and took care of business in the ensuite bathroom while Amy gathered her things. After stripping down to his boxer briefs and brushing his teeth, Justin walked back into his bedroom to find Amy standing at the foot of his bed, holding her stuff and looking confused.

"I'll take this." He plucked the purple toy atop her bundle of clothing and toiletries from her hands. He brushed his lips over her forehead before stepping over to the side of the bed closest to the door. "Do whatever you need to do in the bathroom before bed. But you can leave your PJ's off until after we're done playing with your big girl toys."

"Yes, Boss." Amy saluted him playfully before sauntering into the ensuite.

While Amy was taking care of her nightly routine, Justin pulled back the bedding, sat down on the bed, and pushed buttons on the toy to figure out how to turn it on.

"I probably should've done all that in the other bathroom," Amy mused aloud as she walked out of the ensuite wearing only her bra, panties, and a scarf around her hair.

"You're welcome to use whatever bathroom you want, Sweetheart." Justin ate her up with his eyes.

She dropped what he assumed were her pajamas on the table with his laptop bag before bouncing out of the room to presumably put her things in the guest bedroom and bathroom. She soon returned, no longer wearing the lingerie he'd just fantasized about taking off her with his teeth.

"Fuck, I don't think I'll ever get used to seeing how gorgeous you are." Justin watched as Amy walked to the bed and crawled in beside him, naked except for the scarf around her head.

"You're still wearing too many clothes, Boss." Amy reached for his boxer briefs.

"No, those hafta stay on while I tease you with your toy first, Sweetheart." Justin stilled her hand at his waistband, flipping her over his body to land on her back in the middle of his king-sized bed.

"Oh," Amy squealed, looking up at him in surprise.

"Did I hurt you?" *Fuck, what was I thinking? I hafta be gentle until we know it's safe for her to get a little rougher.*

"No, just surprised me," Amy giggled.

"Good," Justin grinned back at her, moving into a plank position over her. "Now lay still and let me worship you the way you deserve."

Justin covered her mouth with his, not giving her a chance to argue about how he planned to make love to her. The kiss was more reverential than their normal hot and heavy. He shifted his weight to his left elbow, so he could reach for the toy with his right hand, finally pushing the right combination of buttons to turn on both the vibration and suction ends of the almost U-shaped device.

As he continued to make love to her mouth, he teased her titties with the toy. He alternated between rubbing the vibrating end all around her mounds and placing the little suction cup over her taut, taupe nipples.

"Oh, Justin," Amy moaned into his mouth.

"You like that, Sweetheart?" Justin pulled back from their kiss, crawling down her body, so he could get a better view of her reaction to what he was doing.

"Yes," Amy panted breathily.

Justin moved the suction cup from her right nipple to her left, replacing it with his mouth on her right.

"Oh, yes, Justin," Amy moaned as he suckled her, going back and forth so her breasts got equal treatment with his mouth and the toy. "That feels so good, but your mouth feels so much better than the toy."

"You like my mouth better, huh, Sweetheart?" He whispered the words against her skin as he kissed his way down her torso. "I wonder if you'll like my mouth better on your pussy, too, or if you'll prefer the combination of my mouth and the toy."

"I don't know," Amy practically purred. "You'll have to experiment with both separately and together to see what works best."

"Mmm," Justin moaned in agreement, unable to speak as his mouth was occupied licking through her russet-brown folds. He covered her clit with the small suction cup on the toy while he fucked her with his tongue until she cried out his name as she came.

He pulled the toy away as he licked up her juices, knowing her clit was too sensitive for the suction as she came down from her first climax.

"You still with me?" Justin pulled back to watch her face, so he could read her expression, needing to know he hadn't done anything to make her pass out again.

"Yes, Justin," Amy sighed, smiling down at him.

"I need you to tell me if you start to feel like you're gonna pass out again, so I can stop, okay?" It would be torture to stop in the middle of pleasuring her, but he would do it to make sure he didn't risk her health.

"I will, but I'm not gonna pass out again." Amy ran her fingers through his hair, guiding his face back toward the apex of her thighs.

Not wanting to argue when his woman showed him what she needed, Justin flicked his tongue over her clit while turning the toy in his hand to insert the vibrating end in her opening. He moved the toy in and out, mimicking what he hoped to do with his dick soon, while alternating between stroking her clit with his tongue and sucking it into his mouth. It took even less time than before for her to fly over the edge, screaming his name repeatedly as she came the second time. Again, he lessened the suction, lifting his mouth from her cunt to let his breath waft over her clit as he asked once again if she was still with him.

"Yes, Justin," Amy groaned as she shook her head in the negative, contrary to what she was saying. "But I can't take any more of the toy. I need you. Please. Justin."

"You have me, Sweetheart." Justin removed the toy from her pussy and turned it off. He quickly rolled off the bed to lose his boxer briefs and grab a condom from the top drawer of his nightstand. He sheathed himself as he crawled back on the bed between her legs. He lined his cock up with her cunt and slowly sank inside her. "You have absolutely all of me."

Amy wrapped her arms and legs around him, pulling him down close, so they could kiss as they made love. Justin again held his weight off her, resting on one arm beside her head, so he could use the other hand to caress her beautiful body.

He was more gentle than he'd ever been before, reverentially making love to her long into the night. Between kisses, they whispered sweet nothings, mostly about how good it felt, how beautiful he thought she was, and how connected they felt to one another. But Justin bit back the three little words he wanted most to say to Amy — *I love you!*

"Oh, Justin," Amy cried out as her inner walls clamped down on him like a vise.

"Yes, Amy, Sweetheart. Come with me," he replied, holding still as deep inside her as he could go to release his seed into the latex.

As spurt after spurt of sticky cum left his cock, Justin wished it was without the barrier between them. *Fuck! I can't wait to see her, sexy as fuck, her belly round with my baby inside her.*

He gave her one more kiss, making sure her obsidian eyes were open again before rolling off her to go dispose of the condom. He grabbed a washcloth and wet it to clean her honey off her thighs, so she wasn't sticky going to sleep. Once she was cleaned up, he wiped himself up where she'd gushed over more than just the area covered by the condom.

He grabbed his discarded boxer briefs from the floor to take them to the hamper in the bathroom. Then he rinsed out the washcloth and hung it in the shower to dry before heading back to join Amy in his bed.

She'd gotten up and slipped on an oversized t-shirt to sleep in, but Justin opted not to bother with a clean pair of underwear, knowing he'd just strip them off for the shower in the morning.

He crawled in the bed, naked as the day he was born, and pulled Amy into his arms. They cuddled in the middle of the bed before falling into one of the best nights of sleep Justin had ever had.

Chapter Ten

Amy was really enjoying staying with Justin the last couple days, though she wouldn't admit it to him anytime soon. The previous Friday had been the first time she'd stayed overnight with a man, and merging their routines wasn't nearly as awkward as she'd expected. After Monday and Tuesday nights sharing not only Justin's bed, but also his whole house, Amy was starting to feel like she was finally home in a way that even her own house didn't feel like a home.

After her initial argument that he didn't need to clear out half his garage for her to park her car, she'd given in to not only that, but also to everything else he'd planned for making it look like she was using his spare bedroom while actually sharing his bed. Part of her felt guilty for not being the strong, independent woman her mother raised, but it was only a teeny tiny part. Most of her loved just how domestic it felt to live with Justin, spending the evenings watching television after eating and doing the dishes together, like an old married couple.

And the nightly orgasms in his arms are amazing!

She also enjoyed learning more about the quality control lab Justin was setting up in the new methanol production facility. After he finished his initial small-scale experiments with methanol production from cow manure, he oversaw setting up the large-scale production facility. Now he was teaching Amy the processes for spot-checking the methanol produced to maintain the quality they wanted before actually putting the final product on the market for race fuel and using it as an additive in the gasoline produced in the refinery on the western border of the Burlesons' land.

"So, once you're satisfied that the end product is of consistent quality, then what happens to actually market it?" Amy wondered aloud as they finished up another round of testing.

"Our marketing team is already working on branding ideas," Justin replied, smiling at her in a way that made her panties wet. "Once we pick out a brand name, then we'll get our sales team to start contacting the various racing organizations to pitch the more eco-friendly, cost-effective product over what they're currently using. Depending on how receptive the race teams are, we may also start sponsoring a team to get the product name out there."

"What's your favorite of the product name ideas?" Amy's creative juices were flowing as she thought of what she'd use as a brand name.

"Hadn't really thought about it," Justin shrugged. "That's not really my part of the process. I leave that up to the people with more creative minds than mine. Though I wouldn't mind going with the sales team to a few dirt track races to promote the product. Or maybe a monster truck show."

"That's the one where they jack up the trucks super high and make the bodies look like anything but a normal truck, right?" Justin nodded in the affirmative to Amy's question. "Then I have the perfect idea! You should name your manure-based methanol *Moothanol*, and sponsor a monster truck made to look like one of the cows on the ranch."

"Moothanol, huh?" Justin chuckled at Amy's over-excitement for her goofy idea. Amy just shrugged and laughed with him. "I'll be sure to pass your suggestions along to the marketing department."

Before Amy could come up with any more ideas to give him for branding, Justin's phone rang. When he pulled it out of his pocket and looked at the screen, his jovial smile disappeared.

"Justin Burleson." His greeting was clipped when he answered the call. "I'm actually at our facility in Heart's Destiny at the moment. I can be there in an hour as the head of the department, but my lab manager isn't available this afternoon."

Justin paused to let the other person speak, and Amy wished he would've put it on speaker since she was the lab manager he was talking about.

"No, she's outta the office on an unrelated matter this afternoon, but she should be back in the lab tomorrow morning to make any statements you might need from her."

This has to have something to do with Tara, Amy thought as Justin listened to what was being said on the other end of the phone call. *Surely, I don't have to be there for them to be able to arrest her. Do I? Maybe I should reschedule my doctor's appointment this afternoon?*

"Yes, nine a.m. tomorrow morning will be fine," Justin agreed to whatever they were saying before disconnecting his call.

"Nine in the morning will be fine for what?" Amy hated the sharp tone of her voice, but she also didn't like feeling like Justin was making decisions for her without consulting her first.

"A meeting to give your statement to the officers arresting Tara this afternoon." Justin slipped his phone back into his pocket. "I can take you back to the house and get Mom to go with you to the doctor this afternoon, but I hafta head to the office to actually fire her before they arrest her."

"Justin," Amy huffed. "I'm a grown woman. I don't need anyone to go to the doctor with me. Especially not your mother when I'm gonna be asking the doctor about passing out after sex. You asking her to go with me would make it pretty obvious we're more than friends, don'tcha think?"

"Yeah, I know." Justin ran a hand through his hair in frustration. "I just hate leaving you alone until I see her in cuffs."

"But they're gonna arrest her with you there this afternoon, right?" Amy assumed that was why he had to go to the office.

"Yeah, but…"

"No buts," Amy cut off his statement. "You're going up there so they can arrest her, and I'm going to my doctor's appointment by myself, just like I've gone to every doctor's appointment I've had for the last eight years. Now let's go, so you have time to drop me off," *at home,* "to get my car."

Amy barely caught herself to keep from using the words aloud to indicate how she felt like his house was her home. *Everything's going way too fast between us already, I don't need to give him another reason to push for more than secret dates and hot office hookups. My brain's in charge of how fast we progress in our relationship. Not my heart, and certainly not my pussy. So, he's gonna hafta wait a few more months for me to mentally comprehend what we are to each other before I'll be ready to take the next step with him. And even then it won't be moving in.*

"Okay." Justin shook his head like he was stopping himself from arguing the point any longer.

Amy wondered if his silence was because her facial expressions gave away her thoughts as they quickly cleaned up the QC lab before leaving.

"Call me as soon as you get done with Doc Hayes," Justin instructed as they drove between cow pastures on the western part of the ranch to go back to his house. "I'm gonna be worried the whole time we're apart until I know what he says about that passing out spell you had on Monday."

"I'm sure it was just the adrenaline overload from everything that happened." Amy tried to placate his concern. "I haven't passed out since, so I'm sure it's nothing to worry about."

"Yeah, but we've also kept things a little calmer since then." Justin squeezed her hand where he was holding it on the console between them in his truck. "Be sure to ask if it's safe to keep things gentler, or if we need to refrain from all sexual activity until he figures out what happened on Monday."

"Yes, Boss." Amy barely contained her eye roll at how weird he was being about her asking a doctor she was about to meet for the first time sexually explicit questions. *I'm gonna be embarrassed enough telling him about passing out on Monday. Why not make it worse by asking what my sexual limits are to keep from passing out again?*

"And I'll text you about the stuff going on at the office." Justin's words kept her from freaking out about going to the doctor for such a strange reason. "That way I won't interrupt your appointment by calling."

"Sounds good." Amy leaned over to give him a quick peck on the cheek before turning to get out of his truck since they'd just pulled into his driveway.

"See ya tonight, Sweetheart." Justin returned her cheek kiss before letting her leave the truck.

"See ya later, Boss." Amy grinned up at him once she finally got her door open and herself out of the truck.

Since it was only noon when Justin dropped her off at his house and her doctor's appointment wasn't until two, Amy went inside to fix a quick salad for lunch as Justin drove away. *I'm sure he'll get lunch late in the cafeteria after he deals with Tara and the authorities there to arrest her.*

Realizing that Tara would be behind bars in the next couple hours, Amy suddenly felt down, knowing she no longer had an excuse to stay at Justin's house. *What the hell? I'm not ready to move in, or make us official as a couple with his family. So, why do I suddenly wanna cry when I think about going back to my house tonight?*

Amy pondered her feelings as she ate her lunch and repacked her suitcase, trying to figure out how three nights of sharing a bed with Justin was enough to make her want to stay with him all the time. *It's way too soon to think about making this a permanent arrangement.*

Hell, Mom wouldn't even wanna move in after only three nights sharing a bed with someone. She'd barely classify that as taking a test drive on his dick to see if it's a good fit. And she certainly wouldn't be crying like a baby while packing her things to go home after a couple days staying over with a boyfriend.

Recognizing she was acting out of character didn't stop the tears from flowing down her face as she gathered all her things from Justin's house. Once her suitcase was full, Amy wiped her eyes and tossed the remnants of her lunch that she could no longer stomach trying to eat. She rinsed her dishes and put them in the dishwasher before loading her suitcase and laptop bag into her car.

No point in coming back here after the doctor, and risking Justin seeing me cry like a baby when it's time to go back to my house for the night. I'll give him back his extra garage-door opener tomorrow at work.

It was a short drive from the Burleson Ranch to the Heart's Destiny Clinic, so Amy was more than thirty minutes early for her appointment. *Justin should've gotten to the office at least twenty minutes ago,* Amy thought as she grabbed her purse and walked into the clinic. *I wonder how long it'll take for him to fire her and the cops to arrest her before he texts me?*

Amy double-checked her phone was set to vibrate only, before signing in and getting the paperwork to fill out for her first appointment at the clinic. She went through the motions of filling out the standard forms, giving a copy of her insurance card to the front desk person, and paying her co-pay, as her mind vacillated between worrying about Justin being in danger during the arrest and contemplating her unexpected desire to be with him twenty-four-seven.

Her name being called to go back to the exam room by the nurse, who introduced herself as Summer, brought her back to the moment. Though she couldn't say she was completely focused on her surroundings until after the nurse took her vital signs and the doctor walked into the room.

Amy remembered seeing the man the Burlesons all referred to as Doc Hayes at Kay and Anthony's wedding rehearsal, when Anthony wanted him to examine Kay and their unborn baby before going to the rehearsal dinner, but she hadn't been formally introduced to him.

He was an attractive older man, probably around her mother's age. His brown hair had started to turn gray but only at his temples. He wasn't quite as tall as Justin, but the doctor looked like he might outweigh Amy's boyfriend by about twenty pounds or so. His most striking feature was his kind, hazel eyes. Though Amy was sure she'd probably still blush slightly when she told him why she was there, his eyes were already reassuring her that he would compassionately answer all her questions without further embarrassing her.

"So, what brings you in today, Amy?" Doctor Eric Hayes inquired after formal introductions were made.

"I'm relatively new in town," Amy started, returning the doctor's smile. "I just moved here a couple days after Christmas and need to get set up with a local doctor to stay on schedule with my birth control shots."

"Ah, yes, we can absolutely do those," the doctor informed her before turning to his nurse. "Have you gotten her records from her previous doctor yet, so we can make sure we're sticking with the same brand?"

"Not yet," the nurse, Summer, replied. "But Jeri knows to bring them to you when the fax comes through."

"Very well, we can go ahead and do a physical and pregnancy test to be ready once we get them," Doc Hayes decided, turning back to Amy.

"I, uh, also needed to ask you about an issue I had on Monday." Amy felt herself flush as she spoke.

"Okay, and what was the issue you had on Monday?"

"I, um, passed out after…" Amy's words trailed off as she contemplated how to describe when she passed out. "Well, maybe not really after, but more like at the end of having sex. Like in the middle of the finale, if you know what I mean."

"Yeah, I, uh, know what you mean." The doctor lightly blushed, making Amy less self-conscious about telling him. "Is this the only time you've passed out recently?"

"Yes," Amy replied. "The only time I've ever passed out, not just recently."

"Okay, well, there are lots of different reasons why you might've passed out," the doctor advised, turning to his computer to type notes in Amy's chart. "We can rule out pregnancy as a reason with a simple urine test today."

"I don't think that's the reason." Amy shook her head. "Until last Friday, it'd been quite a while since I'd done anything to make that a possibility. Like so long ago I'd've had the baby by now if I'd gotten pregnant before the last few days."

"And when was the first day of your last period?"

"March first," Amy answered the doctor's question.

"And Friday was the first day you had relations with your new partner?" The doctor turned in his chair to look at a calendar on the counter behind him. "The eighth?"

"Yes. We had sex the eighth, the ninth, the eleventh, the twelfth, and this morning." Amy shrugged when the doctor looked at her with a slight grin. "That's the other thing I'm supposed to ask you about. My boyfriend thinks I passed out because we were more intense on Monday evening, so he's been like super slow and sensual ever since. I think it was just because it was the best orgasm I've ever had and more of an out-of-body experience that's completely safe and nothing to worry about. So, he wanted me to ask you which one of us is right to know if it's okay to go a little harder."

"Um, well," Doc Hayes sputtered, his blush deepening.

"Who's your boyfriend?" Summer interjected at the same time the doctor was collecting his thoughts to answer Amy's questions.

Leah Mae Wright

"Um, is that covered under doctor-patient confidentiality?" Amy looked back and forth between the doctor and nurse, trying to determine if the information would get back to Justin's mom or aunt before saying they were dating. "Because we're not really ready to tell anyone we're dating yet."

"Nothing you say in this room will be shared with anyone outside this room," Summer stated matter-of-factly, smiling at Amy.

When the doctor nodded his agreement, Amy finally admitted, "Justin Burleson."

"I told you those Burleson boys were gonna provide enough business to cover the salary of bringing in an OB-GYN," Summer shouted, slapping a hand on Doctor Hayes's shoulder.

Amy couldn't help but laugh at the way Summer called the Burlesons "boys" when she looked to be about the same age as them. Though the doctor and nurse probably assumed her laughter was because of Summer implying there would be a lot of babies born in the Burleson family in the next few years.

"Yeah, they probably will," Doc Hayes chuckled, shaking his head. "But I don't think Amy's issue can be fully answered by having her see our new doctor when she gets here next month."

"No?" Amy suddenly worried her passing out was a much bigger problem than she originally thought.

"No," the doctor replied. "As I was saying earlier, there are several things that could cause someone to pass out. It could be as simple as holding your breath too long while, um, exercising, or as complex as an underlying heart condition."

"Oh." Amy left her mouth in an O shape a few beats too long because she was worried about heart issues in her family after losing her grandmother at only sixty years old.

"At your age, it's most likely because you were holding your breath during the most intense part of your climax," the doctor reassured her, reaching out to pat her hand. "But on the off chance that it could be heart-related, I wanna refer you to a cardiologist in San Antonio for some tests before we say that for certain."

"Okay." Amy was totally freaking out on the inside, thinking of all the tests a cardiologist would want to put her through and worrying about what might be wrong with her.

"Because of the increased risks of heart issues with birth control, I'd rather wait to make sure the cardiologist clears you before giving you the next dose of the shot you've been taking."

"Yeah, that's fine. We've been using condoms, too, since I knew it was due next week." Amy felt slightly numb as the doctor motioned for her to move to the exam table.

The doctor listened to her heart and lungs, and looked in her ears, eyes, nose, and throat while telling her that he thought light activity was safe from what he could see. "If you get too intense with any activity, not just sex, and start to feel light-headed, slow down or stop, and focus on your breathing."

"Okay, yeah, I can do that," Amy agreed before the doctor turned and gave his nurse instructions on who to call to schedule her with a cardiologist, as well as a follow-up with the OB-GYN that would be starting in the clinic soon for after the testing on her heart was completed.

"Let's also do a blood draw," the doctor continued, listing off the various blood tests he wanted to be done that were just a mix of gibberish and letters listed out of order to Amy's ears. "I know even a blood test won't pick up a pregnancy this soon, so schedule her to come back for that blood test at the end of next week."

"You got it, Doc," Summer smiled, turning to exit the exam room, and leaving the door open.

"Okay, Summer will be back in a few minutes with your appointments scheduled and everything she needs to draw some blood," Eric Hayes, M.D. informed her, turning back to Amy. "If you don't have any other questions for me, I'm gonna leave you in her capable hands."

"No, that was all my questions," Amy replied, smiling at the doctor, though it didn't reach her eyes. "Thank you, Doctor Hayes."

"Anytime, Amy," he replied, returning her smile. "Welcome to Heart's Destiny. I'll see you in a couple weeks to follow up once we have all these test results back."

Amy sat there in a daze after the doctor left the room. *Twenty-five is too young to have to see a cardiologist,* she thought, wondering if heart issues ran in her biological father's family. *I know Mom hasn't ever had her heart checked out because she hates going to the doctor. But with Nana and Papa dying from heart issues, maybe there's something genetic in our family that we should all be checked for, not just me. And now I really need to figure out how to contact David Sinclair to find out if there are heart issues in his family, too.* She was so worked up over possibly having a genetic heart condition that she momentarily forgot she wasn't biologically related to her Papa, so his cause of death had no bearing on her predisposition to heart issues.

Summer came back into the room and drew her blood before giving her a stack of papers outlining all the information she needed for the cardiologist in San Antonio, as well as the dates and times of her appointments with both the Heart's Destiny Clinic and the cardiologist.

Apparently, she'd gotten lucky with the cardiologist having a cancellation for the next day, so she could get in there quickly to get started on the various tests.

Lucky me, I get to take off even more time from work when Justin needs me to be there to pick up the slack from firing Tara and needing to hire not only her replacement, but also the quality control techs for the methanol plant.

Amy felt numb as she left the doctor's office and sat in her car, contemplating who she needed to call first — her mother, her sister, or Justin. As much as she felt she needed to call her mother and sister to make sure they got tested, too, in case it was a genetic heart condition, Amy wanted to call Justin more than anything. *I need my Amy Whisperer to help quell my emotions, so I can get through this.*

<div align="center">~~~</div>

Justin hated leaving Amy in Heart's Destiny to go to the doctor alone, but the agents ready to arrest Tara left him no choice. Knowing he wouldn't get a chance to eat lunch if he waited to get something in the cafeteria at work, Justin grabbed a burger on the way out of town, eating it on the drive to the corporate office in San Antonio.

Once he arrived at the office, the rest of his afternoon was chaotic. First, he met the four agents, two from Homeland Security and two from the FBI, in the downstairs security office to put the lab footage on a flash drive for them with Jake instructing him through the process on his cell phone. Justin wasn't sure why they needed a copy from the security room, instead of just accepting the digital copies Jake had already sent them in email, but he followed instructions to give them what they wanted.

After that, they all went upstairs to speak with Jen and take care of all the paperwork she needed in the human resources department to terminate Tara's employment. While in Jen's office, they got back on the phone with Jake to have him cancel Tara's access to their network and deactivate her badge, so she couldn't swipe it to get into the lab any longer. Well, after she left one final time anyway.

Finally, an hour after he arrived at the office, they went down to the lab for Justin to actually fire Tara, right before the agents could arrest her. With the way Tara started throwing a fit when she found out she lost her job, Justin was glad Amy wasn't with him to be in her line of fire.

She didn't just bump into a mostly empty table like she had on Friday. She actually upended one with an active experiment on it, sending glass and chemicals flying across the room. There were several screams and squeals as the rest of the lab techs dove for cover.

"Damn, now I understand why you recommended the lab coat and safety glasses," Justin heard one of the agents say as he stormed by to apprehend Tara.

She tried to put up a fight as one agent held her while a second slapped on the cuffs. The third agent started reading her Miranda rights, adding assaulting an officer to the list of charges for her latest stunt. The fourth agent ushered everyone else in the lab to the other side of the room to start taking their statements.

Within a few minutes, Tara was taken off the premises by two of the agents, leaving the other two to collect all the statements and photograph the destruction in the lab. Justin verified with the team leads that the experiments that were destroyed didn't require lab evacuation or hazmat cleanup before he sat back to wait for everything to be processed, so they could start to clean up the lab.

He was just about to text Amy to let her know what had happened when his phone rang. Seeing Amy's name on the screen when he pulled it out of his pocket, Justin quickly swiped to answer her call.

"Hey, Amy, I was just about to text you." He smiled as he greeted his girlfriend over the phone.

"I, I," Amy stuttered, sounding like she was crying.

"Amy, are you okay? What's going on, Sweetheart?" Justin didn't even care that he used the term of endearment in front of his sister, everyone who worked in the lab, and the two agents still there taking statements.

"I, I need you, Justin," Amy sobbed into the phone.

"Where are you? I'm on my way!" Justin didn't wait for her to answer before he stood to leave.

"Parked out, outside the doctor's office," Amy stuttered, still obviously crying.

"Okay, stay right there. Don't try to drive," Justin ordered while walking toward the door of the lab.

"What's going on?" Jen stepped in front of him and barred him from leaving the lab.

"Hang on a second, Sweetheart," Justin spoke softly into the phone before covering the area he spoke into with his hand to talk to Jen. "Amy had a doctor's appointment this afternoon. She's crying in their parking lot right now, so I'm goin' to get her and make sure she's okay. Hector can supervise the lab clean-up whenever the agents are done."

"Okay." Jen stepped aside. "Call and let me know what's going on once you know she's okay."

"Will do, Sis." Justin practically ran out of the lab as he put his phone back up to his ear to talk to Amy. "Sorry 'bout that, Sweetheart. I'm back now. Can you tell me what the doctor said that has you so upset?"

"He, uh, he said it could be anything from holding my breath too long to a major heart issue." Amy sniffled as Justin ran down the stairs, so he didn't have to wait on the elevator. "They drew blood for all kinds of tests today and I have to see a cardiologist tomorrow afternoon to schedule who knows how many other tests."

"Okay." Justin bolted through the door at the bottom of the stairs, trying to figure out the right words to say to calm her down. "So, he set you up to test for every possibility, but it's most likely the holding your breath thing, right? I mean, it's not likely to be a heart condition in your mid-twenties."

"Yeah, that's what he said." Amy's voice sounded stronger, but not much. "But with my nana dying at sixty from a heart attack, and me not knowing my biological father's family medical history, or my mom's biological father's family medical history, I'm scared that it could be a hereditary thing making me one of the rare few who have heart issues early in life."

Fuck! Fuck! Fuck! I should've been there with her today! Justin berated himself as he stomped out of the building and ran to his truck, grateful his phone automatically connected via Bluetooth to his stereo, so he could drop the handset in the cup holder in the center console and keep talking to her while driving home. *Fuck this on the down-low shit. I'm not leaving her side from now on, and I don't care if that outs us to my family!*

"Well, we can, hopefully, find out some about your bio-dad's history in the information Jake's supposed to be emailing us by the end of the week." Justin hoped being able to answer some of her questions might help ease her worry, so she could stop crying while he drove the hour back to Heart's Destiny to be by her side. "But regardless of what we find with your family health history or the tests the doctors are doing, we'll get through it together. We'll fix it, Sweetheart. No matter what it takes, we'll fix it."

"Thank you, Justin." Amy audibly took a deep breath and blew it out, like she was focusing on her breathing to help calm herself down. "Just hearing your voice is helping me feel better. I think I'm calmed down enough I can drive home now."

"Are you sure?" Justin could hear that her crying had stopped, but he still wasn't sure she wasn't too upset to drive. "I'm already on the highway, so it won't take me that much longer to get there to pick you up."

"Yeah, I'm sure," Amy sighed. "Sitting here in my car kinda feels like sitting in a fish bowl with anyone walking around downtown able to see me break down. But you're welcome to come over tonight and talk some more, or maybe watch a movie or something."

"Come over?" *What the fuck?* "I thought you were heading back to my house after your appointment."

"Did they not arrest Tara? Is it not safe for me to go home yet?" Amy's voice sounded a little more panicked than previously.

"Yes, they arrested her." Justin ran an aggravated hand through his hair. "I just hoped to have one more night cuddling you in my bed. But I can work with cuddling in your bed tonight instead."

"Oh, you think my invite to come over and talk or watch a movie means you're invited to my bed tonight, huh?" Amy didn't exactly laugh, but Justin could hear the lightness in her tone of voice that he'd missed earlier.

"Naw, Sweetheart," Justin replied, grinning even though she couldn't see him. "Opening this conversation with the words *I need you, Justin* was the invitation to your bed."

"That was an emotional need, not a physical one," Amy chided. "I needed you to be the *Amy Whisperer* to ease my worry after everything got to be too much."

"Yeah, and I can't think of a better way to help ease your worry than holding you in my arms and making you forget everything but how it feels when it's just you and me."

"While that sounds nice, I'm probably only gonna be able to give you a couple hours tonight." Justin heard a click on the line and a car door shut. He assumed those sounds meant Amy had gotten home and was walking into her house. "I've gotta unpack my bag from being at your house for the last couple days, call my mom and Ashlyn to tell them what's going on and suggest they get some cardiovascular tests done, and I'll probably spend at least an hour or two soaking in a nice hot bath to ease my stress before bed."

"Fuck, Amy, now you've got me imagining you naked in that big, clawfoot tub," Justin moaned and adjusted his rock-hard cock, so it was a little more comfortable in his pants. "How 'bout this? You go ahead and make your calls to your mom and sister while I'm on my way. Then when I get there, I'll run your bath, soak in it with you, and give you a relaxing massage to put on your lotion before cuddling you all night."

"That does sound enticing," Amy purred. "But how will you get away with staying over when your whole family will wonder why you aren't home?"

"Well, since Jen was in the lab when I ran out just now, I'm sure my whole family already expects me to be taking care of you tonight, either at my house or yours." Justin hoped Amy wouldn't be too upset that he might have just outed them accidentally. "When she tried to stop me from leaving in the middle of the clean-up and giving statements, I had to tell her I was gonna take care of you after your doctor's appointment."

"Oh," was all Amy said, making Justin wonder if she was having a good reaction or a bad reaction to what had transpired in the lab and his subsequent boyfriend behavior that might have given them away to his sister.

"It's not a big deal, Sweetheart," Justin tried to appease her. "While you're calling your mom and sister, I'll call Jen to make sure she doesn't say anything to the rest of the family."

"No, it's fine," Amy conceded, her breath coming out in an audible huff. "It's probably already too late to stop her from telling someone, so we'll just deal with the fall-out if they figure out we're dating."

"I don't think the fall-out will be as bad as you're expecting, Sweetheart." *At least, I hope it won't be. Elation maybe, but definitely not any negative reactions from my family.*

"Yeah, let's hope you're right." Amy sighed. "Okay, I'm gonna call my mom now. And we'll see about you staying over depending on how things go the rest of the night."

"Alright, Sweetheart, see ya soon," Justin agreed as they disconnected the call.

He quickly hit the hands-free button and instructed his phone to call his sister, Jen.

"Hey, Bro, that was a fast trip home," Jen chortled instead of a typical greeting.

"Yeah, I'm not home yet. Amy had to go, so she could call her mom," Justin replied.

"Okay, what's going on? Is Amy okay?"

"She passed out Monday after, uh, everything." Justin couldn't believe he'd almost told his sister about having sex with Amy in his office.

"Yeah, Monday was a pretty stressful day for all of us," Jen concurred in a placating tone.

"Yeah, it was. Anyway, after I barely caught her before she hit the floor and she was out for a few minutes, I insisted on getting her in with Doc Hayes at his earliest opening. That's where she went this afternoon and why she couldn't come into the office for Tara's mess. He's not really sure what could've happened, so he's referring her to a specialist for more advanced testing."

"That's why she called you upset…" Jen started.

"Yeah, and I'm gonna stay with her to take care of her for a little bit, make sure she's not alone if she has another spell." Justin hated lying to his sister, but he hoped it would be enough to keep the dating speculation at bay, so Amy wouldn't have the added stress of his meddling family. "At least until the specialist does all these tests and says it's safe for her to be alone without risking passing out again."

"Okay, I'll let everyone know who needs to know and you let us know if there's anything we can do for Amy while she's dealing with whatever's going on," Jen proffered.

"Okay, just make sure everyone knows I'm doing this as her friend and boss. I don't want Mom or Aunt Hazel to make her uncomfortable with their matchmaking or making comments about weddings or babies or whatever."

"Sure, Bro, I'll tell them you're just being a good friend and boss," Jen giggled. "But you and I both know you wanna be her boyfriend and start planning your wedding and babies with her."

"Jen," Justin groaned.

"Don't worry, Bro, I'm dropping it," Jen replied to his practically growling her name. "But I'm still gonna be hoping for her to see what a great guy you are while you're helping her through this, so she'll eventually give you a chance to be more than her friend."

Damn, her saying shit like that makes me feel guilty for not telling Jen that Amy and I are already more than friends.

"Thanks, Sis," Justin choked out, emotion clogging his throat. "Um, one more thing. Did the agents say anything about the meeting tomorrow with Amy to get her statement? Her specialist appointment is in the afternoon, so we can still come in tomorrow morning if they need us."

"No, but I'll make sure they're good with that."

They quickly said their goodbyes just as Justin was getting off the highway in Heart's Destiny. As much as he wanted to rush straight to Amy's house, he knew she probably needed a little more time to talk to her mother and sister, which she would want to do in private. So, he took the extra time to go by the ranch and pack a bag, or three, to make sure he had everything he needed to stay with her for the foreseeable future.

Justin might have thought telling Jen that he was just going to stay with Amy until she was cleared by the doctor to be alone would throw her off the dating trail, but he also felt uneasy about Amy possibly passing out while home alone. If it was just holding her breath too long while orgasming, she probably wasn't at risk of passing out alone. Well, except if they had phone sex again. But if it was an unknown heart condition, then she could pass out and fall down the stairs, or injure herself in any number of other ways. Justin wasn't comfortable taking the risk with Amy's safety, even though her age made a heart condition the least likely of causes.

Once he had everything he thought he'd need for a couple weeks, Justin went straight to Amy's house. *Fuck, I probably should've grabbed dinner on my way. If she doesn't have anything here I can easily heat up in the microwave, I'll call Jen to bring over some of the frozen meals I haven't eaten in the last month of goin' to dinner with Amy almost every night.*

As he pulled into Amy's driveway, he opted to send her a text, thinking it couldn't hurt to have them already at her house in case she got bad news the next day.

> **Justin: Just got to Amy's house & didn't think about food when I was grabbing stuff at home. Can you bring over the frozen dinners I have in the freezer when you get off work? You know I can't cook & I don't want Amy to have to & risk passing out again.**

> **Jen: Yeah, I can do that. Anything else ya'll need?**

> **Justin: Thanks, Sis! That should do it.**

He pocketed his phone and grabbed his bags before walking up to her front door and ringing the doorbell. When Amy answered the door, Justin's heart broke at seeing her eyes puffy and bloodshot from crying so much that afternoon. He dropped everything just inside the door to take her into his arms.

They stood there in the doorway just hugging for a few long minutes before finally making their way to her sofa to sit and talk. Justin insisted she walk him through all the events at the doctor's office first, before he told her everything that happened at the office.

"So, how did your conversations go with your mom and Ashlyn?"

"They went," Amy replied, shrugging like she wasn't sure how to finish her statement. "Neither one of them seem to think there's a reason to be checked out, even though both of them admitted to having similar experiences in the past."

"Seriously?" Justin couldn't believe that neither her mother nor her sister were worried about Amy. They all seemed so close when they were down to visit her just a couple weeks before. So, their lack of concern seemed out of character for the women he'd met.

"Yeah, they basically chalked it up to really good sex and said to enjoy it, not worry about it." Amy shook her head, like she couldn't believe their reaction either. "I did get them to agree to get checked out if the doctor finds something on my tests, so I'm counting that as a win."

"So, I guess that means you told them about us?" Justin wasn't sure why he felt weird about her family knowing about them when his didn't, but that was a topic to explore another time.

"Yeah, I kinda had to when I was trying to explain when I passed out. But at least they aren't local to out us. Well, until Ashlyn moves down here the first of June." Amy looked at him cautiously. "Though it doesn't really matter since Jen's probably already telling everyone about us."

"Actually, I called Jen as soon as I got off the phone with you," Justin confessed, running a hand through his hair nervously. "I had to tell her you passed out Monday, but I worded it as after *everything*, so she thinks it was from the stress of the day. I also told her that you're goin' to a specialist for more testing, but I didn't tell her what kinda specialist in case you didn't want anyone to know. So, even if she tells my family that I'm staying with you to keep you from risking passing out while you're home alone, she thinks it's only as a friend. I made sure to emphasize that, so Mom and Aunt Hazel don't get any ideas and make you uncomfortable with their romance talk when you've got more important things to worry about."

"Oh, that's a good cover." Amy grinned and playfully slapped his leg. "Just how long do you think your sneaky ways will let us get away with shacking up before they figure it out?"

"At least a week or two, depending on how long it takes for you to get through all the tests," Justin smirked. He was glad Amy seemed to be on board with his idea to spend every night together while they could, even though their sexual activity was limited by Doc's instructions.

Before he could go back and ask her more about how he'd told her to keep her activity light, their discussion was interrupted by her doorbell ringing. Their conversation since he arrived filled his brain, causing him to momentarily forget texting Jen to bring over dinner. "You expecting someone else to come by tonight, Sweetheart?"

"No," Amy replied, shaking her head and looking worried. "You don't think Tara got out on bail already, do you?"

"No," Justin replied, shaking his head and standing from his seat. "But just to be on the safe side, you stay here, and I'll get the door."

"Oh, okay," Amy stuttered out as Justin walked out of the room to the foyer.

As soon as he got to the foyer, he could see several people standing on the porch through the glass in the door. *Fucking hell! Jen couldn't just bring the food by herself?*

Justin opened the door to find a majority of the women in his family standing on Amy's porch, with the exception of Kay and Brook who were both out of town, each of them holding a casserole dish or stack of frozen meals in plastic containers. "Jen," Justin admonished, glaring at his sister. "When I asked you to bring over a couple frozen dinners, I only meant enough to get through tonight, so I didn't hafta leave Amy alone any longer to take care of tonight's dinner."

"Yes, well," Jen hemmed and hawed, pushing past him to walk in like she owned the place. "When I went to do that, I had to explain where I was going. And then when everyone found out what's going on, they were all as worried about Amy as you and I are, so we all had to come check on her."

There was a flurry of activity as his sisters, cousins, mom, and aunts all walked into the house and started spreading out to find Amy and put away the month's worth of food they were carrying.

Justin just stood there dumbfounded with his jaw hanging open, barely registering that he needed to shut the front door, until his mother, Susan, stepped up to him. "Here, take this and show everyone to the kitchen to put away the food, while I go check on Amy."

He turned to catch Amy's eye where she was still sitting on the couch in the living room, mouthing "sorry" to her before redirecting almost everyone to her kitchen. She looked to be in shock, so he hoped he could get everyone to leave quickly after stocking Amy's fridge and freezer. She clearly wasn't prepared for his crazy family to come in and take over her living room for the night.

"We've got this," Justin's aunt, Sarah Harper, insisted once Justin had shown them to the kitchen. "You go find out if Amy wants roast beef, lasagna, or chicken, broccoli, and cheese casserole for dinner tonight, so we can pop it in the oven to heat up for you while we're putting everything else away."

"Oh, uh, okay," Justin sputtered, turning on his heel to go back to the living room, where he found Amy on the couch with his mother on one side and his Aunt Hazel on the other.

"No, there's no possible way I'm pregnant, so that's definitely not what made me pass out," Amy declared, causing Justin to stop in his tracks and grab onto the back of the chair opposite the sofa to keep from falling over in surprise.

"Doc didn't give you any idea what it could be?" Aunt Hazel reached over to take Amy's hand in a way that made him think she was trying to check her pulse to see if she was lying.

"Yeah, too many ideas to narrow it down until after testing for a few things," Amy reported, her voice quivering. "From the stress of the day with figuring out Tara was targeting me and my experiments in the lab causing me to not eat enough to maintain my blood sugar, all the way to several possible underlying heart conditions that I'm having to go see a cardiologist to rule out."

"And what's he recommending you do to prevent the episodes while you wait for all the tests?" Justin's mom rubbed Amy's back in a soothing gesture.

"Keep my stress level down, no strenuous activity, and focus on my breathing if I feel lightheaded," Amy replied. "And since my family's all in Tulsa, he suggested having a friend stay with me in case I hit my head or something if I pass out again."

"And since I've got that covered, why don't we try to get Amy's stress level down by getting everyone outta here, so she can rest." Justin knew he was being rude, but he really wanted everyone to leave, so he could be alone with Amy.

"Yes, we should definitely let Amy get some rest," Aunt Hazel adamantly agreed, her knowing look making Justin uncomfortable. "Did Maggie or Sarah get something in the oven for ya'll for dinner?"

"No, I was sent back in here to ask Amy if she wants roast beef, lasagna, or chicken, broccoli, and cheese casserole, so Aunt Sarah knows what to put in the oven," Justin replied.

"Goodness, I'm not picky." Amy shook her head. "Ya'll really didn't have to do all that."

"Nonsense." Justin's mom waved off Amy's comment, giving her a quick hug. "We take care of family, and we adopted you into the family when you came down for Anthony and Kay's wedding."

"Well, thank you." Amy was obviously fighting back tears as she returned his mother's embrace.

"Justin, what am I putting in the oven?" Aunt Sarah lilted as she walked into the living room, surrounded by everyone who'd put away food in the kitchen. Justin turned to look at Amy, silently asking her what she wanted.

"Whatever's easiest," Amy answered for him. "Like I just said, I'm not really picky when it comes to food."

"Lasagna," Justin decided for them, when his aunt looked to him for an opinion. He would've probably picked the roast beef if he'd been asked his favorite, but he knew Amy loved Italian food, so he opted to go with her favorite instead.

"Lasagna it is." Aunt Sarah turned to go back into the kitchen. "I'll set a timer, so you know when to take it out."

"We actually left instructions for reheating everything as sticky notes on the individual containers," Aunt Hazel told them, patting Amy's hand. "So, Justin should be able to follow those and feed you without burning your house down."

"Hey, I'm not that bad," Justin protested, throwing his hands up in mock outrage. "I know to take food outta the Tupperware before nuking it, so I shouldn't need that many instructions."

"Yeah, but after learning that you didn't even know how to turn your washing machine on, I'm not sure I trust you to mess with my oven," Amy giggled.

His sisters and cousins all laughed with her, several of them making comments about Amy being good at keeping Justin's ego in check. A few minutes later, they were all taking turns giving her hugs and wishing her good luck at her upcoming doctor's appointments before leaving.

"Sorry," Justin apologized for his family barging into her home, sitting back down beside Amy on the couch after closing and locking the door behind his family. "I wouldn't've asked Jen to bring a couple frozen meals outta my freezer if I'd've known I was setting us up for an ambush by all the women in my family."

"It's fine." Amy waved off his apology like it was no big deal. "Actually, I think telling your mom and aunt that there was no way pregnancy was the cause of my passing out really threw them off our tracks."

"Um, about that…" Justin started.

"What about it?" Amy interrupted his train of thought.

"I mean, I know we've used a condom every time, but I also know they aren't foolproof." Justin shifted to look her in the eyes. "Are you really sure that's not possible?"

"Well, it is possible, I suppose." Amy looked down at her hands in her lap for a moment before looking back up at Justin. "But since even the doctor's blood test can't detect pregnancy this soon, I doubt I could have a symptom like passing out already."

"Okay," Justin croaked, drawing out the word while trying to wrap his head around the fact that Amy could be pregnant, even though pregnancy symptoms don't show up in the first few days. *Fuck, she could be carrying my baby right now. And what does it mean for the baby if she has a heart condition? Will she be able to carry to term? Or will it be too much for her heart and risk both their lives?*

"Besides, even if condoms aren't a hundred percent effective, we're doubly protected until the seventeenth when my next birth control shot's due. And it can take up to a year before regaining fertility after going off the shot, so we're probably not at risk, even if I have to skip this shot completely while doing all these heart tests."

"Why would you hafta skip the shot?" Justin really wished he'd have paid more attention to the girls' part of sex education in school, so he wouldn't feel like an idiot asking her a bunch of stupid questions.

"Doctor Hayes said there's an increased risk of heart issues from birth control, so he wouldn't give me my shot today." Amy made her statement as if it was no big deal, but Justin heard *"risk of heart issues from birth control"* and didn't want Amy to risk taking it ever again. "I'm supposed to go back next Friday to have another blood draw for a pregnancy test to rule that out. And then once the cardiologist does all the tests they want, I've got an appointment with the new OB-GYN starting at the clinic next month to see if I should go back on it or not."

NOT! Not, not, not! Justin screamed in his head, knowing if he said it out loud, Amy would balk at his high-handedness.

Before he could figure out how to change the subject without putting his foot in his mouth, he heard the oven timer going off. *Thank fuck! Saved by the buzzer!* Justin stood to go take the lasagna out of the oven.

"Oh, no, mister!" Amy stood to follow him into the kitchen. "You're not touching my oven without proper supervision."

"Yes, mistress," Justin quipped jokingly as they strolled into the kitchen.

"Mistress?" Amy looked at him quizzically. "Is that the kink you discovered you liked by going with your brother to a BDSM club?"

"No," Justin laughed, looking around for a pot holder to be able to remove the lasagna from the oven. "I told you, I just hung out in the bar. I never explored any of the kinks."

"Sure you didn't." Amy rolled her eyes at him before opening a drawer and handing him two pot holders. She then reached over and messed with some buttons on the stove to turn it off. "I think you secretly get tired of being the boss all the time at work and like the idea of relinquishing control to your mistress in the bedroom."

Justin removed the lasagna from the oven, placed it down on the ceramic stovetop, shut the oven door, and placed the pot holders on the counter beside the stove before pulling Amy into his arms. "I wouldn't mind letting you take control in the bedroom once in a while, Sweetheart," he admitted, bending just enough to touch their foreheads together, so they locked eyes as he spoke. "You're more than welcome to take charge and sit on my face or ride my cock whenever you want. But I have absolutely no desire to be spanked or flogged or any of the other stuff I've heard about male submissives enduring."

Justin gave her a peck of a kiss before releasing her to get two plates out of the cabinet for them to eat dinner.

"Oh," Amy squeaked.

Justin grinned at her shocked reaction while he made their plates. They went back to less explicit conversation over dinner. They discussed their schedule for the next day and decided to wait before planning for Friday until after her cardiologist appointment Thursday afternoon.

Once dinner was done, they worked together to clean up the kitchen. "So, do you wanna watch a movie?" Amy requested as they were finishing up.

"No, I think it's time for that long, hot bath and full-body massage," Justin replied, scooping her up in his arms to carry her up the stairs.

"What're you doing?" Amy was giggling as she wrapped her arms around his neck.

"Keeping your activity level light by carrying you upstairs," Justin replied, pecking her nose as they ascended the stairs.

"I'm sure the stairs aren't too strenuous," Amy protested on the second-floor landing. "And I'm too heavy for you to carry all the way up to the third floor." She wiggled in his arms. "Justin, put me down. I can walk up the stairs."

"Sorry, Sweetheart, not gonna happen. You're not too heavy to carry upstairs, and I'm not taking any chances with your health by letting you climb them," Justin disagreed, continuing to carry her up to the third floor.

"I think you should've carried your bags up instead of me," Amy pointed out when he put her down on her feet in her master suite.

"Relax, Sweetheart." Justin gave her another peck of a kiss. "I'll go get them now."

"You'd better hurry," Amy called after him as he descended the steps to retrieve his things from beside the front door where he'd left them. "Or I'll start the bath without you!"

Justin ran the rest of the way, not wanting to miss a minute of her naked in the tub. He took the stairs two at a time on his way back up to Amy, dropping his bags just inside the door once more and beelining to her ensuite.

Amy already had the bathtub filling up and was lighting candles on the vanity when he walked into the room. "Hey, I'm supposed to be the one taking care of you tonight," Justin chastised teasingly, taking the candle lighter from her hand to finish the job and pecking a kiss on the tip of her cute little nose.

Justin felt guilty that Amy had even lifted a finger to start the bath. While he consciously knew it wasn't too strenuous a job for her to do, subconsciously, he wanted to do everything for her, so she wasn't at risk of having a cardiac event that might take her away from him.

"And I'm looking forward to seeing how you take care of me, Justin." Amy's voice dropped an octave as she spoke, indicating her heightened arousal level.

Justin lit the last of the candles she had out before looking over at her by the tub where she was teasing him by slowly removing her clothes. His cock responded to the enticing sight of her standing beside the tub in only a yellow lace bra and panties.

Damn! And I was doing so good at keeping him at half-mast all evening, Justin thought, removing his own shirt as he stalked toward Amy. *I need to focus on taking care of Amy now. I can't think with my dick and do what's best for her at the same time.*

When he reached her side, he stilled her hands before she could reach behind her to unclasp her bra. "Let me take care of you, Sweetheart," he commanded, placing her hands on his shoulders, wrapping his arms around her to pull her closer, and dipping his head to kiss her senseless.

The kiss was soft and sensual at first, meant to be seductive. Justin moved his lips over Amy's in a way he hoped conveyed his love and affection, even though it wasn't as ardent as their norm. He licked through her lips with a sense of reverence that he hoped she understood he felt for her.

"Oh, Justin," Amy cooed when he trailed his lips down the column of her neck.

He deftly unfastened her bra with one hand as his feather-soft kisses trailed lower. He went down on his knees before her, slipping her bra down her arms, lifting her hands briefly to remove it from her body, and flung it back over his head in the direction of the clothes hamper, not caring if it actually made it in at the moment.

Amy slid her hands up into his hair as Justin worshiped her breasts. Amy moaned in pleasure as he lightly suckled her perfect peaks. Justin reveled in her soft sounds, realizing there was no need for words during this sensual moment between them.

While he could've gladly spent the next several hours venerating her with his mouth, Justin knew he couldn't, or she'd never make it into the tub. *Oh, fuck, the tub!* He kissed his way over her abdomen, reaching around her to turn off the water to keep it from overflowing.

Once he successfully prevented flooding her bathroom, Justin looped his fingers through the lace at her hips and slid her panties down her legs. He trailed them with his lips, stopping at her knees as she stepped out of them before kissing his way back up her body until he was standing once again and kissing her russet-colored lips.

He didn't linger long with the soft swipe of his lips over hers, opting to scoop her up into his arms bridal style to lift her over the side of the tub before standing her up in the water.

"Grab a bath bomb outta that cabinet." Amy pointed to the cabinet in question as Justin was unbuttoning his pants.

Justin pushed his pants down as he walked over to the cabinet to do her bidding. When he opened it, he found a basket full of cellophane-wrapped balls like the ones he remembered seeing given as gifts at Christmas. "Do you have a preference for which one, Sweetheart?"

"No, those are all the same, so it doesn't matter which one you pick," Amy replied.

Justin read "lavender and cocoa butter" on the label before ripping it off, tossing the cellophane in the trash, and handing Amy the flowery scented bath bomb. He finished removing his clothing and stepped into the tub, sitting down behind her while she dropped the ball in the bathtub.

The lavender scent filled the room as the ball foamed and coated the surface of the water with a thin layer of bubbles. Justin moved to pull Amy back into his arms, so they could recline in the tub with her back to his front and her head resting on his shoulder, when he realized he forgot to grab her shower cap to keep her hair dry. "Shit, your hair," he vociferated, moving to get back out of the tub.

He looked around the bathroom, trying to remember where she'd left the shower cap she'd worn the past two mornings, when he realized that it was probably still in his master bathroom in his house on the ranch.

"I don't need a shower cap for the bath." Amy smiled at him, where he probably looked like an idiot spinning in a circle in her bathroom, looking for something that wasn't there. "Just grab one of the silk scarves from the top right drawer in my dresser."

Justin rushed out to her dresser, not taking the time to think about the water he was dripping on the floor as he went. He grabbed the first scarf he saw before running back to her in the bathtub. Amy quickly secured the scarf around her head, covering her long ebony locks with the bright orange scarf. Justin stepped back into the tub, sliding his legs around her hips as he retook his seat behind her.

Finally, she leaned back against him, so they could both relax and enjoy the hot soak. Unable to resist touching her, Justin softly caressed Amy's arms and torso. It wasn't necessarily a sexual touch, just his way of reassuring himself that she was safe and healthy there with him. Amy ran her palms over his thighs in a similar manner.

Words weren't necessary as they connected through the light touch. He wasn't sure how long they sat there enjoying their easy affection for one another, but he loved every minute of it. Once the water started to cool, Justin grabbed the bar of soap on the side of the tub and washed them both as best he could without getting back out of the tub to grab a washcloth. He rinsed the suds off their shoulders by cupping water in his hands, directing the flow over their skin, so he didn't risk getting Amy's hair, or the scarf covering it, wet. He helped her to stand before pulling the plug and going to grab towels.

He dried her thoroughly and wrapped the towel around her body before giving himself a cursory once over with the second towel. "Where's your lotion, Sweetheart?" Justin looked around for the bottle as Amy started to walk back into the bedroom.

"Bedside table," Amy replied.

Justin hung his towel over the bar on the door to the shower and blew out the candles scattered around the room before joining her in the bedroom. Amy had laid her towel out on the bed and was lying face down on top of it, clearly ready for the massage he'd promised her. He grabbed the unlabeled bottle on Amy's bedside table, catching a whiff of Amy's signature beachy scent when he opened it and squirted some into his hand.

"Ah, so this is where your beachy smell comes from." Justin rubbed his hands together to spread out the lotion before starting to stroke it over her upper back.

"Yeah, I guess," Amy giggled. "It's actually unscented, but I suppose the coconut oil and cocoa butter in it do smell a little like sunscreen."

While Justin coated her backside with the creamy lotion, Amy went on to tell him how she tried several lotion recipes that she found online before mixing and matching to come up with the one she liked best.

When he asked why she didn't add the essential oils for fragrance that she used in the bath bombs she also made, Amy explained how one of her former coworkers was exceptionally sensitive to fragrance, so she left the scents out of any of her homemade products that stayed on her skin when she went to work.

Justin realized that removing the fragrance from her lotion was just another way Amy showed her consideration of others before herself. She was always doing little things throughout the day to make life easier for those around her, even when it was an inconvenience for her. Her compassion for others was just one of the many traits Justin loved about Amy. *I just hope I can show her the same compassion and consideration that she shows the world every day,* Justin thought as he asked her to flip over, so he could finish massaging every inch of Amy's beautiful, bronze body.

While he'd started at her shoulders and worked his way down on her backside, Justin started at Amy's feet and worked his way up on her front.

"I guess I'm not the only one enjoying this." Amy pointedly looked at his cock, who was standing at attention in response to Amy's moans of pleasure every time he rubbed an exceptionally good spot.

"You're definitely not the only one enjoying this, Sweetheart." Justin's voice sounded gravelly from arousal as he worked his way up her legs.

Justin squirted more lotion onto his hands for the seventh or eighth time before rubbing it into her quads. As he worked his way toward the apex of her thighs, he took a moment to appreciate how the musky scent of her pussy blended well with the soft, beachy scent of her lotion. He looked down to see the wetness coating her lower lips and couldn't resist dipping his head for a taste before massaging any higher.

"Oh, Justin," Amy moaned, arching her back to press her pussy closer to his face after only the first swipe of his tongue.

So fucking responsive, he thought as he worshiped her pussy much like he'd worshiped her breasts before their bath. Long, languid licks, followed by softly blowing on her clit alternated with lightly suckling the needy nub. Justin barely had a chance to repeat the sequence a second time before she was going over the edge and crying out his name as she came. He lapped up her honey like it was the sweetest nectar in the world because to him it was.

"Where all can I use this lotion, Sweetheart?" Justin's breath blew across her clit as she came down from her orgasm high, ramping her back up quickly.

"External use only." Amy breathed out the words so quietly, Justin almost didn't hear her.

"Guess I won't be using my fingers for your next orgasm then." Justin loaded his hands up with more lotion to massage into her hips and pelvic region. He got as close to her slit as he could without risking rubbing the lotion into areas too sensitive for the creamy, white concoction that looked a lot like his jizz.

"No, I need your dick for that." Amy bucked her hips up as he caressed her.

"Mmm, but I hafta finish your massage first, Sweetheart." Justin got out more lotion to massage her midsection while loving her titties with his mouth once more.

Amy continued to moan in pleasure as Justin slid up her body. She wrapped her legs around his waist, pulling their hips together as he finished working the last of the lotion into her skin.

"No more massage," Amy moaned, lacing their fingers together before extending her arms overhead to bring him close enough their lips could finally touch. "I need you inside me now."

"I hafta go get a condom first, Sweetheart." Justin pulled back slightly.

"No, no condom." Amy peppered his face with kisses. "We're still protected for a few more days. We can go back to using condoms tomorrow. I just wanna feel you one time with no barriers between us."

"Fuck, Sweetheart," Justin groaned, wanting nothing more than to be bare inside her, regardless of whether or not her birth control shot was still effective. "Are you sure? It might not be as effective the last few days before the next one's due."

"Yes, I'm sure." Amy sounded breathless as the words whispered out. "I've never done it without a condom. I'm disease-free and I wanna know what it feels like without."

"I'm disease-free, too," Justin admitted, smiling as he looked deep into her obsidian eyes. "And I've never trusted anyone enough to go without either. But I trust you."

"I trust you, too. Please, Justin." Amy's imploring look as she begged for his bare cock was Justin's undoing.

He pressed their lips together as The Anaconda slowly slithered into her tight, wet heat. *Fucking, heaven,* Justin thought as he inched his way in all the way to the hilt.

His long, smooth strokes in and out of her creamy cunt were as much to savor the feeling of being inside her with nothing between them as they were for keeping her activity level down per doctor's orders.

He kissed her the same way he made love to her, softly and sensually, telling her with his body how much he loved her. Justin pulled his head back to look into her beautiful, almost black eyes when he felt the first flutters of her inner walls signaling her imminent orgasm.

"Breathe for me, Sweetheart," Justin gently commanded when he recognized she was holding her breath as she came.

"Oh, yes, Justin," Amy cried out, gulping in a breath both before and after uttering the words.

The rhythmic pulsing of her pussy clamping down like a vise on his cock milked his own orgasm out of him. He held still, buried as deep inside her as possible as he released his semen directly into her womb.

"Amy. Sweetheart. Amy." *I love you!*

As much as he wanted to say the words right then, Justin knew better than to utter them in the heat of the moment. He pecked her lips one more time, not wanting to interrupt her focus on her breathing. Then he rolled to the side, pulling her with him so they could stay connected without him crushing her under his weight.

"That was…" Amy started, her voice trailing off, like she couldn't come up with the right word.

"Perfect." Justin finished her sentence and kissed her forehead. "Just like you."

"I'm nowhere near perfect," Amy argued, snuggling in to rest her head on his shoulder the way he knew she loved to fall asleep.

"You're perfect for me." Justin hugged her close. A moment later, he heard her soft sleep sounds that he couldn't quite call snoring and wondered if she'd even heard him.

Chapter Eleven

Amy felt like she was riding the world's largest emotional roller coaster as she went through her day. From the high of waking up in Justin's arms after their romantic interlude the night before, her stomach plummeted when they arrived at the office, and she had to give her statement to the authorities about everything Tara had sabotaged. Once she got through that, she couldn't actually go back to working on her experiments until all her raw materials were tested to verify they hadn't been contaminated. Which meant she spent the rest of her morning working with Jen to review lab rules and procedures, so they could start taking everyone through retraining to hopefully deal with the other issues Justin had pointed out in watching the security camera footage.

Just as she thought the ride was coming to more of a flat track with her having her normal lunch with Justin, it plummeted once again with going to the cardiologist. She was torn between feeling awkward at Justin insisting on going with her and being grateful that he was by her side throughout the whole exam, holding her hand and being the rock she desperately needed to lean on while worrying about what all the tests would show. *As embarrassing as it was to have him watch while I took off my top and bra for the nurses to have access to my chest for the tests, I'm not sure I could've actually gotten through the appointment without crying or having a panic attack if I hadn't had him there to lean on.*

After the initial exam and electrocardiogram showed no abnormalities, the cardiologist went to see his next patient while Amy was ushered to another room in the office for an echocardiogram. Amy was anxious about the process of yet another test on her heart, but her anxiety decreased dramatically when the technician explained it was just an ultrasound to take pictures of the heart, similar to the ultrasound pregnant women had to see their unborn children.

After the echo, she was taken back to the exam room and told she could change back into her bra and blouse from the hospital gown she'd had to put on for the EKG and echocardiogram. Justin held her hand when the doctor came back in to tell her the tests showed her in peak heart health.

Because her episode had been in the middle of strenuous activity, the doctor scheduled her for an exercise stress test the following week. But he told her it was merely a precaution, just in case there was something going on that couldn't be seen until her heart rate was elevated. Since she'd only had the one time when she'd passed out, the cardiologist believed it was probably from holding her breath, as Doctor Hayes had suggested the day before.

They left the cardiologist's office late in the afternoon, with the recommendation to keep her activity light, at least until after the stress test, just in case the activity was the cause of her syncope episode.

So, basically, the same thing Doc Hayes said yesterday, Amy thought with a sigh. *It's probably just from holding my breath, but I'm not supposed to do anything too strenuous until after another test, just in case there's something wrong with my heart they can't see when I'm not exerting myself. Oh, and focus on my breathing when I orgasm. Like I can think about breathing when I'm mindless from the heavenly things Justin does to my body.*

"You alright, Sweetheart?" Justin squeezed her hand as he posed the question, bringing her back to the moment in his truck as they drove back to Heart's Destiny for the evening.

"Yeah," Amy replied with another sigh. "Just seems like a lot to go through this afternoon to basically be told the same thing as the doctor yesterday."

Justin glanced over at her for a moment before turning his eyes back on the road. Amy wasn't certain from the fleeting expression she caught before he turned away, but she got the impression that Justin didn't feel like the afternoon was as much of a waste of time as Amy did.

"You don't agree?" Amy hated that her anguish was evident in her tone of voice as she stated the question.

Leah Mae Wright

"It's not that I don't agree with you," Justin snapped sharply. Apparently, he spoke more sharply than he intended because he gentled his voice as he continued speaking. "I mean, it sucks that they couldn't do that other test until Monday, but I think they still ruled out most of the heart issues that could've been the cause with the tests they ran today."

Amy thought about Justin's words for a moment, trying to figure out what they could've seen in the tests to diagnose a condition that would cause her to faint. "Ya think?"

"Yeah, the EKG would've shown if there were any signs of nerve signal issues with your heart," Justin replied, nodding. "I don't know if you heard the nurse when she said they could see everything from arrhythmias to heart defects and previous heart attacks with the EKG. Yours was perfect, with no abnormalities whatsoever, so I'm sure they ruled out arrhythmias, prior heart damage, and congenital defects as to why you passed out. And if they didn't rule out the defects with the EKG, the pictures from the echo show everything is the right size and working properly. At least while you're at rest. Now they just wanna look again while you work out to make sure exercise doesn't trigger anything they couldn't see today. But I'd be willing to bet that the two tests today ruled out at least ninety percent of the heart-related possibilities for why you passed out on Monday."

"Maybe," Amy begrudgingly admitted. She still wasn't sure the no-news-is-good-news theory was entirely accurate.

"Trust me, Sweetheart." Justin lifted her hand to his lips to brush a kiss on the back of hers before resting their joined hands back on the center console. "Those tests both being normal is good news. If it was really a heart issue, the doctor would've seen it on those tests today."

"If you say so." Amy gave him a slight smile. *I wish I could be as optimistic as Justin, instead of the "Worry Wart" my mom has labeled me as since childhood.*

"Yeah, I say so." Justin briefly looked over to grin at her before focusing on the road in front of them. "And I'm the boss. So, when I say you hafta quit worrying about it, you actually hafta do what I say and quit worrying about it."

"Sorry, Boss, I think it's gonna take more than you giving me the order to get me to quit worrying." Amy laughed at the incredulous look Justin gave her.

"That's alright, Sweetheart." Justin wagged his eyebrows suggestively. "I've got all kinds of ideas for things we can do to keep your mind off any worrisome topics."

"Oh? Are we stopping at the ranch to pick up your Xbox before going home?" Amy couldn't resist teasing him by acting oblivious to his sexual innuendo. "Or maybe working on a plan for the youth center class we're starting next semester?"

"While I'm more than willing to do both those things in the next few days, I was thinking more along the lines of tying you to your bed, so you can't be too active." The smile in Justin's eyes took on a mischievous glint. "I figured you can practice breathing while you come until it's second nature, and I'll enjoy setting a record for how many times I can make you come in a night."

Yeah, that would probably take my mind off anything I might be worried about, Amy thought, grinning at Justin as he made the turn off the main road and into her subdivision.

"Maybe. But we should probably fuel up with the rest of that lasagna to have the energy for all that. And then, of course, we'll have to wait a couple hours after eating to let our food settle before we can do anything that…" Amy's words trailed off as she paused to think of the right word. "…*jostling* without risking an upset stomach."

"Jostling, huh?" Justin questioned, lightly chuckling as he parked in her driveway.

"Yeah, jostling," Amy replied. "Pushing or bumping into someone in a way that could shake up their stomach contents and make them spew."

"We aren't talking about swimming, Sweetheart." Justin put his truck in park and turned it off. "So, I don't think there's a rule about waiting an hour after eating to avoid cramping up and risking drowning."

"Maybe not officially." Amy shrugged when Justin came around to help her down out of his passenger seat. "But if you don't wanna wait at least two hours after eating, then you're the one responsible for cleaning it up if either one of us vomits from the jostling."

"I'm more than happy to take that responsibility, Sweetheart." Justin shook his head, still grinning, as they made their way into the house. "Because I have no intention of *jostling* you that roughly."

Justin's phone dinged just as Amy got the house unlocked. He pulled it out of his pocket to check his messages just as they walked in the door. When she looked over to see him scrolling on his phone, he had a strange look on his face that concerned Amy.

That doesn't look like a good news text, she thought as she dropped her purse and laptop bag on the table in the foyer. "What's wrong?"

"Nothing's wrong, Sweetheart." Justin pocketed his phone before walking into the dining room and pulling out his laptop. "We just might have a change of plans for tonight."

"No record number of orgasms tonight then?" Amy took the seat beside him as he booted up his laptop and signed in to her Wi-Fi before checking his email.

"Maybe later." Justin grinned wickedly at her briefly before turning back to his screen. "But you might get that two-hour break after eating to talk to your dad."

"What?" Amy exclaimed, reaching over to put her hand on Justin's forearm to help ground her at the thought of contacting her biological father for the first time. She still wasn't sure how she felt about him, much less if she was ready to contact him. *Will he even answer if I call him? Or will he hang up on me as soon as he figures out who's on the phone?*

"I told you Monday that Jake just needed to verify the contact information he had was still current before he sent the report on your biological father." Justin reached out with his free hand to cup her face. "Apparently, it's confirmed. The text was from Jake to tell me to check my email for the report for you."

Holy crap! My father's contact information is in Justin's email. I could actually call and talk to him tonight. Fuck! Shit! Damn! I'm not ready to talk to him tonight!

Apparently noticing the panic written all over her face, Justin leaned over and kissed Amy to bring her out of her head and back to the moment with him. The hand that had been cupping her face slid around to the nape of her neck, holding her head in place for him to plunder her mouth with his tongue.

Amy returned the passionate kiss, sliding her hand up Justin's arm from his forearm, across the slight bulge of his bicep, over his shoulder, and around his neck, where it was joined by her other hand. With his closer arm now free to move, Justin reached around her waist and pulled her into his lap. At least that's what Amy assumed happened when she found herself suddenly straddling him at her dining room table instead of sitting in the chair beside him.

"Better?" Justin arched an eyebrow quizzically when they took a moment to breathe. Amy could only nod, feeling breathless from the way Justin kissed away her worries. "Then why don'tcha sit here and read through this report while I go heat us up some dinner?"

Amy wasn't sure she could handle reading the report without him by her side. She didn't get a chance to voice her fear, though, before Justin read it in her features and settled them down some for her by saying, "Don't worry, Sweetheart. You're just reading a report, not actually calling him. From what Jake's told me, there's nothing in the report that might be upsetting. And if you still aren't ready to call him after reading it, then you don't hafta make that call tonight."

"Okay," Amy finally acquiesced, relaxing a little at not having to make the decision to call right then.

"Okay." Justin smiled at her before pecking her on the nose. He lifted her up and set her back down in her own chair. He then turned his computer to face her, kissed the top of her head, and walked to the kitchen to reheat their dinner.

Amy didn't even question if he was using the oven or just reheating the lasagna in the microwave as she clicked on the attachment in Justin's email from Jake. As soon as the document opened, she read through it to see that her father had been born at the same hospital where she and Ashlyn were born, Saint John's Hospital in Tulsa.

The report went into detail about his early home life, telling her about his parents and siblings. Below that section was information about his education, including graduating from a high school in Tulsa that Amy recognized as the biggest rival of her own alma mater. After the college information her mother had already mentioned, the report went into his employment history.

"Holy crap! We worked at the same company!"

"What was that, Sweetheart?" Justin walked back into the dining room, carrying two glasses of tea and the silverware they would need to eat dinner.

"ATZCorp." Amy pointed at the screen, still dumbfounded at the connection. "He and I both went to work there right outta college."

"Is he also a chemical engineer?" Justin put everything down before reading the report over her shoulder.

"No, he's in advertising," Amy replied, shaking her head. "But it's the only place he's worked since graduating college, so we worked there at the same time. Well, for the same company anyway. He'd moved to the Houston office long before I started working with the company."

"Still a cool thing to have in common." Justin kissed her head once more and went back into the kitchen.

Amy went back to reading the report, which then described his personal life after he and her mom broke up. Apparently, he started dating McKenna Webster right around the time Amy and Ashlyn were born and married her a year later.

She was already pregnant when they got married in June of 1994, Amy realized when she saw the date of birth listed as January 4, 1995, for her half-brother, David Michael Sinclair, Jr., was not quite seven months after David, Sr. and McKenna were married. *I wonder if they got married because she was pregnant? Or if they were like Kay and Anthony and realized they were expecting a few days before their already planned wedding?*

If they got married because of the baby, does that mean he would've married my mom if he knew about Ashlyn and I being on the way? Or would they have still gone their separate ways because she was already in love with Eddie by the time she figured out she was pregnant?

I know Mom says she never told David because she didn't think he could be our father, but how could they have lived so close to each other without him noticing her basketball belly and wondering if her baby was his? Surely, his sister must've known Mom was expecting and would've said something to him. Right?

No matter how hard she tried to accept the story her mother told about how David Sinclair never knew she was pregnant with his daughters, Amy still struggled to believe it. With how often some of Randi's ex-boyfriends had come back around a few months after they broke up to try to get her back, Amy knew it wasn't difficult to keep track of an ex to verify there wasn't an unexpected pregnancy. *Hell, not just Randi's exes, Mom's and Ashlyn's, too.*

The lines on the report about her other half-brother, Richard, who she originally learned about on Ancestry, and a half-sister, Kayley, who was still a teenager, blurred as Amy's eyes filled with tears. She couldn't seem to get past feeling like her father had abandoned her and Ashlyn to go off and raise his other kids.

Amy pulled her feet up onto the edge of the dining room chair where she was sitting to hug her knees into her chest. She put her forehead on her knees and cried for the almost twenty-six years she felt cheated out of having a father.

"Oh, Sweetheart." Justin's voice was soft and soothing as he walked into the room. Amy heard him set their plates on the table before she felt his arms come around her. "I'm so sorry. I didn't think this would upset you, or I wouldn't've suggested you read the report alone."

He lifted her up and placed her on his lap as he took his seat at the table. Amy pressed her face into the crook of his neck and wrapped her arms around him, holding on to her rock while she cried it all out. Justin comforted her by rubbing one hand up and down her back while stroking her hair with the other.

He whispered words like "It's okay, Sweetheart," and "I've got you," but Amy couldn't make out anything else he was saying over the sound of her own sobbing. She didn't know how long he let her sit there crying on his shoulder, but she relished the comfort he provided the whole time. When her tears started to lessen, she finally understood him as he spoke softly in her ear. "Can you please tell me what's got you so upset? I can't figure out how to make it better if I don't know what's wrong."

"See, seeing he ra-raised thr-three other k-kids bu-but not me or Ashlyn," Amy stuttered out, lifting her head to look into Justin's sky blue eyes. "Wha-why could he love them but not us?"

"Oh, Sweetheart." Justin pressed his forehead to hers, their eyes locked on one another. "I don't know how to answer that question for you. I don't think it's possible for anyone to know you and not love you. So, I hafta think he didn't know about you, or he'd have been there for you from day one."

"How could he have not known about us, though? He was still in Tulsa when we were born. He had to have seen Mom at some point when she was pregnant and wondered if he was the father." Amy just couldn't shake the fear that he'd known and willingly walked away because he didn't want to be her dad. "What if he knew and walked away because he didn't want us?"

Justin answered her *What if* question with some of his own. "What if he didn't know? What if he still doesn't know? What if you contact him and find out he's just as upset as you are about missing the first twenty-five years of your life?"

Amy pondered Justin's questions for a few minutes before realization dawned that his "what ifs" were just as plausible as her own.

"He's the only one who can answer those questions for you, Sweetheart." Justin finally broke the silence between them.

"I know," Amy admitted, pulling back to wipe the tears from her eyes that were threatening to make a reappearance. "But I'm afraid of what the answers are gonna be, and if I'm strong enough to handle them if they aren't what I wanna hear."

"Oh, Amy, Sweetheart." Justin shook his head. "You're one of the strongest women I know. Your strength and determination to solve any problem you run into are just a couple of the things I love about you."

Amy was temporarily distracted by his words. *He loves me? Wait, he said those are traits he loves about me. That means he loves the traits I have, not that he loves me. Right?*

"Stop thinking so loud, Sweetheart." Justin smiled at her just before pressing their lips together in a kiss obviously meant to get her out of her own head. Amy returned the fervor of his kiss until Justin abruptly pulled back. "If we keep kissing like that, I'm gonna end up showing you how much I love you right here on your dining room table before we even have a chance to eat dinner."

"You love me?" Amy shocked herself by voicing the question.

"Yes, Amy, I love you. So fucking much."

"I love you, too." Amy grinned at him. Her heart felt lighter at finally being able to say the words to him.

Justin grinned back. "Just so you know and have a chance to wrap your head around it before I propose, I should probably warn you that I'm planning on marrying you and having babies with you because of how much I love you."

Regardless of how serious Justin looked as he said the words, Amy giggled at the thought of him planning their future together. *If anyone had told me four months ago that I'd be in love and excited about a future with my husband and children right now, I never would've believed them.*

"Since that warning is sending you into a fit of hysterics, how about we table that discussion for when you're ready to talk about it and go reheat our dinner one more time?" Justin stood, lifting her off his lap before she could contain her giddiness and reply. He placed her in her chair and picked up the plates he'd previously brought into the dining room, shaking his head at her fit of laughter as he walked back into the kitchen.

Amy felt like a silly schoolgirl finding out her first crush liked her back. Her mood stayed elevated, thinking about her future with Justin. She saw herself walking down the same aisle Kay had four short months before, only to Justin as her groom. He would look like sex on a stick in his classic black tuxedo. She imagined Randi and Ashlyn in yellow bridesmaid dresses and wondered who Justin would ask to be his groomsmen. *His brother? Cousins? Or his two best friends, Aiden and Leo?*

Fast forwarding in her mind, she envisioned herself with her own basketball belly, pregnant with twins, who would be a perfect mix of the two of them. *Will we have boys or girls? Will our kids have his lighter, cool coloring? Or my warm browns? Or maybe some shade in the middle, that perfect mix of him and I?*

I wonder if part of the reason Mom couldn't figure out who was our father is because Ashlyn and I both look like her? If I meet him, will I recognize any of his features in myself? Will he see himself in me?

"Let's actually try to eat this time before it gets cold again," Justin suggested as he walked in, setting their plates on the table.

"Yes, please," Amy replied, grinning at him as she picked up her fork to dig in.

Justin took his seat, and they spent several minutes eating in silence before Amy braved bringing the topic of her father up once more. "Do you really think I'm strong enough to handle whatever happens if I contact my father?"

"Absolutely, Sweetheart." Justin nodded his head to give her a visual affirmative to go along with his words. "But we can talk through it to make sure you feel that way before you make the call."

"Talk through it how?" Amy probed between bites.

"Well, we can start by you telling me what you think the worst-case scenario could be when you call him." Justin shoveled a huge bite into his mouth. Amy knew he'd only taken a bite that big to give her plenty of time to state her worst fear before he was free to talk again.

"That he'll tell me he knew about Ashlyn and I, but he didn't wanna be a father," Amy admitted. Justin kept chewing, so she had to elaborate. "That he still doesn't wanna be our father. That he won't let me get to know my half-siblings. That he'll reject us again, like he did almost twenty-six years ago."

Suddenly no longer hungry, Amy put her fork down and waited for Justin to go into *Amy Whisperer* mode and talk her down.

"And what changes about your life if he does all that?" Justin scooped up another mouthful of food to give Amy the opportunity to answer, but she had to pause and use most of that time to think about the question.

What would change? I don't have a dad now, so it won't be any different if he doesn't wanna be my dad after I contact him. Same with my other siblings. I guess I'll have the closure of knowing where I came from, but nothing about my daily life will actually change.

"Nothing," Amy finally answered.

Justin swallowed and smiled at her before asking his next couple questions. "And what's the best-case scenario? How will your life change then?"

"He'll wanna get to know Ashlyn and I, be a part of our lives. I'll get to know what it's like to have brothers and a sister who's more than three minutes younger than me. I could possibly have cousins, aunts and uncles, and maybe even grandparents to add to my family." Technically, she had all those already, but only as names on a computer screen. If her dad didn't reject her, she could have more people in her family that loved her. More people in her family for her to love.

"So, is the possibility of those good changes to your life worth the risk of a phone call not leading to any change in your life?" Justin raised one eyebrow and gave her a half-smile as he led her to make the decision to contact her biological father.

"Yes," Amy begrudgingly admitted. She picked up her fork and scooped up another bite of lasagna before asking one more question. "Whaddaya think I should do if I call, and he doesn't answer?"

Amy took a bite while Justin pondered the question. "I suppose he might not answer an unknown number. Maybe text him first?"

"And text him what? 'Hi, I'm your daughter' seems like something he shouldn't find out via text," Amy chortled, shaking her head at Justin's crazy idea.

"Well, maybe don't word it that way for the first text," Justin chuckled. "How about asking if you have the correct number? I mean, I know Jake's already verified it's current, but that's a good way to break the ice. Tell him you're trying to reach someone who knew your mom back in the day, then ask if he's willing to talk over the phone instead of texting. Or maybe mention the DNA matches to his family members and ask if he'd be willing to help you figure out how you're related."

"Yeah, I can do that, but maybe we should finish dinner first." Amy looked at her half-empty plate and wasn't sure she could eat another bite without getting sick from how nervous she was about talking to her biological father for the first time. Her heart was racing, and her vision blurred momentarily, making Amy wonder if she was about to pass out again. Or maybe go into a full-blown panic attack. "Or maybe I should wait until after my test on Monday, so I don't have another episode when I'm not being monitored."

"Shit, Sweetheart, are you okay?" Justin looked at her with wide eyes as he stroked a hand over her face as if he was checking her temperature. "Focus on your breathing, Sweetheart. Deep breath, in through your nose, then blow it all out through your mouth."

The instant Justin touched her, Amy's anxiety receded. While her heart rate was still higher than resting, she no longer felt like her heart was going to beat its way out of her chest. She followed his instructions for breathing until she felt completely back to normal.

"Thank you. I feel better now." Amy recognized in Justin's expressive baby blues when he saw the truth in her words reflected in her physical appearance.

"Alright, Sweetheart." Justin leaned back in his chair, breaking their physical connection by dropping his hand from her face. "Shall we finish dinner?"

"Yes," Amy replied, suddenly ravenous.

They ate in silence for a few minutes before Justin finally spoke again. "You know that wasn't the same as when you passed out on Monday?"

"Yeah, I know." Amy sheepishly looked down at her almost empty plate. "That was more like the panic attack I had on New Year's Eve."

"When you ran off the dance floor to go to the restroom?" Justin eyed her quizzically. Amy only nodded in response, embarrassed about having to admit what really happened back then. "I hope I wasn't the cause of your panic that night."

"You weren't," Amy exclaimed, her head whipping up to face him, so he could see that he had nothing to feel guilty about from New Year's Eve. "Not really. It was all from me fighting my attraction to you. You didn't do anything wrong that night at all. I just couldn't admit to myself yet that it was okay for us to be more than friends."

"Well, thank goodness, you don't have panic attacks about that anymore." Justin gave her a boyish grin that made him look a decade younger than his twenty-seven years. "Since that panic-inducing situation ended up turning out pretty good, I think there's a very good chance the current one will, too."

"You're probably right." Amy smiled back at him. "But I still might need you to lean on when I reach out to him."

"Whenever you're ready, Sweetheart. I'll be right there holding you in my arms."

Knowing Justin would be there supporting her, Amy decided to send the text as soon as dinner was over. She told him her plan as they scarfed down the rest of their meals. Justin carried their dishes to the kitchen while Amy grabbed her cell phone out of her purse that was still sitting on the table in the foyer. She finished perusing the report to find David Sinclair's cell phone number.

She heard the water running in the kitchen and knew Justin was rinsing their dishes to put them in the dishwasher before coming to meet her in the living room to sit with her when she sent the first text. She opened up her texting app and input the phone number before walking into the living room to wait for Justin on the sofa.

She contemplated adding him as a contact, but Amy couldn't bring herself to do it before actually talking to him, just in case he didn't want to hear from her again. She typed her initial message, but she waited for Justin to come sit beside her on the sofa and pull her into his arms before hitting send.

Amy: Is this the correct phone number for David Sinclair?

Amy leaned back against Justin, who was reclining in the corner of the couch, resting her head on his shoulder, so he could look at her phone as well. They only waited a moment before the reply came through.

Unknown: Yes. Who is calling?

Amy: My name is Amy. I've recently done my DNA on Ancestry & am a really close match with your sister Donna & son Richard. I wanted to see if you knew Andrea Lawton in Tulsa, Oklahoma back in 1992.

Amy was so nervous, she didn't realize she'd combined the two ideas Justin had given her earlier, inadvertently outing herself as his daughter via text. Justin squeezed her a little tighter as they sat there watching her phone, waiting to see how her father responded.

She noticed the message showed delivered and then read, but the three little dots indicating the person was replying never showed up.

"I screwed up, didn't I?" Tears filled Amy's eyes as she reread her last message and comprehended what she'd sent.

"No, Sweetheart, you didn't screw up." Justin's words were adamant as he kissed the top of her head. "He probably just needs a minute or two to comprehend what your message means to figure out how to respond."

As the minutes slowly ticked by with no response, Amy's tears started to silently fall. Justin turned her in his arms, so he could wipe the streaks from her cheeks. Amy ended up sitting sideways on his lap, dropping her phone in her own lap, so she could embrace the man she loved and who would be there for her no matter what.

"Don't cry, Sweetheart. It's gonna be okay." Justin kissed away her tears. "Remember, worst-case scenario, nothing changes in your life. You still have me, your mom, your sister, hell, my whole crazy family that you can claim as yours."

Amy wasn't sure how long she sat there with Justin comforting her. It felt like hours, but it was probably no more than five minutes before her phone rang in her lap. Amy looked down and recognized David Sinclair's phone number on the screen. She was so surprised that he was calling her that she fumbled and almost dropped her phone before she was able to swipe the screen to answer it.

"He-hello," Amy stuttered in greeting.

"Hey, uh, hi, Amy," the deep, masculine voice of her biological father responded.

The tears were back in full force. Justin kept futilely trying to wipe them away for her, but his efforts weren't very effective.

"I, um, knew Andrea very well back then." David sounded as choked up as Amy felt. "How, um, how do you know Andrea?"

"She's my mother," Amy replied, not realizing she was holding her breath until Justin whispered, "Breathe, Sweetheart," in her ear. She sucked in a deep breath and was blowing it out when her father responded.

"Then I guess, based on those DNA matches, I'm your father," David choked out, almost sounding like he was crying as much as Amy was. "Oh, wow. I, uh, I have another daughter."

"Two, actually," Amy informed him at the same time she heard a woman in the background congratulating him. "I'm three minutes older than my twin, Ashlyn."

"I'm three minutes older." Seriously, what's wrong with me that being older than Ashlyn is the first thing I tell my dad about me?

"Twins!" David exclaimed. "I have two more daughters!"

"Yes," an excited female voice shouted. "Now the women will finally outnumber the men in this family!"

Amy couldn't help but laugh at the voice she assumed was either her half-sister or David's wife.

"What're you screaming about, Mom?" The question was posed by a younger-sounding female voice that Amy assumed was her half-sister.

I guess his wife is okay with the news?

"Hang on a second, Amy," David chuckled as the voices in the background went low enough that Amy couldn't hear their conversation. "I'm gonna put you on speaker, so we can all talk to you."

"Oh, okay," Amy replied, deciding to do the same, so Justin could hear the conversation.

"We should really call DJ and Ricky, so they can meet her, too," the voice Amy believed belonged to McKenna Sinclair advised.

"You call them. I'm on my phone already," David replied, laughing.

"While Mom and Dad figure out how to get our brothers over here, I'm gonna go ahead and introduce myself. I'm Kayley, and I'm guessing you're my sister, but Dad didn't tell me your name."

"Hi, Kayley, I'm Amy."

"Sorry, I was too excited to think about introductions. The other voice you probably heard is my wife, your stepmom, McKenna. She's on the other side of the room calling the boys right now. I don't know if they'll be able to get here while we're still on the phone, but they'll both wanna get in touch with you and your twin as soon as they hear about you."

"Yeah, Ashlyn's gonna flip when she finds out I've talked to you without her here." Amy felt guilty for not making the call when Ashlyn was down visiting.

"You can add her to the call, Sweetheart." Justin pointed at an icon on her phone screen that Amy wasn't familiar with.

"How?" Amy turned to Justin to have him show her how to add her sister to the call at the same time Kayley asked, "Who's there with you?"

"Oh, yeah, I probably should've mentioned I have ya'll on speaker and am here with my boyfriend, Justin."

Kayley burst out laughing. Amy looked at Justin, wondering what was so funny that she apparently missed. Justin just shrugged, giving her the impression that he didn't know what was funny either.

"Oh, dear," McKenna chuckled along with her daughter.

"Good to know it's not just me causing Dad to make that face," Kayley snorted, still laughing.

"What face?" Amy couldn't stop herself from asking the question, assuming her father's expression was what Kayley and McKenna found funny.

"The *I-don't-like-the-idea-of-my-daughter-dating* face," McKenna growled, lowering her voice to try to imitate an angry father.

"Sorry, David, but you hafta like me," Justin smirked. "If it weren't for me, Amy wouldn't've found you."

Amy giggled at the irony.

"Oh, that sounds like a story we need to hear," McKenna lilted.

"Justin gave his cousin, Charlotte, a couple dozen DNA tests for everyone to do at her birthday party back in January," Amy explained, smiling. "One of which was the one I took, which led me to finding out Mom miscounted how many weeks back Ashlyn and I were conceived, and identified the wrong man as our birth father for the last twenty-six years."

"Not only that, but I also got my other cousin to track down your phone number for her to be able to contact you." Justin finished Amy's statement when she paused to take a breath before explaining the rest.

"Sounds to me like I should be thanking your cousins," David stated sternly. Amy wasn't sure if she was hearing a little laughter in his voice or not. "So, I can still wait to pass judgment on you when we meet in person."

"Wait, the twins are twenty-six years old?" McKenna faltered.

"We'll be twenty-six on June sixteenth," Amy explained.

"So, the night we met, it was their mom you were telling me about?"

"Yeah," David chuckled. "I guess I was wrong."

"What?" Amy barely squeaked out the question, unable to fully elaborate her inquiry about what David said to McKenna about Andrea almost twenty-six years ago.

"The night I met McKenna," David explained, his voice still sounding light. "I had to work hard to convince her to go out with me. She said she was holding out for the man of her dreams. So, I told her that the surefire way to find the man of her dreams was to date me for six months, then the next guy she dated would be the man of her dreams and give her babies and the whole happily ever after, just like my last girlfriend, your mom. I told her about dating Andrea from Saint Patrick's Day to mid-September, then hearing from my sister that Andrea met the love of her life a couple weeks before Halloween."

"You said something about giving her babies." Amy was barely able to choke out the words to the question she was dreading hearing the answer to. "So, you knew Mom was pregnant with us?"

"Not until Donna mentioned it the following Valentine's Day," David answered, his tone turning serious. "She also said your mom was planning to marry her baby's father when he got home from deployment, so I assumed she really had met the love of her life a month after we broke up and he was the one who got her pregnant. Had I realized there was a possibility that I was your father, I'd've insisted on paternity tests, so I could've been there for you and your sister from day one."

Amy was stunned into silence as she comprehended what he said. *"Had I realized there was a possibility that I was your father, I'd've insisted on paternity tests, so I could've been there for you and your sister from day one." He knew Mom was pregnant. But he thought she planned to marry the man who fathered her children. He didn't know he was our father. He didn't abandon us, not really. He would've been there from day one if he'd known.*

"Amy, Sweetheart." Justin brushed his hand down her arm, bringing Amy out of her own head for a moment. "Why don'tcha hand me your phone, so I can add Ashlyn to the call. She needs to hear this as much as you do."

"Oh, yeah." Amy was in a daze as she handed him the device. She let her father's words sink in once more while Justin told everyone to hold on a second, so he could get Ashlyn on the line with them. *He actually wants to be our dad. Not just that, but with the way he reacted to hearing Justin's my boyfriend, he's already acting like our dad, and he's barely known we exist for five minutes.*

"Hey, Sis, what's up?" Ashlyn's voice rang through the phone to bring Amy back to the moment.

"Is it on three-way?" Amy asked Justin, who nodded to let her know their father and his other family could hear both her and Ashlyn. "Hey, Ash, I have you on a three-way call, so you don't miss out on our first phone call with our dad."

"Holy shit! Seriously?" Ashlyn shouted.

"Yep, she's definitely your kid," McKenna chuckled.

"Hi, Ashlyn," David greeted her sister, sounding choked up again. "I hear your mom and I were both bad at counting and didn't realize I'm your father."

"Seriously? You too?" Ashlyn laughed. "I figured I got my horrid math skills from Mom, but Amy's excellent ones had to come from you."

"Well, maybe," David chuckled. "I didn't actually try to count the months back then. I just believed my sister when she told me your mom was marrying the love of her life and having his baby."

"They must not have stayed in touch after we were born." Ashlyn's tone didn't sound quite as excited as before. "Or she'd have known Mom never got married."

"Oh?" Amy couldn't interpret the meaning behind her father's utterance.

"Yeah, Eddie, the guy she thought was our father, died in Somalia a month before his deployment was over," Ashlyn confided, somberly.

"Oh, I, I'm sorry to hear that." David's voice sounded as bleak as Ashlyn's. "From what my sister told me about him and your mom, they were very much in love. I know it's a lotta years too late, but please pass along my condolences to your mother the next time you speak with her."

"I will. I'm sure she'll appreciate that. Now, tell me all about you and the brother of ours that Amy found online."

Shit! I should've told Ashlyn about the report Jake compiled, so she'd know already that we have two half-brothers and a half-sister.

"Actually, Ricky is not your only brother," David chuckled. "And Amy isn't your only sister."

"Nope, we girls bookend the boys," Kayley interjected, laughing again. "Hi, Ashlyn, I'm Kayley, your other sister."

"Oh, wow, is the whole family on the phone?" Ashlyn sounded surprised.

"Not yet, but the boys are on the way," McKenna informed them. "I'm McKenna, your stepmom."

"Oh, cool, nice to meet you," Ashlyn replied.

"And the boys are actually DJ, David Jr., who just turned twenty-four in January," David added, his smile evident in his tone of voice. "And Ricky, who just turned twenty-one in December. Ricky is actually the one with his DNA online. He did that last year as part of a class he was taking in genetics."

"Oh, so Ricky is the brainiac like Amy," Ashlyn laughed. "How old are you Kayley? 'Cause you sound like you might be the fun one like me."

"Fifteen and a half," Kayley replied. "And I'm definitely the fun one. So, it sounds like it's your closet I need to raid when we finally meet face to face."

"Only if you wanna give Dad a heart attack," Amy joked, laughing.

"Who wants to give Dad a heart attack?" a strange male voice asked.

"Definitely not me," another strange male voice replied.

"Amy says I'll give Dad a heart attack if I borrow clothes from Ashlyn's closet," Kayley giggled.

"Sorry, little sis, as much as I'd love to hook you up with my bangin' wardrobe, I'd kinda like to get to know Dad, so I can't let you give him a coronary."

"Thanks, I think," David chuckled once more. "Now, let me introduce you to your brothers."

"How about we introduce ourselves, Dad, since they can't see us? I'm DJ, AKA David Jr., the oldest."

"Not anymore," Kayley laughed. "The twins are almost twenty-six."

"Sweet, now you're the middlest of middle children," the other male voice, who Amy assumed was Ricky, quipped. "I'm Ricky, by the way."

"Hi, guys, I'm Amy, the actual oldest," Amy greeted her brothers for the first time.

"Only by three minutes," Ashlyn pouted. "And I'm Ashlyn, the fun one like Kayley. And Amy's the brainiac like Ricky, so which one are you, DJ?"

"I'm both, smart and fun," DJ declared, his tone sounding happy.

"Whatever, Bro," Ricky huffed. "DJ's actually a jock who got the cheerleaders to do his homework for him."

"You'd have flunked out if you went to school with us," Ashlyn chuckled.

"Are you saying you wouldn't've helped your brother with homework?" DJ teased.

"No, just that you'd have been going to the wrong sister for help if you came to me because I was a cheerleader," Ashlyn scoffed. "The only reason I graduated high school is because Amy helped me with my homework."

"What've you each done since high school? Where do you live? Still in Tulsa? I wanna know everything about you." David started in with the getting-to-know-each-other questions Amy hadn't imagined she'd ever get to answer with her father.

"I took some secretarial classes to keep from being stuck in a waitressing job," Ashlyn informed them. "Now I'm a receptionist at Bama in Tulsa, but I'll be moving down to Texas with Amy the first of June."

"You're in Texas already, Amy?" David sounded hopeful that she was close to his location.

"Yes, I moved here right after Christmas," Amy replied. "I went to OU for a degree in chemical engineering and worked in the product development lab at ATZCorp for the last three years. I came down to Heart's Destiny for my best friend's sister's wedding in November and met Justin and his family, who offered me a job in the lab at Burleson Incorporated that I started in January."

"You worked for ATZCorp? What a coincidence. That's where I've worked ever since college."

Amy didn't mention to David that she already knew that from the report Jake had sent her about his life.

"I've heard of Burleson Incorporated, but I'm not sure where Heart's Destiny is," David continued after telling them about his various jobs at ATZCorp that Amy already knew about.

"We're about an hour southwest of San Antonio," Justin filled them in on the location of his hometown.

"So, only about five hours from us here in Houston," David replied. "We'll definitely have to plan a weekend when we can meet since we're so close together now."

"Dang, I wish I hadn't taken my vacation at the end of February now," Ashlyn pouted. "'Cause now it'll be June before I can meet any of ya'll in person."

"Or we can plan a trip for Spring Break," Kayley suggested.

"Our Spring Breaks don't all line up on the same days," DJ contended, sounding bummed that wasn't an option.

"Are you still in school, DJ?" Amy was curious about why her brother, who was only two years younger than her, was talking about Spring Break.

"Yeah, I'm doing my MBA at Rice," DJ bragged.

"And what're you studying that required a class in genetics, Ricky?" Amy wanted to know all about her brothers.

"Biochemistry and biophysical sciences at the University of Houston," Ricky told them. "I'm sure a few of my classes cross over with your chemical engineering, but I'm more focused on working in a medical lab when I get done."

"Do you have any idea what you wanna study in college, Kayley?" Ashlyn inquired.

"I wanna go to cosmetology school," Kayley replied. "Not to work in a salon or whatever, but to be a makeup artist for movies and TV shows."

"That sounds like a cool career that would be right up my alley," Ashlyn agreed, laughter evident in her tone of voice. "Hey, Justin, do you think Jen and Becky can hook Kayley and I up to do the makeup for the movies Burleson Entertainment is gonna start putting out?"

"Not my department, Ashlyn," Justin chuckled. "You'll hafta ask Jen and Becky about that."

They went on for another hour talking about all the things they had in common with their father and siblings, along with a few differences. By the time they finally hung up the phone, they'd all exchanged phone numbers and started a family group text to keep sharing information about their lives on a daily basis.

Amy also had a complete family medical history to give her doctor on Monday. Well, as much as it could be complete when she still didn't know who her mother's biological father was, even with all her recent work on the Ancestry website trying to figure it out from her DNA matches.

While her father had wanted to plan a weekend trip so they could meet two days later, Amy put off their get-together for another week. She not only didn't want to miss Brooklyn and Bobby's joint bachelorette and bachelor party, but she also wanted Justin to take her to Houston. She wasn't comfortable inviting her father and his family to stay the night at her house after only one phone conversation. Plus going to meet her biological family gave her and Justin another excuse to spend a couple nights in a hotel together without the prying eyes of his family.

When they finally climbed the stairs to go to bed for the night, she was almost too tired to do more than sleep. Almost. After not passing out the night before when he reminded her to breathe, Amy wanted to test her ability to be more active in bed. Breathing when Justin told her to the night before made her think her episode on Monday was just from holding her breath. She certainly hadn't felt like she was going to pass out from an elevated heart rate earlier when she was anxious about contacting her dad.

They quickly went through their nightly routine of brushing their teeth and getting ready for bed. Amy wrapped her hair as she usually would, but she skipped putting on anything else to sleep in, stripping down to nothing but her scarf before crawling into bed with Justin.

She rolled over to cuddle with him, where he was already laying in the bed. Amy rested her head on Justin's shoulder, and he brought his arm around her, pulling her even closer. She laid her palm on his chest, where she felt the steady beat of his heart.

"Goodness, Sweetheart," Justin crooned as he trailed his hand down her bare back, settling on her butt and giving it a light squeeze. "If I'd've realized you were gonna come to bed naked, I'd've left my boxers in the bathroom hamper with the rest of our clothes."

"It wasn't my original plan." Amy trailed her hand through his perfect smattering of chest hair down to tease across his chiseled six-pack abs. "But as I was wrapping my hair, I got to thinking about how my heart raced earlier tonight, but I never thought I was gonna pass out as it happened. Then I thought back to last night when you reminded me to breathe as I was starting to come and holding my breath."

"Yeah?" Justin prompted her to go on when she paused in explaining her thought process.

"Yeah, and the more I thought about it, the more I realized that passing out wasn't brought on by getting my heart rate up or being too active." Amy turned her face so she could brush her lips across Justin's pecs. "I'll still go for the test on Monday just to be sure, but I wanna try being a little more active tonight with you. If you remind me to breathe anytime I start to hold my breath, I think it'll be fine, without any episodes of passing out."

"Mmm, and just how do you wanna be more active tonight?" Justin rubbed the side of her breast, the only part available since the rest was smashed into his torso.

"I figured I'd indulge your love of country music." Amy lifted up, kissing her way up his chest to his throat and rolling on top of him, so she could whisper in his ear. "Follow the advice of that song about saving a horse and ride my cowboy."

"Fuck, Sweetheart, that sounds amazing," Justin growled, his hands sliding up from her butt to the sides of her face, so he could push her up far enough their eyes could meet. "But are you sure it's not a risk? We can still wait 'til after your tests next week for you to do more than relax while I do all the work."

"I'm sure," Amy replied, leaning down to peck his lips with hers. "Besides, I think I'm supposed to be the one doing all the work while my boss sits back and supervises. So, are you ready to supervise, Boss?"

"Fuck, yeah, Sweetheart." Justin pulled her back down for a toe-curling kiss before pushing her up to a sitting position.

Amy felt her cream coating his abs, but she didn't have a moment to think about being embarrassed over it as Justin was barking out orders to her.

"You hafta stay sitting up, so I can play with your tits the whole time," he commanded. "And watch for any signs that it's too much and I need to take over."

"Yes, Boss." Amy grinned as she slid back to straddle his thighs.

"Take my cock out, Sweetheart."

Amy did as she was instructed, sliding his boxer briefs down as far as she could without asking him to get up to actually take them off.

"Now rub that creamy cunt all over my cock. Get me nice and lubed up before you take me inside you."

"Oh, yes, Boss!" Amy quickly walked on her knees back up to where she could lower herself over his erection. She reveled in the feel of his satin-covered steel stroking through her folds, especially the pressure he put on her clit when his dick twitched between them. She kept rocking her hips against him, ramping up to where she thought she might come before they were even joined.

"Fuck, that feels amazing." Justin's voice was deep and gravelly as he plucked at her nipples with both hands. "But not nearly as amazing as it's gonna feel when I'm balls-deep inside you."

Amy moaned in pleasure, unable to vocalize her agreement at the moment.

"Breathe, Sweetheart," Justin ordered, both hands moving down from her breasts to grip her hips and slow her movement. "And don't you dare, fucking, come until I'm deep inside you."

"Then you need to hurry up and get inside me," Amy retorted.

"Gladly, but you're doing all the work this time, remember," Justin smirked.

"Oh, yeah, sorry, Boss," Amy giggled, lifting up on her knees, so Justin's dick was no longer trapped between them.

"Line me up, Sweetheart, so I can slide home," Justin commanded, still gripping her hips and darting his eyes from hers down to where they were about to be joined as one.

Amy reached down and stroked his cock a couple times before angling him, so the bulbous purple head was centered at her slit. As she started to sink down on him, Justin controlled her speed of movement with his hands on her hips.

"Please, Justin, don't rein me in this time," Amy pleaded, not wanting him to keep things slow and gentle when she had so much passion to unleash on him. She knew he needed their unbridled intensity just as bad as she did, but he was still trying to be too careful with her out of fear.

"Fuck, sorry, Sweetheart," Justin cursed, letting go of her hips to let her control their pace. "But you hafta promise to let me know if it feels like too much and you need me to take over."

"I will, Justin, I promise." Amy leaned over just enough to rest her hands on his pecs as she slid all the way down, so she was filled with him from root to tip. "But just as I'm trusting you to remind me to breathe when I start to hold my breath, I need you to trust me to tell you when we get close to my other limits."

"Fuck, yes," Justin groaned, his hands coming back up to palm her breasts once more. "I trust you completely, Amy."

Amy smiled as she gazed down into his baby blues. No more words were needed as she lifted back up and sank back down. She sped up the pace, bouncing up and down his dick in a hard rhythm.

She angled her hips, so her clit hit his pubic bone on each downward stroke, ramping her back up to almost climax in mere moments.

"Fuck, you're so beautiful, Amy." Justin watched intently where they were joined, seeing his cock stretch her open as he plunged into her pussy. "I love watching you ride me. Seeing you take what you need is so fucking hot."

Amy couldn't talk and focus on her breathing at the same time, especially not when she was controlling the brutal pace of their fucking.

"Breathe, Sweetheart," Justin reminded her as the pressure built in her core. "I love you, Amy. I need you to stay with me and keep breathing while we come."

"Yes, Justin, yes, I love you, too," Amy chanted between panting breaths as she felt like she was imploding. Her orgasm washed over her like a tidal wave, causing her to crash down on top of Justin at the same time he cried out his own release.

He wrapped her in his arms, smashing her breasts into his chest as they floated together in orgasmic bliss. "I got you, Sweetheart. Just breathe."

Amy followed his instructions, syncing up her breathing with his slow, deep breaths. Once they'd both come down from their high, Justin rolled her to lay on her side beside him. He pulled out of her before bounding out of bed and heading into the ensuite bathroom.

Amy heard the water turn on in the bathroom and rolled onto her back to luxuriate in the experience of Justin cleaning her up after sex. It was one of the little ways he took care of her that showed her that even when they were having a rough, hard fuck, they were making love.

~~~

Saturday, March 16, 2019

Justin wasn't sure how he was supposed to keep his feelings for Amy hidden when they went to Bobby and Brooklyn's joint bachelor and bachelorette party at Tully's Roadhouse on Saturday evening. Yeah, everyone knew he was sticking by her side twenty-four-seven until
~~~

after her medical tests were completed, but he wasn't sure he could keep up the friends-only façade once everyone started drinking.

Not that everyone would be drinking since both the bride and her matron of honor were pregnant. Justin and Amy had even talked beforehand and planned to only have one drink each to toast the happy couple at the beginning of the night. It was their plan for maintaining their sobriety enough to keep from outing their couple status to everyone accidentally.

What Justin was actually worried about was how he could control his inner caveman if one of his friends got drunk and asked Amy to dance. As her friend and boss, he should have no reason to object to her dancing with another man. But as her boyfriend, he very much objected to anyone else dancing with his woman, regardless of the fact that nobody was supposed to know about their relationship status just yet.

I could insist that Amy doesn't dance tonight to keep her activity level low like her doctors have recommended, Justin thought as they walked into the bar. *But that's a total douchebag way to handle it, especially since I know Amy loves to dance.*

Since they separated into the two main rooms of the bar, Justin didn't have to worry about the guys hitting on Amy for the first part of the party. Just like at Anthony and Kay's party back in November, when Justin first met Amy, the guys went to the back room to play pool while the ladies stayed up front to play the bachelorette party games the guys didn't want to witness.

"You can't tell me you don't have a problem with your fiancée playing the pin-the-dick-on-the-dude game." Luke Walker was pointing at Bobby when Justin walked up to the group after leaving Amy in the front room of the bar with the women. "There's no way you're okay with Brook touching another man's dick, even a cartoonish picture of one."

"Dude, it's just a picture, and not even of a real dick." Bobby shrugged. "Besides, she already knows mine's bigger, so she wouldn't be satisfied with the picture even if it was real."

"Please tell me none of the paper penises the girls are gonna be touching tonight actually touched your junk when ya'll were making comparisons." Justin went a little green at the thought of Amy or one of the women they were both related to touching anything that had made contact with Bobby's cock.

"Don't worry, Cuz," Bobby chuckled. "Comparisons weren't needed, just a brief look from across the room with Brie holding one up and laughing at how little the pieces for the game are compared to the real thing."

"How 'bout we change the subject, 'cause I don't think any of us really wanna know about the size of your cock." Anthony shook his head at his oldest brother, Bobby.

"Yeah, we should definitely be grilling Justin on how things are going with living with Amy this week." JJ smirked. "Just how comfortable is her couch, little brother?"

"Comfortable enough." Justin shrugged, hoping he pulled off convincing his family and friends that he and Amy were just friends. *But not nearly as comfortable as her bed.* "At least for the hour or two we spend there every evening. I've actually been sleeping in her guest bedroom, just like when she stayed with me when I was protecting her from Tara before she was arrested."

That's not technically a lie, right? Since we've slept together in the master bedroom at both places, saying it's the same at both locations is the truth. Just because I'm the only guest who gets to sleep in her room with her, doesn't mean I can't call it a guest bedroom since I'm sleeping there and I'm a guest in her home. Only we don't hafta fake messing up the guest bed at her place to keep anyone from figuring out we're sleeping together, since she doesn't have anyone coming by to clean her house for her like I do.

"Yeah, right." JJ shook his head. "As far up her ass as you've been all week, I'm surprised you've let her outta your sight for this party."

"I'm not up her ass," Justin groaned at his brother. *Though I wouldn't mind sticking my dick in her juicy ass.* "Besides, she's not exactly alone in the other room. She's got plenty of people to help her out if she gets lightheaded tonight. And if she does need me for any reason, she'll call my phone, just like she does at night to let me know she's done in the bathroom and has made it safely to bed without passing out."

Yeah, that was a blatant lie, but it couldn't be helped. I hafta let them know we have a system when we're in separate rooms at night or they'll figure out we're sleeping together.

"Leave him alone, Cuz." Bobby pointed at JJ. "We all know he's not nearly as up her ass as he wants to be, so don't make him feel worse about being stuck in the friend zone."

"I'm not trying to make him feel bad." JJ held his hands up in surrender. "I'm just trying to give him the kick in the ass he needs to take advantage of all this extra time he has with her to get outta the friend zone."

"I'm not gonna take advantage of her having a medical issue," Justin objected, though after the last couple days, he was convinced her medical issue was just her holding her breath when she orgasmed.

"Of course not, Cuz." Anthony shook his head disapprovingly at JJ. "You're doing the right thing by being there for her as a friend. When the time's right, I'm sure she'll see how much closer ya'll are and will let you know when she's ready for more."

"Alright, enough with the romantic drama that would be better suited to be in the other room with the womenfolk," Luke grumbled, picking up a pitcher of beer and starting to pour a few glasses. "It's time to toast Bobby for giving his balls to Brooklyn."

"Dude, he's getting married, not giving up his balls," Anthony objected. Being the only married man there, Justin thought it was appropriate his cousin was the one to correct Luke's misconception.

"No, Bro, he's right," Bobby argued, shocking them all. "I'm more than happy to give Brie my balls on a daily basis because of how good it feels when she plays with them while…"

"Bobby Burleson, you'd better not finish that sentence," Brooklyn shouted, cutting off whatever Bobby was about to say.

"What're you doin' back here, Brie-Baby?" Bobby grinned as several of the men turned to see Brooklyn and Kay walking up to the table they were gathered around.

"The girls are doing a couple rounds of shots," Brooklyn explained, pointing with her thumb over her shoulder. "And since we can't imbibe, Kay and I thought we'd come see what ya'll are doing before starting on the games."

Anthony threw his arm around his wife at the same time Bobby embraced his fiancée. Justin wished Amy would've come back with them, even though he couldn't hug up on her like his cousins were with their women. At least, not until she was ready to tell everyone they were together.

"We were just about to toast Bobby for giving you his balls," Luke told the ladies as he started passing out plastic cups of beer to the guys.

"So that's why Bobby was describing what sounds like it should be a scene in one of our books," Kay giggled, grinning as she turned to look directly at Brooklyn. "If he likes whatever you do to his balls enough to brag about it to his buddies, you should definitely write it out to give our readers some new ideas."

"Please tell me our mothers aren't reading ya'll's books." Bobby looked a little green at the thought.

"Or our sisters," JJ added, also looking uncomfortable at knowing the content was graphically sexual, which was funny to Justin considering JJ's proclivities.

"Didn't you know all the Burleson women are our beta readers?" Brooklyn somehow kept a straight face as she looked up at Bobby. "Along with several of our friends around town."

I wonder if their books are where Amy got some of her ideas last weekend? Justin couldn't help but chuckle at the mortified expressions on his brother and cousin's faces.

"Brooklyn, we need our bride back, so we can get these games started," Becky shouted, sticking her head into the back room.

The distraction of the women being called back to the front room was enough to get the guys to move on from the conversation to spread out and play a few games of pool. They did a couple toasts to the groom before everyone finished their first beer, knowing that Bobby wouldn't drink more than one before switching to water for the rest of the night.

Justin also switched to water after the one beer, as was the plan for him and Amy. *I wonder if she was able to only have one? Or if the girls doing shots pushed her to drink more than we planned?*

Not that he could really go and check on her when he knew the ladies were playing the bachelorette party games. He ended up alternating his time between playing pool and eating a basket of chicken fingers and fries while hanging out with the rest of the guys.

After a while, a few of the women migrated back to the pool hall and started challenging the guys to games. Bobby and Anthony ended up being dragged to the front to dance with their significant others. When Justin didn't see Amy come back with his sisters, he asked them how she was doing, hoping they wouldn't pick on him too much about being overprotective of her in their obviously tipsy states.

"She's fine, Justin," Jen slurred, shaking her head at him as she walked by to go pick a pool cue.

"She was going to the bathroom when we headed back here." Julie told him while following their sister, not sounding as inebriated as Jen.

"By herself?" Justin knew he was being ridiculous worrying about Amy going to the ladies' room alone, but he couldn't stop himself.

"Yes, Justin, by herself." Julie rolled her eyes at him. "She is a grown woman, fully capable of peeing without any help."

"I know that." Justin threw up his hands. "But did anyone go with her in case she has another fainting spell?"

"I don't know," Julie shrugged. "But I'm sure there's someone in there already or who will go in there right after her, so she won't be alone long if she is."

Not trusting that Julie was right, Justin took off out of the back room, through the front room, and down the hall beside the bar that led to the restrooms and storage rooms.

He knocked on the ladies' room door while calling out Amy's name to check that she was okay. He heard someone moving around inside, but he couldn't make out the muffled response of whoever was talking on the other side of the door. Just as he was about to push the door open to verify it was Amy answering him, the door flew open, being pulled from the inside.

"Whoa, Boss, what's wrong?" Amy looked up at him with wide eyes.

"I just wanted to make sure you're okay." Justin ran a hand through his hair nervously. "I know you haven't had another fainting spell since Monday, but you also haven't had any alcohol either. I didn't know if the girls pressured you into drinking as many shots as you did at the last one of these parties. And I worried that you might've passed out in the bathroom alone."

"I'm fine, Justin." Amy placed her palms on his chest and pushed against him like she wanted him to go further down the hall. "I had two shots, but I switched to water when they were passing out the rest of the rounds."

"Okay." Justin relaxed slightly, holding her hands against his chest as he walked backwards in the direction she seemed to be trying to push him. His irrational panic seemed to be dissipating the longer she had her hands on him.

"In fact, I'm feeling so good that I wanna try something just a little wild." Amy wagged her eyebrows suggestively and smiled up at him. "If that storage room isn't locked, anyway."

"Oh?" Justin raised an eyebrow inquisitively as his back hit the storage room door. "Whaddaya have in mind, Sweetheart?" *Fuck, I hope it's the same thing I'm thinking.*

"Check that doorknob, and if it's unlocked, I'll tell you when we're alone inside," Amy directed.

Justin dropped one of his hands from hers to check the doorknob to the left of his ass. Once he opened the door, he pulled Amy into the storeroom with him, and quickly closed the door so nobody would catch them.

"Now, what were you thinking, Sweetheart?" Justin backed her against the door. He knew it couldn't be locked from the inside, so if they did anything they didn't want anyone to walk in on, then they needed to do it against the door.

"A public quickie." Amy grinned, sliding her hands down from his chest to his waistband, unbuttoning his jeans faster than he could even formulate a response.

"Thank fuck, you're wearing a dress," Justin growled before crashing his lips to hers. He pulled his wallet from his back pocket, just before Amy shoved his jeans and boxer briefs to his knees. He pulled out the condom they'd already discussed going back to using until she could get her next birth control shot.

Amy took the condom from his hand and expertly sheathed him while he struggled to get his wallet back in the pocket of his jeans. As soon as he was covered, he pushed her dress up to her waist and ripped off the tiny scrap of lace that was in his way. Then he grabbed two handfuls of her luscious ass, lifting her up so she could wrap her arms and legs around him and he could slide into her wet pussy.

Knowing they didn't have time for the foreplay he preferred, Justin took a couple shallow strokes first, barely pushing the head in, so she had time to adjust to his sizable invasion before he plunged all the way inside her. He covered her mouth with his, trying to keep them both quiet so they wouldn't get caught.

He plunged his tongue into her mouth, mimicking the way he was fucking her against the door. Amy returned his kiss with ardent passion, rocking her hips in time with his thrusts. They were both panting through their noses as they chased their mutual climax.

Not sure if panting provided enough oxygen to Amy's brain to keep her from passing out, Justin pulled back from their kiss to allow her to breathe. "God, I fucking love you so much, Amy," Justin whisper-shouted as her inner walls started fluttering around his cock.

"I love you, too, Justin," Amy whispered back before biting down on the side of his neck where it met his torso as she went over the edge.

Justin's thrusts became almost frantic as he fought to move inside her vise-like grip, loving the feeling of her marking him as she came. "Breathe, Sweetheart," Justin reminded her, knowing she couldn't with a mouth full of his trapezius.

She released her bite and sucked in a deep breath, sending Justin into his own orgasmic high from obeying his command, even in the throes of her own orgasm. Justin held still as deep inside Amy as he could get, filling the condom with jet after jet of cum.

Amy rested her head on his shoulder as they took a moment to come back to earth. "I hope you know," Justin whispered in her ear. "That even when we have a quick and dirty fuck, I'm still making love to you, Sweetheart."

"I know, Boss," Amy replied, lifting her head before dropping her feet to the floor.

Justin took a step back to give them room to right their clothes, making sure she was steady on her feet before releasing Amy from his hold. He removed the condom and tied it off before pulling up his boxers and jeans and quickly buttoning up.

"I guess these are useless now." Amy picked up her ruined panties from where Justin had dropped the scrap of lace on the floor.

"I'll buy you some new ones." Justin took the red panties that matched her dress from her hand and stuffed them in his front pocket.

After making sure her dress was back down to cover her, Justin barely opened the door to peek out and make sure nobody saw them exiting the storage room. "The coast is clear," he informed her as he opened the door the rest of the way. "Let's do a quick cleanup in the bathrooms before meeting back here in the hallway."

Amy grinned at him as she walked past him to head back into the ladies' room. Justin quickly shuffled into the men's room and dropped the used condom and wrapper in the trashcan on his way to a stall.

He took a piss while wiping any residual cum off his cock with toilet paper. Once he was as clean as he could be without a shower, Justin buttoned back up and exited the stall to wash his hands. He noticed the bite mark on his neck when he looked in the mirror as he was turning the water on, so he adjusted his collar to cover it as best he could before actually washing his hands.

The door opened as he was shutting off the water, making him glad he'd adjusted his collar before anyone came into the restroom.

"I was wondering where you ran off to." JJ made his way to a urinal.

"Didn't run off," Justin alleged while drying his hands. "Just had to take a leak."

"Damn, I was hoping you'd found a place to hide away and make out with Amy."

Justin schooled his features, not wanting to give his brother any clues that he'd just done a whole lot more than making out with Amy, and walked out of the men's room without replying.

Amy joined him in the hallway, and they walked side by side back to the party, with nobody having a clue what they'd just done.

Chapter Twelve

Friday, March 22, 2019

Amy was anxious as she and Justin walked into the Heart's Destiny clinic for her follow-up with Doc Hayes and the blood draw for a pregnancy test, now that it was a week after her prime window for ovulation, so it would be accurate. Not that she was worried it would be positive. She knew that even if her shot from December was at the end of its effectiveness when she and Justin had gone bare on Wednesday and Thursday of the previous week, it could still take up to a year to get pregnant after going off the shots. Besides, they'd gone back to using condoms every time on Friday of the previous week, two days before her next shot was due, so it was extremely unlikely that she'd end up pregnant.

What had her worried was that the cardiologist had cleared her of any heart conditions that could've been the cause of her fainting spell, but he also said that her primary care doctor may have other options to test before giving her the all-clear. As much as she loved having the excuse for Justin to stay with her twenty-four-seven, she really didn't want to have to go through more testing when she thought she and Justin had well and truly proven that her one episode was from holding her breath.

She also felt a little strange at the inquisitive looks she was getting from everyone in the waiting room, including Jeri at the front desk. *It has to be because Justin's with me,* Amy thought after signing in and having a seat. *We're not even holding hands or doing anything to give us away as a couple, but it's clear everyone's trying to figure out if we are or not.*

"Relax, Sweetheart," Justin whispered, putting a hand on her knee to keep it from bouncing. "I'm sure after seeing the specialist's report that nothing could be found on any of those tests, Doc Hayes is gonna agree with our observations for the last week and give you the all-clear to resume your normal daily activities."

"I hope so," Amy whispered back, hating the loss of comfort when Justin lifted his hand from her knee. She really wished she could lean her head over on his shoulder and have him wrap his arm around her to reassure her, but that wasn't possible in a room full of witnesses that would tattle on them to the Matchmaking Mommas of Heart's Destiny. So, Amy sat stoically waiting for her name to be called when it was time for her to go back to the exam room.

When Summer finally came to the door and called her name, there were several raised eyebrows around the room as the other patients watched Justin stand up and follow her. *I wonder how many small-town rumors we just started?*

"Just so you know," Summer stated once they were all in the exam room. "Doc Hayes and I won't say a word to anyone about why ya'll are here together, but doctor-patient confidentiality doesn't cover whatever's said by nosey neighbors."

"Don't worry about it, Summer," Justin chuckled. "My whole family knows I'm barely letting Amy outta my sight to go to the bathroom, until we know how to keep her from passing out with nobody around to catch her and keep her from hitting her head if she's standing up when it happens. They'll quash any rumors and let anyone who tells them about seeing us here together know I'm just being a good friend and boss."

"Uh-huh, sure you are." Summer grinned and shook her head as she set up to take Amy's vital signs. Once those were done, along with all the check-in questions, Summer drew a vial of blood from Amy's arm before leaving them alone in the exam room to let Doc Hayes know they were ready for him.

Justin reached over and took her hand in his, lightly squeezing to remind her he was there for her as they waited. She returned the comforting squeeze before taking a moment to lean on him like she'd wished she could do in the waiting room. Justin released her hand to put his arm around her shoulders, making everything seem more bearable with his one-armed hug.

Amy sat up abruptly when Doc Hayes knocked once on the door before walking on in, but Justin wouldn't let her sever their connection by moving his arm. He kept his arm around her while the doctor took his seat and greeted them. "Hello, Amy and Justin. Good to see you both."

"Hey, Doc," Justin replied. "Good to see you, too. But you can make it great to see you, if you've got some good news for Amy."

"Ah, that I do," Doc Hayes chuckled. "All your blood work from last week came back normal. And the cardiologist's report came back clear as well."

"Yes, he told us that on Monday after my stress test." Amy hoped all these normal test results meant she didn't have to be tested for anything else. As much as she liked the excuse to cover up her relationship with Justin, so they could have their privacy for a little while longer, she was really tired of worrying about there being something medically wrong with her.

"Have you had any other fainting spells?"

Amy shook her head indicating a negative response to the doctor's question.

"We've, uh, monitored her breathing whenever her activity level is up." Justin turned a little pink as he spoke, obviously uncomfortable talking about their sexual proclivities with the doctor. "Even going so far as me reminding her to breathe whenever she starts to hold her breath. And that seems to have prevented any recurrence."

"Excellent," the doctor smiled. "If you keep that up, then I see no reason why Amy can't go back to more vigorous activity."

"So, I don't have to have any more tests to make sure it's just me holding my breath?" Amy's tone of voice reflected her hopefulness as she asked the question.

"Well, we could still run a tilt-table test," Doc Hayes postulated, dashing Amy's hope to be done with testing. "But I think it'd be a waste of time since all the other tests show you're as healthy as can be."

"So, that's it? No more need for a follow-up?" Justin asked the questions Amy was too afraid to voice herself.

"Well, for this," Doc Hayes replied. "Obviously, come back in if you start passing out again, but I think you've got a handle on that for now."

"And when can I get my next birth control shot?" While Amy didn't mind using condoms, she wanted to be able to ditch them with Justin.

"We'll call you next week when we get the results of your pregnancy test to schedule that. We have to have that confirmation that you aren't pregnant before we can administer it."

"Okay." Amy's shoulders slumped at having to come back for yet another appointment.

"It won't actually take a full appointment for Summer to give you the shot," Doc Hayes advised, reading her mind. "Once we have those results, she'll just give you a call to stop by on your way home from work, so she can give the injection without you even having to see me or the gynecologist we have starting on April first."

Amy returned the smile the doctor gave her, though she hated having to wait another week for her birth control.

"Do you have any other questions for me? Or are ya'll ready to get outta here?"

"I don't have any other questions." Amy turned to look at Justin. "Do you?"

"Nope, I'm good." Justin removed his arm from her shoulders to extend his hand for the doctor to shake. "Thanks, Doc."

Amy and Justin followed the doctor out of the exam room, then stopped at the front desk for Amy to pay her co-pay. There was a different group of patients staring at them as they exited through the waiting room. *Great! More busybodies to out us to the Matchmaking Mommas.*

"Ready to head to Houston?" Justin inquired as they got in his truck.

That was the other reason Amy was anxious. They'd packed for their weekend trip before going to work that morning, leaving their suitcases in Justin's backseat all day, so they could go as soon as her doctor's appointment was over.

"As ready as I'll ever be." Amy buckled her seatbelt. *Though, maybe our night in the hotel will relax me enough that I won't be so nervous tomorrow when I meet my dad in person for the first time.*

~~~
~~~

Justin was glad Amy finally seemed a little more relaxed as he pulled up to the valet stand at the Lancaster Hotel in Houston. Just like the first time he'd gotten a hotel room for he and Amy, Justin picked the top-of-the-line deluxe penthouse king suite for their two-night stay in Houston.

He wasn't sure what had made her so anxious at the doctor's office, especially since she got a clean bill of health. But he was thankful that their easy conversation as they drove across the state seemed to be all she needed to relax.

"Valet?" Amy looked at him questioningly as they unbuckled their seatbelts and got out of the truck. Justin just shrugged as he tucked the valet slip into his pocket and walked around the vehicle. He pecked a kiss on her forehead before reaching back into the extended cab to grab their bags and place them on the bellman's cart. "You're seriously spoiling me with these fancy hotels."

"Good." Justin grinned at her as he took her hand in his and they walked into the hotel. "You deserve to be spoiled."

Amy was awfully quiet as they checked in and made their way up to their suite. Justin hoped he hadn't offended her by wanting to spoil her, since he knew she was fiercely independent. So much so, that she'd insisted on alternating who paid for their dates. It took some serious effort on his part to pay for their more expensive outings before she did, while letting her pay for the less expensive activities to make it seem like they were really alternating between who paid.

It wasn't just that he was raised to be a little old-fashioned in thinking the man should pay for everything on dates. He also had an inner caveman he was constantly fighting that wanted to provide for his woman's every want, need, and desire. Besides all that, he also knew how much money she made compared to him. While she was well paid with a six-figure yearly income, it was still significantly less than what he made between his salary, dividends, and investments. And she had a mortgage to cover that he didn't.

Knowing she had more expenses and less income than he did made it impossible for him to feel comfortable with her shouldering the added expense of any pricey outings with him, like hotels and fancy dinners. Though if tipping the bellman made her feel that she was doing her part, he'd swallow his pride to let her exert her independence.

Once the bellman left, Justin carried their bags into the bedroom and Amy promptly started unpacking. "Whaddaya wanna do for dinner?" He joined her in taking their toiletries into the opulent, marble bathroom.

"Whatever," Amy shrugged, rotely moving to hang up her clothes to prevent wrinkling. "I don't really have a taste for anything particular."

"Hey, are you okay?" Justin stopped Amy from going back to her suitcase to unpack anything else, stepping into her path and gripping her shoulders, so she had to look at him while they talked. He didn't know what was going on, but he knew Amy wasn't acting like herself, and he wanted to fix whatever was bothering her if he could.

"Yes, no, I don't know," Amy sputtered, shaking her head before bringing her arms around his waist and burying her face in his chest.

Justin held her to him, rubbing his hands up and down her back to comfort her as she collected her thoughts. He wanted nothing more at that moment than to shoulder all her burdens and take away all her stress.

"I've been so stressed with everything lately." Amy wasn't quite sobbing, but she wasn't sounding like her normal self either. "And figuring out the medical stuff just lifted one worry off my shoulders. I'm still freaking out about how tomorrow's gonna go, how we no longer have an excuse to give your family so we can keep having sleepovers, and how many people saw us together at the doctor's office that are probably gonna spread all kinds of rumors."

"Oh, Amy, Sweetheart," Justin cooed, kissing the top of her head. "You don't need to worry about any of that. Tomorrow's gonna be a fabulous day. Your family already loves you from just a few phone calls and texts, so they'll just love you more when they finally meet you in person."

"I hope so." Amy's voice only slightly quivered, so Justin believed she was taking his reassurances to heart.

"I know so." Justin rested his cheek on the top of her head, just needing the contact with the woman he loved. "And yeah, it's gonna suck to go back to my lonely bed without you when we head home on Sunday. But we'll still figure out ways to be together, whether or not we have sleepovers. Nooners in my office. Overnight dates we don't mention to anyone, like when we got the hotel room in San Antonio a couple weeks ago. And of course, our after-work dates."

"You're right," Amy admitted, pulling her head back to turn and look up at him with her lips turned up in the cutest grin. "And I do love our nooners in your office."

"Me, too, Sweetheart." Justin grinned down at her before kissing the tip of her nose. "Though I think I might prefer fucking you in my office after everyone else has gone home, so we don't hafta be quiet."

"You just don't like having to cover up the marks on your neck where I bite down to keep from screaming," Amy laughed.

"Yeah, well, as much as I love having you mark me," Justin confided, wagging his eyebrows suggestively. "We're gonna hafta come up with a better way to keep you quiet in the office because I can't keep wearing turtlenecks much longer."

"Yeah, I guess those will give us away since it's so much warmer here than I'm used to in Tulsa. Maybe we can find some time this weekend for me to take you shopping for some concealer and teach you how to apply it."

"No, I'm not wearing makeup," Justin objected, causing Amy to laugh even harder. "We'll just hafta bite the bullet and let the Matchmaking Mommas know they were right about us all along, so I can proudly wear your marks without having to cover them up."

"Or maybe I just need to start marking you on your chest and shoulders where they're easier to hide."

"You can mark me anywhere you want, Sweetheart," Justin replied, smiling at her to cover up how he was feeling a little down that she still wasn't ready to openly date him. "In fact, why don't we order room service and stay in tonight practicing being strategic in how we mark each other?"

"Oh, I like the way you think, Boss." Amy's voice was husky with desire, making Justin's cock harden even more than he already was just from being in the same room as Amy.

Justin kissed her once more, keeping it more chaste than he really wanted, before going out to the sitting room to look for the room service menu, pulling Amy by the hand behind him. As soon as he had the menu in hand, he took a seat on the sofa, pulling Amy down into his lap, so they could peruse their dinner options together.

Once they picked their entrée options, Justin looked at the dessert menu and got a wonderful idea for how he'd like to spend the night playing with Amy. "How about the Make Your Own Sundae for dessert?"

"How are we supposed to make our own from room service? Don't we have to go down to the restaurant for the sundae bar to do that?"

"No, they'll bring the toppings in separate containers, so we can pick and choose what we want on our ice cream." *Or whatever else we wanna eat them off of, like your delectable nipples and sweet pussy.*

"Oh, well, that sounds good then." Amy turned her head to kiss his cheek. "I'm gonna go finish hanging up our clothes while you place the order."

Amy hopped off his lap and practically skipped back to the bedroom, while Justin picked up the phone and called room service. As soon as the order was placed, he joined her in putting away their things, chatting while they waited.

Though she didn't seem as anxious as before, she still asked him about the possibility of the town's busybodies spreading gossip about them, and whether or not his family would believe it.

Justin reassured her that even if someone said something to his mom about him going to the doctor with her, his mother already knew he was being a good friend by accompanying her to her appointments. Finally, with lots of reassurance that she had nothing to worry about, Amy seemed to relax about the time their food arrived.

Amy teased him about thinking she was going to get dessert first, so the ice cream wouldn't melt, and playfully pouted when it arrived in a cooler to keep it frozen. *Fuck! She's adorable.*

"But, Sweetheart, I have special plans for how we're gonna eat our dessert tonight." Justin pulled out her chair for her, bending down to whisper in her ear once she was seated. "And we need to fuel up, so we have plenty of energy for what I have planned."

"Oh, really?" Amy arched an eyebrow at him, her interest obviously piqued.

Justin just smiled in response, taking his seat at the table across from her. With their napkins in their laps, they ate in silence for several minutes before Amy's patience faltered.

"Please tell me what you have planned," she begged.

Leah Mae Wright

"Patience, my adorable Amy." Justin cut another bite of his steak, taking his time to savor the flavor of the perfectly prepared beef before finishing his thought. "I know you struggle with it. But I promise my plans for tonight are worth waiting for."

~~~

Oh, yes, these plans were definitely worth waiting for! Amy thought as she laid back on the table, naked save for her scarf currently being used as a blindfold, and waited for Justin to surprise her with what he was going to eat off her body first.

"Open, Sweetheart." Justin pressed a cold spoon to her lips, indicating her mouth was what he wanted her to open for him.

But it'd be so much more fun to open my legs.

Amy opened her mouth as instructed and enjoyed the flavor of the creamy vanilla ice cream mixed with a decadent warm fudge sauce that Justin fed her. "Mmm," she moaned as she swallowed. "Why are you feeding me? I thought I was gonna be your sundae bar."

"And you are, Sweetheart." Amy felt the cold ice cream being spread across her breasts, followed by the warmth of the fudge sauce. The juxtaposition of cold then warm against her sensitive skin was exceptionally arousing, but Justin's tongue lapping up the sticky sweetness was even more so. "I just wanna make sure you get plenty of dessert, too, so your ice cream doesn't melt while I'm feasting on you."

Justin fed her another bite of ice cream, this time covered in a warm caramel sauce. As she was savoring the flavors on her tongue, Justin repeated his earlier spreading of cold ice cream and warm sauce on her breasts, this time focusing exclusively on her nipples and areolas.

"Mmm, that feels so good," Amy moaned as Justin sucked her nipple into his mouth, lightly scraping her flesh with his teeth. Amy wasn't sure if it was to make sure he got all the ice cream and caramel off her, or if it was to increase the range of sensations for her, but she liked the feeling immensely.

"You taste so good," Justin murmured against her skin before pressing a piece of fruit to her lips. Amy bit into the ripe strawberry as Justin took his time arranging what felt like several different fruits and
~~~

other toppings on her torso. "And you look so beautiful decorated with our dessert."

Amy's anticipation built as Justin alternated between his ice cream ritual and feeding her a piece of fruit, cookie, or various candies with him eating the same from where he'd laid them out on her midsection. The lower he moved with tasting the solid toppings on her torso, the more she looked forward to him eating some part of their dessert from between her thighs.

It was truly the most erotic dessert she'd ever had. Possibly the most erotic experience of her life thus far. And he hadn't even touched her pussy yet. Amy was so turned on, she was afraid she'd come instantly with the first touch of his tongue between her folds, or maybe even as he was covering her mound with the food before eating it off.

"Oh, Justin, please." Amy wasn't sure what she was begging for, more erotic torture from Justin's mouth on her breasts or for him to finally eat her pussy to make her come.

"Please, what, Sweetheart?" Justin ate what felt like the last piece of fruit from her lower abdomen, causing Amy to buck her hips up, trying to get him to move his mouth lower. "You want me to eat your sweet pussy now?"

"Yes, Justin, please!" Amy couldn't stop the rocking of her hips, desperately needing him to apply just a little pressure to her clit to send her flying. "I'm so close. Please, eat my pussy and make me come. Please!"

"Fuck, I love hearing you beg for me like that." Justin spread her legs before shaking a can and covering her mound with whipped cream. The lightweight topping wasn't nearly enough sensation to send her over the edge, but Amy knew it would only be moments before Justin took her there. "Open one more time, Sweetheart."

Justin gave her a small squirt of whipped cream to taste before diving between her legs to eat her for dessert. He barely touched her with his tongue at first, delicately removing the whipped cream from her pubic bone before licking through her labia.

When the tip of his tongue finally touched her bundle of nerves, Amy's hips shot up off the table as her orgasm exploded from her core throughout her whole body, leaving a tingling sensation in its wake.

Every muscle in Amy's body seemed to spasm at once, leaving her unable to vocalize coherent words as she writhed in pleasure.

She barely registered Justin telling her to breathe as she floated, weightless, in ecstasy. It was like fireworks going off behind her closed eyelids when Justin removed her scarf.

"You still with me, Sweetheart?" Justin brushed his fingers from her temple down to her jaw, then over her neck as he asked the question, almost as if he was checking for her pulse to make sure she was still alive.

"Mmm," Amy moaned, her eyes fluttering open to look into his bright, baby blues. "I might've died and gone to Heaven."

"Watching you come like that was certainly heavenly." Justin smiled down at her.

"Now it's time for me to take you to Heaven with me." Amy pushed herself up, first on her elbows and then to a fully seated position on the edge of the table. "Is there any more of that whipped cream left?"

"A little." Justin sat back down in the chair, his dick standing at attention. He reached over to the room service cart to grab the can of whipped cream, eating her up with his eyes as if trying to decide where to eat it off her next. "Where do you want me to squirt it, Sweetheart?"

"All over your cock," Amy replied, placing her feet on the floor before lowering to her knees between his spread legs. "It's time for me to eat my dessert now."

"As you wish, Sweetheart." Justin shook the can before drawing a line of whipped cream up the underside of his erection from his balls to circle over the bulbous head, covering the precum leaking from the slit.

Amy bent down, tilting her head to the side, so she could follow the same path he had. She swirled her tongue over his balls first, glad he manscaped so there weren't any long pubic hairs mixed in with her creamy dessert. Then she flattened her tongue to lick up the line of whipped cream over the main vein of his dick. She pulled back just before hitting that sensitive spot where the shaft met the head, so she could swallow the whipped cream she'd already laved off him.

"Fuck, that feels good," Justin growled, one hand squeezing the can of whipped cream and the other squeezing the arm of the chair.

Amy extended her tongue, lightly lapping up the cream on his frenulum and enjoying the way his cock twitched each time she applied just the tiniest amount of pressure on the super-sensitive spot.

"Fuck, fuck, fuck!" Justin's hips bucked as she teased him.

It was a heady feeling being the one pushing him to the edge of his control, but Amy reveled in it for only a moment. She didn't want to tease him too much before ending the erotic torture. She opened her mouth wide, closing her lips over the ridge where his head met his shaft and sucking hard to swallow the whipped cream mixed with his salty precum.

Justin dropped the can of whipped cream, his hands both coming to the back of her head as he groaned in pleasure. He didn't grip her hair hard or try to take control of her movements, just weaved his fingers through her hair, like he just needed the contact to ground him as she gave him the ultimate pleasure.

Yum! Amy thought as she swirled her tongue over him to make sure she completely cleaned him off. *The perfect salty-sweet snack.*

Amy kept her eyes open and locked on his as she bobbed up and down his length. She sucked him as far back in her throat as she could without triggering her gag reflex before hollowing her cheeks and increasing the suction as she pulled back to where only his head was still in her mouth.

Justin alternated between praising her for her blow job skills, complimenting her beauty, and saying, "I love you," as she continued to suck his cock. She cupped his balls with one hand while stroking the base of his dick that wouldn't fit in her mouth with the other.

Just as Amy felt his balls draw up in her hand, signaling he was about to come, Justin released her hair and moved his hands under her arms to lift her off of him. "Fuck, Sweetheart, as amazing as your mouth feels, I wanna be in your pussy when I come."

He sat her on the table before retrieving a condom and quickly sheathing himself. He stood between her spread thighs, kissing her passionately while lining his cock up with her opening.

Amy tasted the mixture of their arousal and the sweet, whipped cream as their tongues tangled. He gripped her hips as he slowly pushed into her. When he bottomed out inside her, Justin broke the kiss to remind her to breathe.

He trailed open-mouthed kisses down her neck to her chest as he increased the pace of his thrusts. Amy dug her fingers into his scalp, guiding his mouth to her nipples as she relished their passionate coupling. With his mouth otherwise occupied by suckling her breasts, Amy took over the whispered praise and sweet nothings, chanting "I love you, Justin" repeatedly as she flew over the edge once more.

Justin pushed in as deep as he could, his dick feeling like it was swelling inside her as he held her hips still. His back arched as he released her breast, shouting out his orgasm as he came, pushing her to her third climax of the evening.

Amy wrapped her arms around Justin's shoulders, clinging to him with her head resting on his chest. She listened to the steady thrum of his heartbeat as they each caught their breath. Justin lifted her from the table, his cock still inside her, before she'd fully recovered.

"What're you doing?" Amy wrapped her legs around his waist, so it was easier for him to carry her out of the sitting room.

"Figured now that I've got you good and dirty, it's time to clean you up." Justin confidently strode through the bedroom and into the bathroom. He sat her down on the smooth marble bench in the shower before stepping back out to dispose of the condom.

"Grab my shower cap while you're out there." Amy stood to get out of the spray of the water as she turned it on to set the temperature.

"Yeah, um, about that." Justin looked at her sheepishly as he stepped back into the shower without her shower cap in his hand. Though she did notice he had a couple condom packages with him that he placed on the ledge beside her shampoo. "We're gonna hafta wash your hair today instead of tomorrow."

"Why?" Amy didn't understand why she couldn't go through her normal routine the next day since they weren't scheduled to go to her father's house until noon.

"Because I don't think you wanna sleep with whipped cream in your hair," Justin replied, pointing to a spot just above her forehead while failing to stifle his chuckle.

Amy turned to stick her head out of the shower and looked at herself in the mirror to see a white splotch reminiscent of the cum used as hair gel scene in the movie ***There's Something About Mary***. Amy couldn't contain her giggle as she turned back to Justin.

"I guess we should limit food play to Saturday morning sex from now on." She continued giggling as she stepped closer to the spray of the water to double-check the temperature.

"Mmm, who needs pancakes, waffles, or French toast when I can lick syrup off you for breakfast?" Justin pulled her into his arms and spun her around under the rainfall shower that was, thankfully, not too hot or too cold.

"Surely, you can be more creative than just syrup for breakfast food play, Boss." Amy ran her palms over Justin's biceps before sliding them over his shoulders. Amy loved the feel of Justin's body. Though he was lean and nowhere near as bulky as some of the other men in his family, his muscles were solid from the time he spent working with the horses on the ranch.

"Don't worry, Sweetheart." Justin bent his head to lightly brush his lips over hers, their breath mingling as he continued speaking. "I'm not just thinking about maple syrup. I've got several flavors in mind, a few jellies, maybe even a little cinnamon, and powdered sugar. Oh, and we'll hafta ask Kara for her donut glaze recipe, too."

Before Amy could protest asking their friend for restaurant recipes, Justin sucked her lower lip into his mouth, giving it a little nibble before tangling their tongues. His erection pressed into her belly, and she couldn't believe he was already able to go again.

All thoughts of future food play flew from her mind, along with all her worries, as she focused solely on the man in her arms and how he made her feel. Amy loved Justin more than she'd ever dreamed she could possibly love another. And when she was with him, it was like nothing and nobody else existed in the world. Just the two of them, connecting in a soul-deep manner, as two truly joined as one.

~ ~ ~

Saturday, March 23, 2019

Amy was nervous as she and Justin left their hotel to go meet her biological father and his side of her family. She wasn't sure why she was so anxious, considering she'd talked to her dad daily since the night she first contacted him over a week before. But it was the first time they would actually see each other in person, so Amy assumed that was the cause for her anxiety.

Maybe this wouldn't be so difficult if we were meeting up somewhere public? Amy wondered, second-guessing the plan to have their first meeting be for a backyard barbeque at her father's home. *This kinda feels like I'm going into enemy territory. Or trying to push myself into their family unit when I don't really belong there.*

"Breathe, Sweetheart." Justin gave her hand a reassuring squeeze as he drove through the gate leading into the upper-class neighborhood where her father lived. "You already know you're gonna get along just fine with all of them from the long phone calls and group texts this last week. There's nothing to be nervous about."

"I know," Amy replied, returning the comforting squeeze of his hand. "But it's the first time I'm gonna actually see what he looks like, the first time he's gonna see what I look like, so I can't help but worry we won't see anything of ourselves in each other."

"Yeah, I still don't understand why you haven't exchanged pictures, or at least friended each other on social media to see pictures of each other." Justin arched an eyebrow in a questioning manner as he turned into the driveway of an elegant brick home.

"Because we wanted to see each other for the first time in person, not on a phone or computer." Amy answered his statement as if it was a question, feeling silly for having that idea in the first place. She was still surprised she'd gotten Ashlyn to go along with it, much less the rest of her newfound family members.

After Justin parked, he came around to help her down from the passenger seat of his truck. Instead of taking her hand like he usually did, Justin crowded into her space, pulling her in for a hug and pressing his lips to hers for a brief kiss first.

"What was that for?" Amy questioned when he released her and reached for her hand like normal.

"Figured you needed a moment to get outta your own head and quit worrying, Sweetheart," Justin smirked. "And just 'cause I couldn't keep my lips off yours for a second longer."

"You really are good at taking my mind off things." Amy giggled as they walked up to the front door hand in hand.

She barely had a chance to reach out and ring the doorbell before the door was opening. They were greeted by a man in his late forties, who stood about six feet tall with sandy-brown hair and hazel eyes. They stood there just staring at each other for several long moments.

My dad looks more like Justin than me, Amy thought momentarily before looking deeper than just hair, skin, and eye color. Then she noticed her facial shape was obviously from her father, more oval than her mother's heart-shaped face. She also inherited her lip shape from her father. Where her mother's lips were both fuller, Amy, Ashlyn, and their father each had a fuller bottom lip with a thinner top lip.

"Amy?" He quavered at the same time Amy choked out, "Dad?"

"Yes," they chimed in unison. Then they chuckled at their similar timing before her father turned to look at Justin. "And you must be Justin."

"Yes, sir." Justin extended his hand to shake her father's.

Amy felt awkward and wondered if she should've shaken her father's hand, too, instead of just staring at him. When the men released their handshake, Amy started to extend her hand to her father, but she stopped when he spoke.

"If it's okay, I'd really like to hug my daughter for the first time." David's eyes were welling up with tears as he opened his arms for her to step into his embrace.

"That's more than okay." Amy stepped closer and threw her arms around her father for the first time in her life. It was such a poignant moment that Amy couldn't contain the tears streaking down her face.

They hugged each other tightly, both of them crying for all the years they'd missed being a part of each other's lives. Justin stepped back, leaning against the brick half-wall surrounding the porch to give them their father-daughter moment.

"David, was that not them?" McKenna called out, breaking their solemn moment.

"Yes, it's them." David released Amy from the embrace to turn in the direction of his wife's voice and wiped his eyes on the sleeve of his polo shirt.

"Well, don't make them spend the whole day on the porch." McKenna's voice was coming nearer as she spoke, alerting Amy that she was walking down the hall toward the door. "Let them in so we can all meet them."

"I was about to, Kenni." David shook his head at his wife. "But I had to hug my daughter first."

Amy giggled as she wiped her tears with her fingers before Justin stepped up and finished the job for her. She was so glad he was there with her, especially since he seemed to innately know when to step back and when to be right there for her.

Justin took her hand in his as they turned to look back at her father, who was still standing in the doorway.

"Sorry, please come in." Her father stepped back to allow them entry into his home.

That was the first moment Amy caught a glimpse of McKenna and, apparently, the first moment McKenna caught a glimpse of Amy.

"You're Black," McKenna gasped.

David glared at his wife, obviously unsure how to handle the situation.

Amy was shocked at the exclamation and stopped in her tracks just inside the door. *What the hell? Did he not tell her that he'd dated a Black woman before her? Did Ricky not compare our racial breakdown on Ancestry to figure that out, if dear old dad didn't tell them in advance? And how the hell am I supposed to respond to finding out my father's wife is apparently a racist?*

Sarcasm, Sis, Amy imagined hearing her sister, Ashlyn, saying in her head. *It always works for me.*

"Really? I hadn't noticed," Amy quipped, channeling her sister's sarcastic tendency as she looked down at her arm beside Justin's. Then she looked up at Justin and smirked. "Did you realize I'm Black and not lily-white like you?"

"Hey, don't lump me into the lily-white category." Justin raised his free hand in surrender and feigned being insulted. "I'm one percent African, too, ya know."

Amy almost laughed at Justin's response, but she somehow managed to keep a straight face as she tried to think of a witty retort.

"I'm sorry," McKenna apologized before Amy could come up with anything else to say. "I didn't mean that as a bad thing. I was just surprised is all. Please, come in and I'll try to keep my foot outta my mouth for the rest of your visit."

Amy looked at Justin while trying to decide if spending the day with her father and half-siblings was worth possibly being uncomfortable with McKenna being there, too.

"Entirely up to you, Sweetheart." Justin smiled at her when she looked up at him to help her decide what to do, apparently reading her mind.

Lord, can this man be any more perfect? He's willing to go if I want, or stay if I want, even knowing this could totally turn into a complete clusterfuck. He's here to back me up, no matter which way I choose to go. He's totally the rock I can lean on to give me the strength to make any decision I ever have to make in life.

"Please, Amy, don't go," her father pleaded. "This is my fault. I should've reminded McKenna of what I told her about my dating history back when we first started dating. But it was over twenty years ago that I told her I'd mostly dated African American women before we met, so I can see how it would've easily slipped her mind."

"Yes, please stay," McKenna practically begged, an earnest look in her eyes. "He did tell me that way back when we'd only been dating for a few weeks. I just put it outta my head because I didn't like to think of him dating anyone but me back then. And when we found out about you last week, it never even crossed my mind to ask about your mother's race because it didn't matter. You're his daughter. That's all that matters. Please don't let my shock at seeing such a beautiful, African American woman when I expected someone as pasty-white as my husband, be the reason you don't wanna stay and get to know your family."

Amy assessed her stepmother, then looked to her father, who looked hurt at the thought of her leaving. McKenna certainly did seem apologetic for her misspoken words. And even though she barely knew him, Amy couldn't leave and be the reason for the hurt look in her dad's eyes.

"Of course, we're staying." Amy smiled and hoped to defuse the situation with a little levity. "After all, it's not really a family get-together without the black sheep of the family showing up. Though you really should've expected the black sheep to actually be Black."

Her father smiled then. "You're not the black sheep, Amy. And technically, you're only half Black."

"Actually, I'm only thirty-five percent Black. Apparently, I got some of my European heritage from Mom, too."

Leah Mae Wright

"You and Ricky should compare notes on what you found on that site." David led them through the house to the backyard, where her half-siblings were waiting.

Amy wasn't sure what kind of lawn game they were setting up, but she was glad she'd opted to wear her casual khaki capris and sneakers instead of the dress she'd originally thought to wear the first time she met her father, so she was prepared to learn.

Time to find out what all I missed out on by not being a part of this family when I was a kid.

~~~

Justin was truly having a good time getting to know Amy's newfound family. After the initial awkwardness with McKenna, the rest of the day seemed to be going off without a hitch.

None of her half-siblings said a word about their racial differences. They all welcomed her into the fold as if they'd known and loved her all their lives. Hell, Justin even felt welcomed as if he was another brother.

They laughed and joked around and generally had a good time learning to play croquet. Kayley got the same adorable look on her face that Amy got whenever she got irritated, pointing out that with Justin along the guys still outnumbered the girls and made it hard to divide into teams for the games.

"It won't be next time." Amy tried to placate her little sister. "When Ashlyn gets moved down here, we'll easily beat the boys at everything."

"How 'bout I go help your dad with the grill while ya'll play brothers versus sisters?" Justin pointed over his shoulder to where David was starting the grill, having left the lawn and creating the uneven number of players.

"You actually know how to grill?" Amy looked at him quizzically, like she wasn't sure he knew any more about grilling than he did about operating an oven or doing laundry.

"Oh, Sweetheart, I may not know much about household appliances," Justin drawled, grinning at her as he walked backwards
~~~

toward the patio. "But it's impossible to grow up on the Burleson Ranch and not learn how to throw a slab of beef on the grill."

"Wait, you're one of the Burleson Beef Burlesons?" DJ looked at Justin with a confused expression on his face. "I thought you were one of the Burleson Oil Burlesons, and I was gonna ask you about internship possibilities when I get to my last semester of my MBA."

"Actually, I'm both," Justin shrugged. "Burleson Oil, which is now Burleson Energy, and Burleson Beef are just two divisions of Burleson Incorporated."

"Wow, okay." DJ looked slightly embarrassed. "Guess I should've done a little more company research before asking about an internship."

"Naw, you're still in the early stages yet, so it's not expected that you'd have done a ton of research on my family business before meeting me at a backyard barbeque." Justin wanted to reassure the younger man. "But when you get ready to actually apply for an internship, let me know. I'll give you my sister Jen's number. She's in charge of human resources and will be the one you need to impress with your company knowledge."

"Thanks, Justin." DJ's lips barely lifted in the slightest smile as he gave Justin a chin lift of gratitude. "I appreciate that, but I'd rather just have the information on how to apply like everyone else. Dad's already said he could get me an internship where he works, but I'd rather earn it on my own, ya know. Not just get it handed to me because of who my dad is or who my sister's dating."

Justin had a whole new sense of respect for Amy's younger brother. Even though he'd spent his summers throughout high school and college working in more entry level positions in the family business, he'd always felt a little guilty for just walking into his vice-presidential role at Burleson Incorporated right out of school, so he understood DJ's feelings about not wanting to be given a job he hadn't earned on his own merit.

"Understood." Justin lifted his chin to DJ in the same way the younger man had just done. "But you'll still hafta ask Jen, 'cause that's not my department. I just won't tell her to be expecting your call, so there's no possibility of favoritism being shown when you apply."

Leah Mae Wright

With that, Justin turned and walked the rest of the way to the patio where David was manning the grill. "Anything I can help with?" Justin nodded toward the grill, where David had a dozen burgers spread out to cook.

"Looks like you've already helped more than you know." David dipped his head in the direction of his children, who were actively debating who should take the first turn.

Did he hear my conversation with DJ from all the way over here? Or is he talking about helping Amy find out about him? Or letting her make the decision about whether or not we stayed earlier? Justin raised an eyebrow inquisitively instead of asking any of those questions.

"It seems I have a lot to thank you for," David stated in response to Justin's unasked questions. "Not just for helping Amy connect with our family, or what you just said to DJ."

Justin didn't quite know how to respond. He hadn't done anything all that remarkable. He was just following his natural instincts. Neither of the two things David mentioned being thankful for were things he wouldn't have done for anyone else. But he couldn't really reject the man's gratitude without coming off as a prick, so he just stood there silently waiting for David to change the subject.

"I may have only recently connected with my oldest daughters," David confided, his voice low like he was trying to keep anyone else from hearing their conversation. "But in the discussions I've had with Amy and Ashlyn in the last week or so, I've come to realize that we wouldn't be seeing the more outgoing side of Amy's personality if it weren't for you."

"I don't know about that." Justin shook his head to show his disagreement, not believing he had that much of an impact on Amy's personality. "Amy only seems to be really shy when she first meets people. Once she gets to know them, she's more comfortable being herself. So, I don't really think I've had any kinda influence on how she interacts with ya'll."

"You may not see it because you're around her every day." David turned his back to Justin, so he could flip the burgers. "But I've been watching her closely all day, wanting to remember everything about my first time meeting my daughter, and I've seen the way she looks to you before making a decision. And you've shown me that you're a good man, who will respect her decisions in life, even when they aren't what you'd choose if you were in her shoes."

Justin shifted uncomfortably, glad David was focused on flipping the burgers and not looking at him as he continued speaking.

"But even though you aren't making the decisions for her, she looks to you for the courage to make them. Just knowing you're there for her, no matter what, gives her the strength to say and do the things she might not be brave enough to say or do on her own."

Justin took a moment to really let David's words sink in. *Do I really give her strength and courage that she doesn't possess on her own? No, she's definitely strong and courageous on her own. But maybe knowing I have her back, no matter what, helps reassure her to believe in herself enough to act on her inner strength. Yeah, that's gotta be it. She's too independent to need me to provide her strength and courage. I just help bolster her confidence to be herself with the rest of the world.*

"I think you're good for her," David concluded, bringing Justin back out of his own head.

"Thank you, sir," Justin replied. "She's good for me, too. Makes me wanna be a better man to be worthy of her."

"I guess I should be asking what your intentions are with my oldest daughter then." David turned back to face Justin and glared like any overprotective father should at his daughter's boyfriend.

If it was anyone else asking Justin's intentions, he'd probably feel uncomfortable answering honestly. Had any of the fathers of the girls he'd dated before Amy asked that question, they'd have hated hearing he was only interested in a good time for a little while. But Amy was different. Or rather, Justin's intentions with Amy were different than with anyone he'd dated before. So, he could proudly answer David with honesty.

"I love Amy more than anyone or anything else on earth." Justin smiled at her father. "And I fully intend to marry her, raise a family with her, and spend the rest of my life doing everything I possibly can to make her happy."

"Damn, I can't very well run off a good man with love and intentions like that," David chuckled, shaking his head and smiling. "Guess I'll have to save the shotgun for whoever comes around trying to date Ashlyn and Kayley."

"Feel free to bring them to the ranch if you need any backup to help run off the lowlifes," Justin chuckled.

"Deal." David extended his hand. Justin reached out and shook it. "Welcome to the family, son. You be sure to let me know when you're ready for that proposal. If you don't already have something picked out, I'd love to pass down my mother's engagement ring to Amy."

"Wow, thank you." Justin was exceptionally touched by David's gesture. "I, I don't have anything picked out," he stuttered, running his hand through his hair after releasing their handshake. "And I'd be honored to ask her with your mother's ring. I'm sure Amy will love it even more than anything I could pick out, especially knowing where it comes from."

"Do I need to get it for you now? Or do I have time to take it to be cleaned and polished for you before you pop the question?"

"Considering she's not even ready to tell my family we're dating," Justin chuckled. "I think you have plenty of time to have it cleaned and polished."

"Why won't she tell your family you're dating?" David raised a quizzical eyebrow. "Will they not accept her for some reason?"

"No, no, nothing like that." Justin raised his hands, palms out, to punctuate his statement. "My mom and aunt have actually been trying to fix us up since we first met back in November. But we've fooled them into believing we're just friends, so they don't get too full of themselves with how successful they are at matchmaking."

"I take it your mom and aunt do that often." Justin nodded in agreement with David's assumption. "So, have they been successful with more than just you and Amy?"

"I'd say they're less successful than they'd take credit for, but they did fix up my cousin Bobby with his fiancée, Brooklyn."

"You talking about the Matchmaking Mommas?" Amy surprised Justin as she walked up, making him wonder how much of the conversation she'd overheard.

"Yeah, I was just telling your dad that if he makes a trip to Heart's Destiny anytime soon," Justin fibbed, throwing an arm around her shoulders, and kissing the top of her head. "Not to mention us being anything but friends."

"I don't understand why you don't want them to know they're right in pairing up the two of you."

"Because they've stepped up their matchmaking for everyone in town since my cousin Anthony got married in November," Justin explained as David removed the burgers from the grill and the rest of the family joined them at the table to start making plates. "And they're driving my cousins, siblings, and I crazy with their scheming."

"So, being successful with matching up Anthony has turned them into matchmaking monsters?" McKenna mused aloud.

"Oh, no, they didn't have anything to do with Anthony and Kay getting together." Amy giggled lightly as she shook her head. "They met in Tulsa and fell in love at first sight."

"But when Anthony brought Kay and her daughters to Texas to keep them safe from her abusive ex," Justin continued the story Amy started. "Aunt Hazel started planning their wedding just a couple weeks after they met. And she claimed credit for getting them together when they were married, and Anthony had adopted Kay's daughters within two months of when they met."

"The Matchmaking Mommas also claimed credit for Randi and James getting together, too, even though they also met and fell in love at first sight in Tulsa on the same night as Kay and Anthony." Amy went on to explain how her best friend and former roommate virtually dated James from September to November, when they finally saw each other in person again once they were all in Heart's Destiny for Anthony and Kay's wedding. She also listed out all the other couples they tried to match up the week of the wedding.

"So, let me get this straight in my head." David used his fingers to reference people so he could match them up correctly. "Your best friend's sister married Justin's cousin?"

"Yes, Kay and Anthony," Amy replied, nodding her head to show he was right so far.

"And your best friend met Anthony's best friend the same night and started dating him on the computer, but the matchmakers are claiming credit for getting them together because they were paired up together for the wedding and all the events leading up to it."

"Yes, that's Randi and James," Amy confirmed once again.

"That same week they were pairing the two of you up." David pointed back and forth between Justin and Amy.

"Not just that week, but at every event in town since Amy moved down, too," Justin interjected.

"They also matched up your siblings and cousins with wedding guests from outta town?"

"Well, the girls anyway, since most of the out-of-town guests were male," Justin elaborated. "And since the woman my brother is interested in was also a bridesmaid, they tried to make JJ jealous by pushing her towards James's twin brother, who was the other groomsman. Then when they realized that strategy backfired, they went back to just trying to match up couples at Christmas and every birthday party and church potluck ever since."

"And that's how they matched up your other cousin?" David questioned Justin.

"No, actually Aunt Hazel hired Brooklyn to help clean all the houses on the ranch and moved her into Bobby's house." Justin chuckled at the memory. "But that was back when we all thought she was Brie."

"Wait," DJ interjected. "Who's Brie?"

"Brie and Brooklyn are the same person," Amy explained. "She's Bobby's fiancée."

"Oh my gosh!" McKenna exclaimed. "Are you talking about Brooklyn Barns?"

Justin and Amy nodded in unison.

"I read about her," McKenna practically shouted. "She's the heiress from Georgia who disappeared back on Thanksgiving and then turned up in Texas after running away from her crazy father, who was trying to marry her off to one of his cronies."

"Didn't her dad just go on trial for that huge embezzlement case?" DJ queried.

"Yeah," Justin confirmed. "Bobby and Brook have had to go back to Georgia a couple times to appear in court. How'd you know about that and not who she was?"

"One of my professors mentioned it," DJ clarified between bites of his burger. "He was trying to figure out how he could be charged with embezzlement when he was the sole owner of the company and could legally take a draw from his owner's equity account."

"But Bradley Barns wasn't the owner of Ashbury Enterprises." Justin shook his head. "He was the trustee of the Ashbury estate and given the CEO position at Ashbury Enterprises until Brooklyn met the conditions of her mother's will to inherit everything. And he wasn't just embezzling from the company, he was also stealing the monthly stipend Brook was supposed to receive to cover her living expenses."

"Ah, well, that explains how they were able to convict him." DJ nodded his head. "So, I guess Brooklyn owns it all now. Damn, between Ashbury Enterprises and Burleson Incorporated, their kids are gonna be set for life."

"Actually, Brooklyn sold Ashbury to Burleson." Justin grinned, enjoying educating the kid on the family business. "She wanted to make sure all her kids and their cousins could share the wealth."

"Brooklyn is much happier being an author," Amy elaborated, reaching over to squeeze Justin's hand. "Than she ever would've been trying to run a company."

"So, back to the whole matchmaking thing." David brought their conversation back to the original topic. "Bobby and Brooklyn are the only couple your mom and aunt can actually take credit for pushing together besides the two of you?"

"Yes, but they're working really hard with some of their friends to make more matches," Justin confirmed after taking his last bite of the delicious burger. "Especially with my cousin Charlotte and the guy who just started teaching English with her at the middle school in January."

"And the bridesmaids and groomsmen who're being paired up in Brooklyn and Bobby's wedding in a couple weeks," Amy added. "So, we don't wanna give them any more success stories to give them the confidence to do more than making people sit together at birthday parties and wedding showers. At least until we can get through James and Randi's wedding on the first of June."

Thank fuck! She just gave me a deadline for when we can stop hiding that we're dating!

Chapter Thirteen

Wednesday, March 27, 2019

Justin hated that Amy wasn't with him as he walked into the conference room for the first board meeting after adding all the Avington cousins to the board of directors at Burleson Incorporated. It seemed only fitting that she should be with him as he got to know his newfound relatives the same way he was by her side the previous weekend when she met her biological father and half-siblings. But since she still wasn't ready to let everyone know they were dating, he knew he couldn't ask her to accompany him to any of the family dinners they were planning while their cousins were in town, much less the board meeting that even his mom didn't normally attend.

As he took a seat between his brother, JJ, and his cousin, Jake, Justin noticed that Kay and Brooklyn were both in attendance, which was rather unusual. *If Anthony and Bobby get to bring their women, I should really be able to bring Amy.* Justin shook off the jealous thoughts, knowing he was being petty, since his situation with Amy wasn't the same as his cousins bringing their wives. *Wanting her to be my wife doesn't count the same, especially since I know she's nowhere near ready to take that step with me. Hell, if I can't even convince her to let everyone know we're dating, it'll be a long fucking time before I can convince her to marry me.*

Justin knew the majority of his irritated mood was the fact that he was missing Amy, and not animosity toward his cousins for having their happily ever afters already. He'd gotten so used to being at her side twenty-four-seven the previous two weeks, that him having to go home without her, once she got a clean bill of health from the doctor the previous Friday, was one of the hardest things he'd ever had to do in his life. He was thankful for having two extra nights with her at the

382

hotel in Houston, but sleeping alone since Sunday was starting to wear on him.

Or rather not sleeping when he was at home in bed alone. He tossed and turned and couldn't get comfortable to go to sleep without Amy in his arms. *We're gonna hafta let everyone know we're together soon, or I'm gonna be a zombie trying to work on no sleep from not being with her every night.*

As his dad called the meeting to order, Justin tried to tune back in to what was going on around him. Introductions were made for anyone who hadn't been to the family dinner they had the night before to welcome the Avingtons to town. While they were specifically for Josh and Jake, who'd just arrived in town that morning, Justin was glad to get a refresher of who was who in the Avington family.

"Wow, ya'll are as bad with the B-names as we are with the J-names." Josh chuckled after being introduced to Byron, Barrett, Blaine, Brady, and Blake.

"Hey, we don't all have J-names," Becky objected.

"No, but six outta ten for our generation definitely makes it the most popular first initial in our family," Josh replied, shaking his head. "I just thought it was funny that it was a similarity among our family to pick a letter like that and stick to it."

"Yet another reason for me to veto the name Jimi Hendrix Burleson for this little one." Kay rubbed her hand over her baby bump as she looked at Anthony.

"Then I'll hafta veto Braden." Anthony shrugged. "So we don't steal a name one of our cousins might want for their kids to keep up the B-name tradition."

"As much as I'd love to know what ya'll are gonna name my first nephew, I don't think we have time for ya'll to figure it out right now." Jake smirked across the table at his brother and sister-in-law.

"Yes, we do need to get this meeting started," Justin's dad, Jon, declared before getting them started with reports from the various division heads.

After Julie told them all about how things were transitioning with a couple companies they'd acquired since the last board meeting in December, JJ reported on the increased energy production that quarter from the various wind and solar farms they'd brought online following the environmental cleanup of former oil well sites.

"In addition to increased revenue from wind and solar energy production, we expect to have our new methanol production facility fully operational within the next month, so sales of the new product can be scheduled for the beginning of May," JJ bragged, completing his report.

"I actually need to pass along an idea for a brand name for our manure-based methanol." Justin smiled at the memory of Amy giving him the name. "Moothanol."

"Moothanol?" His dad raised an eyebrow as he questioned the suggestion. "Where on earth did you come up with that idea?"

"Amy actually gave me the idea when I was showing her the quality control lab at the new facility." Justin was unable to stop himself from smiling as he said her name. "She also suggested sponsoring a monster truck made up to look like one of the cows on the ranch to promote it."

"That's actually a pretty clever idea." Jen grinned at him.

"Who's Amy?" Barrett Avington questioned.

"Our lab manager," Justin replied. *And my girlfriend, so back the fuck off, Cuz.*

"And the girl Justin's pining over, so don't even think about asking her out," Bobby added, giving their new cousins the warning Justin couldn't without breaking his word to Amy that he wouldn't tell his family about them dating.

"Wouldn't dream of it." Barrett held both his hands up in surrender. "I was just wondering who she was to try to figure out why she couldn't give her suggestions straight to the marketing department."

"Amy's had a lot going on the past couple months," Jen informed their newfound cousins. "Now that life's calming down some, I'm sure she'll be able to send them an email with her suggestions."

"Speaking of the issues Amy's had to deal with since starting to work here," Jon segued the discussion, turning to look at Justin and Jake where they were seated side by side. "What's the latest on the lab tech we had to let go?"

"She's still sitting in jail awaiting trial," Jake answered.

"And luckily, she hadn't contaminated any of the other supplies in the lab," Justin continued for his cousin. "So everyone else was able to get back to work within a week of her arrest."

"And the other issues you found on the security footage have been resolved?" Byron Avington queried.

"Yes," Justin replied, nodding his head.

"I actually spent the week, when they weren't able to run experiments, assisting Amy in retraining everyone in the lab on the rules and regulations of their jobs." Jen smiled at the oldest Avington cousin. "Though, it probably wouldn't hurt to keep up some spot checks on those cameras to make sure they all listened."

"Yeah, I'm still remotely checking those each day," Jake admitted.

"And I made sure they all know that if I catch anyone horsing around in the lab or playing phone games when they're supposed to be working, they'll be next in line to lose their job, just like Tara," Justin added.

"Maybe not just like Tara," Jen giggled. "I mean, we can't exactly have them arrested for playing phone games."

"You know what I mean." Justin shook his head at his sister. "They've been warned, and the written reprimands are in each offender's HR file, so if they're caught not paying attention to active experiments while playing on their phones, they all know they won't have a job anymore."

"Very well." Justin's dad put an end to the lab discussion. "Now, what've we got going on in the entertainment division?"

"Actually, that's why Kay and Brook are here today." Becky pointed to her sisters-in-law. "They came to me with a suggestion about content for the streaming service we want to develop. And the more I look at the costs for acquiring outside content, and the vast number of other streaming services that already carry the same content we'd only be able to purchase limited rights to carry, the more I agree with them that we need to produce our own original movies to set us apart from the competition."

"So, you wanna produce movies as well as the theatre productions you've been focused on?" Becky's dad, Bob, inquired. Justin was surprised that Becky hadn't already informed her father of her intention to add movie production to the entertainment division, since she'd mentioned it to Amy's sister back when she was in town and looking at job opportunities at Burleson Incorporated a month before.

"Yes," Becky answered, smiling at her dad. "Starting with adapting Brook and Kay's books into movies we'll release in theaters all across the country, until we have enough content to fill a streaming service."

"This seems like a rather expensive endeavor that won't have any return on investment for at least a few years with trying to make enough content to fill a streaming service." Byron's blank expression matched his words, indicating he wasn't supportive of the idea.

"Yes, that's why we wanna release the movies to theaters at first." Becky's smile and positive attitude never faltered as she explained her thought process. "We'll make back our production costs with box office sales and the streaming service will be almost a hundred percent profit when we finally roll it out. I have a PowerPoint breaking down all the numbers to show this option is, in fact, much more profitable than purchasing the rights to share other people's content and competing with a dozen other streaming services, some of which are free to the consumer."

"Please, set that up to show us." Jon motioned for Becky to hook her laptop up to the SmartScreen on the back wall of the conference room.

"Just how many books do you have ready to be made into movies?" Blaine Avington asked.

"I have five out so far," Brooklyn replied.

"I only have one published," Kay professed, her lips turning up in a half-smile. "But I already have a dozen more plotted out that I just need to finish writing."

"Same here." Brooklyn backed up her soon-to-be sister-in-law, also smiling. "And we both know other indie authors, who would love to have their books made into movies as well."

"But we'll have to buy the production rights for books by other authors." Byron scowled, obviously not liking the idea of adding a production company to their entertainment division. "Which brings us back to the same problem with spending a fortune on the rights to content that could be sold to other streaming services as well as ours."

"Technically, we have to buy the production rights to Kay and Brook's books, too." Charlotte stood up for her sisters-in-law to be paid what they'd earned by writing the original content for the movies.

"And production rights are different than distribution rights." Becky pointed to the slideshow she'd started. She skipped forward a few pages in her PowerPoint to one outlining the differences. "When we buy the production rights to a book, the author can't sell those same production rights to another movie producer for the specified term of the contract with us. And as the production company for the movie, we have full distribution rights for that movie. But if we buy distribution rights to movies made by other production companies, they don't have to be exclusive in who they allow to stream their movies."

"So, the authors won't have the right to distribute the movies we make from their books elsewhere?" Byron looked pensive as he posed the question.

"No, because the movie is actually our product that we've made," Becky answered. "The production rights contracts I've looked over do have a provision for the authors to earn residuals from the sales of the movies made from their work, but they have no say in how we distribute our work product."

As Becky closed out of the slideshow option for displaying the PowerPoint to be able to go back to the beginning of the presentation, Justin noticed the time at the bottom of the screen. *Shit, I'm gonna miss having lunch with Amy today. I'd better message her and let her know, so she doesn't worry when I don't show up in the cafeteria.*

<div align="center">~~~</div>

As Amy was shutting down her latest experiment to get ready to head down to the cafeteria for lunch, her tablet dinged with an intraoffice message. She finished putting away her supplies before swiping the screen to read the message.

Justin: Still in the board meeting, probably won't make lunch.

Yeah, I kinda figured that was gonna be the case when you told me the one in December lasted all day and ya'll had to order in lunch, Amy thought, smiling at how Justin took the time to notify her, just in case she hadn't realized what was going on, so she wouldn't worry about why he wasn't there for their normal lunchtime together. *Such a thoughtful man.*

She quickly typed back a reply before heading to her office to grab her phone, wanting to check her messages while she ate, just in case the doctor's office had called to schedule her for her birth control shot.

> **Amy: NP. If ya'll don't run too late & I don't have to run straight to Doc's office after work, maybe we can meet for dinner?**

> **Justin: Sounds good. Even if all that happens, I can grab a pizza & stop by on my way home.**

> **Amy: K. Have fun in your meeting.**

Amy agreed to him coming over for pizza later even though she knew he'd probably have to cancel to spend time with his new cousins that night, just like he'd had to do for the past couple nights.

Amy barely sat her tablet down and pulled her purse out of her bottom drawer when her phone buzzed inside it. She quickly pulled it out and recognized the doctor's office number flashing on her screen.

She quickly swiped to answer the call, saying "hello" as soon as the call connected.

"Hi, is this Amy Lawton?" the voice she recognized as Summer from Doctor Hayes's office inquired.

"Yes, Summer, this is Amy," Amy replied, sitting down in her desk chair to talk in the privacy of her office, instead of heading out to the cafeteria.

"Oh, goodness, you've been here too much recently if you recognize my voice over the phone." Summer laughed lightly.

"Well, I've been expecting your call." Amy chuckled with the nurse. "I'm assuming you're calling to tell me I can come in this afternoon for my birth control shot?"

"Um, well, not exactly." Summer sounded a little tentative about the news she was about to impart. "I'm actually calling to schedule you with our OB-GYN next month."

"Oh, I thought Doctor Hayes said I didn't need to see the gynecologist just to get my birth control?" Amy's words came out almost sounding like a question, though she meant them as a statement.

"Well, normally, no, you wouldn't." Summer sounded sheepish in her response.

"Oh-kay…" Amy drew the word out to three syllables. *Just spit it out already!* Amy inwardly shouted, wondering what could possibly be wrong with her latest round of bloodwork that warranted her now having to see another doctor. "Just tell me what's going on, please. Is there something wrong with my bloodwork that could be why I passed out?"

"No," Summer practically shouted. "Well, not that would've affected you as early as when you passed out. But maybe if you've had another spell."

"I haven't had another spell," Amy reassured the nurse. "But there is something wrong with my bloodwork that's making it necessary for me to see the gynecologist before I can get my shot?"

"I'm not really supposed to give you the test results over the phone." Summer's tone sounded pensive, like she was thinking about doing it anyway. "But I'm trying to schedule you with our new doctor for her services as an obstetrician more than a typical gynecologist visit."

"Ob-obstetrician?" Amy stuttered out the term, clearly sounding like a question. "Like for delivering a baby instead of just doing my yearly pap smear?"

"Yes," Summer stated matter-of-factly. "Are you available at four o'clock on Monday, April fifteenth?"

"Wait!" Amy exclaimed, closing her eyes and taking several long, deep breaths to regain her composure before asking for clarification on what she was realizing as she sat there. "I can't get my birth control shot today and need to schedule with an obstetrician because my pregnancy test on Friday came back positive?"

"As I said, I'm not allowed to give you test results over the phone." Summer took on a much more professional tone of voice than she'd ever had at the office. "But if you'd like to stop by the clinic on your way home from work, I'll have the lab report for you to pick up in a sealed envelope at the front desk."

"Summer," Amy practically growled. "I work in San Antonio and don't get off work until five, so I won't be able to get there before you close today. I'm not asking you to read me the report. Just answer one question, yes or no, so I don't toss and turn all night from freaking out about the possibilities."

"Oh-kay…" Summer drew out the word the same way Amy had earlier.

"Am I pregnant?" Amy barely whispered the question, not quite sure which answer she wanted.

"Yes," Summer squeaked out, just as quietly.

Holy shit! How is that possible? I was supposed to be covered until the seventeenth. We should've been good to go condom free on the thirteenth and fourteenth. And what the hell happened to it taking a year to become fertile again after being on the shots?

How the hell am I gonna tell Justin? Oh, Gawd, his family doesn't even know we're dating and now we're having a baby together. Does he even want kids this early? I know he wants them eventually, but he seemed to be talking about a long time in the future before even discussing starting a family.

Will he be pissed? Think I got pregnant on purpose to try to trap him? Shit, he's gonna think I'm a gold digger, trying to get a chunk of that Burleson bank. Hell, even if he doesn't think that personally, I'm sure there'll be rumors like that around town, and here at work, especially.

"Amy, are you still there?" Summer's worried tone brought Amy back out of her head to realize she was still sitting there holding her phone to her ear.

"Yes, I'm still here." Amy shook away her negative thinking and pulled up the calendar app on her tablet. "Monday, April fifteenth, you said?"

"Yes, at four p.m. if that works for you," Summer replied.

"Yes, that works for me." Amy added the appointment to her calendar. "Thanks, Summer."

"You're welcome. See you in a couple weeks." Just as Amy was about to say goodbye to the nurse, Summer spoke again. "And try not to stress out too much between now and then. It's not good for you or the little one. I know it's a shock to your system to find out right now, but it's really a good surprise. It's obvious to anyone who looks at you and Justin together that you're madly in love. Ya'll are gonna be amazing parents. So, just relax and enjoy your miracle."

"Thanks, Summer." Amy took a deep breath as she tried to embrace Summer's outlook on her situation.

Amy sat at her desk for several long moments after they said their goodbyes. *I'm pregnant,* she thought, trying to really let it sink into her brain.

I'm having Justin's baby. Or maybe babies if I have twins like Mom did. Summer's right, this really is a miracle. Not only did Justin's super sperm override my birth control, but they also overcame the year I was supposed to be infertile after going off the shot. That could only happen if we're really destined to be together as a family.

Amy covered her still flat abdomen with both hands, as if she could feel the life growing inside her at that moment. *I'm not sure how bad your Daddy is gonna freak out when I tell him, but your Mommy loves you already. Now, whaddaya say we take advantage of Daddy being tied up in his board meeting for Mommy to teach you the joy of having cake for lunch?*

Amy's stomach growled at that precise moment. "I guess that's a yes," Amy laughed as she grabbed her purse, shoved her phone in it, locked her office, and went downstairs to the cafeteria.

~ ~ ~

Sunday, March 31, 2019

Amy still hadn't figured out how to tell Justin about the baby as she walked into Hazel and Bob's house for Josh and Jake's birthday party. It didn't help that she hadn't really had any time alone with Justin in the last week. Not only had he gone back to his own home after she got a clean bill of health from the doctor, but he'd also been expected to be on the ranch for quality family time every night with his new cousins coming to visit.

Amy had stopped by the clinic to pick up the lab report the morning after she got the call from Summer. She couldn't wait to read it, not even caring if taking the time to do so while sitting in the doctor's office parking lot made her late for work. And one of her biggest pet peeves was being late for anything.

Leah Mae Wright

She'd been surprised to see the report had more than just the one line saying she was pregnant. It also listed her hCG level at seventy milli-international units per milliliter, which according to the charts she'd found online indicated she was approximately three weeks pregnant. But Amy knew that wasn't possible, since she'd taken the test only two weeks after her first time having sex with Justin. She had to wonder if her levels were higher than normal because of the possibility she was having twins.

With me being a twin and Justin having three sets of twins in his family, the odds of us having twins are probably pretty high. Yeah, I definitely shouldn't tell him tonight at his twin cousins' birthday party.

I'm sure one baby will be enough to freak him out. And clueing him in on the possibility of twins too soon will only make that worse. Besides, I'd rather tell him when we're alone than when his whole family and all our friends are with us. Telling him with everyone else around will inevitably out us as more than friends.

Speaking of everyone being nearby, she looked around the room and noticed there were even more people there than had been at JJ's birthday party at the beginning of the month, which had consisted of mostly family members. In addition to several people she'd met and hung out with as part of Justin's crowd of friends, the Avingtons were all in attendance, as well as several women she didn't recognize. *I wonder if Justin's party will be this crowded next week?*

It was so overcrowded that Amy couldn't locate Justin in the mass of humanity in the dining room where almost everyone seemed to be gathered. She politely said "hello" to the people she knew as she weaved her way through the crowd to see if she could find Justin in the kitchen.

Even if he's not there, I'll at least be able to get a glass of water. If I didn't know it's too soon to have cravings, I'd swear this baby is making me crave ice water.

"Oh, Amy, it's so good to see you." Justin's mother, Susan, pulled Amy into a motherly hug. "I was so relieved when Justin told me all your tests came back normal and that fainting spell was just a fluke from the stressful situation in the lab the other week. We were all so worried about you."

"As you can see, I'm perfectly fine." Amy returned Susan's warm embrace.

"So, what're you doing out here instead of hanging out in the dining room with the rest of the party?" Susan released Amy and stepped back, so she could examine Amy's expression.

"I was just coming to get something to drink."

"Oh, we've already put the tea and soda out in the dining room," Susan replied.

"Along with all the plastic cups," Hazel added from behind Susan where they were finishing putting the candles on the cakes.

"Oh," was all Amy could come up with to say in response. *Now how am I supposed to avoid caffeine and get the ice water I'm craving?*

Quit being so damn shy and ask for what you want, Amy heard her sister, Ashlyn, shout in her head.

"I'm actually supposed to be upping my water intake and cutting caffeine since it can be dehydrating." Amy shrugged when both of the Burleson matriarchs looked at her quizzically. *Surely they can't tell by looking at me and hearing I'm avoiding caffeine that I'm pregnant. Right?* "The doctor seemed to think I was dehydrated when I fainted."

"Oh, well then definitely grab a bottle of water from the fridge then." Hazel pointed Amy in the direction of the massive appliance. Amy still couldn't believe Hazel had a restaurant-sized refrigerator in her kitchen.

"Thanks." Amy crossed the room to get her water before heading back into the chaos of the party.

This time when she entered the dining room, she easily spotted Justin standing with a couple of his Avington cousins. *Thank goodness he's not in the middle of that group of women with Jake and Josh.* Amy blocked herself from going down that jealous thought path and walked over to Justin while sipping her water.

Justin reintroduced her to Blake and Brady, who she'd met earlier in the week when they came into the lab as part of their tour of the Burleson Incorporated headquarters.

After several minutes of meaningless small talk, Amy finally voiced the question that would give her an idea of when she'd be able to have some alone time with Justin again. "So, how long are ya'll staying in town? Or are you moving here now that you're part of the Burleson board?"

"I only have a couple weeks left on my leave time." Blake shook his head. "So, I'm going back on the tenth. But with Jake and Josh trying to convince Pop to integrate Avington Security as a division of Burleson Incorporated, instead of just farming out the accounting paperwork, there's no telling where the rest of the family will end up living."

"We're all planning to go back to Georgia on the tenth as of right now," Brady replied. "Even if we end up relocating the company, we'll hafta have time there to hire more people to cover the jobs we'd normally handle before we can expand as much as they're talking about."

Justin asked questions about how they'd integrate their security company, but Amy wasn't really listening to how his cousins answered. That was all corporate stuff she wasn't interested in and way outside her job description.

So, Amy excused herself from their group and meandered over to the group of women she'd enjoyed getting to know at the bowling alley a few weeks back. After hugs from Kara, Lexi, and Kayla, and updates on how they were all doing, Amy asked who the women at the party she didn't know were.

"That's the Thirsty Threesome." Kara rolled her eyes.

"They were cheerleaders when we were in high school," Lexi added, shaking her head. "They were always after whichever one of the Burleson boys they could get their claws into, even going so far as to offer to all three do him at once."

"And apparently, they still wanna be the bread in a Burleson beefsteak sandwich," Kayla continued the explanation, making a gagging face.

Amy giggled at how high school they were acting nearly a decade after graduating. Even though she knew she'd turn into a jealous bitch if the Thirsty Threesome were blatantly flirting with Justin the way they were with Josh, she couldn't help but laugh at how uncomfortable the badass SEAL looked, trying to escape their advances.

"We should probably go rescue Josh." Lexi grinned as she watched him fidgeting to get away from the girls.

"But it's so much fun watching him squirm," Kayla replied, giggling with Amy.

"Too bad Ashlyn's not here," Amy mused, thinking aloud. "She'd gladly save him from them, but he'd probably be in more trouble with her than he's in now."

"Your twin from the wedding shower?" Kara tilted her head inquisitively.

"Yeah, she'd offer the threesome consolation prizes from her sex toy business, and then proposition Josh to show her how long SEALs can hold their breath while muff diving." Amy slapped a hand over her mouth, surprising even herself by blurting out something Ashlyn would say if she was there.

The girls' raucous barks of laughter gained them the attention of all eyes in the room. Amy felt her cheeks heat and was glad when it seemed to only be a moment before everyone had returned to their previous conversations.

"What's so funny ladies?" Leo Walker threw an arm around both Amy and Kara as he pushed his way into their circle. "You know you can't keep all the best jokes to yourselves, so you'd better start sharing."

"Nothing." Amy shook her head, too embarrassed to repeat her words a second time.

"We were filling Amy in on the antics of the Thirsty Threesome," Lexi told him, not letting Amy off the hook.

"And Amy told us what her sister would do to rescue Josh if she was here." Kayla grinned like a loon as she explained.

"Oh, shit. Yeah, I don't wanna know," Leo whisper-shouted, shaking his head. "After meeting Ashlyn, I imagine it'd involve knocking them all over the head with a giant purple dildo."

"Something like that," Kara chortled as they all laughed once more at the mental image Leo had just given them.

Amy was laughing so hard, she had tears in her eyes, keeping her from seeing how Justin glared at Leo from across the room.

"Yo, Cuz, you might wanna let go of Justin's girl," Aiden grumbled, sticking his head between Amy and Kayla to motion with his eyes at Leo to look across the room to where Justin was standing.

"Shit, sorry," Leo shouted, raising both hands off of Amy and Kara's shoulders and holding them up in surrender. "No harm, no foul. Just a friendly gesture."

Amy removed her glasses and wiped the moisture from her eyes before she finally recognized Justin's jealous expression when she put her glasses back on. She gave him what she hoped was a reassuring smile, while secretly reveling in knowing she wasn't the only possessive one in their relationship.

"I'm surprised he's not got you glued to his side," Leo told Amy. "To stave off the threesome's advances, as well as to keep all us guys from getting too close to you."

Shit! Our jealous tendencies are gonna give us away!

"No, it's not like that. We're just friends." Amy was shocked to hear the words "just friends" said in unison with her by everyone in their small circle.

"Ya'll can keep saying you're *just friends* all you want," Kara remarked, pointing to Amy. "But we all see how the two of you look at each other when you think nobody's watching. You both wanna be more than friends, even if you're fighting it."

"You should really quit fighting the inevitable," Kayla added, nodding her agreement with Kara. "Ya'll are obviously meant for each other."

"Though, maybe you should let him sweat it out for another week," Lexi whispered, leaning in close to Amy with a mischievous gleam in her eyes. "Then give him the birthday present he really wants."

"Whaddaya think he really wants for his birthday?" Amy couldn't stop herself from posing the question.

"You," Lexi replied, smirking. "Wearing nothing but a bow."

"Ya'll are as bad as my sister." Amy shook her head and laughed with her friends. *Though, if I can get him alone to give myself to him like Lexi suggested, maybe I could take the opportunity to tell him about the baby, too. If only I was sure he'd consider our baby news a good birthday present.*

It wasn't that she really thought he'd be upset by finding out she was pregnant. It was more that she was afraid he'd think she got pregnant on purpose to trap him. She didn't want Justin, or anyone else in town, lumping her in with the gold-digging women he'd told her about having to deal with when they first talked about their dating histories.

I hope he knows me well enough to know I'm not that kind of girl, Amy thought as her friends continued talking around her. *If not, I'm probably gonna end up with a broken heart when I tell him about the baby. And that's exactly what I've spent most of my life trying to avoid.*

Yeah, I'm gonna put off telling him for as long as I can. I need to at least make a few more memories with him to carry me through the rest of my life without him.

~ ~ ~

Saturday, April 6, 2019

Justin wasn't sure what was wrong with Amy, but she hadn't been acting like herself for the last couple weeks. The fact that they were constantly being cock blocked by his family since they came back from their trip to Houston didn't help his chances at figuring it out either.

He wasn't just missing out on their dates by having to attend family dinners on a nightly basis while the Avingtons were in town. He was also missing his one-on-one lunches with Amy because of his brother, sisters, and cousins barging in to join them, regardless of whether they ate in the cafeteria or ordered in to eat in his office.

They still talked every night. But by the time Justin got home from whatever family plans he'd been stuck in all evening, Amy was too tired for the Skype sex he was trying to talk her into and kept their conversations brief.

Justin was starting to worry that she was going to break up with him before they ever admitted to his family that they'd even been dating. It was like they went from domestic bliss while dealing with the craziness at work, her health scare, and family drama, to a total dating drought once life seemed to mostly calm down. Well, at least for her. He was still dealing with evolving work and family dynamics, and he wished she could be there for him to lean on while he went through the transition.

Thank fuck, Mom and Aunt Hazel are still trying to push us together by seating us side by side at Bobby and Brooklyn's wedding reception. Maybe I can figure out how to get a few minutes alone with her for some quiet conversation, even if it has to be whispered on the dance floor.

"That was a beautiful ceremony." Amy was making small talk with his sisters and Becky, who were seated at their eight-person round table along with JJ, Dusty Deere, and Nick Martin. "And the dress was gorgeous. I really liked how Brooklyn bucked tradition by having the blue accents on her dress."

"Yeah, I was surprised she picked that dress, but it's beautiful on her," Jen agreed, smiling at Amy.

"I wonder what's taking them so long to get here from the church." JJ looked around the room at the tables of guests, who were patiently waiting for the arrival of the wedding party to start the reception. "I don't remember it taking this long between the wedding and reception when Anthony got married."

"I know they're taking pictures both at the chapel and out in the garden here." Becky also looked around for a moment before waving over to someone behind Justin. "But I know just the man to let us know how much longer it's gonna take."

Her friend, Nico, who worked with her at the Destiny Playhouse and was married to the photographer, Philippe, walked up and gave Becky air kisses on both cheeks. "You look gorgeous as usual, darling." The flamboyant theatre director complimented Becky in greeting before turning to look at the rest of the people at the table. "As do all of you lovelies. Wow, this might be the hottest table in the room." He fanned himself with his hand. "If only Philippe and I were seated here with you."

Since getting to know the gay couple in the year they'd lived in Heart's Destiny, Justin had gotten used to being lumped in as one of the *lovelies,* as Nico was fond of using the term to describe any group of attractive people, regardless of gender identity or sexual orientation.

"Speaking of your handsome husband," Becky started, grinning at their friend. "How long do you think he'll be taking pictures before we can finally get the reception started?"

"Well, since the wedding party is starting to filter in…" Nico trailed off as he pointed out where a few of the groomsmen had entered the ballroom. "I imagine he'll just take a few more pictures of the bride and groom before packing up his camera and coming in to set up for their grand entrance. Speaking of, I'm supposed to figure out where he can set up the tripod to cover most of the action. Care to join me in scoping out the room?"

"Absolutely," Becky grinned, standing and looping her arm through Nico's. She motioned around the table with her free hand as she suggested, "Go get a drink, guys. It'll take at least thirty minutes for Philippe to break down his outdoor setup and get it all put back together in here."

"Shall we?" Justin extended his hand to Amy, hoping to sneak a few minutes alone with her in one of the rooms off the ballroom while everyone else made their way to the bar.

"Let's!" Amy giggled as she placed her delicate hand in his much larger one. Justin chuckled at the way she acted as if they were extras in a Disney princess movie during the big ball scene. He played along as if he was escorting her onto the dance floor, but he quickly bypassed it, as well as the bar that now had a long line, opting to take her out a side door that led into the dining room where the Hunters served breakfast to the B and B guests.

"Where're we going?" Amy wondered as they stepped out of the ballroom.

"Someplace private," Justin replied, looking for an alcove or empty room, so he could finally get his lips on hers again.

"Oh," was all she said as he pulled her along to an empty parlor that was normally used as a conversational space for guests, but wasn't being used during the wedding reception.

As soon as they entered the space, he spun her around and pressed her back against the closed door, reaching down to flip the lock. "Fuck, I can't go two weeks without kissing you again," Justin growled, his words flowing against her lips right before he kissed her passionately.

Amy returned his fervent kiss, wrapping her arms around his neck as their tongues dueled for dominance. They made out like horny teenagers, grinding against each other in a primal mating dance that would be much better naked.

Justin slid his hands up her thighs, pushing up the soft satin of her bright yellow dress. He needed to feel her skin on skin. He palmed the globes of her ass and gave them a little squeeze before sliding his right hand down the silky string of her thong to delve his fingers through her wetness.

"Oh, Justin," Amy moaned, the soft sound going straight to his cock. Justin's dick was as hard as he'd ever remembered being, but Amy's aroused utterance of his name made him feel like he'd grown another inch.

"I need to be inside you so, fucking, bad, Sweetheart," Justin growled, lifting her leg with his left hand to wrap it around him and thrusting his erection against her pussy.

"Yes, please, Justin. I need you, too."

Just as he was about to unfasten his slacks and impale her on his cock, Justin realized he didn't have a condom on him. "Fuck," he whisper-shouted, not wanting anyone else but her to hear him. "I don't have a condom with me, but I can still take care of you, Sweetheart."

Justin released his hold on her to drop to his knees, allowing her flowy skirt to fall back down to her knees and planning to satiate her with his mouth.

"No, we don't need one." Amy grabbed his arms to pull him back upright.

"You got your birth control shot?" Justin hated that they hadn't even had enough alone time lately for her to have had the chance to tell him when she did it.

"No, not exactly." Amy dropped her hands from his arms and looked down at the floor between them. "This isn't quite how I planned to tell you this. Although, I haven't really come up with a plan for how to tell you either, so this is probably as good a chance as any."

Amy's voice was so soft that Justin almost couldn't hear her words. "When Summer called to give me the test results, she said I can't take the shot anymore for a while."

"Wait." Justin held up a hand to stop her from speaking while he tried to wrap his head around what she was saying. "They found something wrong on your last test results? Is that why you passed out? Why didn't you tell me as soon as you found out?"

"It's not anything wrong exactly," Amy mumbled. "Just that I can't take birth control because I'm already pregnant."

"Pre-pregnant?" Justin stuttered, completely shocked by her statement.

"Yes," Amy whispered, still looking down at the floor and not up at him. "I guess my last shot wore off sooner than I thought it would. If I'd've realized it was no longer effective, I never would've suggested going without condoms. I'm so sorry, Justin. I know this isn't part of our plans for right now, but I really didn't get pregnant on purpose."

Fuck! She sounds like she's about to start crying and thinks I'm pissed about having a baby with her, which is so not the case. I'm fucking elated that we're having a baby!

Justin stepped in close to Amy and tipped her chin up, so she had to look him in the eyes. He was sure he had the biggest, goofiest grin on his face when their gazes finally locked. "Don't you dare apologize, Sweetheart. This is the best thing that's ever happened in my life. The woman I love more than life itself is having my baby. *You're having my baby.*"

"You're really not upset?" Amy tilted her head and looked at him with surprise in her obsidian eyes.

"Upset? Fuck, no! I'm fucking thrilled." Justin dropped his hand from her chin, picked her up in his arms, and pressed his lips to hers. He kissed her with every ounce of love he held in his body, telling her with his kiss what he was about to tell her with words. Pulling back slightly, he continued, "I love you, Amy."

He placed her back down on her feet before dropping to his knees. Wrapping his arms around her, he kissed her belly where he assumed their unborn child was resting in her womb. "I love this baby. I'm looking forward to spending the rest of my life adoring you and our children."

"Justin Lee Burleson, don't you dare propose because I'm pregnant!" Amy arched her back and pushed on his shoulders to indicate she wanted him to let her go.

"I'm not, Sweetheart." Justin chuckled as he released her, so he could stand back up and kiss her once more. "I can't propose right now anyway, because I hafta wait until after I see your dad again to pick up your grandmother's engagement ring that he's having cleaned and polished for me to ask you with."

"What?" Amy's eyes went wide, and she covered her mouth when it dropped open at his statement.

Justin chuckled at her adorable actions in response to hearing about her grandmother's engagement ring. "Yeah, we talked about more than just the matchmaking mischief my mom's been up to while he was grilling the burgers. After asking my intentions with you, he gave me his blessing, and said he wanted to pass his mother's engagement ring down to you if I hadn't already picked one out. Since I figured it'd be a few more months before you'd say yes, he's having it cleaned and polished, so it'll be ready whenever we are. We should probably let him know your ring size, so he can have it sized first, too."

"Wow!" Amy still looked shocked. "I knew you were talking about us dating long term, but I didn't realize you've already thought about marriage and babies for us."

"Sweetheart, I've been thinkin' about marrying you since the day we met." Justin grinned at her before making his next confession. "And before we started making love, the most intense orgasm I'd ever had was while imagining getting you pregnant while jacking off in my shower."

"That was the shower fantasy you wouldn't tell me about?" Amy's eyes practically bugged out of her head as she referenced one of their earliest phone sex experiences.

"Guilty as charged." Justin raised his hands in surrender. "But I couldn't exactly tell you that fantasy when I'd barely convinced you to go on a few friend dates with me and I wasn't sure I'd get you past phone sex yet. I knew you weren't ready to think about forever with me then. That's the same reason I didn't say *I love you* the first two dozen times I thought it. I know you're skittish about this whole love thing, so I've been trying to let you set the pace. And I'm gonna keep doing that. If you're ready to get married before the baby's born, we'll do it. If you wanna wait until after the baby's born, that's fine, too. Hell, if you wanna wait ten years before we get married, I'll wait. But I do wanna put a ring on your finger just as soon as you'll let me, so the whole world knows you're mine."

"I guess this means we'll have to tell your family we're dating, huh?" Amy's lips lifted in a shy smile as she looked up at him.

"Yeah, we should probably do that pretty soon." Justin pulled her back into his arms, just because he needed to hold her. "That way they won't be wondering who knocked you up when you start showing."

"Speaking of wondering about us, we should probably head back into the reception before Brooklyn and Bobby make their entrance, so it's not so obvious we've skipped out together." Amy reached under her dress to adjust her panties before reaching up to straighten his tie.

"Yeah, probably," Justin replied, hating that he didn't have more time to make love with the mother of his unborn child before heading back into the ballroom.

"I need to go to the ladies' room before we go back into the ballroom," Amy announced, leading him a different way back, so she could make her pitstop.

As they approached the foyer for Amy to duck into the ladies' room between it and the ballroom, Justin overheard voices that sounded suspiciously like his mother, aunt, and his friends' mothers. While Amy did her business, Justin slinked closer to hear exactly what they were plotting.

"So, who all have you set up together tonight?" Karen Walker inquired.

"All the bridesmaids and groomsmen," Justin's Aunt Hazel replied.

"Well, except Anthony and Kay," Justin's mother corrected.

"And we're still pushing Charlotte and Ian together, both here and at school," Lisa Walker, the principal at Heart's Destiny Middle School, admitted.

"I made sure a couple of your boys were sitting at their table, so maybe one of them will fall for Ian's sister, Cait, since none of our boys seem interested in her," Aunt Hazel confessed their plotting.

"And we put Justin and Amy together again," his mom sighed, sounding a little irritated. "Though I'm beginning to wonder if maybe we should try to match them up with other people, since they already spend so much time together at work and don't seem to be interested in being more than friends."

Justin had to stifle a chuckle as he realized how successful he and Amy had been at hiding their relationship from the matchmaking mommas.

"What're you doing?" Amy whispered her question as she walked up behind him.

"Listening to the plots of the matchmaking mommas," Justin whispered back.

Amy leaned in close beside him to listen in, too.

"And we seated Lexi, Cassidy, Kayla, and Sierra with the rest of your boys, hoping we'll find a match there, too," Aunt Hazel confessed. "But maybe we should've introduced one of them to Amy, instead of seating her next to Justin again."

"Why would they do that?" Amy looked confused as she mouthed the question to him.

Before he could respond, his mother answered Amy's inquiry with more of their plotting. "We'll try that at the next wedding if they don't get together by then. Even if it's not a great match, maybe it'll be enough to make Justin jealous, so he'll step up and stake his claim on the woman he obviously wants to be with."

"Guess it's a good thing we're planning on telling them we're dating before James and Randi's wedding." Amy grinned as she took his hand and pulled him back the way they came, so they wouldn't get caught eavesdropping on the mommas.

"Howdaya think we should tell 'em?" Justin probed as they snuck back through the guest dining room to the back entrance to the ballroom. "Do you think we should blatantly announce it? Or just let them catch me kissing you on the dance floor tonight?"

"No, not tonight," Amy objected, shaking her head. "It's Brooklyn and Bobby's night tonight. I don't wanna take the spotlight off them at their wedding reception."

"Okay." Justin paused just outside the ballroom door to press their lips together one more time while they were still alone. "Tomorrow at my birthday party?"

A mischievous smile spread across Amy's face, making Justin hard at all the ideas she could be thinking about doing to make his birthday special. *Fuck, maybe I'll let everyone know we're dating by throwing her over my shoulder to carry her outta the party, so I can unwrap her as my birthday present back at my house.*

"Yeah, I think that'll work." Amy released his hand as they walked into the ballroom.

By this time tomorrow, I'll get to officially claim Amy as mine to the whole world.

~~~
~~~

Amy was feeling a sense of déjà vu as she walked into Justin's birthday party to find it just as overcrowded as Josh and Jake's was the previous week. Though it looked like Susan and Hazel had decided to save her several trips to the kitchen for bottles of water by having a cooler stocked at the end of the drink table for anyone who didn't want a caffeinated beverage at the party.

I wonder if Hazel's pregnant daughters-in-law mentioned needing caffeine-free options after the last couple family events?

Amy didn't want to alert Hazel or Susan to her own pregnant status by asking them, so she just smiled politely as she got out a bottle of water before mingling with the other guests. She might have been able to hold off on getting something to drink until after finding Justin in the crowd, but she was exceptionally thirsty after parking her car at his house and walking over to his aunt and uncle's home at the other end of the main grouping of houses on the ranch.

Why couldn't they have had his party at his parents' house just across the gravel drive from his place? It seems strange to have his aunt and uncle host his party instead of his parents. But I guess they did the same thing last month for JJ's birthday party, so I shouldn't really be surprised.

She wouldn't have had such a long walk if she hadn't wanted to park at Justin's house, so her car would be there to leave for work in the morning. As she was getting ready to come over to the ranch, she realized that telling everyone they were dating at the party would make it possible for her to spend the night with him. So, she'd packed an overnight bag and put on the sexy red lingerie under her matching red dress that she wanted to wear for him as an extra special birthday present.

A small smile lifted her lips at the thought of her plans for Justin that night. She'd ordered the red corset, thong, and garter set from her sister's website the day they got home from Houston. After using her scarf as a blindfold for their food play, she'd decided to order a red bondage set, which she also ordered that day, to give Justin for his birthday, and she couldn't resist the matching lingerie. The bondage set included four soft cuffs to go around wrists or ankles without leaving a mark, a satin blindfold, and a feather for sensation play. It wasn't hard-core, whips and chains, like she imagined couples who were really into BDSM would use, but it was perfect for the lighter play she was finding she liked with Justin.

Now we just have to figure out which one of us is being tied up and teased first.

Before she could decide between him taking control, as she typically preferred, and tying him to the bed to give him a birthday spanking, Justin found her in the crowd. He walked up to her and took her breath away in his tailored black slacks, crisp white button-down, and a red tie that matched her dress. "What's that sexy smile for, Sweetheart?"

"Just thinking about how much you're gonna like your birthday presents tonight," Amy replied, reaching up on her tiptoes to press a kiss to his cheek.

"Yeah, which box is from you?" Justin slipped an arm around her waist and dipped his chin in the direction of the table of presents. "I'll open it first."

"Oh, my present for you isn't on that table," Amy whispered, hoping only he would hear her. "It's in my car, parked at your house, and for your eyes only."

Justin grinned at her before opening his mouth to reply, but he held his words back when their intimate conversation was interrupted by several of their friends surrounding them. After multiple "happy birthdays" were expressed, Aiden finally pointed out to the room how cozily they were standing together.

"I see you're staking your claim, so nobody else can hug up on Amy at this party." Aiden nodded down at Justin's arm around her waist with his hand possessively on her hip.

"Yeah, something like that," Justin replied, looking at Amy and grinning.

"So, are ya'll dating now, or are you still sticking to the *just friends* line that none of us have believed for months?" Lexi teased.

"What's this about dating?" Justin's mother, Susan, prodded, pushing into the circle of friends around them.

"You wanna tell 'em, or do ya want me to?" Justin asked Amy.

"It's your party, so you get to do the honors." Amy grinned back at her boyfriend.

"Amy is officially my girlfriend," Justin announced, not taking his eyes off Amy's face, even though he was directing his comments to the crowd around them. "We've actually been dating for a couple months now."

"You've been dating for months and didn't tell any of us?" Justin's mother screeched, bringing her hand to her chest like she was shocked and gripping at her own heart.

"It's not a big deal, Mom. We wanted to spend some time together and see how we really feel about each other, without the pressures of work or family swaying us one way or another."

"I can't believe you didn't even tell me." JJ grinned at Justin and Amy as he put an arm around his mom. "I mean, I understand not wanting anyone interfering in your relationship until you knew it was solid, but you know I wouldn't've done anything, but help you keep it a secret."

"Hey, I did tell you when I was planning to ask her out," Justin protested his brother's words.

"But when I asked if you'd actually asked her and what her answer was, you were noncommittal." JJ pointed at Justin, shaking his head. "I thought you'd chickened out on asking."

"Naw, just needed to keep my girl all to myself for a while." Justin leaned over to peck Amy's lips. "Now let's get on with this party before I decide I'd rather have a private party at home with my Sweetheart."

~~~

As much fun as Justin had at his birthday party with all his friends and family in attendance, he was really glad to have Amy all to himself when they walked into his house afterward. He was also really glad she'd kept his garage-door opener in her car since her brief stay on the ranch the month before and had used it to park at his house when she came to the ranch for his party.

"I need to grab my stuff outta the car," Amy informed him as they walked in the front door.
~~~

"Leave it." Justin wrapped her in his arms and nuzzled her neck. "We'll get it tomorrow. It's been too long since I've been inside you and I need you in my bed right now."

"But your birthday present is in the car," Amy argued, gripping his shoulders as she returned his open-mouthed neck kisses. "Well, half your present is in the car. And I can't give you the half I'm wearing without the rest of the gift."

"Fuck," Justin groaned as he licked the sensitive spot on her throat just above her collarbone, The Anaconda desperately trying to slither out of his slacks to get to her. "Does that mean you're wearing some sexy lingerie under that prim and proper dress?"

"Yes, Boss," Amy purred as she nibbled on his neck. "But you hafta unwrap the other part of your present before you can unwrap me."

"Then we'd better go get it outta your car." Justin let his hands roam down her body, gripping the perky globes of her ass to lift her into his arms and carry her out to the garage. Amy wrapped her legs around his waist, neither of them wanting to stop making out long enough to make the trip alone. "But I don't know if we'll make it outta the garage before I'm opening both my presents. We might just hafta see how comfortable my truck bed is for our first round."

"Oh, no!" Amy arched her back to pull out of his arms just as he took the two steps down into the garage. "We need to be in your bed to use the spindles in your headboard and footboard for what I have planned for tonight."

Justin wasn't exactly sure what Amy had planned, but he hoped his antique wooden bed frame was sturdy enough to handle the picture his mind had just conjured of her bound to the bed for him to pleasure. He put her down on her feet when they got to the floor of the garage, not having much choice since she'd released her legs from around his waist and was pushing on his shoulders, instead of clinging to them as she had previously.

Amy turned and sauntered to her car, leaving Justin standing there to ogle her ass that was just round enough to poke past the boxy straight lines of the t-shirt dress. With the way the asymmetrical hem covered her almost to her ankles in the front, he hadn't realized she was wearing flesh-tone stockings until he saw her calves where the back of the dress was not only cut higher but was also lifted by the curve of her ass.

Fuck me, that was a garter belt I felt when I picked her up, not cheeky panties. Yeah, she'll be leaving that on for a little while. Along with those fuck-me red stilettos.

Justin was enjoying looking at Amy's legs and ass so much, he was practically entranced by the view as she bent over to grab her things out of the back of her car. It wasn't until she returned to an upright position and turned around that he realized he was falling down on his job as a gentleman. He quickly closed the space between them to take her bags and the small, wrapped box from her hands, so he could carry them inside for her.

"You know I'm perfectly capable of carrying my things inside, right?"

"Yes, Sweetheart." Justin brushed his lips over her forehead as he removed the bag straps from her shoulders to put them on his own. "But until we see the doctor to find out if there are limits on how much weight you can lift while pregnant, I'm gonna take care of the heavy lifting for you while you take care of growing our baby."

"Fine, but since you've got my purse, laptop bag, and suitcase, I'll carry your birthday present." Amy pushed up on her tiptoes to kiss away his scowl. "Don't worry, it doesn't even weigh two pounds."

Fuck, what kind of sex toys did she get that are so light? Scarves for me to tie her up and blindfold her again? Or maybe that remote control butterfly vibrator she mentioned wanting to try when we played with her other toys?

"That's fine, Sweetheart." While he wanted to carry everything for her, he wouldn't argue with such a light load and spoil the mood for the night.

Justin followed Amy back into the house, all the way back to his master bedroom before he finally put her bags on top of his dresser. Amy sat on the side of his bed, still holding the box, and patted the bed beside her for him to join her.

Don't hafta ask me twice, Sweetheart! Justin thought as he took his seat, eager to get on with their night. She handed him the box, which he wasted no time ripping the paper off of, so he could see the gift he'd been anticipating all night.

"Holy fuck!" Justin couldn't believe his eyes when he saw the four faux-fur lined red leather cuffs, matching satin sleep mask, and feather tickler. "Just what exactly did you have planned for tonight, Sweetheart?"

"Just a way to keep you still, so I can give you your birthday spanking." Amy grinned at him mischievously.

"And what if I'd rather use these on you?" Justin dangled the wrist and ankle cuffs by the small chains connecting them on his finger between them as he returned her grin. "I'm the birthday boy, so I should get my way tonight. Don'tcha think?"

"Oh, you'll definitely be getting your way," Amy purred, her voice husky with desire as she ran a finger over the fur lining of one of the cuffs. "I figured we'd be taking turns using these tonight."

Justin wasn't sure he'd enjoy being the one tied up, but if that was what Amy wanted, then he'd gladly let her bind him. Lightly spanking her was a lot more appealing than her spanking him, but since the kit she bought didn't come with a paddle or whip, he thought he could handle whatever she'd do with her hand.

"Then we'd better dispense with some clothes, so you can have your way with me first." Justin handed her the cuffs and loosened his tie. "And I hope you're ready for a long night because once I get you tied to my bed, I'm not letting you up until sunrise."

Amy's eyes widened at his statement as she sat there watching him start to undress. Once Justin removed his tie, he pulled his dress shirt from his waistband, where it was tucked in, and started unbuttoning it.

Amy stood, dropping the cuffs on the bed beside him as she moved to stand facing him at the side of the bed. "Aren't you gonna unwrap the rest of your birthday present?"

Damn, how could I forget the need to uncover her lingerie? Justin left his unbuttoned shirt on as he moved his hands to the hem of her dress and slowly started to slide it up. He revealed the tops of her thigh-high stockings, then the garters they were attached to before pushing the material of her dress up to her waist to expose the matching red garter belt and tiny G-string.

"You're so fucking sexy," Justin growled as he pushed the material higher to reveal the matching red satin corset that was essentially acting as her bra for the night.

"So are you." Amy lifted her arms for him to completely remove her dress, which he promptly tossed to the floor beside them.

Justin buried his face in her cleavage as Amy pushed his shirt off his shoulders. Once his arms were free of the sleeves, Justin wrapped them around her, holding her still as he explored her with his mouth.

Not one to be patient, Amy reached between them to unfasten his belt and slacks, much to his cock's delight. Eager to be inside her instead of confined to the cotton prison of his boxer briefs, Justin released Amy from his hold long enough to stand, toeing off his shoes and socks at the same time he shoved the rest of his clothing down his legs to the floor, allowing his dick to act like a divining rod and point directly at Amy.

Once he stood before her naked, Justin looked at Amy and asked, "How do you want me positioned for this birthday spanking?"

"I'm thinking face down on the bed with your arms and legs extended so I can hook the chain between the cuffs around the spindles of the bed."

Justin carefully got into position as Amy fumbled with putting the cuffs in place around the center spindles of his headboard and footboard. He didn't see how she was going to do more than spank him in that position, but he figured Amy would release him to flip over if she wanted to ride him before letting him have his turn tying her up.

Once she got the cuffs buckled around his wrists, Amy moved to the foot of the bed and attempted to put the ankle cuffs on him. "Can you move your feet closer together? The cuffs won't reach with them where they are now."

"Sweetheart, I already brought my legs as close together as they can go without smashing my balls," Justin chuckled.

"Wow, okay," Amy huffed, backing away from his feet to kneel beside his hips on the bed. "This worked so much better in my head."

"Yeah, we should probably get some rope or something to tie the individual cuffs to the corner posts instead of leaving them chained together." Justin turned his head to look at her the best he could while lying face down.

"Probably, but I can't exactly trek out to the barn dressed like this to get it now." Amy waved her hand over her torso to indicate her sexy as fuck lingerie.

"No, I guess not," Justin laughed. "But we can just skip the ankle cuffs for tonight and grab some rope before next time."

"Yeah, and maybe it won't feel so awkward next time." Amy laughed with him before slapping his bare ass cheek with her palm. She barely smacked him hard enough for him to feel it, but she pulled her hand back and rubbed her palm with the other hand like it was more painful for her than it'd been for him. "Ow! This isn't nearly as hot as I thought it'd be."

"Then why don't we trade places, so I can show you how hot you are," Justin suggested, already unbuckling the cuffs since his hands were close enough together that he could unfasten them himself.

"Wow, I didn't really have you restrained at all, did I?" Amy giggled when she realized that Justin was already free from her restraints.

"I don't think these are really meant to be escape-proof." Justin grinned at her as he rolled out of the way for Amy to take his place in the center of the bed. "But I would've stayed there as long as you wanted if I thought you were really enjoying having me tied down and at your mercy."

Amy grinned as she giggled while laying down on the bed, face up instead of face down like he'd been. "I see what you mean," she acknowledged while helping him buckle the cuffs around her wrists.

Justin grabbed the blindfold and feather tickler from the open box, enjoying the view of Amy spread out on his bed for him a moment before covering her eyes with the sleep mask. "Let's see if you enjoy this as much as you liked being my dessert a couple weeks ago."

He trailed the feather from her wrist down her arm, across her shoulders and collarbones before going back up the other arm. Amy giggled when he found her ticklish spots and moaned when he followed the feather with his fingers applying a little more pressure.

He repeated the process with the feather and then his fingers over her cleavage before pushing the cups of her corset down to expose her breasts. Her nipples hardened as he ran the tickler over them. She arched her back and cried out his name when he replaced the light tickler with his mouth and sucked on her sepia tips.

He was so turned on by the way she writhed in pleasure, his dick seemed to grow even harder than it already was just from being the one to bring her to the brink. Needing her too bad to keep playing for long, Justin moved down her body. He trailed the feather over her inner thighs, causing her to spread her legs wide for him as he positioned himself between her thighs.

His shoulders held her open for him to dip his head to the apex of her thighs. He pushed her tiny G-string to the side, so he could lick his way through her soaking wet folds. He ate her pussy like a starving man, devouring her for their mutual pleasure. He dropped the feather tickler to the bed, so he had his hands free to finger-fuck her while suckling her clit.

With two fingers inside her, he bent them just right to stimulate her G-spot, taking her over the edge for the first time that night. He lifted his head to remind her to breathe, seeing the smile of pure bliss on her face as she floated back down from her high.

His cock was weeping precum and he couldn't wait a second longer to be inside the woman he loved. Justin pushed up on his knees between her spread thighs. He stroked his hands over her stocking-clad legs, lightly gripped her ankles, and propped her sexy as fuck stilettos on his shoulders before lining his dick up with her slit and sliding home inside her slick, wet heat.

They moaned in ecstasy and whispered words of love and affection as he gripped her hips to control the way he thrust inside her. As always with Amy, it was pure heaven to make love to her, but it was even better being able to be bare. He loved knowing there were no barriers between them.

With one hand he reached up and removed the blindfold, wanting to see her obsidian eyes as they came together as one. "Fucking heaven," Justin groaned, wanting her to know how he felt being inside her. "So wet. So perfect. You're my everything, Sweetheart."

"And you're mine," Amy replied as her inner walls contracted, milking him of his own release.

They moaned each other's names as they peaked together, with their moans turning to grunts and incoherent gibberish as they each lost the ability to form words at the height of their excitement.

Not wanting to fold her in half or risk hurting her or their baby by collapsing on top of her, Justin released her legs and rolled to lay beside her. He immediately felt the loss of their connection, but she couldn't exactly roll with him while her hands were bound and immobile.

Leah Mae Wright

"Wow, that was so much hotter than when I had you tied up." Amy was breathless from their exertion.

Justin chuckled lightly, not able to respond otherwise as he was still catching his breath. He reached up to unfasten the cuffs, releasing her from the bonds that held her to the bed, so he could pull her into his arms.

Best birthday ever!

Chapter Fourteen

Justin wasn't sure what to expect as he sat in the waiting room with Amy at the Heart's Destiny Clinic for the second time in less than a month. The first time wasn't nearly as nerve-racking since it was just a follow-up when he pretty much knew what the doctor was going to say. But they weren't there to see Doc Hayes, the family doctor he'd seen for as long as he could remember. No, they were there to see a new doctor, an obstetrician, to start prenatal care for their baby.

Or babies, he thought, wondering how soon they could find out if they were having twins, since they apparently ran in both their families. *Is she far enough along that we can do an ultrasound today? Could we leave here this afternoon with a picture of our babies?*

"Amy Lawton," a nurse Justin didn't recognize called out from a doorway on the opposite side of the front desk from where they normally called patients to go back for Doc Hayes.

"Hi, I'm Amy." Amy raised her hand to wave at the nurse as they stood and walked to the doorway where the new nurse waited.

"Nice to meet you, Amy. I'm Arden Snyder, and I'm going to be your nurse whenever you come for a visit with Doctor Magnum." The nurse turned her attention to Justin before asking, "And you are?"

"I'm Justin, Amy's boyfriend." Justin ran a hand through his hair nervously, not being used to having to introduce himself to anyone in his hometown.

"Nice to meet you, Justin." Arden smiled at him before turning. "Right this way."

Justin took Amy's hand as they followed the nurse through a part of the building he'd never seen before.

Leah Mae Wright

"Excuse our mess." Arden directed them past a room that still looked under construction. "We're still getting a few things set up down here after focusing on the new birthing suites upstairs first."

"I don't think I've ever been in this part of the building before." Justin looked around the hallway before they stepped into an exam room that looked similar to the ones on the other side of the building.

"Yeah, I don't know what was in this part of the building before Doctor Magnum decided to move her practice here." The nurse took a seat at the small desk, logging into the computer to start charting Amy's vital signs.

I wonder if the obstetrician recommends Magnum brand condoms? Justin snickered at his mental quip as he and Amy took their seats beside the desk.

"Did you work with Doctor Magnum before she moved the practice?" Amy inquired as she extended her arm for Arden to take her blood pressure.

"Yes, in San Antonio. But when we had more than one patient mention how worried they were about making it to the hospital in time to have their babies, she looked over her patient records and realized that more than half her patients were driving from here. So, it just made more sense for us to move the office and set up a birthing center than to expect that many patients to drive over an hour to get to us."

I wonder if Kay or Brooklyn were the patients who mentioned being worried about making it all the way to San Antonio to give birth? Not that I can ask them if they were, since Amy doesn't wanna tell anyone about the pregnancy until after the first trimester.

How long is a trimester? Justin did some mental math from the basics about pregnancy that he remembered from the sex education class he took in middle school. *Three months. And we only started making love a little over a month ago, so I can't say anything to my family for two more months.*

How soon until the baby starts showing? Anthony and Kay found out about their baby in November, and I noticed her baby bump in February. That's three months. Shit! Will my family figure it out before Amy's ready to tell them by noticing our baby bump?

Wait, that was three months from when they found out about being pregnant, not from when the baby was conceived. I wonder how far along she was then? It had to be at least a month, right? For her to know she'd missed a period to take a test? So, if Kay didn't start showing until the fourth month, then maybe Amy won't start showing until at least four months along, so we can keep it from everyone until after the first trimester.

Justin was so lost in thought that he didn't realize Arden had finished her part of the appointment and left the room. It wasn't until Dr. Devon Magnum introduced herself that Justin escaped his mental rabbit hole to focus on what was going on around him.

"I wanted to ask you about the hCG number on the blood test Doctor Hayes ran on the twenty-second of March." Amy's worried tone drew Justin's attention. He watched her face intently as she explained. "Everything I've read online says that seventy milli-international units per milliliter is normal for someone three weeks pregnant, but it was only possible for me to be one or two weeks along on that day."

"Don't worry about those charts." Dr. Magnum waved her hand as if she was waving away the charts she was talking about. "They don't have estimates for weeks one and two because they are actually the two weeks between the first day of your last period and the day you ovulate. We'll estimate your date of conception based on the first day of your last period and when you had sex during your prime fertility window."

"My last period was on March first." Amy glanced in his direction with a shy smile on her lips. "And we started having sex on March eighth."

"That puts your prime fertility window between the ninth and fourteenth, with the most likely date of ovulation being the fourteenth. With those dates, you'd be considered three weeks pregnant on the twenty-second, even though it was actually only a week since conception."

"So, we probably conceived on the fourteenth when we went without a condom," Amy whispered. "But I thought my shot had me covered until the seventeenth…"

"Unfortunately, while it's advertised as being effective for three months, that last week or so, when it's mostly worn off, is what drops the effectiveness of Depo-Provera down to only ninety-four percent." Dr. Magnum patted Amy's hand in a comforting manner. "That's why

I recommend using condoms the last two weeks before the next shot is due for my patients on it."

"Yeah, my last doctor didn't tell me that." Amy looked down at her lap, slightly shaking her head.

"While I'm not set up for them here, there are other options if you're not ready to have a baby at this time of your life," the doctor offered, her voice way too calm for what Justin thought she was suggesting.

No fucking way! Justin thought at the same time Amy shouted, "No! It's a surprise and not what I was planning for at this point in my life, but I'm absolutely keeping my baby."

"*We're* keeping *our* baby," Justin corrected, his left hand covering Amy's over her still flat stomach while his right arm went around her shoulders to pull her into his side protectively.

"Okay, good to know," the doctor placated, her lips turning up in the smallest smile as she turned to the computer and started clicking the mouse. "Then let's use an estimated date of conception of March fourteenth. That will give you a due date of December sixth. We'll do a pelvic exam today, but it's too early to see anything on an ultrasound. I prefer to do the first one around the twelfth week, unless there are issues that require one sooner, so we'll schedule you to come back in about six weeks for that. That would be the last week of May."

"There's no way I can do it the last week of May." Amy didn't even bother pulling out her phone to check her calendar. "That's the week of my best friend's wedding and I'm sure she's gonna monopolize all my free time that week."

"Then we'll schedule it for the week before or the week after." Dr. Magnum clicked something else on the computer before standing. "Just let them know whichever works best for you when you check out. Now I'm going to step out so you can get undressed from the waist down."

She handed Amy a paper sheet to cover herself with before actually walking out of the room.

"Um, you don't have to stay back here for this part." Amy shyly turned away from him, standing from her chair and walking over to the exam table. "Unless you want to."

"What's she gonna do?" Justin wasn't sure what was about to happen, so he couldn't be sure if he wanted to stay or not.

"Stick a speculum in my hoo-hah to open me up enough she can reach inside and feel around," Amy stated, deadpan, as she toed off her shoes and unfastened her pants.

"She's gonna what?" Justin wasn't sure how Amy maintained a straight face as she explained once more what all a pelvic exam entailed while stripping off her pants and panties. He felt a little lightheaded at the thought and was grateful he was a man, so he never had to endure what sounded like a painful exam.

"Like I said, you don't have to stay for this part if you don't want to." Amy's face remained blank as she hopped up on the exam table and covered her lower half with the paper sheet.

"It's not about what I want, Sweetheart." Justin stood and walked across the room to stand by her side. "If you want me to step out and give you privacy for this, I will. But if you want me to stand here holding your hand to help you deal with what sounds like a painful exam, I'll do that, too. It's entirely up to you."

"You really wouldn't mind staying?" Amy looked up at him, her obsidian eyes imploring him to stay.

"No, Sweetheart, I don't mind." Justin wrapped his arms around her and dropped a kiss on the top of her head. "I'm not gonna like seeing you in pain, but I should probably get used to it before December. I wanna be by your side for every part of this pregnancy and any others we have in the future."

"Then stay up by my head." Amy hugged him back quickly before releasing him and laying down on the exam table. "That way you won't see what the doctor's doing."

"Deal," Justin agreed, taking a step toward the head of the bed, and taking Amy's hand in his, just as the doctor knocked once on the door and reentered the room. "Does that go for when the baby's born, too? Because if human babies being born look anything like when horses or cows are born, I'm not sure I'll be able to handle seeing the carnage between your legs."

"What is it with this town and all the cowboys comparing childbirth to birthing livestock?" Dr. Magnum shook her head as she chuckled.

"It's the only birthing we see being raised on a ranch, ma'am," Justin drawled, playing up his Texas twang. "And when you see the vet reach elbow-deep inside a cow to turn the calf so it can be born, it kinda sticks with you."

"Oh, Lord," Amy exclaimed, covering her mouth with her free hand. Justin wasn't sure if it was because she was shocked by his graphic description or if she was trying to keep from vomiting after picturing it in her head.

"Well, you don't have to worry about ever seeing me elbow-deep in one of my patients." Dr. Magnum grinned. "I only go wrist-deep when I do a C-section and we don't let Daddy watch that."

"Yeah, I'll stay up by her head." Justin nodded down at Amy, feeling a little queasy at the thought of the doctor having to cut her open for their baby to be born. "I don't need to see anything you're doing, just Amy and our baby once it's safely born."

"Relax, Dad, the only hard part for you will be if you want to cut the umbilical cord and see the baby before we clean them up." Dr. Magnum wasn't reassuring Justin as much as she seemed to think she was. "Now, Amy, let's have you scoot down to the end of the table and put your feet up in the stirrups, so I can examine you."

Amy got into position as the nurse came back in, pushing a tray table with sterilized instruments on it. Justin briefly glanced at the tray of instruments, but when he didn't recognize any of them or what they were for, he decided to keep his gaze locked on Amy's face instead of asking about them.

Amy smiled up at him as she laid there while the doctor did her thing, only briefly squeezing his hand a little tighter during what he assumed was the most painful part of the exam. He used his free hand to wipe her brow in a comforting gesture, but he kept his smile in place instead of grimacing like Amy was.

"Everything looks good," the doctor finally said, snapping her gloves off to dispose of them. "I'd say you're definitely in the sixth week of your pregnancy, approximately four weeks from conception. We'll get you started on prenatal vitamins today and see you back in six weeks, unless you have any issues that arise that we need to check out before then."

"Issues?" Justin felt like his heart skipped a beat at the thought of there being issues with Amy's pregnancy. He wondered what he needed to watch out for to make sure Amy and their baby were safe.

"Abdominal cramping, more than a little spotting from today's exam, or any kind of outside factor that might make you concerned about the health of your baby," Dr. Magnum replied while sliding the stirrups back into the table and motioning for Amy to sit back up.

"I understand the cramping and spotting…" Amy trailed off, looking concerned and squeezing Justin's hand again as she pulled herself into a sitting position. "But what other outside factors should I be worried about?"

"There's nothing specific you should be worried about," the doctor sighed, shaking her head. "Sorry, I didn't mean to make it sound like there are issues. I just meant things that could happen to anyone, pregnant or not, like car accidents or falls, that kind of thing. If an accident happens, it's not just you who needs to be checked out now."

"Oh, yeah, okay." Amy finally smiled again. Justin returned her smile, though he was now worried about how to keep her safe from any accidents too.

"Do either of you have any more questions for me?"

"No, I think that's everything," Amy replied.

Justin shook his head. Even though he knew he'd probably come up with a dozen questions as soon as they left the doctor's office, he couldn't think of a single one in that moment.

"Excellent." The doctor stood and used the hand sanitizer dispenser beside the door. "Then I'll let you get dressed and get outta here. Arden will have your vitamin prescription with your paperwork and new-parent bag at the front desk when you check out."

"Thanks, Dr. Magnum," Justin and Amy said in unison as the doctor and nurse both left the room.

As soon as the door closed behind them, Amy used the paper sheet to wipe between her legs before getting off the exam table.

"Why'd you do that?" Justin waved his hand in the general direction of her crotch to indicate what he was asking about.

"Wiping off the rest of the lube the doctor used to insert the speculum." Amy gave him a sexy grin as she got dressed.

"Damn, ya'll didn't mention there was lube involved in this exam." Justin faked a disappointed look, shaking his head. "I might've enjoyed watching that part."

"Perv!" Amy giggled.

Leah Mae Wright

"But I'm your perv," Justin replied, hugging her to his side as they exited the exam room.

"Yeah, you are." Amy wrapped her arm around his waist and leaned her head against his chest as they walked back up to the front desk to check out.

They stopped at the counter just before exiting the back area to go through the waiting room, where Arden was waiting with what looked like an insulated lunch bag full of paperwork and baby stuff.

"So much for not announcing we're expecting before the end of the first trimester," Amy mumbled. "As soon as we step in the waiting room with a baby bag, half the town will know, and word will get back to the ranch before we can even drive over there to be the ones to tell your parents."

"Naw, I got this." Justin smirked, taking the bag from Arden. He moved the baby bottle from the small side pocket to the middle, rearranged the pacifier and diaper samples, and folded the paperwork, so it would all fit in the inside compartment that he could zip closed. "Now it just looks like I'm carrying a little yellow lunch bag."

"You know that'll only work if the people in the waiting room haven't received their own little yellow lunch bag, right?"

Justin shrugged at the same time Arden informed them, "No worries. Ya'll are our last appointment of the day, so the waiting room is empty."

"See, problem solved." Justin smirked once more. "And anyone who sees me carrying it to the truck will think I'm just being gentlemanly and carrying your lunch for you."

The ladies both chuckled before setting their next appointment for Monday, June third.

Damn, it's gonna be hard to wait that long before seeing a picture of our baby.

~~~

Amy was glad to have the chance to talk to Randi on one of the rare days when she wasn't flying on a Saturday morning. Instead, her BFF
~~~

was hanging out in her hotel room while waiting for her allotted time to make her appearance at the fan expo being held the day before the GWA's *No Remorse* pay-per-view.

"It feels like ages since I've gotten to actually talk to you," Amy lamented into her phone. Though they texted almost daily, their texts were all lighthearted and superficial. Actual phone conversations, discussing the meaningful things in their lives, were few and far between because of Randi's crazy work schedule. "And I have so much I need to catch you up on that I didn't wanna tell you in a text."

"Yes, I need all the updates on your daddy drama and how things are going between you and Justin," Randi professed, her voice going up a couple octaves from her excitement. "Last time we talked you couldn't tell me much other than what your mom said about your real dad and that dating was on hold while your mom and sister were in town."

"Yeah, well, I've not only found out more about my dad, but I've also actually met him," Amy started before telling Randi all about how Justin had gotten his cousin Jake to locate her biological father and all the conversations and visits they'd had since then. She also went into detail about the Tara situation at work before circling back to discuss dating Justin. She hit the highlights of their dating timeline, glossing over the actual acts as she informed her friend that their relationship had progressed between the sheets and ended up causing her to have a health scare when she passed out during an intense orgasm.

"Wow, so ya'll had his whole family fooled into thinking he was just being a good friend and taking care of you, when he was really there rocking your bed every night?" Randi giggled as she posed the question.

"Yeah, but they all know we're dating now." Amy chuckled with her friend a moment before sobering. "Oh, that's something I should probably warn you about since you take the same shot I used to."

"Shot? You mean our birth control shot? And whaddaya mean by you *used* to take it?" Randi's voice took on a sharp tone and she no longer sounded jovial.

"Yeah, um, during the whole testing and doctor visit phase of figuring out I passed out from holding my breath, it was also time for my shot." Amy wondered if she could tell her friend to use condoms the last two weeks before hers was due without telling her about the baby yet. "They got a new OB-GYN here in Heart's Destiny that I saw, and she told me to be sure to use condoms the last two weeks because it's not as effective then as it is the first ten weeks after getting it."

"Seriously?" Randi shouted. "Why didn't anyone tell us that before now?"

"No clue." Amy shrugged even though her friend couldn't see her through the phone. "But maybe it was because neither one of us was serious about anyone we were dating to go without the condoms before now."

"And now we're serious enough to ditch the condoms, so it's seriously need-to-know information." Randi's voice sounded muffled as she called James's name, so Amy waited for her friend to finish telling her boyfriend when he'd need to wrap it up in the future. When she finally came back on the line sounding as clear as before, Randi announced, "Thankfully, it didn't seem to matter for us back in January and a couple weeks ago, but I'm glad you told me before we get to the ten-week mark on the latest shot. I want at least a few years under my belt as a wrestler before I have to take time off to have a baby."

"I know, that's why I wanted to make sure I warned you like my new doctor warned me." Amy was glad her friend seemed to have forgotten the comment about her no longer being on the shot. "So, what's new with you? Special plans for the pay-per-view tomorrow?"

"Are you trying to get spoilers outta me?" Randi laughed.

"No, not really, just wondered what I'm gonna miss since I can't be at this one." Amy enjoyed watching her best friend living her dreams on the weekly Tuesday night televised show when she didn't have plans with Justin. But since they'd officially announced they were dating, Justin had insisted she spend her Sunday evenings at his family dinners, so Amy didn't think she'd be home to be able to order the pay-per-view to watch it live.

"Yeah, you're not the only one who isn't gonna be at this show." Randi sounded a little down. "It's gonna be my first pay-per-view without a single family member in attendance, since Kay's maternity leave started."

"Oh? I didn't think she was due until July." Amy wondered why Kay started maternity leave so early. She didn't think that would start until the baby was actually born.

"She's not, but she's thirty weeks along on Monday," Randi replied. "And between the issues she had with preterm labor with the girls and the fact that her job requires flying daily, the doctor grounded her six weeks earlier than most pregnant women would be told to stop flying."

"While I hate that she's missing your show this weekend, I'm glad to hear they're being proactive and not taking any risks by having her fly too close to her due date."

"Yeah, me too. But I still miss them." Randi sounded more like she was worried about her sister and the baby than just the normal melancholy of missing her family. "Hey, maybe since you're spending so much more time on the ranch now, you can check in on her for me?"

"Of course." Amy wondered if Kay already had plans for the day or if she could pop over there to ask her a few pregnancy questions and put Randi's mind at ease at the same time. "I can head over there now if you want."

"You wouldn't mind?" Randi's voice lightened, like Amy's offer lifted a weight from her shoulders. "I don't wanna put you out, but I worry about my sister, and she doesn't always tell me everything when I'm not looking her in the eyes."

"I don't mind at all," Amy replied, smiling even though Randi couldn't see her through the phone. "I consider her another sister of the heart, just like you, so it'll be nice getting to visit with her more regularly."

"Thanks, I appreciate it."

They said their goodbyes with promises to call later that evening to chat some more after Randi was through with her commitments at the fan expo and Amy had returned home from her visit to talk with Kay.

Once they hung up, Amy swiped through her contacts in her phone and called Kay.

"Hey, Ames, what's up?" Randi's sister sounded upbeat, like she didn't have a care in the world, making Amy wonder if Randi's worry was misplaced.

Leah Mae Wright

"Not much," Amy replied, matching her happy tone to Kay's. "Just got off the phone with Randi and she told me you're officially on maternity leave."

"And she wants you to come check on me because she's being a worry wart." Kay completed Amy's sentence in a way she hadn't planned on admitting.

"Something like that," Amy chuckled, wishing she could be as close with her sisters as Randi and Kay were.

"Well, come on over." Kay laughed along with Amy. "You can keep me company while I'm relegated to only directing traffic, instead of actually moving my things myself."

"Oh wow, I can't believe your house is ready already!" Amy exclaimed, shocked that their castle-like home was completed only five months after their wedding.

"Yes, the Walkers have to be the fastest construction workers on the planet." Kay's tone sounded giddy at being able to move already, when they didn't expect to be in the new place before their baby was due in July. "Not only did they finish our place, but they also fixed up the south bunkhouse here on the ranch, while still covering their other projects in town."

"Wow, and I thought what they'd done at the B and B before your wedding was amazingly fast." Amy was in awe at the speed with which Walker Construction completed such quality work.

"Yeah, I guess that should've clued us in that our ten-month timeline would be cut in half." Kay laughed. "You know how to get to our new place on the ranch?"

"I know how to get to the south bunkhouse." Amy wasn't really sure how to get from there to Kay's new home, but it was the closest landmark on the ranch that she knew how to get to, and she only knew how to get there from the day they'd gone there for a barbeque over five months before.

"Might be better if you just go to the house between Hazel and Susan and follow one of the trucks coming down here moving our stuff." Kay offered Amy the best way to go see her without getting lost on the ranch.

"I'll do that." Amy sighed with relief. "See you in a few."

They said their goodbyes and Amy freshened up quickly before heading to the ranch. She knew Justin wouldn't let her lift a thing to help with the move, but she still dressed comfortably, thinking she'd at least try to make herself useful by helping Kay unpack and set up her kitchen, if nothing else.

It didn't take her long to get to the ranch, pulling up in front of the house Kay had called home for the last six months. As she was getting out of her car, JJ and Justin walked out the front door, each carrying one end of a sofa that they promptly loaded in the back of Justin's truck. The man was certainly stronger than he looked, and watching him working hard enough to make the muscles in his forearms flex very quickly made her panties wet.

"Hey, Sweetheart," Justin called out, jumping down out of the back of his truck to stalk over toward her. He pulled her in for a hug and a quick, chaste kiss. "What're you doing here? I didn't think I'd get to see you 'til this evening."

"Yeah, I'm not here to see you." Amy playfully pushed him away. "After talking with Randi this morning, I called Kay to plan a time we could catch up now that she's home for a few months. So, now I need to follow the next load of stuff going to her new place, so I can keep her company while she's supervising the move. I know I'm useless when it comes to the heavy lifting, but I thought I might be able to help with unpacking and setting up the kitchen or whatever."

"Sounds good." Justin dropped another kiss on the top of her head. "Give us a few more minutes to finish loading up my truck and you can follow me."

"I don't have space for furniture, but ya'll can fill my car with boxes, too." Amy waved her free arm toward her car as Justin was walking back toward the house, pulling her along by the other hand.

"Amy, good to see you," Anthony greeted her as they walked in the front door. "Did you just say you have space in your car?"

"Yes," Amy replied, looking up to her friend's husband, who towered over both her and his cousin beside her. "I have a big trunk and wide open back seat."

"Excellent!" Anthony turned to look up the stairs before shouting. "Girls!"

"Yes, Daddy," Tia and Maria hollered back in unison from somewhere upstairs a moment before they both appeared at the top of the stairs.

"You mind loading the girls and their clothes in your car?" Anthony asked Amy. "They've been chomping at the bit all morning to start setting up their new bedrooms, and I haven't been able to oblige them yet because of having to get the big stuff while I've got the manpower here to do the heavy lifting."

"Not a problem." Amy smiled up at the girls before releasing Justin's hand to head up the stairs.

"No heavy lifting," Justin commanded, pointing at her when she was only a few steps away from him.

"Don't worry, Boss." Amy gave him a mock salute and winked at him over her shoulder. She swung her hips a little more than necessary as she sashayed up the stairs, knowing he'd have his eyes glued to her ass the whole time she was walking away from him. "I'm more than capable of carrying a few outfits at a time."

"Auntie Amy," the girls greeted her with hugs as she reached them.

"Morning, girls. I hear we have some clothes to move in my car."

"Thank goodness you're here." Maria grabbed Amy's hand to pull her toward her room. "Daddy doesn't understand that girls have to move clothes first, so we have something clean to change into when we get our first outfit dirty while moving."

Amy couldn't help but chuckle at the precocious eight-year-old. It took a dozen trips each but the three of them eventually filled up Amy's trunk and back seat with their clothes, still on their hangers and ready to go straight to their new closets.

Once the guys had the three trucks filled up with furniture, they caravanned down to the south side of the ranch to the castle Anthony had built on a beautiful bluff for his new family. They pulled up just as three other trucks and a couple cars pulled out.

I guess Bob, Jon, and Bobby took the first load with all the beds before I arrived to see Justin, JJ, and Anthony loading the downstairs furniture. Amy knew it would still take most of the day to get everything else packed, moved, and unpacked, but the Burlesons had made a huge dent in the moving by starting with the furniture.

She pulled through the circle drive and parked off to the side once she passed both garages, where she and the girls could unload her car without getting in the way of the guys carrying the furniture, and appreciated the view of the creek below the bluff at the back of the house for a moment before grabbing her first armful of clothing and carrying it to the room where Maria directed her to put it in the closet.

Once the clothes they'd brought on that load were all put away in their proper closets, the girls directed Amy through the maze of the upstairs of their new home down a back set of stairs to the kitchen, where she found Kay fixing glasses of iced tea for everyone there.

Great! How am I gonna get outta drinking it with everyone here?

"Mom, can we have some strawberry lemonade?" Tia asked her mother, opening the fridge to grab the pitcher before her mother even had the chance to agree.

"Of course," Kay replied to her daughter. "I was just getting the tea ready for the guys because I know that's the first thing they're gonna ask for when they get done unloading."

"Actually, strawberry lemonade sounds better to me, too." Amy smiled, grateful for Tia's assistance, even though the teen had no idea she'd given Amy the opening she needed to avoid the caffeine.

"I'll fix you a cup, too, then, Aunt Amy." Tia poured three red plastic cups about three-quarters full of lemonade before putting away the pitcher and handing Amy and Maria each a cup.

"Thanks." Amy took her cup and sipped the perfect mixture of tart and sweet liquid.

When Justin, JJ, and Anthony brought a table and chairs into the kitchen, they all took a seat to enjoy a refreshing beverage before getting back to work.

"So, what's left to move?" Kay leaned into Anthony's side.

"Just a bazillion boxes, only half of which are packed up so far." Anthony dropped a kiss on Kay's forehead. "And the furniture that hasn't been emptied of its contents yet."

"We didn't get ya'll's clothes yet either." Maria pointed to her parents.

"Your sisters were all planning to focus on boxing stuff up when they left here a few minutes ago." Kay motioned to Anthony, Justin, and JJ to indicate she meant all the Burleson women of their generation. "But with it only being the four of them packing and six of you moving stuff, you might need to give them a little head start to keep from standing around waiting for a box to be ready to load up."

"Or Maria and I can help with the packing so it's an even race," Tia grinned.

"Whaddaya want me to do?" Amy wanted to do her part to help her friends.

"I want you to stay here and help me unpack the boxes the girls brought down earlier." Kay smiled at Amy. "I'm not allowed to use the step-ladder to put away the kitchen stuff that goes on the top shelves, so I need someone a little taller than me to help me out with that. Besides, you can't very well tell Randi to quit worrying about me, if you don't at least spend a couple hours watching me like a hawk for her."

"True." Amy laughed with Kay.

A few minutes later, the guys all left with Kay and Anthony's daughters in tow. As soon as they were alone, Kay turned to Amy and insisted, "Okay, now that there are no little ears to tattle to the Mommas, spill."

"Spill?" Amy looked down at her half-empty cup of strawberry lemonade in confusion at Kay's words.

"Talk…" Kay drew out the word for added emphasis. "Spill your news. Tell me the details. Like how far along are you and when's the baby due?"

"Wha-what? Ha-how?" Amy stuttered, glad she hadn't just taken a drink of her lemonade or Kay would've been wearing it from Amy's sputtering.

"Anthony and I had an appointment with the OB a couple weeks ago to see the new facility here in town," Kay explained, reaching over to squeeze Amy's hand reassuringly. "As we were leaving, we saw you and Justin walking back to an exam room together. And we both know you don't take your boyfriend to the OB-GYN with you unless you're expecting. I know it's gotta be driving you nuts to not have your mom and sister here to talk to about it, and it's too early in your relationship with Justin for you to feel comfortable talking to his mom or sisters. So, talk to me. I already consider you family, and you've known me long enough to know I won't say a word to anyone until you're ready."

Amy relaxed and let out a breath she hadn't realized she'd been holding since Kay first said the word *baby*. "You're right, I do need to talk to someone," Amy finally admitted, leaning over to hug her friend. "As much as Justin's been there for me to talk to about things, he's just as clueless as I am about what's normal and not normal in pregnancy."

"I'll give you a list of baby books for you to pass along to him." Kay reassuringly patted Amy's back as she returned the hug. "They've worked wonders for getting Anthony to calm down and not freak out about every little thing I wanna do while pregnant."

"I'll definitely take that list." Amy pulled back from her friend to wipe her eyes before the tears escaped. She hadn't realized how stressed she'd been or how much she'd needed a friend who understood what she was feeling. "I was worried he'd overreact about me helping today and spill the beans to his whole family. I don't even wanna tell my mom until I'm outta the first trimester, much less his mom. And since he's come up with a dozen questions in the last two weeks that he should've asked the doctor at our first appointment, I was afraid I'd have to wait until my next appointment in June to get him to chillax a little."

"Girl, I understand." Kay finally stood up to start working on the kitchen when the dishwasher finished the last cycle. "Anthony was the same way and with Doc Hayes not really being equipped to answer his questions, those books saved my sanity until I could get in to see Dr. Magnum in San Antonio."

Amy followed Kay to the other side of the kitchen and helped her put away the clean dishes. "I guess you were one of the people responsible for getting her to move her practice here?"

"Yeah." Kay chuckled as she moved to the stack of boxes beside the island to start unwrapping more dishes to run through the dishwasher. "That was probably more Anthony and Bobby than Brooklyn or I, but I'm sure her move is a hundred percent because the Burlesons are procreating. So, that was your first appointment back on the fifteenth?"

"Yeah, well, my first appointment with Dr. Magnum," Amy clarified as she worked alongside her friend. "I actually saw Dr. Hayes for a fainting spell in mid-March. In trying to figure out what caused me to pass out, he did some tests and referred me to a cardiologist for some more tests. While talking about my cycle to figure out if pregnancy could've been the cause, he determined it was too early in my cycle for pregnancy to have been the reason because a pregnancy test wouldn't even be effective for another week. Turns out

I got pregnant the day after that appointment since he wasn't comfortable giving me my birth control shot until after getting the test results back from the cardiologist."

"Seriously?" Kay looked at Amy with wide eyes at her revelation.

"Yeah, I thought I was still covered with my last shot until the seventeenth, but apparently it's not as effective the last couple weeks of the twelve-week cycle." Amy shrugged. "So, I got pregnant on the fourteenth, went back for more bloodwork on the twenty-second, and got the news on the twenty-seventh that I couldn't come in for another birth control shot, even after all my cardiology tests came back perfect, because I was already expecting."

"So, you're just now as far along as I was when Anthony and I got married," Kay stated, matter-of-factly.

"Yeah, I guess." Amy shrugged once more, not sure how accurate that was without being privy to Kay and Anthony's date of conception.

Kay's movement stilled as she looked momentarily lost in thought. "So, that puts you about five months behind me in your pregnancy, which would give you a due date in early December?"

Ah, she was doing some mental math, Amy realized as they both moved on to the next box to unpack. "Yes, December sixth." Amy paused for a moment before finally confiding in her friend about what most worried her about her pregnancy. "But with me being a twin, and twins being so prevalent in the Burleson family, I'm not sure how accurate that date really is, since twins tend to be born a month early."

"Oh, I didn't think about the possibility of twins for you." Kay didn't look as concerned as her tone of voice implied. "But twins aren't hereditary on the father's side, just the mother's. So, while you have a strong chance of having twins because of being a twin yourself, the prevalence of twins in the Burleson family doesn't actually increase your chances of having twins any."

"That's good to know." *So, now if I have twins, I can't share the blame with Justin.* "I guess I can shelve my worry about preterm labor and premature birth until after my ultrasound."

"Absolutely, and even if you find out you're having twins, don't worry about that either. I had early labor with both my girls. While it's boring as hell to spend the last few weeks on bed rest, it really does work to keep the kiddos in there cooking 'til they're fully developed."

"Thanks." Amy gave Kay a sincere smile, relieved of a little worry at hearing about her friend's previous experience. "Now, what can you tell me about when to expect to have morning sickness? And do you have any tips for dealing with it while keeping it hidden from nosy coworkers who might tip off Justin's family?"

"Morning sickness could actually start anytime." Kay made a face that made it obvious she disliked that part of pregnancy. "And it's not limited to just in the mornings. Crackers and ginger ale helped settle it best for me. Though Brooklyn swears by peppermint tea for hers. As for hiding it from the Burlesons, all I can do is wish you good luck with that."

Both ladies laughed at the truth in Kay's words, dropping the subject when they heard the guys arrive with the next load of boxes being moved. Amy enjoyed spending the rest of the day helping Kay unpack and sneaking in pregnancy talk when everyone else was working at the other house.

<div align="center">~~~</div>

Justin enjoyed seeing how well Amy fit in with his family as they all worked together to get Anthony, Kay, and their daughters moved into their new home. While it was tiring work, getting to sit with his girl beside him whenever they took a break easily alleviated his exhaustion.

Once everything was moved, Justin's mom, Susan, and Aunt Hazel brought dinner down to the new house to feed everyone. Apparently, when Anthony designed the castle he'd had built for his girls, he set up the kitchen, breakfast nook, and family room to be one open space, which was much bigger than the formal dining room and even bigger than the one in his parents' house. He'd also ordered enough folding tables and chairs to seat at least a hundred people, having them set up before anything else was moved into the home. According to Anthony, when they folded up the tables and chairs and put them on the rolling carts, which were similar to what the Hunters used at the bed and breakfast for moving around all the furniture needed for various events in the ballroom, they took up one entire space in their three-car garage.

Leah Mae Wright

I guess that's why they added the two-car garage attached to the house by a portico going over the circular driveway, so they'll have a place for their kids' vehicles when they get old enough to drive. Though maybe they should've made that a three-car garage also, since they're about to have their third child.

"I suppose we'll be moving all the family parties down here now." Jen motioned around the room as they took their seats to eat.

"We can if ya'll want." Anthony shrugged as he put a plate in front of Kay, who looked too exhausted to get up to make her own. "But this room was actually the girls' idea to make sure we have room for everyone in the GWA to visit, when the baby's born and Kay's not gonna have the energy to go over to the B and B to see them."

"Oh, are they all coming to town when you have the baby?" Hazel questioned Kay as Anthony walked away to go fix his own plate now that he had his wife taken care of.

Damn, I probably should've done the same for Amy, Justin thought, feeling guilty for just following her through the line to get food instead of taking care of her.

"Depends on when this little guy gets here." Kay rubbed her round belly. "They're on break from June twenty-ninth to July seventh. And I'm sure several of them will be in town for the wedding on the seventh. So, if he comes before our July eighth due date, then I'm sure we'll be overrun with visitors wanting to meet him while the company is off to celebrate Independence Day."

"Have you figured out what you're gonna name him yet?" Justin couldn't stop himself from asking the question, curious about what his cousins were planning on naming their children, so he could cross those names off his own mental list of baby name ideas.

"I'm leaning toward the name Samuel." Kay glowed as she said the name, obviously loving the name for her son. "With him being due around Independence Day, I wanna give him a patriotic name. And what's more patriotic than Uncle Sam?"

"Washington, Lincoln, or Kennedy are all strong patriotic names," Aunt Hazel interjected.

"I'd suggest Jefferson, but you've already said no J-names," Charlotte added. "But what about Franklin?"

"Oh, even better, Hamilton!" Becky shouted.

"You're as bad about theatre names as your brother is about musician names." Kay pointed at Becky while giggling at Becky's suggestion.

"And I still prefer Hendrix or Wright," Anthony interjected, kissing Kay on the top of her head before taking his seat beside his wife.

"I know Hendrix is after your favorite guitarist." Julie looked quizzically at their cousin. "But why Wright?"

"Wait, let me guess!" Jen waved her fork around to get everyone's attention on her. "After the Wright brothers?"

"Ding, ding, ding, we have a winner!" Kay pointed at Jen and grinned. "I had to let him have Wright as an option after vetoing Orville and Wilbur."

"Actually, Maria and I vetoed Wilbur," Tia pointed out between bites. "We don't want our little brother to be named after the pig from **Charlotte's Web**."

Her comment brought a round of laughter throughout the room, after which Justin asked Bobby what he and Brooklyn were considering for their baby's name.

"We're waiting until after the next ultrasound to narrow down our options," Bobby answered, shaking his head. "Since we couldn't tell if we're having a boy or a girl at the first one."

Justin remembered the fuzzy black-and-white pictures his cousins had shown everyone after their ultrasound visits and wasn't surprised it was hard to tell the sex of the baby. To him, the images looked like a stationary shot of the fuzzy screen on the television when the cable went out. *Fuck, I hope we can see more than that when we get to see our baby for the first time.*

"Has the doctor mentioned the 3D ultrasound for you yet?" Kay queried Bobby and Brooklyn.

"No, she just said we'd be able to determine if we're having a boy or girl at our twenty-two-week scan in June," Brooklyn replied. "But she didn't mention it being 3D."

"The twenty-two-week scan isn't 3D." Kay shook her head. "It's an extra, elective scan that she doesn't have the equipment for in her office. She only told us about it two weeks ago and referred me to a place in San Antonio that does it. We're going this week to get it because I want pictures of our little boy as soon as I can get them."

"Don'tcha already have pictures from the ultrasounds you've already had?" Amy asked Kay, looking confused.

"Yes, but just the grainy, black-and-white ones," Kay replied. "The pictures from a 3D ultrasound look more like portraits from a professional photographer."

"Oh, then I definitely wanna go get those done," Brooklyn proclaimed excitedly.

So do I, Justin thought, squeezing Amy's hand under the table to silently impart his thoughts. With the way she returned his gentle hand squeeze, Justin believed Amy understood his meaning and agreed to wanting those more realistic pictures of their baby in utero as well.

Dinner progressed with more conversation about preparing for the arrival of the two Burleson babies the rest of the family knew about, while Justin started thinking about what he and Amy needed to do to prepare for their own.

My house is too small for raising more than one child. While my spare bedroom could easily be made into a nursery, it won't be big enough for long if we have more children in the future. I wonder if Amy will want me to move in with her at her house? Or should I look into building something bigger like Anthony did for his family?

And what about when her sister and mom move down here? Her house is only three bedrooms, so there won't be a room for our baby if she still intends for them to live with her.

And what're her thoughts on baby names? Will she think I'm narcissistic if I wanna name my son after myself? Does she have names she likes already? People she looks up to that she wants to name our baby after?

Justin was so lost in thought he didn't realize dinner was breaking up and everyone else was starting to leave until Amy leaned over and kissed him on the cheek.

"I'm gonna head home and get ready for our date," she informed him as she pulled her lips back from his skin. "You still planning to pick me up at seven?"

"Ye-yes, Sweetheart," Justin stuttered, momentarily flummoxed by her question.

"Good, see you then." Amy smiled before pressing her lips to his for the briefest peck.

Justin reached up and slid his hand around her nape, pulling her back in for a deeper kiss now that he'd recovered from his mental baby trance.

"Get a room," Tia quipped, interrupting the moment for Justin and Amy.

He chuckled lightly as he pulled back from the kiss, which was probably inappropriate for where they were anyway. Amy smiled at him before backing away.

"Leave them alone, Tia," Maria argued, surprising Justin. "Maybe if they canoodle enough we'll get another cousin next year."

Amy's eyes went wide as Justin burst out laughing at the uncanny accuracy of Maria's statement.

"I'll see you in a couple hours," Amy blurted, quickly turning on her heel to exit the room.

Before Justin could figure out how to explain to his family why Amy suddenly bolted, Anthony saved him from needing to cover for her and their baby news. "Hey, Justin, do you have time before your date tonight to help me get the girls' game room set up?"

"Yeah, sure." Justin stood and cleared his place at the table before following his cousin to the game room upstairs.

They worked in silence for the first few minutes, detangling cords and laying out the components to figure out the best way to wire them up in relation to the position of the outlets and where the girls had already dictated the furniture should be placed.

"So, um," Anthony hemmed and hawed, breaking the silence, even though he looked nervous about saying whatever he was about to say. "Anything going on that you might wanna talk about?"

Justin wasn't sure what Anthony was getting at, but it was obvious he thought he knew something and wanted to be there for him if Justin needed to vent. As Anthony was the youngest of his cousins, Justin hadn't ever thought to go to him for advice about anything in the past. But since he was the first of their generation to figure his shit out and settle down with a family, Justin quickly realized that maybe he should.

"Things are going great with Amy, if that's what you're asking." Justin focused on the task at hand instead of looking his cousin in the eyes.

Leah Mae Wright

"Yeah, I got that based on seeing you two together." Anthony chuckled without stopping what he was working on either. "But I thought you might wanna talk to someone about why ya'll were at the baby doctor together a couple weeks ago."

Thankfully, Justin had already set the Xbox down and was working on running the cord through the back of the entertainment center when Anthony spoke. Otherwise, he might have dropped and broken it. As it was, his head snapped up to look at his cousin at the same time his jaw, and the cord in his hand, dropped to the floor.

"Don't freak out, Cuz." Anthony held one hand up, palm facing Justin like a stop sign. "The only reason Kay and I saw ya was because we were leaving the exam room at the same time ya'll were headed back to one. And neither one of us has said a word to anyone about seein' ya'll there."

"Please keep it that way." Justin knew Amy didn't want to tell anyone until they were out of the first trimester. But he also knew he could trust his cousin to keep their confidence until she was ready to announce their pregnancy to the rest of the family. And Anthony was right, Justin really did need to talk to someone other than Amy about everything he was feeling about their relationship and his impending fatherhood, without worrying about censoring his words. Since Justin knew he could trust Anthony to be there as a friend, as well as family, he said the words aloud for the first time. "We're having a baby."

"Congratulations!" Anthony's wide smile showed how much he meant that.

"But she's just as nervous about telling everyone about the baby as she was about admitting we're dating," Justin stated, going back to work routing the electrical cords to the power strip. "I'm trying to be the supportive boyfriend and let her set the pace for everything because I know she's been skittish about relationships all her life. But it's killing me to not shout it through a bullhorn that she and the baby are mine."

"I know that feeling," Anthony chuckled. "But at least you've got over the major hurdles already. She finally let you tell everyone you're dating. And she won't be able to keep the baby a secret once she starts showing."

"True," Justin laughed with his cousin. "Since you've already gone through that part of pregnancy with Kay, maybe you can give me an idea of when the baby bump develops, so I'll have an idea of when I can quit trying to keep it a secret."

"It was obvious to me at three months, but only when Kay was naked. She had to buy bigger clothes by four months, but it wasn't obviously a baby and not just a little weight gain until month five."

"Shit, we're barely a month and a half in. I thought I'd be able to tell everyone at three months. I'm gonna go insane if I hafta add two more months to the month and a half I'm already struggling to make it through without telling anyone."

"Well," Anthony drawled, slapping a hand on Justin's shoulder. "I guess it's a good thing Kay and I figured it out then. So, whenever you need to talk about the baby, just give me a call."

"Thanks, Cuz," Justin replied, returning Anthony's one-armed, back-slapping bro-hug. "Now, what can you tell me about pregnancy, so I know what to do to help Amy through it?"

"Hmmm, let's see." Anthony scratched his chin thoughtfully. "Keep crackers and ginger ale handy to settle her stomach after morning sickness. Hold her hair back and get her a cool washcloth, if she'll let you help her when she pukes. And maybe keep a travel toothbrush and toothpaste for her in the office."

Damn, I should probably be writing all this down, Justin thought as they finished setting up the gaming system and mounted the television.

"Don't complain about extra bathroom breaks because it's entirely your fault that your kid is sitting on her bladder."

Justin chuckled at what sounded like something Kay had blamed Anthony for in their pregnancy.

"While you're making sure she's eating enough for two, eat enough to keep up your own energy levels." Anthony grinned. "Because you'll need the fuel to be able to keep up with her during the second trimester."

"Whaddaya mean?" Justin couldn't figure out how her energy level could go up while she had a baby growing inside her to sap her energy.

"After they get over the majority of the morning sickness in the first trimester, the second trimester is when their systems are flooded with sex hormones, and they become insatiable. It's the part of pregnancy that I like to call the hobbit-sex phase because a pregnant woman's sexual appetite starts to resemble the normal appetite of a hobbit. She wants sex before breakfast, after breakfast, elevenses, a nooner, as a mid-afternoon snack, before dinner, after dinner, and as a midnight snack. Every. Fucking. Day."

Justin couldn't believe his cousin kept a straight face as he listed off a sex schedule that sounded next to impossible to maintain.

"Damn, is it even possible to have sex that many times a day?"

Anthony's mouth widened into the biggest grin Justin had ever seen on his cousin's face. "It's hard to do with kids and a job, but it is possible."

Maybe Amy and I will just hafta take a few months off work...

Chapter Fifteen

Saturday, May 25, 2019

Amy felt like she'd really settled into life with Justin in the last month. They'd seamlessly fallen into a routine of being together constantly for work, their volunteer opportunities at the youth center, trips to visit her family, and especially at home, since they were practically living together. After talking about needing more space for their family than his house on the ranch provided, Justin had basically moved in with her, even if they hadn't officially told anyone they were living together yet.

They still hadn't agreed as to whether they would set up a section of the master suite for their baby, since the room took up the whole top floor, or if they were going to convert one of the second-floor guestrooms into a nursery. Amy didn't like the idea of being a floor away from the baby at night, and Justin didn't like the idea of not having a wall between their room and the baby's room.

He claimed he didn't want to share their room with the baby, so their nighttime activities wouldn't disturb the baby's sleep, once they were able to resume after the baby's birth. But Amy thought Justin was really just trying to come up with every excuse he could think of to convince her that neither of their houses would meet the needs of their growing family.

Crazy man needs to realize that my house is just fine. We don't need to build another huge house on the Burleson Ranch to raise our family in, when mine is plenty big enough for our needs. Yeah, it's gonna be a little crowded when Ashlyn gets down here next week, and again in a couple years when Mom moves down. But it's not like either one of them will be permanently living with us. They're just planning to stay with me for a couple months while finding a place of their own.

Hell, Ash will have moved in and back out again before the baby's born, so it's not a big deal if we don't convert her room into our child's room anytime this year. And I'm not talking about forever sharing our room with our kid, just while he or she is a newborn and I'm a nervous new mom. Six months, maybe a year, that's not too much to ask, is it?

Amy looked across the truck at Justin, examining his profile as he drove them across town to Tully's Roadhouse, where James and Randi's joint bachelor and bachelorette party was being held. He was so handsome, he took her breath away every time she looked at him.

With as often as I want him, maybe he's right about needing some separation between our space and the baby's. And I can't even blame our insatiable sexual appetites for each other on pregnancy hormones, since I'm not in the second trimester yet. We might be the first people to overdose on sex if the second trimester makes me any hornier than Justin already does.

Before Amy's thoughts could veer into naked, sexy time with Justin, he parked the truck at Tully's and brought her back to the moment. Justin was ever the gentleman, insisting she wait for him to walk around and open her door to assist her down from the tall vehicle. They were walking hand in hand into the bar when she realized she had no idea how she was going to avoid imbibing without alerting everyone around her to her pregnancy.

"Justin, wait!" Amy stopped walking and pulled back on his hand to get him to stop with her. "What am I gonna drink tonight that won't make it obvious I'm avoiding alcohol?"

"Shit, I don't know," Justin replied, shaking his head, like he hadn't thought about that problem beforehand either. "I just assumed you'd order whatever mocktails Kay and Brooklyn are drinking."

"Yeah, but won't that make it obvious, if I'm the only one drinking the same thing as the pregnant ladies?"

"Probably, but I don't know what else to do." Justin ran a hand through his hair in frustration. "And we probably should've discussed this somewhere other than in the middle of the parking lot right outside the bar where all our friends and family are waiting for us."

"Too late now," Amy muttered, shaking her head. "Oh, I know, you can stay up front with me and take my shots when the girls aren't looking."

"Sweetheart," Justin huffed out the endearment in a way that made her feel like he was exasperated with her. "First of all, there's no way you can distract two dozen women at once to keep them from realizing I was taking your shots for you. And second of all, there's no way I can choke down a blow job shot, even if you could keep them from seeing it."

"Fine, then we'll just both only drink water all night and tell them we're in training for a 5K or something." With that decided, Amy turned back toward the bar and started walking again.

"Wait!" Justin stopped her forward momentum by pulling her back into his arms. "Why do I hafta only drink water all night?"

"Because if it's just me avoiding alcohol, it'll look suspicious. But if we're training together, it'll be our cute, couple's thing." Amy pushed up on her tiptoes to peck his lips before turning back toward the bar.

"Fine, but if I do this for you, then I need another quickie in the storeroom tonight," Justin leaned down to whisper in her ear as they reached the entrance.

"Deal!" Amy wagged her eyebrows and grinned at him as she agreed, hoping they could not only make their lie believable, but also sneak away for that quickie without getting caught.

"Two waters, barkeep," Justin hollered, flagging down Leo behind the bar to get their first drinks before they split up to join their separate groups for the first part of the party.

"Don'tcha normally start with a beer before switching to water?" Leo arched his eyebrow curiously as he passed two bottles of water over the bar to Justin.

"Yeah, but we're training for a marathon, so I'm cutting it out until after the race." Justin passed one of the water bottles to Amy before sliding a couple bills across the bar to Leo.

Not a marathon! Amy screamed in her head. *I said a 5K, so it'll be a believable story. It'd be tough for me to even do that with my lack of desire to run. There's no way I could ever complete a marathon. Not even a fictional one to sell this story.*

"I didn't know you were a runner." Jen surprised Amy by walking up beside them with her twin right behind her.

"I'm not really. It's something new I'm trying for Justin. And it's a 5K, not a marathon." Amy glared at Justin, hoping he got her hint to tone it down.

"There's actually gonna be a 5K, a 10K, a half-marathon, and a marathon that weekend." Justin grinned mischievously. "We're still trying to decide which race we'll be ready for by then."

"But you've never been a runner either." Julie pointed at Justin. "Why on earth would you decide to take it up now, in the heat of the summer?"

Shit, I really should've thought this through a little better!

"We didn't think it up to start in the heat of the summer." Justin shook his head at his sisters before taking a sip of his water. "The cardiologist recommended it as a good form of exercise for heart health back in March."

"And I've just let Justin talk me into it in the last couple weeks." Amy seamlessly continued Justin's lie like it was second nature for them.

"Whatever." Jen threw up her hands, dropping the subject before placing her order with Leo.

Justin gave Amy a quick peck of a kiss before they parted ways to go to the separate areas of the party.

Amy immediately hugged Randi as soon as she got close to the group where the bride-to-be was seated. She was then introduced to the other bridesmaid, Allissa Walters, and a couple other women who wrestled for the GWA that she hadn't met before.

"Time for the first round of shots," Becky shouted, carrying a tray of tall shot glasses topped with whipped cream.

"I'll stick to my water thanks," Amy declined when Randi tried to pass one to her.

"You can't toast to my wedding with water," Randi objected, still trying to hand her the shot glass.

"But Justin and I are in training and keeping our diets clean," Amy protested, not even pushing her hand out to signal her negative answer, so Randi wouldn't have the opportunity to force it into her hand. "And that means no alcohol."

"James and I are in training year round for wrestling, so you can't use that excuse with me, Ames," Randi argued, still trying to hand Amy the shot glass.

Fuck! Shit! Damn! Amy internally panicked, racking her brain for any other plausible excuse to not drink without telling her best friend about the baby while half of Justin's family was at the table with them. *When did my reserved friend become as pushy as Ashlyn?*

"No!" Amy shouted louder than she intended, but she was at her wit's end with the whole situation. "I'm not drinking tonight. Every time I come to one of these parties, ya'll push the shots. And then I wake up the next morning with no idea how I even got home. And I have plans with my man tonight that I'm gonna be stone cold sober to enjoy!"

"Dang, girl, way to let that freaky side out!" Randi hollered, downing the shot she was holding before lifting her free hand to high five Amy. "But we've still gotta order you something to sip tonight, so you don't have to toast my marriage with water."

"I'll go get her something," Kay offered, smiling at Amy as she stood from her seat. "I may not be able to drink for another few weeks, but I'm gonna at least order a drink at my sister's bachelorette party."

"Thanks, Kay!" Amy smiled at her friend. Since Kay knew about her pregnancy, Amy knew she could trust her to bring her a non-alcoholic drink without making it obvious to everyone else. "I'll trust you to not get me too drunk to ride my cowboy tonight."

Randi burst out laughing, along with several of the other women around them. "Who'da thunk you'd move here and fall for a cowboy and start sounding more like Ashlyn than my quiet, reserved bestie?"

"Probably the same people who never expected you to come outta your shell after meeting James," Amy replied, laughing along with her friends.

"Speaking of Ashlyn, when's she gonna get here?" Jen inquired.

"Her last day at Bama was yesterday," Amy explained. "I don't know how long it's gonna take her to pack everything and move, but her lease is up on the thirty-first, so she'll leave Tulsa sometime between now and then."

Leah Mae Wright

"Excellent," Jen replied. "I know she said she'd be here for her first day of work on the third, but I thought she'd give herself a little more time to get settled in here than just next weekend."

"If she's here in time, you have to bring her to the wedding." Randi grinned and Amy imagined it was because of how she expected Ashlyn to be her outrageous self and shock the rest of the Lees at the reception.

"Oh, um, I'm not sure what her plans are for the weekend. But I think she said something about spending it with our dad and half-siblings in Houston."

"Oh, well, invite them all to the wedding then." Randi leaned over to hug Amy. "Besides, they aren't really family 'til they meet your bestie. And what better time to meet the rest of us loony toons than when we're all on our best behavior for the wedding."

Amy returned Randi's embrace, giggling along with her tipsy friend. "Good point. I'll give them a call tomorrow to extend the invitation."

Kay returned to the table and sat a glass layered with red and orange liquid down in front of Amy. "Thanks." Amy smiled at her friend as Kay returned to her seat.

"Ooh, tequila sunrise." Randi pointed at Amy's glass. "Good choice, Sis. Now we can start the toasts."

Knowing her glass only contained orange juice and grenadine, Amy lifted it in the air to start off the toasts for the night. "To Randi and James and their long, passionate life together!"

"To Randi and James!" The girls all clinked their glasses together before taking a sip or downing another shot.

And to really good friends who understand the need for secrets until we're past the riskiest part of pregnancy!

~ ~ ~

Saturday, June 1, 2019

"Hey, Justin!" Justin was surprised to hear a deep voice calling his name as he made his way through the church to the room where the groom and groomsmen were supposed to wait before the ceremony.

He was even more shocked to see Amy's father was the one calling out to him when he turned toward the voice.

"Hey, David, good to see you." Justin extended his hand to greet the older man as he walked up to where Justin had stopped in the middle of the aisle. He was actually stunned to see him, not realizing he and his family had been invited to Amy's best friend's wedding.

"You look surprised to see me," David commented as he shook Justin's hand.

"Well, yeah, maybe a little," Justin chuckled.

"I thought it was your idea to invite the whole family." David looked around the room before he reached into his pocket. "Figured you needed me to bring you this for whatever you had planned that required both Amy's mother and I to be here today."

David pulled a black velvet ring box out of his suit coat and handed it over to Justin, while looking around as if to make sure nobody saw the exchange. Justin couldn't resist opening the box to look at the diamond solitaire set on a gold band that had previously been worn by Amy's grandmother.

Understanding why David was acting so suspicious as he passed it to him, Justin quickly closed the box and slipped it into his pocket before any of his family could catch on to the exchange.

"I appreciate this, and while I'm definitely ready for it, I don't have anything planned yet."

David raised an eyebrow at Justin's statement, like he wasn't sure he believed it.

"Seriously, I had no idea you were gonna be here today, much less Andrea and the rest of your family." Justin shook his head. "And while I love the idea of ya'll being here when I ask her, I don't wanna steal James and Randi's spotlight today."

"Yeah, I understand that." David nodded his head. "We're staying at the bed and breakfast tonight, and I know Andrea is visiting with Amy and Ashlyn for at least a week. Maybe you can plan something for tomorrow while we're all still here in town?"

"Maybe," Justin chuckled, grinning at his, hopefully, future father-in-law. "I'll, uh, try to think of something while I'm doing my groomsman duties today."

Leah Mae Wright

"Ah, you and Amy are both in the wedding party." David motioned at Justin's black tuxedo. "That explains why you're wearing the tux that I thought was just you being spiffy to propose to my daughter."

"Yeah, and I kinda need to head to the groom's room now, so we can get this party started." Justin looked around briefly and saw his parents walking into the chapel to take their seats. "But let me introduce you to my folks first. If anybody can come up with a spectacular last-minute proposal plan, it's my mom. So, as you're getting to know your future in-laws, maybe pick her brain for ideas for me?"

"Are you asking me to infiltrate the Matchmaking Mommas?" Justin saw the same mischievous gleam in David's eyes that he often saw in Amy's.

"Hey, if ya can't beat 'em, join 'em." Justin grinned as he led David over to make the introductions.

The older man laughed as he motioned for his family to follow him.

"Mom, Dad," Justin called out, waving his folks over to them. "I'd like you to meet Amy's father, David Sinclair. David, these are my parents, Jon and Susan Burleson."

"Nice to meet you." David extended his hand and shook Justin's father's hand.

"I'll let you finish introducing the families, since I need to head back." Justin tilted his head in the direction of the room on the side of the church, where he quickly headed before they even had the chance to return the pleasantries.

"What took you so long getting here?" Dean questioned as soon as Justin stepped into the room.

"Ran into Amy's dad on my way and had to introduce him to Mom and Dad, since he doesn't really know anyone else here today," Justin replied.

"Thank fuck, you're here." James pulled him in for a back-slapping bro-hug. "I was beginning to worry that Randi had gotten you and Amy to help her run away before the ceremony."

"Dude, I already told you, Randi's not running away." Anthony shook his head at their obviously nervous friend. "Because if she was, Kay and I would've been the ones she called to help her."

"Naw, if she didn't wanna marry you, she'd have her dad help her get away from here," Dean chuckled.

"Fuck, don't even joke, Bro." James was clearly distraught as he glared at his twin. Then he turned to look at Anthony and asked, "You don't think Charles is gonna try and talk her outta this, do ya?"

"No, he's not." Anthony tried to reassure the anxious groom. "Besides, even if he does, Kay already has a plan to feign labor pains to distract him until the ceremony starts."

Justin was impressed with his cousin's deadpan delivery of the preposterous plan, but he couldn't stop the involuntary chuckle that escaped him. "Relax, man," Justin suggested when he stopped laughing. "Randi's not gonna let her dad or anyone else keep her from walking down that aisle to become your wife."

"He's right," Dean agreed, slapping a hand on James's shoulder. "She'd have married you the last time we were in Vegas, if you'd have proposed a month earlier. So, I'm sure she'll practically run down the aisle to get hitched with you today."

"Yeah, I'm seriously regretting not suggesting that Vegas wedding back in January." James shook his head. "That would've been much less nerve-racking than waiting for today."

Thankfully, James didn't have to wait much longer since the pastor knocked on the door to tell them it was time. They lined up right outside the room as the processional music changed to the song signaling it was time for the guys to enter the chapel. The pastor led the way through the side door of the chapel to the pulpit, followed first by James, then Anthony, then Dean, and finally Justin.

They took their places at the front of the church and turned with the rest of the guests to look at the back of the room to observe the ladies walking down the aisle. Justin knew from attending the rehearsal the day before that Amy would be the first to walk down the aisle, followed by Allissa, then Kay, then Tia and Maria acting as both flower girls and ring bearers, before Randi made her grand entrance on her father's arm. But when the double doors at the back of the room opened and Amy stepped through the doorway in her red, satin bridesmaid's dress, Justin couldn't focus on anything but her for the rest of the ceremony.

She's fucking stunning! Justin thought as he watched her glide down the aisle. Though she was dressed in red, he pictured her in a white wedding dress walking down the aisle to become his wife. It was all he could do not to drop to one knee and propose the moment she reached the end of the aisle before she turned to take her place for the next bridesmaid to make her entrance.

Once she stood on her mark, their eyes met, love shining brightly between them. Justin didn't take his eyes off Amy, even when the other women walked between them to take their places at the altar.

As the preacher spoke, Justin imagined his and Amy's wedding. When James and Randi said their vows, Justin imprinted them on his heart, as if he was saying them with Amy at that moment. It wasn't until the preacher pronounced James and Randi as man and wife that Justin came out of his trancelike state to move out of his position and walk Amy back down the aisle to the back of the church.

They stopped in the vestibule so Kathy Harrison could position them in a receiving line and all the guests could leave the chapel to head to the reception at the ballroom of the Hunters' Bed and Breakfast. As their duties at the church were winding down, Philippe snapped picture after picture before ushering the ladies away to the restroom. "Take a moment to dry your tears and freshen your faces so we can get the rest of these gorgeous photos."

"Dude, you look as nervous as James did before the wedding." Dean slapped a hand on Justin's shoulder as the guys relaxed a moment while waiting on the women to come back for the rest of the pictures.

"No, not nervous." Justin shook his head and tried to figure out how to explain to his friends exactly how he was feeling in that moment. "Excited maybe? Ready to pop the question and afraid I won't be able to make myself wait until after the reception to do it. But definitely not nervous."

"Seriously? You wanna propose to Amy at our reception?" James grinned at Justin, as if he actually liked that idea.

"I almost dropped to one knee when Amy got to the end of the aisle before your wedding even started," Justin chuckled. "But I'm trying my best to hold back, so I don't steal the spotlight on your special day."

"Are you kidding? Randi would love it if her best friend got engaged at our wedding." James's smile widened. "And if you're really ready to do it, I say we rig the bouquet and garter toss like Anthony and Kay did. So you can ask her in the middle of the reception."

"You wouldn't mind?" Justin looked at James quizzically, unsure he could believe his friend was serious.

"I would consider it a wedding present to be able to include my bride in the plan." James grinned and chuckled.

"Do you have a ring yet?" Anthony asked Justin.

"Yeah." Justin pulled the box from his coat pocket. "Her dad gave me his mother's ring to use, so he could pass it down to Amy."

The guys huddled around to look at the ring for only a moment before Justin had to hide it in his pocket again because the women were coming back from freshening up to take more pictures.

"What're you guys whispering about?" Randi asked as the ladies joined them.

"Just telling them about the plans I have for our honeymoon, Angel," James lied, pulling Randi into his arms.

Before Randi could call James out on his lie, Philippe stepped in to direct them where to stand and how to pose for pictures. They took several shots at the church before driving over to the bed and breakfast to take even more. Justin drove Amy over in her car, so she didn't have to struggle to get in and out of his truck in her form-fitting dress. It was almost an hour later before they made their entrance to the reception.

With the wedding party being seated at the opposite end of the ballroom from the wedding guests, Justin didn't get a chance to alert Amy's father that he now had a plan for the proposal. *Fuck, I hope her family is at least close enough to see what's going on after the bouquet and garter tosses.*

Justin wasn't even sure how James was going to tell Randi their plan, since they didn't have a moment alone during the first half of the reception. *Unless he told her in the ten seconds they were in the hall alone before entering the ballroom? Or he whispered it in her ear when they had their first dance as husband and wife?*

Fuck! I hope he didn't tell her then. Surely he had more romantic things to whisper to her while they were dancing.

Regardless of whether James filled Randi in on the plan during one of those moments or when they were whispering at the table during the speeches, he somehow managed to get Randi on board. At least that's what Justin thought based on the way Randi turned and fast-pitched the bouquet straight at Amy. Amy had no choice but to catch it before it smacked her in the face.

Justin couldn't contain his grin at the look of shock on Amy's face when she realized that throwing up her hands to protect her face caused her to end up with the bouquet.

"Jeez, Randi," Kay shouted while laughing. "I wasn't nearly that blatant when I threw my bouquet to you. Or as deadly with the toss."

"Sorry, Ames, didn't mean to almost poke your eye out with the roses," Randi yelled across the room, laughing with her sister.

"I'm just glad you had the foresight to have the thorns removed," Amy hollered back, laughing along with the rest of the people in the room.

"And now it's time for the single gentlemen to line up for the garter toss," the emcee announced.

Justin moved into position along with several of his friends and relatives, including Amy's two half-brothers. He nodded over to them and noticed the rest of Amy's family off to the side, where they would have a very clear view of his proposal.

Randi took a seat in the center of the dance floor as James got down on his knees at her feet. As he was lifting the hem of her dress and bending further, as if he was going to dip his head under her wedding gown, Anthony called out, "Remember there are children present!"

"Guess that means I hafta use my hands and not my teeth to remove the garter," James joked, wagging his eyebrows up at his bride.

"Please don't slobber on it before you toss it at us, Bro," Dean yelled, inciting a round of laughter throughout the room.

"For real," the wrestler Justin had only been introduced to as Crockett, even though this was the second wedding the wrestler had attended in town, shouted. "Randi's the only one who wants your bodily fluids flying at her."

"Dude, I don't want him to spit on me either!" Randi squealed over the roar of laughter.

"I don't think that's what he meant, Angel." James chuckled as he slid his hands up under Randi's dress. "But I promise I won't be sharing any bodily fluids, even the ones I know you do want shooting at you, while we're here in front of an audience."

Randi's face turned beet-red when she finally realized what Crockett and James were both referring to. "Oh" was all she said before covering her face with her hands and folding down to touch her forehead to the top of James's head.

James pulled his hands out from under her dress, holding the garter in one and reaching up to move her hands away from her face with the other. He whispered something unintelligible before pressing his lips to hers briefly.

"Now, let's get this show on the road!" James stood up and looked around the room. "I'm ready to get started on our honeymoon!"

Without any warning, James wrapped the garter around his fingers as if they were a slingshot, aimed directly at Justin, and let it fly. It was an easy one-handed catch for Justin, who was glad everyone seemed to know better than to try to fight him for the garter.

"Fabulous! Time for the bouquet and garter photo!" Philippe clapped his hands to get their attention before pointing at Justin and Amy to direct them to the center of the dance floor where the chair was now sitting empty. "Miss Amy, if you would please have a seat."

"Oh, I thought Justin was supposed to sit first with me on his lap, like at Kay and Anthony's wedding." Amy looked so cute in her confusion that Justin almost gave in and followed her instructions.

"Oh, no, that pose is so last year." Philippe waved his hand around. "The trend now is for him to make it look like he's gonna put the garter on you as if you're getting ready for your own wedding."

"Oh, okay." Amy still looked slightly confused as she sat down in the chair for Philippe to arrange the bouquet in her lap the way he wanted it for the pictures.

When he stepped back, Justin dropped down on one knee in front of her. Instead of presenting her with the garter and pretending to put it on her, Justin swapped the garter for the ring box in his pocket. He took her left hand in his, opening the box with his right hand before presenting it to her.

"That's not a garter!" Amy pointed out the obvious before he could even utter the first word of his proposal.

"No, it's not," Justin chuckled. "But I still hope you'll let me put it on you tonight."

Amy opened her mouth as if to speak but quickly closed it and nodded at Justin to continue.

"Amy Edwina Lawton, I fell head over heels in love with you the first moment I saw you back in November. Getting to know you as a friend and coworker just made me fall deeper and deeper in love with you. Dating you these past few months has only shown me that I was right to give you my heart from day one. I know this is sooner than you expected and I'm willing to wait through a long engagement, if that's what you need. But I can't wait a moment longer to call you my fiancée. Please, Sweetheart, will you marry me?"

"Yes!" Amy shouted, dropping the bouquet on the floor as she threw her arms around his neck.

Their lips met in a kiss that quickly became too passionate for their audience. Justin barely kept the ring box in his hand as he wrapped his arms around the love of his life, picking her up as he stood to spin her around.

Shouts of "congratulations" finally sank into Justin's brain, reminding him that they weren't alone. He placed Amy back down on her feet and withdrew the ring from the box.

"How did you get it to fit?" Amy asked as Justin slid the ring on her finger.

"That was actually the work of your dad and Ashlyn," Justin confessed.

"Yeah, Dad called me and asked our ring size since you wouldn't tell Justin." Ashlyn pushed between them to hug her sister.

"It's not that I wouldn't tell him," Amy protested even as she hugged Ashlyn. "I just don't know it and haven't had the chance to visit a jewelry store to have my finger sized."

More people crowded around them, offering their congratulations by shaking Justin's hand and hugging Amy before they finally made their way back to their seats to finish out the reception. As much as he tried to push the focus back on their friends who'd just gotten married, Justin still felt like he was floating on cloud nine with his bride-to-be by his side.

<div style="text-align:center">~~~</div>

Amy couldn't take her eyes off the ring on her finger the rest of the night. If she did, it was only to gaze lovingly at her handsome fiancé. She still couldn't believe Justin had taken the first opportunity to have both their families in the same room together to propose to her.

Looking back at her life, especially how she'd believed she would never find true love for most of it, she was so glad to realize just how wrong she'd been.

Falling in love with Justin was her most secret dream come true. He didn't just show her love and affection in a physical sense. He admired her intellect and valued her opinion, both professionally and personally. It wasn't just when they were making love that he made her feel adored. It was every moment of every day.

But I still can't wait to get him alone so we can make love for the first time as an engaged couple, she thought as they exited the ballroom after James and Randi's wedding reception.

"Hey, Boss, think we can go to your place tonight?" Amy squeezed his arm where she gripped it as they walked down the stairs toward the lot where her car was parked.

"Sure, Sweetheart, if that's what you want." Justin looked at her quizzically. "But I thought you wanted us to live at your place from now on."

"Well, yeah, your place is too small for us long term," Amy admitted as Justin opened her passenger door for her to get in the car. "But Mom and Ashlyn are both at my place tonight, and I'd rather not have them overhear our bedroom activities when we still have access to a private place to be alone."

"Then my place it is, Sweetheart." Justin bent over to kiss her forehead once she was seated. He then closed her door and walked around the vehicle to get in the driver's seat. "You know we can stay at my place for the next few months while our house is being built and let your mom and Ashlyn have yours for as long as they want it, right?"

"You're never gonna give up on this building us a house thing, are you?" Amy gave him the side eye as they buckled their seatbelts, knowing he was going to be stubborn and continue trying to convince her to let him build her dream home for them.

"Nope." Justin popped the p as he pulled out of the parking space.

"Why are you so set on building a house for us when there are so many houses for sale in town that would meet our needs?" Maybe if she understood his motivation, she could finally give up her own stubborn streak to agree to his plans.

Leah Mae Wright

"Mostly because I love you and I wanna give you the house of your dreams." Justin didn't take his eyes off the road as he answered her. "But there's also a part of me that wants to raise our kids on the same land where I was raised, and several generations of Burlesons were raised before me. I want our kids to be close to their cousins and feel that connection to their legacy."

Well, damn, how am I supposed to argue with that?

"Fine," Amy huffed, no longer able to think of a valid reason that they should stay in her house. "But pick a place for our house down by Kay & Anthony and Brooklyn & Bobby, since their kids are gonna be closest in age to ours."

"Really?" Justin glanced at her briefly, as if he was trying to check to see if he heard her correctly.

"Yes, really." Amy nodded as Justin glanced over at her while he was stopped at the gate to enter the Burleson Ranch. "But I reserve the right to change my mind if you build our house close enough to your cousins that they hear me when you make me scream at night."

"Deal. And I'll make sure to add extra soundproofing to our bedroom, just in case." Justin lifted her hand from where he was holding it on the center console and kissed the back of it as the gate opened for them. "Or I could just make sure to keep the screaming orgasms to daytime hours, so there's no chance they'll hear you at night."

"Justin Lee Burleson!" Amy turned in her seat to glare at him. "You would not deny me nighttime screaming orgasms!"

"You're right, I wouldn't." Justin laughed as he drove through the other houses on the ranch to get to his. "So, quadruple soundproofing for our bedroom it is. Hell, if I have it done right, our own kids won't even hear us from down the hall in the same house."

Amy had to giggle at her ridiculous fiancé. "So, how long do you think it'll take to build our house? Will we be able to move in before the baby's born, or should we set up your guest room as a nursery for now?"

"It only took the Walkers five months to build Anthony's castle," Justin reminded her as he parked in his garage. "So, if we can decide on what we want in the next month, we might be able to move in before the baby's born. But I don't know how much of that speed was because Anthony dipped into his trust fund to pay for it. If I don't have enough saved from my salary the past few years, we might hafta wait until after we get married, so I can use my trust fund to speed up the build."

Amy was suddenly worried about not being able to contribute much toward their home, since she'd depleted her savings when she made the down payment on her house in town.

"Hey, don't look so down, Sweetheart." Justin took her hand to pull her up out of her car and into his arms. "I've got excellent credit, so I'm sure I can get a loan for anything over what I have saved, and will be able to pay it off in a couple years, when I turn thirty and get my trust fund, whether you're ready to marry me yet or not."

"I'm not worried about that," Amy mumbled, shaking her head even as her arms went around Justin's waist. "I just don't feel like I'm pulling my weight as your partner, since my money is all tied up in my house."

"You and your damn independent streak," Justin groaned as he scooped her up in his arms and carried her bridal style into the house. "If I promise to love and support you in being so fucking independent ninety-nine percent of the time, will you let my inner caveman have his way to provide for our family by covering all the costs of building our dream home?"

"I suppose I can do that," Amy giggled. "Since I don't really have the excess funds to argue with you about paying my part anyway."

"Good. Now, do we have anything else to discuss before I make love to my fiancée?" Justin dropped her in the middle of the bed, following her to cover her body with his.

"I suppose we could figure out when we wanna get married." Amy put one finger to her mouth like she was really thinking hard about their wedding date to tease him a little before starting to strip his clothes off.

"The weekend between Christmas and New Year's," Justin whispered against her skin as he kissed his way down her neck. "I'll let you pick the year, so we can have as long an engagement as you want, Sweetheart."

"You want a winter wedding?" Amy was surprised by his choice of wedding date.

"I'd marry you tomorrow, Sweetheart." Justin slipped the thin straps of her dress off her shoulders before kissing his way down between her breasts. "But at Bobby and Brooklyn's wedding shower, you told me you wanted a Christmas wedding, and I've been picturing it in my head ever since."

"You've seriously been imagining our wedding since the end of February?" Amy pushed on Justin's shoulders to make him lift up enough to look her in the eyes.

"Yeah, Sweetheart." Justin smiled brightly at her. "Though I'm still not sure how I'm gonna convince the florist that it's not a bad omen to make your bouquet outta yellow carnations."

"What?" Amy was confused by Justin's plan for the flowers at their wedding.

"Have you ever wondered why I always get you red, white, and pink carnations, but not yellow, even though I know it's your favorite color?"

Amy thought about it for a moment before nodding. She'd wondered about the flowers he always picked for her, but just assumed it was because the florist didn't have any yellow ones available.

"It's because none of the florists I've been to carry yellow carnations. In fact, more than one florist has told me it's because they symbolize rejection, whereas the other colors symbolize love, romance, and affection. So, I'm hoping when the time comes I can convince Florence that we don't believe whatever old wives' tale that says yellow carnations mean rejection to be able to get your favorite flower in your favorite color for our wedding."

Amy was so touched by his thoughtful planning to get what he thought she'd most want for their wedding that she instantly decided not to make him wait for a long engagement.

"Oh, Justin!" Amy gripped his face with both hands and pulled him down for a kiss. Their tongues tangled passionately for several long moments before she finished her thought while they took a few seconds to breathe. "We're getting married at the end of December this year, whether you can convince Florence to give us yellow carnations or not."

"Thank fuck!" Justin peppered her face with kisses between his words as Amy returned his affection in a similar fashion. "Because I don't think I'd survive having to wait longer than that to make you my wife."

"Oh, you're gonna make me your wife, huh?" Amy pushed him to roll over so she could be on top. "What if I wanna make you my husband?"

"Works for me either way, Sweetheart." Justin rolled them the rest of the way off the bed to make it easier to remove their clothing. He shrugged off his tuxedo jacket and toed off his shoes while Amy started to unbutton his dress shirt.

She made a mental note about how much easier it was to get him naked with the mandarin collar than when they had to fight with removing his tie first. *Maybe we'll go with similar tuxes for our wedding.*

Justin unzipped her dress, pushing her hands from his pecs momentarily to slip the straps off her arms, so the dress could fall to a puddle on the floor. No more words were necessary as they started to shed their clothing, though they each still whispered words of love and praise for one another as they kissed each newly exposed section of flesh. Amy basked in the feelings evoked by hearing how beautiful Justin thought she was between their whispered I-love-you's and hoped he liked hearing how hot she thought he was in return.

Amy had to give up on removing anything other than his shirt as Justin bent to worship her breasts after deftly removing her strapless bra. He laved them with his tongue and suckled lightly, keeping the intensity of his oral affection within the limits she could handle, since pregnancy made her breasts so much more sensitive than before.

Amy ran her fingers through Justin's hair, luxuriating in the sensations he was creating as he caressed her body. His hands roamed down her back, over her buttocks, and down her legs before making a return trip to her hips. He looped his fingers through the lace of her panties and slid them down her legs as he trailed open-mouthed kisses down her torso.

Justin went down on his knees and spent extra time kissing every inch of her tiny baby bump before dipping his head lower. "Sit back on the bed, Sweetheart," Justin directed, his hot breath blowing across her labia.

"Yes, Boss." Amy did as instructed, allowing Justin to take control the way they both enjoyed most.

Justin slipped her shoes off as soon as her feet left the floor. He looked up into her eyes and started rubbing her left foot.

"Justin, you don't have to do that now," Amy protested, ready for him to quit teasing her and get to the main event already.

"But I know your feet hurt from wearing heels all through the wedding and reception." He switched to the right foot, giving it the same treatment he'd just given the left. "I wanna make sure they don't cramp up."

"Like I can even feel my feet when you're making love to me." Amy playfully rolled her eyes at him as Justin grinned up at her. "When you're inside me, all I can feel is you, and where we're touching each other. And I really need you inside me right now."

"And I'll gladly give you what you need, Sweetheart." Justin stood abruptly, quickly shucking the rest of his clothes and crawling on the bed to lay on his back beside Amy. He arched an eyebrow as he looked over at her. "Unless you'd rather take what you need instead?"

Amy wasted no time in rolling on top of her fiancé, too eager to have his cock inside her to debate who should be on top. Justin took her face in his hands, pulling her down for a panty-melting kiss. Well, it would've been if she'd still been wearing panties for him to melt.

Amy let Justin take control of the kiss, feeling completely claimed as he devoured her mouth. She reached between them to grip his dick, adjusting her position to line him up with her opening. She swirled his tip through her folds, spreading her arousal over his cock before sliding down to take him all the way to the root.

Justin broke their kiss to shout, "Fuck! Amy, you feel amazing!"

"You're the one who feels amazing, Justin." Amy pushed up to a seated position, posting up with her hands on Justin's pecs, so she had better control of her movement as she bounced on his cock.

Justin let her control their coupling, focusing solely on fondling her breasts. "Fuck, Sweetheart, I love watching your tits bounce in my face like this." He lifted his head from the mattress, so his mouth could join his hands on her breasts.

Amy felt her climax building inside her as she rode her cowboy. She increased the speed with which she moved up and down his long length, grinding her clit on his pubic bone every time he bottomed out inside her. The stimulation to her clit and cervix at the same time kept bringing her closer and closer to the edge.

"Fuck, Justin," Amy cried out, arching her back as she imploded.

"Don't stop, Sweetheart." Justin grabbed her hips and took control, thrusting up into her at the same time he pulled her down on him. "Breathe through it and keep coming on my cock."

Between his words and his actions, Justin prolonged her orgasm and kept her conscious, even though it was one of the most intense yet. Their eyes locked on one another as Amy's inner walls clamped down on Justin's dick.

As her whole body spasmed for a second time, Amy wasn't sure if it was the first orgasm continuing, or if Justin had fucked her into a second one with the way he was masterfully making love to her. She collapsed onto his chest, feeling boneless as the waves of ecstasy rolled over her.

Justin rolled them, so Amy was on her back, and he was able to thrust more freely. He switched the rhythm, slowing things down as he brushed feather-light kisses down her neck and across her chest.

"I love you, Amy." Justin's voice was reverential as he repeated the words with each sensual slide inside her.

"I love you, Justin." Amy dug deep to find the energy to wrap her arms around him, needing to hold him close to show him how she felt as she was telling him.

Justin kissed his way back up her neck to whisper in her ear, "You and me, forever."

"Forever and always," Amy whispered back as he pushed in deep, holding still balls-deep inside her as they mutually climaxed.

While she thoroughly enjoyed every orgasm with Justin, regardless of whether they came from a fast and furious fuck or a slow and sensual screw, nothing compared to the times it felt as if their very souls were joining as one when they came together. They floated in nirvana, looking into one another's eyes, with no awareness of anything but their connection.

Being with Justin was pure bliss, her personal heaven on earth, and Amy couldn't believe she was lucky enough to get to spend the rest of her life with him.

Once they caught their breath, Justin rolled off her to head into the ensuite bathroom. Amy smiled when she heard the water turn on. Justin soon returned to clean her up with a warm washcloth and dry her off with a hand towel.

After he cleaned them both off and returned the dirty linens to the hamper in the bathroom, Justin rummaged through his dresser until he found one of her scarves that she'd apparently left there at some point. He pulled her up to sit on the side of the bed and insisted on wrapping her hair for her.

"You know I can do this without having to go look in the mirror to do it, right?" Amy arched an eyebrow questioningly at Justin.

"Yeah, but I like taking care of you." Justin grinned as he took his time positioning the scarf to make sure all her hair was covered for them to go to sleep. Once he had it just the way he wanted it, Justin pulled the bedding back to shift Amy under the covers and crawled into bed with her.

Amy rolled onto her side to rest her head on Justin's chest. He wrapped an arm around her shoulders as she laid her arm across his ribs and entwined her legs with his. "So, about this wedding between Christmas and New Year's. Do you have a specific date picked out?"

"Whatever date falls on Saturday?" Justin kissed the top of Amy's head.

"I guess we'll hafta wait until we have the energy to get up and look at one of our phones to pick the actual date," Amy decided as she yawned.

"Or we can just send out the invitations with the last Saturday in December listed as when we're getting married and let everyone figure it out for themselves," Justin joked.

"You say that like your mom and auntie aren't gonna take over all that for us," Amy chuckled.

"You're probably right about that." Justin chuckled with her. "You think helping to plan our wedding will be enough to convince your mom to go ahead and move down here, instead of staying in Tulsa until she can retire?"

"I don't know." Amy thought about it for a moment, not sure if her mom would be swayed that easily. "While I'm sure she'll love working with your mom to plan our wedding, I think it might take more than that to get her to move this year."

"The baby?"

"Yep, definitely the baby. There's no way she'll be able to stand being the only grandparent living so far away from our little one." Amy couldn't contain her grin at thinking about how excited both their mothers would be when they found out about the baby being on the way.

"Have you thought anything about names? Or whether you want a boy or a girl or one of each?"

"A little." Amy was nervous about what Justin would think of her ideas for baby names, so she skipped over elaborating. "I've thought more about the possibility of twins. But whether we have them one at a time or two at a time, I don't care if we have boys or girls or one of each. I just want them to be healthy."

"I agree, healthy babies are all that matters." Justin kissed the top of her head once more. "If we have a boy, I'd kinda like to name him after my Pappaw Jerry. And if we have a girl, after my Memmaw Judy."

"I was thinking the same thing about my grandparents," Amy confessed, pushing up to look into Justin's eyes. "Tom and Shanae."

"Tom or Thomas?" Justin arched an eyebrow at her.

"I guess his name was actually Thomas, but he went by Tom."

"Well, then, if we have one of each, we have both their names picked out." Justin pecked her lips with his. "Jerry Thomas Burleson and Judy Shanae Burleson. Unless you prefer Thomas Jerry or Shanae Judy?"

Amy scrunched up her nose as Justin said the second options. "Jerry Thomas and Judy Shanae. Thomas Jerry sounds too much like *Tom and Jerry* and would lead to our kid being picked on about being named after the cartoon by his classmates in school."

Justin's chest rumbled under her cheek as he laughed at her silly observation.

"If we have two boys, would you wanna name our other son after your dad?" Justin inquired while rubbing a hand up and down her back.

"As much as I'd like to, he already has DJ named after him. Maybe we could use David as a middle name? Or find out more about his parents and use one of their names?"

"We can definitely do that." They laid there in silence for a long while before Justin finally broke it with another baby name suggestion. "If we have a second son, I'd kinda like to name him after my third-great-grandfather, Jonah."

Leah Mae Wright

"He was the first Burleson to settle here, right?" Amy yawned once more.

"Yeah, the son of a slave born in captivity, who came west to be a cowboy after his mom died," Justin explained.

"I would love to name our son after him. And if we have two daughters, we'll name one after his mother."

"Her name was Mary." Justin went on to tell her their history and how Jonah had named his daughter after his mother. Amy drifted off to sleep as he told her once more about the second Mary Burleson who went off to war and started the Avington line of their family tree, dreaming about the strong men and women they planned to name their babies after.

Epilogue

Monday, June 3, 2019

Justin was a lot less nervous about Amy's second appointment with
the obstetrician than he was the first time. Though he still felt like he
was bouncing off the walls as they walked back to the exam room, it
was pure excitement at knowing they'd be seeing their baby for the
first time with the ultrasound. He knew it would only be the grainy,
black-and-white pictures this time and not the clear 3D ultrasound
pictures like Anthony and Kay had for their little one, but he was still
really looking forward to seeing his and Amy's child for the first time.

After reading the books that Anthony recommended for him, he
also knew he'd be able to hear their baby's heartbeat at this
appointment, so he was excited about that, too. He was practically
bouncing in his seat as Arden went through the initial steps of the
appointment with Amy.

"Are all expectant Daddies this jittery when they come to these
appointments?" Amy asked Arden.

"Unfortunately, no," Arden replied, shaking her head before
smiling at them. "But all the best Daddies are as excited as Justin."

"See, Sweetheart, I'm doing my job by being excited enough for
both of us, so you don't have to get your blood pressure up while
you're pregnant." Justin wrapped his arm around Amy's shoulders
and pulled her into his side, so he could kiss her temple.

"Maybe, but just watching you bouncing around today is tiring me
out." Amy giggled along with Arden as the nurse stood to exit the
room.

"Dr. Magnum will be with you in just a few minutes." Arden
grinned at them as she left.

Leah Mae Wright

Before Justin could ask Amy if there was anything he could do to make her more comfortable for the appointment, Dr. Magnum knocked once before entering the room. After pleasant greetings, she asked Amy to get on the exam table.

"Your weight gain looks good, three pounds since I saw you last and five pounds since your initial appointment with Dr. Hayes in March." Dr. Magnum snapped on purple exam gloves.

Amy moved to sit on the end of the exam table as the doctor was speaking and Justin got up to stand beside her and hold her hand, unsure what all was going to happen, since Amy hadn't been instructed to disrobe this time.

"Ideally, you should probably gain about a pound a week from now until your baby is born," the doctor continued while pulling a tape measure out of her lab coat pocket. "Amy, please lay back and lift your shirt, so I can take some measurements. Justin, if you wouldn't mind stepping to the other side of the table, so Arden can get the ultrasound machine in on this side."

Amy laid back on the table as Justin walked around to the back side, standing between the table and the wall to hold her hand. Arden came back in, pushing a cart with what Justin assumed was the ultrasound machine on it, placing it in the spot where Justin had just been standing.

As soon as Amy's shirt was lifted, Dr. Magnum used the tape measure in her hand to take some measurements of Amy's belly, which wasn't as flat as it used to be, but she didn't have an obvious baby bump yet either.

The doctor called off numbers that the nurse entered into the computer, going through what he assumed was their standard routine for a prenatal exam.

"Everything looks to be progressing right on schedule." Dr. Magnum put away her tape measure and picked up a bottle of blue goop from the ultrasound cart. "Now let's get that first look at your little one."

The doctor squirted the blue goop on Amy's belly before rubbing it around with the ultrasound probe. Justin leaned a little over Amy to try to see the screen even though he wasn't sure what he was looking at while the doctor clicked a mouse with one hand and repositioned the probe with the other.

While the doctor remained quiet as she clicked and appeared to be measuring blobs in the fuzzy image on the screen, Arden's eyes widened as she said, "oh" while looking at the monitor.

"Oh?" Amy questioned, looking back and forth between the doctor and nurse before turning to look up at him with concern. Justin shrugged, not sure what the nurse was seeing that he couldn't decipher by looking at the ultrasound screen. "Please tell me that's a good *oh* and not a bad *oh*."

"Sorry, just something I hadn't seen before," Arden explained at the same time Dr. Magnum said, "It's all good."

"Can you please clarify what we're looking at so we can quit worrying that something's wrong?" Justin couldn't make heads or tails of the images on the screen, and he didn't think Amy could either, since she was trying to look at it from a worse angle than he was. So, he really wanted the doctor to point out what they were looking at to set both their minds at ease.

Dr. Magnum turned the cart, repositioning the monitor so Amy could see it better. She pointed to what looked like a black circle with a small white blob at the bottom of it. "This is the amniotic sac," she explained as she pointed out the black part of the circle before moving the pointer on the screen to the white blob at the bottom. "Holding baby number one."

"That clump of white squiggles is our baby?" Amy asked, neither of them registering the end of the doctor's sentence or the meaning behind it.

"Yes, one of them." Dr. Magnum pointed to a second black circle with a second clump of "white squiggles" as Amy had described their first baby. "And this is the amniotic sac holding baby number two."

"Ta-two?" Justin stuttered. "We're having twins?"

"Yes, you're having twins." Dr. Magnum smiled brightly at them. "Technically, you're having monochorionic-diamniotic twins because they share a placenta but have separate amniotic sacs."

"That's what I hadn't seen before," Arden clarified. "Because the only other twins I've seen on ultrasound were fraternal, so my 'oh' earlier was because I got excited to see my first set of identical twins."

"I guess that makes sense, since I'm an identical twin," Amy smiled first at the monitor then up at Justin.

Leah Mae Wright

"Now let me turn the volume up, so you can hear their heartbeats."
Dr. Magnum reached over and adjusted the sound on the machine.

Fuck yes! Justin thought as they all got quiet to listen to the
thumping of their babies' hearts softly coming from the speakers on
the machine. *I can't wait to tell Bobby and Anthony how much more
potent my swimmers are than theirs, since more than one of mine
pushed past Amy's birth control to make our babies.*

Oh, wait, no, that would be the case if they were fraternal twins,
Justin suddenly remembered. *Identical twins just require one egg and
one sperm, and split into two babies after fertilization.*

*Yeah, I'm still gonna tell 'em my sperm is better than theirs since it
only takes half of one to make a baby.*

The doctor moved the probe over Amy's belly again, changing the
angle so they only heard one heartbeat, instead of the two together.
She explained that she wanted to listen to them separately to make sure
there were no issues with either baby. She then moved the probe once
again to listen to the second heartbeat on its own.

Once she confirmed there were no issues with either baby, Dr.
Magnum printed off several pictures of their babies from different
angles, typing in "Baby A" and "Baby B" over the circles, so they
could tell which was which when they showed them to their families
and friends.

They finished out the appointment by asking all the questions Justin
hadn't already found the answers to in the books he'd been reading
before being instructed to schedule their next appointment in four
weeks.

Amy took a minute to wipe the excess goop off her belly after the
doctor and nurse left the room, while Justin tucked their babies'
pictures in the pocket of his button-down over his heart.

"Guess it's time to tell everyone now that we have pictures to show
them." Amy smiled up at him as they walked hand in hand out to the
front desk to check out and schedule their next appointment.

"Yeah. Think we can convince your dad to come back to town
tonight, so we can tell them all at once?"

"I don't know, since he just went home yesterday," Amy replied as
they stopped at the desk to wait for the receptionist to be available to
check them out. "But maybe we can get him to bring the whole family
back next weekend?"

"Sounds like a plan." Justin smiled before bending down to give Amy a quick peck before the receptionist turned to them.

As Amy was making their next appointment, Arden walked behind them and opened the door to the waiting room. "Charlotte Burleson," she called out, getting Justin's attention.

Shit! Why's Charlotte here? Is she gonna out us to the family before we have a chance to plan a time to tell everyone? Or will she keep our secret because she's here for the same reason we are and won't want us to tell anyone we saw her here either?

Sure enough, a moment later his cousin stepped through the door to follow Arden back to an exam room. Charlotte's eyes went wide as they met Justin's. Justin smiled at his cousin as she walked past them, but they didn't otherwise acknowledge each other.

Justin waited until they were ensconced in the privacy of his truck and driving away from the doctor's office before voicing his questions to Amy.

"So, why do you think Charlotte was visiting the obstetrician? Do you think she and Ian are getting closer than she wants any of us to know?"

"Oh, I didn't even think of that possibility!" Amy exclaimed, covering her mouth with her hand, like she was shocked at Charlotte's potential pregnancy. "I just assumed she was going for an annual gynecological exam and pap smear."

"Yeah, I guess that could be why she was there." Justin ran a hand through his hair before reaching over to clasp Amy's on the center console. "But as much as she complains about Ian, I can't help but wonder if the English teacher doth protest too much, trying to cover up what's really going on between them."

"Are you suggesting that instead of hiding behind friendship like we did, they're hiding their relationship behind being frenemies?"

"Frenemies?" Justin laughed at Amy's strange hybrid word.

"Yeah, you know, enemies who sometimes act like friends," Amy clarified.

Justin thought about her definition for a moment as he looked back at the various interactions he'd witnessed between his cousin and her coworker whenever Ian came to the ranch to pick up his sister and son, when the Campbells had stayed with his aunt and uncle while their house was being repaired from a water leak and Ian helped rescue

Charlotte, or when they attended the same events in town. "Yeah, I see what you mean." Justin nodded in agreement with Amy's assessment. "They do act a lot like friends whenever Brody's around."

"I just can't tell if their over-the-top fighting whenever he's not there is real, or their way of flirting without being obvious to the Matchmaking Mommas."

"Fighting as foreplay, maybe?" Justin raised an eyebrow at Amy.

"Maybe," Amy giggled.

"I suppose if she says anything about seeing us at the baby doctor today before we have a chance to let the family know, then we can assume she was just there for an annual exam and the fighting with Ian is real." Justin started thinking out loud.

"And if she pretends she didn't see us today because she doesn't want anyone to question why she was at the baby doctor too, we can assume the fighting is foreplay." Amy finished vocalizing his thoughts.

"Wanna bet on whether they get married before or after we do?" Justin joked.

"Depends. What're the stakes?" Amy looked at him with a mischievous gleam in her eyes.

"If they get married before our ceremony in December, then the first month when we're allowed to have sex again after the babies are born, I'll eat your pussy until you come at least three times every night before I finally sink inside you. And if they don't, you'll suck me off first for that same month." Justin grinned, knowing they'd both enjoy whichever outcome happened.

"You've got yourself a bet, Boss."

Want More of Amy and Justin?

Visit https://leahmaewright.com/aa-bonus-scenes to download your free copy of ***Adoring Amy Bonus Scenes***, which contains three bonus epilogues in the story of Amy and Justin, including their wedding, their honeymoon, and their first day back at work after their parental leave ends, and should be read after reading ***Adoring Amy***. While these scenes are primarily about the main characters in ***Adoring Amy***, they do take place during ***Dion's Dream Girl***, ***Destined for Deanna***, and ***Lights, Camera, Ashlyn*** and may include spoilers for those books. Normally, I'd suggest reading those books before reading these bonus scenes, but since ***Destined for Deanna*** and ***Lights, Camera, Ashlyn*** are still being written and edited and haven't been published yet as I'm writing these scenes, I can't exactly do that this time. Therefore, I'm going to ask you to please read the ***Heart's Destiny Series*** through ***Dion's Dream Girl*** before reading this eBook, and consider any mention of the events in ***Destined for Deanna*** and ***Lights, Camera, Ashlyn*** as teasers for those books instead of spoilers. And be sure to watch your email for my newsletter announcements when those books will be published.

DISCLAIMER: This multicultural, best friends to lovers, office romance book contains profanity, graphic sex scenes, and emotional moments interacting with long lost family. It is intended for adult readers (18+) who are not easily offended.

Playlist

As I'm writing, I often have Pandora playing for background noise. I thought some of my readers might want to know what songs I noted as inspiration while writing this book, so here are the ones that stood out while I was writing **Adoring Amy**.

Marry That Girl by Easton Corbin
Best Shot by Jimmie Allen
Last Night Lonely by Jon Pardi
I Don't Know About You by Chris Lane
Yours by Russell Dickerson
The Good Ones by Gabby Barrett
Light Switch by Charlie Puth
Havana by Camila Cabello featuring Young Thug
Sweetest Pie by Megan Thee Stallion & Dua Lipa
Levitating by Dua Lipa featuring DaBaby
To The Moon by Jnr Choi
Sunshine by One Republic
Heartfirst by Kelsea Ballerini
Butterflies by MAX and Ali Gatie
When We (Remix) by Tank featuring Ty Dolla $ign &
Trey Songz
Come On by Jhenè Aiko
Best Shot by Jimmie Allen
Speechless by Dan + Shay
Rumor by Lee Brice
You by Dan + Shay
Hrs & Hrs by Muni Long

Face Down by Vedo & OG Parker
Lotus Flower Bomb by Wale featuring Miguel
Everything by Ella Mai featuring John Legend
All This Love by Trey Songz
It's In The Mornin by Robin Thicke featuring Snoop Dogg

Coming Next: <u>Fighting for Fiona</u>

Galactic Wrestling Association Series
Book 1

Rick Robertson lived his dream life as the second-generation owner and promoter of the world's most successful sports entertainment company — the Galactic Wrestling Association. As a single dad and billionaire boss, his life was spent traveling the world with his twelve-year-old daughter and the crew he considered a second family. But seeing his staff and talent falling in love made him realize there was still one thing missing in his life — his soulmate.

Fiona Harrison was tired of living the sheltered life of a preacher's daughter in a small Texas town. She craved adventure and excitement, like she read about both with her middle school English students and alone at home. She wanted to get out of Heart's Destiny and see the world. And maybe meet a man who could make her feel more than the friendly affection she felt with the guys she grew up with.

Fiona jumped at the chance to travel with the GWA when her coworker and friend told her about the traveling English teacher position. She interviewed for the job when the GWA was in Heart's Destiny for a wedding over Thanksgiving break. She was scheduled to start her new job at the beginning of the new year, and hoped the instant attraction she felt when she interviewed with the owner of the company wouldn't make the working conditions too uncomfortable.

Rick didn't think his attraction to the new English teacher, who was ten years his junior, would be a problem. She was too young to be interested in a single father with too much responsibility on his shoulders to ever have time to take her out and treat her the way a beautiful young woman like her deserved. He considered himself to be more than man enough to appreciate her beauty from afar and keep all their interactions professional.

Then he went home to New York over Christmas break and hired a male history teacher closer to Fiona's age. When the two new teachers both started work in the new year and seemed to be spending an awful lot of time together, Rick struggled to fight his natural alpha tendency to claim Fiona as his own.

Which battle would Rick win? The battle with himself not to pursue Fiona? Or the fight for Fiona's heart?

DISCLAIMER: This single dad billionaire boss, teacher, age gap, sports romance book contains references to fertility issues, profanity, and graphic sex scenes. It is intended for adult readers (18+) who are not easily offended.

Coming Next in Heart's Destiny

<u>Charlotte's Wedding</u>

Heart's Destiny Series Book 5

Former DEA agent Michael Ian Campbell struggled with civilian life after leaving the agency when his wife was killed after blowing his cover with the Rodriguez Cartel. He barely made it out alive the day he and his family were ambushed in a drive-by ordered by Rojo Rodriguez to take him out, so he retired from the DEA and took a job as an English teacher at one of the local schools.

Until the day he got word that Rojo Rodriguez had escaped, when the rest of the major players in his cartel were captured in a raid in South Texas, that is. With limited resources keeping the DEA and local law enforcement from having someone actively looking for the cartel kingpin, Ian moved there to help find the man responsible for his wife's death.

Charlotte Burleson didn't know the new English teacher she had to work with was actually a friend of her brother, Jake, and a former undercover DEA agent. She only knew him as a one-night stand she thought she'd never see again, and the most infuriating man she'd ever met.

Ian wasn't sure how to deal with finding out the hot-as-hell one-night stand he had on the night he interviewed for his new job was with the sister of a man he'd worked with on a joint task force and considered a friend. Or that she was also the other English teacher at the middle school where he started his new job in Texas. He had to keep his cover and not let on to anyone in town that he knew Jake Burleson before moving there. Not to mention the fact that he couldn't tell his friend Jake that he'd slept with his sister. He had to keep his growing attraction to Charlotte to himself, unwilling to risk getting burned if Rojo Rodriguez caught wind of his presence in town and went after her, the way he had Mari.

As danger loomed, the couple fought their instant attraction and growing connection, not realizing that standing together was the only way they could win in the end.

DISCLAIMER: This single dad, teacher, brother's friend, instalove, alpha male, romantic suspense book contains references to past gun violence and child abuse, as well as the kidnapping and rescue of a main character, profanity, and graphic sex scenes. It is intended for adult readers (18+) who are not easily offended.

Books by Leah Mae Wright

Heart's Destiny Series

Galactic Wrestling Association Series

Glossary of Professional Wrestling Terms – Free eBook
Fighting for Fiona – Rick Robertson and Fiona Harrison
Dean's Darlin' – Dean Hunter and Allissa Walters
Mistakenly Married? – Liam Connery and Rylie Long, Brent Crockett and Aiken Pearson, & Josh Parker and Teagan Shields
Winning Rylie – Liam Connery and Rylie Long
Claiming Cage – Cage Dalton and Jaxon Nolen (MM Romance, Coming Soon)
Blade's Botched Bump – Brandon "Blade" Braddock and Caitlyn Sullivan (Coming Soon)

About The Author

Leah Mae Wright lives in Florida with her husband and fur babies. Her head has been filled with romantic stories for as long as she can remember, beginning with fairy tales as a small child growing up in Oklahoma and carrying through to countless ideas of her own throughout the years, as she's moved around to live in several different states. Now that her children are grown and life has slowed down, she's letting them out of her head, so they can join the libraries of her fellow fans of romance. Leah's literary world is a wonderful place that has no Covid, no real politicians, and a few unreal towns. Her favorite part about her characters living in her literary world is knowing that they are guaranteed a happily ever after.

You can keep up to date with Leah's future book plans at: www.leahmaewright.com – Be sure to sign up for the Newsletter to receive emails about new releases, sales, and freebies.
www.facebook.com/LeahWrightAuthor
www.amazon.com/author/leah_wright
https://www.instagram.com/leahmaewrightauthor/
https://www.pinterest.com/LeahMaeWrightAuthor/

Provide your feedback to the author at:
Leah's Literary World Facebook Group
LeahWrightAuthor@gmail.com
Leah@LeahMaeWright.com

You can also review Leah's books on Amazon, Apple Books, Barnes and Noble, Bookbub, Fictiondb, Goodreads, Google Play Books, and Kobo.

www.ingramcontent.com/pod-product-compliance
Lightning Source LLC
Chambersburg PA
CBHW010555310726
48969CB00009B/2443